AIN'T NEVER NO SNOW IN ATLANTIS

a novel

Ain't Never No Snow in Atlantis

(c) 2024 Bobby Burnett Lee
All Rights Reserved

No part of this book may be used or reproduced in any manner whatsoever without permission except in the case of brief quotations embodied in critical essays or reviews.

This is a work of fiction. Any references to historical events, real people, or real places are used fictitiously. Other names, characters, places, and events are products of the author's imagination, and any resemblance to actual events or places or persons, living or dead, is entirely coincidental.

Attention schools and businesses: for discounted copies on large orders please contact the publisher directly.

Kallisto Gaia Press Inc.
PO Box 220
Davilla, TX 76523
info@kallistogaiapress.org
(254) 654-7205

Cover Design: David Graham and Bobby Burnett Lee
Interior Design: Paul Baillie-Lane
ISBN: 978-1-952224-40-9
Distributed by Ingram Lightning Source

Library of Congress control info available on request.

AIN'T NEVER NO SNOW IN ATLANTIS

a novel

BOBBY BURNETT LEE

*For the Indigenous peoples of Texas,
namely those from the valleys of what we now call
the Red, Sulphur, and Cypress rivers.*

PART ONE

WHAT HAD HAPPENED WAS

Catch yourself looking for answers on jail cell walls, you done messed up a long time ago. No news there. But this thing? This latest thing? That's stretching the limits of loserdom, bud.

    I showed up to Steve's funeral as drunk as physiology allowed. Why the hell not? Only person I cared about caring about that was dead. Murdered, the hell what the papers said. Then some of them so-called mourners took offense at being called out by the town's off-white, once-was, has-been in front of God and Steve's dead body, resulting in my current residence: the Caddo County jail. Directly situated—not even kidding here—across Dewey Street from the home of my late teens: Steve's house, in which a not-yet famous version of myself (80s rendition, acid-washed jeans and all) used to live. I'm not one for acronyms or initialisms or whatever-the-hellisms, but FML.

    It's easier to forget the dump where you came from when you're not detained there. *Dump* excluding my deceased adoptive father and a sprinkling of others who for some damn reason remain in Atlantis, TX. But now Steve's gone, drowned and six feet down. Can't say about the rest, scorched bridges and all. This being the East Texas redneck shitshow it is, I've erred on the side of Austin these years, although back when I was on tour and still musically somebody I always made sure to swing through Atlantis with middle fingers held high in a band bus with my name on the side in elaborate, fuck-off cursive. Good times. Sadly, flipping off crackers ain't the same when you're solo in a 70s pickup with dwindling royalties and a voice that crapped out years ago.

I stare at Steve's place through the cell's tiny window, Plexiglass scratched with dozens of half-familiar names, arguable axioms, disembodied genitalia of dubious size, and a handful of *For a Good Time Calls*. 867-5309. I shouldn't have done that at the funeral. I shouldn't have come.

My cellmate stirs on the lower bunk a few feet behind me, having been somnolent and immobile since they chunked me in. He looks like a cave troll from *Lord of the Rings*—bald, scabby, maybe five feet tall, and with shoulders as wide as our dingy little cage. He thumb-rubs his eyes, squints my way.

"Hey," he says.

"Howdy."

"Well, goddamn."

"You're telling me," I say.

"Bobby? That you?"

I don't say anything. And then I say, "Nope."

"It's me, Bobby. It's Chuck."

I turn back to the window and its scratchy insight. Maybe Chuck will slide back into his coma for the remainder of my stay. Over at Steve's, the wind is having fits in the ancient pecans. I can almost hear the shells dropping and cracking underfoot.

"Charles Tender?" he tries again. "I know you remember me..."

His name is like an old rag my mom kept under the sink. Chuck wears a stained Dallas Cowboys jersey with a 54 on it in torn-up, navy blue. Looks like a muumuu that's been shat on by mustard-eating crows.

"We was Merfeet together back in the day," Chuck offers. "On the O-line with Red and that colored fella."

"Sofa," I say. Now Sofa, I remember. You don't typically forget folks named after furniture.

"Yeah, Sofa! And then it was Red and old what's-his-name, too," Chuck muses. "That one went off and got famous. That mixed boy? Half Gypsy, I think."

Gypsy... Just one from the stock of slurs: *Wop, Beaner, Coonass, Canuck...* Nobody knew, so everybody guessed. Dark hair, weird eyes. Maybe something off with the nose.

"Sam," I say, unclenching my hand. "Sam Sorrow."

"That's it!" he shouts. "Whatever happened to that old boy?"

Sam Sorrow, born Robert Samuel Soreau, and thereafter Bobby to all. Named after his technical father who stuck around just long enough to be technically named after.

"That's me, buddy," I say. The used-to-be singer, the crashed star.

"Nah," Chuck scrunches his nose. "You were... Nah, see, the one I'm talking about was that singer? Got them records?"

I raise my hand in a visual sigh. I know what's coming next by that look. Can't get away from it, not even in here.

"Okay," Chuck says, turning his head from side to side like he's working out the rust. "Guess I can see it now... It's just... You don't sound right. Your voice..."

"Yep."

"Don't recall that fella sounding like Macho Man Randy Savage."

Through the marks in the window, what's left of the yellow leaves tries to hold on, hold on. Pecan pie, Steve's favorite. When was the last time I had some decent pecan pie?

"Okay," Chuck says. "It's you, I guess. So... it was me and you and Red and Sofa and... who was that played center?"

He's talking more than twenty years back. No, thirty. More than thirty. Goddamn.

"I know you remember that fella," he says, cheering up. "I was there when you beat the ever-living ugly off him that one time at Nirvana. You remember that?"

I don't even bother shaking my head. My head hurts and I want my hurting head to die.

"Or maybe it was Red?" Chuck considers. "Whatever one of you it was, Nirvana's for sure where it happened."

"Nirvana," I say, trying to recall it. "That place still out there?"

"Well, sure! Where's it supposed to go?" Chuck grins. "Weren't nothing but a bunch of gravel out there in the woods in the first place. Anyway, back to this fella I can't remember—"

"I remember," I say, still no idea who we're talking about. "Surprised you didn't hear."

"Hear what?"

"His old lady shot him," I say. "Right in the back of the head. Left him face down in an alley like a dog. Like a dog who is dead."

"No..."

I nod. Oh yes, Chuck. *Oh yes...*

"Goddamn," he frowns and shakes his head at the floor. "Goddamn. Never turn your back on a woman, man."

"I won't," I say, but I will.

"Kinda how I got in here," he confides, taking a preparatory breath.

Walked right into it. And there's nobody responsible for the suffering to follow but my own conversation-encouraging ass.

"Caught me off guard," Chuck cracks his knuckles. "See, it all started—"

"They serve chow in here yet?"

"See, what had happened was," Chuck begins, "is I'm out there at *Seven Sirens* getting a lap dance from this new girl called Sedona. You know Sedona? Course, Sedona is just her dancer name. Told me her real name in confidence once, but all I recall is that it's sort of like Sedona. You know, like Winona or Verona... Corona. Ramona, maybe. Anyway, Sedona's new to the game, see—a peach-fuzz in the trade, as we say—and this might be my fourth, fifth time with her, and still—*still*—she ain't exactly learned to control the pace of the action, if you get me. So in the course of this adult entertainment I'm referencing here, ended up there was some extra moisture involved, on account of my enthusiasm, see? And Sedona, well… she might've acquired a little extra moisturizer up in her hair, if you get me!"

It's my own damn fault that I do.

"So, that's the long and short of it, so to speak," Chuck claps his mitts with finality. "How I got chunked out of the Sirens and thrown off in here like a goddamn criminal. What you gonna do, though?"

"Not jizz on strippers?"

"Hey," he says suddenly. "Know who I see out there sometimes? The Old Man. You believe that? Coach."

Coach has been old and *Coach* for so long that few people know his actual name.

"There's somebody I haven't thought of in a long-ass time," I say.

"*Long-ass time…*" Chuck snorts. "Remember how we used to say a *coon's age?* That's how we measured a long stretch of time, on account of raccoons living so long."

"I'm not sure they do, though."

"Actually ain't so sure myself," Chucks considers. "All I know is you can't say shit like that no more. PC Nazis, man. It's like *1984* up in here."

"Parachute pants and all."

"Naw, man. I'm talking that Orwall book! Thought police, totalitarianism, head boxes with rats in em, fucking uppity liberals…" Chuck takes the obligatory look around the cell, in which we remain the only visible inhabitants. "If you want to know what I think…"

The rest of what Chuck Tender thinks involves chem-trails and Jews and N-word lizard people and the Deep State (including the Caddo Club—our local chapter of the Illuminati, per Chuck) and some new drug lord in Atlantis who everybody good and well knows is a CIA stooge. It's like Alex Jones shat out a Tolkeinized replica of himself and left it in here to die.

Now I remember Chuck, who's apparently hell-bent on remaining the kid who never shut up. Along with me and Red, he belonged to the sports-oriented *powhitetrashes* (PWTs) of town, but Chuck lacked the charisma and functional intelligence to aspire otherwise. He was also an unrepentant bully, only topped in high school assholery by Red and myself.

But my primary memory of Chuck is from back when my mom was still alive, two or three years before Steve adopted me. Back then, Steve was just our history teacher and my mom's best friend. It was in history class that Chuck lapsed into thinking a person could actually fuck with Steve Berkey, that a mere child could refer to Steve's uncloseted sexuality in derogatory fashion—something of the *cock gobbler* variety, muttered-but-not, something us kids maybe would've laughed at were we all off somewhere else in whispered hiding. Thing was, Chuck had just come out and said it, right there in class, and loud enough so other humans could hear it. The rest of us sat there chin-dropped like we'd just seen a nun get slapped.

You were supposed to know. What Chuck had done wasn't just off limits; it was real-world bad for your health. Steve's father was Beau Berkey himself, notoriously protective of his only gay son (well, his only son—like me, Steve was an only child). Beau employed a good portion of the county, he headed up the Caddo Club, and more than once he'd sent goons to readjust the knees of somebody who'd addressed Steve's homosexuality in audible form.

Even so, no physical tragedy befell Chuck as a result of that day, no doubt due to Steve's intervention. But what Steve did to Chuck was a dozen times worse for a kid like that: he made Chuck deliver a series of oral reports in front of the whole class, and by *series* I'm talking Discworld-length or those novels I can't remember the name of with that guy with a leopard head. For a flunky like Chuck, getting up there day in and out for months was way worse than any beating, which he was probably getting at home anyway.

Chuck's academic reports were mumblecore hell for the rest of us to sit through. They were all Caddo-related, because Steve was the only adult in the area code invested in teaching us about the native people who'd previously lived for thousands of years in the surrounding region and county that bore their name. If you fucked off in class, Steve gave you the Caddo treatment, but we'd never seen him do anything like he was doing with Chuck. The report I most recall was "The Man Who Lived Like a Woman"—one of Steve's favorites.

It went like this: The man who lived like a woman stayed back with the ladies of the tribe when the men went off to fight, and some of the men didn't like it much. They said it was shameful, so they picked at the man for years. Eventually, one of the elders told them to let the man who lived like a woman be, to just let him stay behind with the other women and live the way he wanted, but the warriors wouldn't listen. Look, the old timer warned, this man who lives like a woman was created that way by the Great Father, and the Great Father has given him powerful medicine. If you do him harm, there'll be a price to pay that none of y'all will live long enough to settle. But the men didn't listen. In fact, they killed the man who lived like a woman, or tried to. On their first go at it, his corpse just climbed out of the grave and zombie-walked back to the village and put the fear in everybody by carrying on as if nothing unusual had happened. Like, he was still the man who lived like a woman, only dead. So, the men tried again, only this time they cut his head off and weighed it down in the river under some kind of magic rock, and then they burned what was left of his body on the shore. But as they were doing all that, the men began to bicker. Their bickering turned violent, and the fighting got worse and worse until, wouldn't you know it, they killed each other off, one by one, until not a one of them was left breathing.

I'd heard Steve tell that story in other versions. In one, there was something strange about one of the man's fingers, and the other men couldn't kill him until they removed it from his hand; in another, the man who lived like a woman didn't die at the end. He married within the tribe and settled down to live out the rest of his years with his husband. I asked Steve why that was. What's the real story? You know, the official story—the one all others are based on. Like, lots of folks got a "Hallelujah," but it's always Leonard's song.

I can't remember what Steve said. I can't remember half of what he ever said. But when Chuck's reports came to an end, he was a different sort of child from then out, at least in class. And he never put Steve's name in his gabby mouth again.

But oh, is that mouth gabby now. On and on about Hillary and her all-mighty emails, something called *Love Jihad*, more N-word lizard people, and some gobbledyfuck about Nelson Mandela and the Berenstein Bears. I know I'm supposed to step in and set Chuck straight with all the diplomacy and wokeness you'd expect from a maybe mixed personage who's also Steve Berkey's adopted son, but I don't. Just like all the other things I'm supposed to do in life and don't. I just let the tape roll and look out at Steve's three-story Victorian and hope to God my ability to hear takes a cue from my larynx and just up and unexpectedly dies.

There's a new tree in Steve's yard. No, not a tree—a man. A man in a colorful shirt, or maybe it's just color in his arms—kaleidoscopic and bushy. He's got a bouquet. It's flowers.

"Hear what I'm saying?" Chuck demands, huffing hard. He's been at it for a while.

"Sure," I say, squinting at the stranger in Steve's yard. "Berenstein Bears…"

Chucks pouts over next to me and breathes through his mouth. "What you keep looking at out there?"

"Where I used to live," I point. "Up in that attic."

Chuck strains to see it. "I thought you came up in that trailer park with Red."

"I did," I say. "Before. You remember Steve Berkey? Beau's son?"

Chuck shuffles back to his bunk and lies down. "Can't remember shit no more. My head ain't right."

When I turn back to the window, the bouquet man is gone, and the yard is once more pecan trees, shrubbery, regret.

"Don't matter," I mutter. "That was long time ago. A long-ass time ago."

"Exactly," Chucks replies. "That's how you know none of it matters."

"I didn't say none of it matters. I didn't say that."

"No," Chuck says firmly. "Listen: It's the past, right? And the past is gone. You see it around here anywhere?" Chuck gestures around the cell, like, *Do you behold the times of yesteryear upon the toilet? Beneath mattress or pillow of this here bunk?*

"No," Chuck answers for me. "You do not. Which is why they call it the past—cause it done *passed*. And what's gone and passed don't matter no more. At all. None of it. Zero. The past don't even exist no more."

THE PAST DON'T EVEN EXIST

It was a day back, maybe two, and I was tying one on at my crappy apartment in Austin, continuing the liquid arc of my long decline, when somebody called to tell me Steve—my not-quite father, but the only father who ever cared one whit—had died. And just like that, Steve was dead. This was the night before the funeral.

"Who's this?" I asked. It would take days for the shock to set in, way longer to get an answer.

"He would want you to know," the man said in an accent I couldn't place. "Tomorrow at noon. I believe the name of the cemetery is Hillcrest, yes. There is a family plot there."

"Yeah, I know, but—"

"I am sorry," said the stranger, who hung up.

I stuffed a duffle with random gear and peeled out of South Austin right after sunset, just drunk enough to drive. A horizontal stretch of purple and orange sky saw me out of town, and by the time I hit Atlantis it was well after midnight. I grabbed a room at the Best Western and spent a couple of hours hitting the Julio and calling people I didn't know anymore, running down a list of names I knew had long erased me from connective existence. Not one of them picked up. But despite getting respectably trashed that night, there were still numbers I managed to avoid. Functional drunkenry for the win.

The funeral was about what you'd expect—casket gilded with flowers, radiating rows of plastic eggshell chairs, the somber and well-dressed guests. Jack Tanner (the town's fifth-gen undertaker), flanked with his minions in functional, black Skechers. A preacher mouthing all the appropriate nonsense. More mourners than I could count, waves and waves of them, all of us mumbling together when prompted like a discordant, middle school choir. *Mumble, mumble. Amen, mumble.*

I'm the only family Steve had left. They put me solo front and center of what remained of him. Behind me—over half of them standing—must've been a record number for a funeral in Atlantis, mostly students (current and former), teachers and staff, and local luminaries, such as we have in a place like this. The mayor was there. Coach, too. The members of law enforcement who would soon escort my drunk ass out of there. And then, off to one side with their stupid little secret society pins, members of the Caddo Club, several also upper management and/or shareholders in Berkey International. One nodded my way with a nod that was more of a wink. I saw people I used to know and lots of people I didn't. I saw the grown-up version of my very first girlfriend, wet-eyed and stunning, and—a couple of rows behind her—Meredith. Looking right at me like she was reading something written upside-down on the inside of my skull. And if it weren't for the tequila'd haze, I wouldn't have been able to shake her gaze or stop myself from walking over there and doing something stupid. Well, something stupider than what I ended up doing. On either side of Meredith and behind were a little girl two-knuckles deep in her nose, a trio of earnest teen boys holding baseball caps over their hearts, a small cluster of gender busters in black, including one with crazy rainbow hair, but I didn't see the somebody I was looking for—the somebody who was Red.

I didn't realize I'd been holding my breath until I let it out in an annoyingly loud sigh. Meredith, I could handle. Probably. But

Red was something else. And when I recognized the raw relief I felt regarding his absence—that Red not being there was more pressing to me than Steve being dead just feet from my face—a surge of guilt and shame came over me as if summoned from a nightmare sea, and the sudden rush of it almost kicked me out of my chair.

People were quietly crying or pretending to. Either that or they were looking at the ground or staring at the pamphlets in their laps that told us all about Steve and his celebrated saintliness in an exhaustive review of his charitable works. *Survived by his adopted son...* And the preacher rambled on and on with a stack of gorgeous, pomaded hair that would make Johnny Cash blush. *God is good*, he said. *His arms encircle all. Into his heavenly grace,* he said. *By the light of his son. That we may rise. And be together whole. God is good*, he said. *What Steve hath done. His works live on. Without charity is naught. Despite our faith. God is good,* the preacher said, and said it again, and then there were mumbles, and then mumbles more, and then it was quiet.

I don't know how long I'd nodded off for. It was my name on repeat at increasing volume that woke me up. *Sam, Sam...* It was Steve's voice. "Sam," he said, much louder this time. But it wasn't Steve; it was that preacher.

"Yessir," I said, unslumping myself.

"Say a few words?"

If that preacher wanted me to say something, he was the only one. I looked around at everybody and then back at him. Clearly, he was new in town. I shook my head *no* for all our benefits and I was all set to sit there and maybe go back to sleep and ride the damn thing out in polite disassociation until everybody left, but then it happened.

A couple of rows behind me, somebody fake-coughed. Then, across the way, somebody fake-cleared their throat in response. Then a third joined them over from the Caddo Club section, only his was bolder and a straight up snicker. I couldn't locate the exact mouth it came from, so I just glared at the CC section in general. A collective sphincter-tightening came over the crowd. That's when I staggered up to the stage.

I nodded at the preacher and put my Stetson back on and looked around for my mic and guitar, and I was genuinely confused when I couldn't find my mic and guitar where they were supposed to be. And I was just about to yell at the roadies when I saw Steve's body again—supine, haloed with lilies and roses—and his body was dead. I wasn't on stage; I wasn't about to perform. That wasn't even a thing anymore. I was at a funeral, and it was Steve's, and he was absolutely and utterly no longer alive. I stood there and looked at his face and shook my head.

"I don't know," I said, my voice like burnt plastic. "I just found out and drove here and... Thanks for coming, I guess. Steve would like this, seeing all y'all. Not being dead, but knowing y'all were here, having these flowers and trinkets and... That pamphlet kinda says it all. His accomplishments and charities and all that, but them words... they don't... I mean, who he was, you know? Not that words could. Everybody here has their story about Steve. Most of y'all know mine. How he took me in after mom died. Gave me a roof, adopted me, sent me to college, paid for... shit, everything. If you didn't know, now you do. All the gossip at the time. Not that Steve gave a damn. Maybe he did, I don't know... Ain't one good thing ever happened in my life I can't trace back to Steve. Career, hit songs, them videos... You ever meet somebody who treated you the way Steve did? I mean, most of us say we don't care about color and money and religion and all that, but that's just what we say. You gotta see how it plays out and... Why was Steve even here? Like, his dad had more money than all of us put together. Steve could've done anything. Gone off, been a professor, travel the world. Why stay here and teach redneck high school, for fuck's sake? In Atlantis. Atlantis, Texas. Caddo County. Where we loved him so, so much. Where we all treated him with... Let's see a show of hands, huh? Lemme see them hands! There you go... up, up... that's right, up... Now, see, what I was gonna say—what I was gonna say was—show of hands if you ever called Steve *faggot* behind his back... Down, down, down... Y'all serious? Not a one of you? Not even whispered to friends? It's okay... Look here. I'm raising mine. I said it plenty. Faggot, butt-pirate, all of it... But not y'all, huh? I'm just... just fucking with y'all. Like, you know, it's true and everything, but... Guess y'all don't need it today. Except maybe you Caddo Club boys. What's that y'all in over there, anyway—VIP section? Y'all up in the funeral booth? Woot woot! Hey, it's okay... Papa Berkey ain't around to slap y'all down no more. Call Steve whatever you want now. Ain't nobody gonna stop you. Maybe now y'all can pull in some of that oil money, huh? Now that Beau ain't around. And Steve. Say, that reminds me, was Beau's death also under suspicious circumstances? I mean, did Beau also drown out there in Lake Atlantis like Steve did? A lake he was terrified of? No? Hold off, officers... Just give me a... I ain't done! Listen! You think I drove all this way to make peace with you redneck, hate-criming, mouthbreathers? Fuck y'all! I came to make the sword... *bring* the sword. To bring it, y'all hear? Unhand me, officer! I ain't.... Paper says suicide? In that lake? Fuck that shit. That ain't even—"

EVER SINCE I TOUCHED THAT PYRAMID

"Shouldn't a done that," Chuck tells the wall.

"Yeah, well..."

I've stopped looking at Steve's house. I'm just sitting on the floor, waiting for nobody to post my bail.

"Bad idea," Chuck says, this time to me. "You ever, like, *what was I even thinking?*"

I'd give every last penny of what's left of my royalties to make Chuck disappear.

"Only telling you because you and Red is friends," he says.

Last thing I want to think about right now is Red. I don't know what I want to think about right now, but it sure as shit ain't Red.

"Don't tell him I said it," Chuck says.

"No problem."

"But, you know, if Red does come for you? Don't say nothing about what I said about her, but, I don't know... Put in a good word. Maybe he'll go my bail, too."

"Red ain't going my bail."

"Red ain't coming for you?" Chuck asks, more distressed about it than I am.

"Not in that way."

"Oh," he says, looking down. "Might as well tell you the rest, then. Wasn't going to on account of—"

"Know what, Chuck? Let's just—"

"On account I don't think he knows this one part about his old lady."

"Which part?"

"Exactly," Chuck says. "Only, *witch* ain't the proper term. *Medicine woman* is more like it. On account of her being Indian and all? Native American? You know, like—"

"Red's old lady is a witch because she's Native American?"

"No! That ain't—" Chuck recoils. "Man, you making it sound like I'm Indian racist or something. I ain't Indian racist!"

"Okay."

"Hell, I'm part Indian myself! Like you."

"What?"

"Cherokee," Chucks says, knuckles proudly thumping his heart.

Let the record state that Chuck Tender is most definitely not any part Cherokee. A remarkable percentage of rednecks claim at least an eighth of native blood—sometimes more, but rarely exceeding a quarter—and nearly all allege Cherokee heritage.

"I just mean…" Chuck sits up. "She's got powers, man. Look here: I seen her nekkid one time. Never seen such beautiful titties my whole life… A little on the small side, but perky, which happens to be my preference, and with these little brown nipples, just like you'd imagine an Indian would have. Little perky Indian nipple princess. Goddamn…"

Chuck lies back on his bunk in reverie of perky witch breasts, squinting with a look of simultaneous confusion and contentment.

An hour later, they bring us lunch. We each get a tray with two white bread bologna sandwiches, a bruised slice of cantaloupe, and an eight-ounce carton of skim milk. It's not delicious. I dig in. Chuck doesn't touch his plate.

"Ain't you hungry?" I ask.

"My tummy's been off for a while now," he says softly. "Plus, I'm on that gluten free."

"Want my cantaloupe?"

"Nah, go on ahead. Starting to think... I don't know, maybe she might've poisoned me."

"Who, Hillary?"

"Shit, I'd like to see her try! No, I'm talking Rain."

Red's girlfriend. Who was it told me about her before? I eat all four bologna sandwiches and wait for the remorse to set in.

"I got them headaches, too," Chuck grumbles. "From football. All them concussions we got? Supposed to be every game is like a car crash. You know that? Course, they don't tell you at the time. You get em? Headaches?"

"I didn't play all the way through," I say.

"Red's got em worse. But he was all college and NFL. Famous and shit. Look at him now, though. Worse off than me! Giant bastard can barely walk. But you already know that... Anyway, mine's getting worse, too. My head, I mean." Chuck's voice is weighty with regret. "Ever since I touched that pyramid."

Nearly everybody around these parts has some kind of Bigfoot story, but claimed sightings of our lake's mythical pyramid are rarer than a steak in mid-moo. Chuck stands up from his bunk, hands arranged in front of his body in something between a triangle and oversized football. He moves the shape around the room as he paces, checking in with his paws from time to time, trying to get the shape just right, eyebrows squeezed with effort.

"It was out near that big island in the lake..." he begins quietly. "Nighttime. Water lower than usual. Remember how it does that sometimes? How they can't explain it? Well, that's how it was that night, with me out in this Jon boat. I saw something peeking up over there in the dark near that big island, the one with the rocks, but closer to one of them little ones out there. And I seen there was this object in the water, kinda peeking up. Looked like a rock or something. Only, the rock was triangularly shaped. And it wasn't sticking up all that much, just maybe a foot above the water line. Not even. Maybe eight inches, seven. No… like, five inches. Five-and-a-half. Anyway, I pull up aside it to see this stone was flat on all sides and sorta rough. Slimy, too. Gray, pointy on top, but rounded off a little. And I got up close—I mean, right up next to it—and I seen it was etched with strange designs all around it. Like a talisman. Ancient and powerful and…"

"You're saying you saw the pyramid?" I ask.

"I ain't saying, I'm knowing. And it wasn't just seeing. I touched it," Chucks whispers.

The air in our cell has gone expectant and solemn. Chuck rubs the palm of his right hand and looks at it with concern.

"When?"

Chuck shakes his head. "That there's a question I can't rightly answer. Time's gone all squirrelly since it happened. Might've been a month ago, could've been just last night in a dream. Whenever it was, I touched that sumbitch with this here hand. The same pyramid them Spaniards and Frogs talked about back in them olden days. Look at my hand, Bobby. Look at it…"

Chuck shoves his right hand just inches from my face. It smells like a hot dog lost a fight with a fart. I back away to focus and clear my nose and Chuck holds the hand steady, fingers up and palm out like the Buddha statue my ex once kept above our fireplace in Austin. Except that Buddha didn't have farty hot dog hands.

"See?" Chuck asks. "That triangle?"

All I see are callouses from decades of hard labor. "Damn," I say, "look at that."

Chuck returns his hand to his jerseyed torso. "It won't stop burning, Bobby," he says. "It burns me something bad."

"You should ask for some lotion or something," I suggest.

"It burns, though."

"Lotion might help, is what I'm saying."

"Another thing is, right after I touched it?" Chuck continues. "The rain come up, just like that. Like it was a consequence or something. The rain come up and the wind did, too, and the water got choppy, choppier than you would think it could, so much so it knocked me out that sumbitch. The Jon boat. Just about sank it tryin to climb back in. Might've drowned too, if I weren't so close to one of them little islands where the water's all shallow. The ones them gators like. But there weren't a gator one that night. And when I turned around? Weren't no pyramid no more, either. It was just… gone. Like it had never even been there. That's when I realized it's alive. It's sentient. Know what that means?"

"It don't like being touched?"

"Means it's got a mind of its own," Chuck confides. "Means it could have struck me dead, but it did not. It just scalded me as a warning. As punishment. I have been marked, see. I wronged it with my touch, and this damn thing ain't stopped burning ever since. I think it's getting worse, Bobby."

"Maybe try that lotion?"

Chuck regards his hand one last time with a mutter before Al Bundying it down inside the waistband of his sweatpants. Then he turns to the wall next to his bunk and goes quiet. It's so quiet I can almost hear his hand burning.

"Thank you for listening, Bobby," he says. "You're a good listener."

"Well."

"I touched it," he says. "Shouldn't a done that…" Then he adjusts his too-big jersey, curls into himself like a forlorn bear, and falls asleep.

Sightings of that pyramid have been part of local lore even before one of De Soto's flunkies wrote about it in 1542. He'd separated from the rest of the flock (likely deserted, Steve said), paddled upriver, and air-quotes discovered our neighboring lake. The Spaniard stayed through summer and returned downstream in fall, feverish and yammering, with rough sketches of a partially submerged pyramid made of gold, capped with jewels, and inscribed with a form of writing that most resembled Phoenician. His superior sent back an exploratory band of homesick vets who found zero pyramids but an unusually large lake where it didn't make sense there would be one. The elongated body of water stretched out into hundreds of tributaries and was populated with more islands than they could count, none larger than a couple of acres. On one of the bigger islands, the Spaniards found a rough circle of stone menhirs surrounding the remains of a deserted village.

Steve taught us that was code. In explorer-speak, *deserted* meant *littered with corpses*—that whole *can't handle smallpox* thing. Some say that initial Spaniard brought it with him, single-handedly wiping out the lake-dwelling Caddo, and that he'd most likely been the one to erect the stone circle. With no gold to be found, his buddies probably hung him. And the only thing they returned with were unreliable maps of this part of East Texas and the name *Atlantis*—that fabled Shangri-la first mentioned by Plato and given legs a thousand years later by codpiece-wearing aristocrats.

Anyway, that's how this town got its name.

Of course, the Caddo called it something else. They had different stories about the lake and how it got there, too. And just like the legends Chuck was forced to report about in front of Steve's history class, there were multiple versions, but most went something like this: Long before honkeys started calling it Lake Atlantis, the people who lived on its shores called the place the Lake of the Rock of the Big Man. But there was a before time—a time when it had just been a river—and in those times, they say a lone hunter canoed upstream and camped on a high bluff overlooking the river, and when the hunter went down to the bank for some water, he saw the Big Man fishing out there in a wide spot on an enormous mossy rock, and the Big Man waved the hunter away with an urgent gesture of his giant hand. The hunter had never seen one of the Big People before and he was frightened. He hauled ass back to his village and told the Kahdi all he'd seen and the Kahdi held a council to find out what it meant. One of the grandmothers knew about the Big People from stories she'd heard as a child. She said what the hunter had seen was a bad omen, or at least a warning from the Big People, and they all needed to leave for the hills at once. So that's what the village did—they picked up and left. A week or so later, on the next full moon, the earth shook so hard that it leveled trees for miles and the river rose up and washed away what remained of where they had lived, and the place where the hunter had seen the Big Man was transformed into the lake we have today. In time, the people moved back and the lake became famed for its bounty of fish and deer. But the Caddo also encountered strange phenomena there: the sky would turn unnatural colors for no reason, some of the islands seemed to move around when no one was looking, there were tall stones piled in strange arrangements, and sometimes traders or hunting parties were unable to find their way back home after returning from afar, sometimes needing to backtrack for days, and sometimes, it's said, coming back to a river where their village by the lake was supposed to be. The people of the lake also believed you shouldn't speak while out on the lake, especially when the moon was out. It was said to anger the water.

MAN FROM ATLANTIS

Turns out I don't have do my full stay with Chuck. Even better, it isn't Red who bails me out.

"I need a drink," I tell him.

"What you need is a goddamn shower," Coach says. The Old Man, ever-present whistle and all.

"What took you so long?"

"Ungrateful little shit," he scowls. "Knew I shoulda left you in there. Was hoping you'd sober up more before I pulled you out."

We drive away from the county jail in Coach's new Raptor F-150— shiny, red, all kinds of loaded. We drive right by Steve's house on the corner of Falway and Dewey, where the past doesn't even exist.

"What you over there mumbling?" Coach asks.

"Something Chuck said," I say. "According to him, the past doesn't exist."

"Well, first of all, that's nonsense. Second, who the fuck is Chuck?"

"Tender. Chuck Tender."

"That ugly sumbitch?"

"Says he sees you on the regular out there at Sirens. Also says he's seen that pyramid out at the lake. Touched it even."

"I bet he has," Coach nods at something out on the street. "Proba- bly climbed inside that pyramid, went back in time, and butt-fucked a dinosaur while he was at it. That boy ain't right. Crazier than a shithouse rat. What's he doing in there?"

"Talking."

"Always was a bit chatty," Coach says. "What's he in for this time?"

"Shot his load on a stripper."

"Oh, for fuck's sake," Coach huffs. "You can't be going around doing that sort of thing. Who'd he hose down?"

"Verona, I think. Madrona?"

"That ain't a name," Coach says. "Regardless, it's ungentlemanly. Which bring us to you, shitbird. You need to go back to finishing school? Learn how to act decent in public? I know your boyfriend taught you better. Just because he's dead and gone don't mean you can go full heathen on us now."

I've always thought that Coach didn't feel one way or the other about Steve being gay until Steve took me in my senior year. Coach didn't take my not returning to football too well, and he likely blamed Steve for encouraging my other interests (music, namely). It's a wonder why Coach even spoke to me after that. As far as he's concerned, there are only two types of people in the world: football people and who-the-fuck-cares.

"What's wrong with your voice, anyway?" he asks. I haven't run into him since it went bad. "You sound like a Mongolian throat singer who ain't singing."

"That would probably just sound regular."

"Naw, *Sling Blade!*" Coach shouts, convinced he's the first person in existence to suggest it. "*Well, I used to sing real purty, mm hmm, but now I sound like shit. French fried taters, mm hmm... That's what you fucking sound like!*"

"I know what I sound like."

Coach passes the quickest way back to my hotel, keeping on Falway, right down the middle of *Blacklantis*—the black part of town.

"What happened? Used to sing like a bird," he says. "That's what they tell me, anyway."

Like a bird who was once called Alt-Country's Elvis Costello. But then that bird fucked it all away and woke up with a voice like this.

"I appreciate you bailing me out," I say.

"Trying to change the subject," Coach says. "Well, you're welcome. But it ain't a gift, you know. I ain't that generous. Gonna expect you to cough that cash up before too long. Ain't exactly made of gold or nothing."

"Truck says otherwise."

"Looks are deceiving," he replies. "Anyway, I was surprised to hear you were still in the can. Thought your lady friend woulda got you out."

"Shit," I say, powering down the window, "if it was up to Mere, I'd do the whole 48 in there and then some."

"Wonder why," Coach smirks. "But I wasn't talking about her. I was referring to the other one. You know, your rich nigger girl?"

Coach is one of these codgers who live just for the sheer joy of getting under people's skin. Well, that and football. The slur isn't merely racist assholery; it's him trying to get a rise out of me. I lean my head outside the truck.

"What's wrong?" Coach asks. "What you doing over there?"

"You know better than to say shit like that."

"I know. I'm sorry," Coach says solemnly. "Old habits die hard, son. Let's try again... Rich... nigger *woman*. How's that?"

"The worst part is you thinking you're funny."

"I am funny," he grins. "And I still don't understand why I can't say it! They call each other that and way worse in my very presence. You know how it is in that locker-room!"

"How about you let me out at the next stop?"

"Aw, now," Coach says. "Don't be like that, snowflake. I'm just pulling your chain. Daisy chain, by the look of it. You over there pouting? That city life making you soft, city boy? Seriously, you shoulda called her—Sonya, that is. Your African-American love interest of yesteryear. You know she owns half Atlantis these days, and the other half is lookin to sell."

So that was her at the funeral. Sonya Tyson. Goddamn.

We stop at a red at one of the only lights in Blacklantis, maybe half a mile before Falway hits the highway. There's a Texaco on the southwest corner of the intersection that looks brand new, where two black kids in letter jackets pump diesel into the side of an elongated Ram truck, both looking down into their phones as they lean back on the truck and wait. Coach lays on his horn and the young men jump. One drops his phone. When they see that it's Coach, they laugh at each other and clap and point at Coach and he laughs and points at them, too. The light turns green, but Coach just sits there, shout-talking with them about practice later today and some reference to *Luke Cage* I don't catch.

"See?" Coach says, driving on. "I watch *Luke Cage, Martin, Jeffersons*... all that."

"How about *Atlanta?*"

"Too surreal for my tastes."

"You know what's surreal? You telling me how broke you are when I know for a fact you get a brand-new truck like this every year."

"Surreal ain't the right word for that. Besides, it's every other year. Maybe."

"What they run you? Seventy K? Eighty after taxes?"

"Can't recall, exactly. I get em on special," he says to passing traffic.

"CC Special," I say, knowing it might be the only thing in the known universe that could get under Coach's wrinkly, liver-spotted skin. "Still under their thumb, huh?"

"I ain't under nobody's thumb," he mutters. "And what the fuck is that supposed to mean, anyway?"

"It's an expression."

"An expression of what—stupid?"

"An expression of you being somebody's dog after all these years. Weren't you supposed to get yourself free? Go off and retire or something? But here you are, still driving another man's truck..."

"You know what you really sound like, Billy Bob?" Coach replies after composing himself and spitting out of his window. "You sound like a bunch of sour grapes got caught up in your throat right along with all them dicks you been sucking. You trying to wash that dick down, boy? Don't taste too good? Maybe you should use some grapes that ain't so sour. Ever thought of that, grapey dick boy? Or maybe—here's a thought—maybe you should stop sucking so many dicks. Or, if you just have to keep sucking dicks, maybe don't throw your career down the toilet so's you can afford the right kind of grapes for your dicky throat."

It's always *Tom and Jerry* with Coach. Tom pulls a knife, Jerry's got a rifle. Tom grabs a bazooka, Jerry's in a tank. At some point, you just have to give the geezer the round, but I'd be lying if I said that last jab about my career didn't sting.

"Hey," he says, checking me out sideways. "I missed your ass. You know that, right? You know I'm just funnin."

"I know I need that drink," I say. "Why ain't you to the Bestern?"

"Ain't going there straight," he smiles sideways. "Want to know where we're going first?"

"Mainly I want to know how you know so much about sucking dicks."

"Don't ask, don't tell!" Coach laughs, slapping his knee. "Still got it, huh? Ain't too many that can fun it up like you and me. Around here, you were always one of the few. Gets lonesome without other actual men around. We're a dying breed, you know that? Soon we'll all be gone."

"Some sooner than others."

"Now you gonna crack at my age?" he hoots. "You ageismizing

me? Gonna have to do better than that, son. Everybody knows age tends to flatten a man. Hell, I hardly recognize myself in the mirror sometimes... Mainly cause I keep gettin better lookin!" he shouts and punches me in the arm with glee. "Not you, though. You look like shit. Smell like it, too."

"I'm getting drier by the second over here and I'm just gonna keep smelling until you get me back to that hotel."

"To the point," he nods. "I respect that. Real man shit. Well, here's the thing, Bobby—"

"It's Sam," I say. "You know my name is Sam."

"Whatever, Bobby. See, here's the thing," Coach coughs. "It's about them CC boys you called out at the funeral. The same ones you have rightly identified as my ongoing benefactors. Same ones who line my short pockets with just enough long cash to do shit like bailing you out."

"The CC paid my bail?"

Coach takes a right off Falway into a dead-end street that cul-de-sacs two blocks up. I don't remember it at all. We're still in Blacklantis, somewhere under the big hill that marks the south side of Hillcrest, but we must be at least a half mile from the highway. Coach pulls over in the semi-circle and kills the truck. The street is empty. Whatever homes used to be here were razed years ago.

"I'll take this dramatic pull-off as a yes," I say.

"Don't," Coach replies, rolling down his window. "Or maybe do, but only in a roundabout way. But you should very much not roundaboutly shut your mouth about the CC being responsible for what happened to Steve and Beau, at least for the remainder of your stay."

"Well, that's not suspicious. And I ain't staying long enough for there to be much of a remainder."

Coach nods at the trees. "Look, I know what it sounds like. But, first of all, you're wrong. About Beau, about Steve, about all of it. Which you, in a hopefully less drunken state, will realize. But right now? I'm just saying... Caddo Club ain't the sort that appreciate being fucked with. I mean, I'll do what I can, but... there's consequences."

"Yeah," I say, "I've heard the stories."

"Okay, then."

"One in particular about Orv Morris's dad. You remember him, don't you, Coach?"

"You know I do," he says quietly.

"Morris Sr. gets in deep with the CC and the old boy can't pay it off and, well... next thing you know, cops are pulling him out of Lake Atlantis, only he's wearing these brand new cinderblock shoes. You hear that story?"

"Wasn't just a story," Coach inhales. "But a coincidence in this matter. Meaning the lake. Because if the CC did murder Steve? What would stop me from telling you right here, right now? I mean, really. You forget who I am, son. Ain't much happens around here I don't get word of first, and the CC might put a little jingle in my pockets on occasion, but I bought these big boy jeans myself."

"So, you're telling me Steve killed himself. That what you're saying?"

"Whether he did or not isn't relevant to this conversation. All I know is the CC weren't behind it," he says.

"CC are behind everything around here."

"Maybe back in the day," he snorts. "Back when they were the only show around. Back when they didn't have all this competition. Used to be things were relaxed and everything went on smooth behind the scenes and people knew their place. Somebody occasionally got out of line or thought they could get away with skipping a payment or two—or, in Morris's case, about a dozen—and then said particular dumb fuck would get invited fishing. And after that, everybody would remember who was running the show and start acting right again. Order restored."

"You inviting me fishing, Coach?"

He breathes out slowly and looks out at the street where nothing is happening.

"No," he says. "I'm inviting you to hold off on the asshole act just a little bit—"

"I'm an asshole?"

"Hardly anybody at the funeral knew who the fuck you were until you opened your asshole mouth! But the CC remembers, Bobby. They know exactly who you are. And if you keep poking that bear in the balls, don't act surprised when he buttfucks you with your own pecker. Especially the way things have been going as of late."

"What do you mean *as of late?*"

"Like, recently."

"I fucking know that part, man. I'm asking—"

"It's just bad, okay? CC have been on a tear ever since Papa Berkey died and left your gay uncle in charge. They took a hit when Steve came in and revamped the whole operation, and before you make an even bigger deal of something else that ain't, listen: Berkey International is just one piece of this whole country-ass puzzle. You heard about our little meth problem, right? Well, for every dollar the BI makes, this new meth king makes five more, maybe ten. That's a whole new operation going on around here without the CC's consent, not to mention them not seeing a dirty penny of that money. Then top it all off with your old lady friend. Every damn day she's buying up some new business or house or property around here, even places ain't nobody want in the first place. This street, for example. What she gonna do with a street like this? And the CC ain't exactly doing back flips about a black woman charging them rent for this and that in a town they been accustomed to running since way back. You feel me?"

Even ten years ago, Sonya had more pull in the county than anybody in the CC would have voluntarily allowed. Steve had a hand in that, despite his dad running the Caddo Club ever since coming back from the Korean War and transforming the CC from a ball-less social collective of honkey businessmen into an aboveground mob of whites-only politicians, judges, and done-good rednecks (fewer pinky rings, nicer trucks) who ran every penny through Berkey International—legit as it comes, and by far the largest employer in all of East Texas. Which brings me back to Coach.

That under-their-thumb comment hit the way it did because Coach has wanted to hang up his whistle for decades now, but the CC always finds a way to yank him back in. Coach might have paid for his big boy jeans, but the CC were the ones who sold them to Coach at cost. It's no secret that high school football in Texas is a for-profit endeavor, and football in Atlantis has been a CC cash cow since the 70s, especially with Coach at the teat-squeezing helm. Some people are inclined to a particular greatness; Coach's is orchestrating the sanctioned violence of high school ball, for which he is compensated by the CC above his schoolboard-approved salary and under just about every table imaginable. There are more original football minds out there, but few of them can match Coach's record, his district and state championships, his on-field aura, his skill at manipulating teenage brains, or his penchant for exploiting an opponent's weak links. There's not much to say for growing up in Atlantis, but making Coach's Merfeet squad is an exception. To unquestionably bleed your way into the starting Merfeet lineup is to walk the halls of Atlantis High like a bruised and burnished god, ridiculous mascot be damned.

That's right, the Merfeet. Originally, it was *Mermen*—because, you know, Atlantis and all. Originally, the mascot was part iridescent fish (the bottom) and part Aryan muscle-bound youth (the upper), but then that Bigfoot craze of the 70s hit and our Merman morphed into its current form, mostly due to Caddo County also being famed for elusive hominids of unusual size (aka, the *Big People*). Folks my age and older recall film crews setting up shop around the lake and cranking out documentaries and B films of variable merit, as well as waves of tourists who briefly made Atlantis a Bigfoot trinket boom town. That was also the CC's doing. And it was Beau's idea to change our mascot into something of a more Sasquatchic demeanor—shaggier, sneering, yet still aquatic and armed with a trident. After Bigfoot fever died, the image just stuck. Makes sense. Who'd go back to being a plain-ass Merman after that?

"Hey!" Coach shouts. "You asleep over there?" He powers down his window and shoots a nose puppy out on the pavement.

"Just thinking how bizarre a Merfoot is. I mean, the bottom is a fish and the top is some hairy, mythical ape."

"Ain't no ape," Coach snorts, starting up the truck and pulling out of the cul-de-sac. "Ain't mythical, either. You know better than that."

Locally, our legendary pyramid might be viewed as questionable, but Bigfoot? Around here, you don't talk shit about Bigfoot.

Coach continues. "You think I got to consider how bizarre a Merfoot seems to outsiders? I am constantly reminded every damn game. You remember the sideline banners: *Murder the Merfeet, Mangle the Merfeet, Massacre the Merfeet...* Each one so fucking convinced of its own cleverness. Kind of like you, come to think of it. Same ones, year in and year out. Actually, there was a new banner last week I ain't seen before: *Marinate the Merfeet.* Someone had drawn a Merfoot trying to get out of an oven with an apple its mouth, herbs and spices and shit all over it while it was being cooked by some drastic looking eagle in a chef's hat."

"Well, that's taking it too far," I say.

"Agreed. First of all, eagles don't cook their food. Second, there ain't any damn eagle within a hundred miles of these parts. Therefore, a Merfoot—when you think about it—is equally as realistic as some kind of monster, football-related, chef-eagle."

"Never thought of it that way."

"Nobody does," Coach says.

THE BEST LITTLE SHITHOLE IN TEXAS

In Blacklantis, as well as the white parts of Atlantis that surround it, the streets are named either for non-native trees or the Civil War deities of the town's postbellum pioneers, who fled the deeper South after Sherman reverse-alchemized their crops into charcoal. Coach has just made a right onto Davis Street, as in Jefferson Davis—President of the Confederate States of America. Most of the black churches I remember here are gone now, and Ant's—the grocery store/auto shop/social hub of Blacklantis—is all boarded up. We pass one abandoned and condemned house after another, then even more at increasing intervals when we turn onto Judge Street (after Judge John Campbell, who served on the US Supreme Court until he decided to battle Reconstruction with his native Georgia—like anybody else who had Steve as a teacher at Atlantis High, I only know these crumbs of secret history because of him).

"Jesus," I say. "Get me to the Bestern already. You already delivered the message."

"That was business," he says, driving slower and squinting to examine one of the shanties that line Judge Street. "This here's social. Hell, I might be dead next time you roll through."

We're at the highest elevation of Atlantis now, in the hills that were Caddo hunting grounds for thousands of years. Most of the roads in and out of town follow native trails that once spidered out in all directions and connected hundreds of villages in a bountiful web, but other than Caddo County itself, the names of those people have never been registered in the textbooks of time, as it is for the slaves and descendants of slaves who built our downtown and worked the soil until it yielded enough cotton and corn to make their effort worthwhile for the men who drove them. There is one exception to the rule: Frederick Douglass Elementary, originally built as the black school in Atlantis, and only desegregated in the 1960s. Now it, too, is shuttered and abandoned.

"When did that happen?" I ask.

"The elementary? Oh, there's a new one over next to the high school now. Named it after Dubya," Coach laughs.

"Of course. Ain't nothing changed around here. Same ole, same ole."

"Tell that to the kids who've got AC now. You remember what a shithole that old one was. It was like a sauna for possums and rats up in there."

"I don't remember possums."

"There was possums," Coach says. "And rats as big as possums. And now there ain't. So, in actuality, things change plenty around here, and for the better."

"Depends on how you look at it."

"Yeah, whether you're outside looking in or inside looking out."

"Some of us are stuck with both."

"Ain't nobody can do that," Coach says, rubbing the back of his neck. "A man can only be in one place at a time, and you picked your spot a long time ago."

We drive away from the old school on Hickory Creek Drive alongside a ditch that passes for the neighborhood's sole creek that hasn't seen a hickory tree since forever. Coach slows down in front of an overgrown, two-acre lot that used to be a trailer park. That's where I lived with my mom.

"Look there," Coach points. "That ain't change?"

"Keep driving."

The road curves back to Dewey Street, where Coach hooks left and heads north through Old Atlantis where Beau Berkey's grandparents and the other Old Money families built their estates in the 1800s. We roll by what was once the city park and pool that glittered in the Texas sun with the unending vanity of summer. They bulldozed it years ago and put in a playground where nobody plays.

Finally, we hit the spot where Dewey terminates into 59 on the north end of town. There, in the face of incoming traffic, a billboard reads WELCOME TO ATLANTIS, BEST LITTLE TOWN IN TEXAS. To verify the claim, the Chamber of Commerce and CC placed one just like it on the highway as you come in from the west. As a child, I took that brag as factual, as if some larger governance had decreed Atlantis supreme among the other five billion similar shitholes in Texas.

Coach loops back south on the highway in the direction of the Bestern. He points out the new businesses on 59 with a pride suggesting he had a hand in their construction. Another E-Z Mart, a Pizza Hut, a Pep Boys, the Denny's… each adjacent to a deserted version of older establishments that smelled like the future when I was a kid. Coach has lived in Atlantis all his life.

"Why didn't you go live somewhere else for a while?" I ask. "Get out and see the world?"

"I saw Nam," he says. "That count?"

"I'm not talking about that."

"No," Coach replies. "Most people don't."

"I'm talking about traveling on purpose, checking out how other people live. Trying out something that doesn't suck for a while."

"Not all of us think like Gypsies, Bobby."

"*Roma*," I say. "And it's Sam."

"Roma what?"

"That's how you reference the people you just referenced."

"You daddy was Roman?"

"I don't know what the fuck he was, but what you say is *Roma* or *Romani* or—"

"Is this how you are now?" Coach huffs. "Like, perpetually uptight? What'd you do back there in County—stick your finger up the wrong person's ass?"

He's going several miles under the speed limit in the fast lane. A trucker buzzes by on our right, looking down on me like I'm slow-motion roadkill.

"The main reason people say shit they ain't supposed to say," Coach explains, "is to help people like you to get over your uppityness."

"Asking for basic respect ain't uppity."

"Basic respect?" Coach coughs. "That's rich, coming from you."

"Meaning?"

"Meaning you publicly trashing this town every goddamn chance you get? How many of them songs you gonna write about us? Always tearing us down... Think none of us got MTV? There was a goddamn town hall about that one video with them burning crosses and chicks in Bigfoot bikinis and—"

"'Man from Atlantis,'" I chuckle. It was one of my hits back when I had hits.

"Why you gotta do shit like that, Bobby? We already know what you think about us a hundred times over, but you just keep running up the score."

"You're no stranger to that."

"Fair enough," he replies. "And just like you, I will meet my reward for it. But you really ought to take people's feelings more into account."

"Like the CC's feelings?"

"Not just them," he replies absently. "Everybody. By and large, people who grow up around here—black, white, striped, polka dotted, whatever—love this place. That's why they stay. Which happens to also be why they don't take kindly to you shitting on it."

"I grew up here, too."

"Yeah, well... It ain't like your people are from here, is it?"

"And yours are?"

"As a matter of fact, yes," Coach says. "Mine hit Texas in the 1820s, and lots of others' folks did, too. That's a lot of history in one damn place, son. We built this place."

"Slaves built this place," I point out.

"I ain't... Man, I'm talking before that! Like, years—"

"It was slaves from day one, Coach, and if you really want to talk about before times, you know this was all Caddo land for thousands—"

"Shit, them Caddo came in and stole it from whoever lived here before them. Everybody knows that! That's human nature, son. And none of that's got shit-squat to do with my people, because them Caddo was already gone when we got here. I feel sorry for them. Really, I do. And you might not know it to look at me, but I've got some of that Cherokee blood myself."

"What, an eighth?"

A woman in the next lane waves at Coach and smiles as we pass. If they allowed soccer in East Texas, she'd be the redneck version of your archetypal soccer mom. Coach waves back and she nearly creams herself. Everywhere we drive, that's what it's like. Waves, thumbs up, the three-fingers-held-high hand sign indicating the Merfoot's trident... each of them returned by Coach with a smile for his admirers and a victorious smirk for me. He holds up the whistle on his chest.

"Here's your real answer, though," he says. "This whistle belonged to my daddy when he was Coach." Nobody's ever seen Coach without his whistle on. The joke used to be that Coach bangs his wife and all his ample side action with nothing but that whistle on, tweeting it full blast upon ejaculation. "I ever tell you how he died?"

Coach flips back north on the highway at the point where 59 begins its long waggle out toward Houston. We're about a mile from the Bestern now. The fingers on my right hand are starting to shake. It's been years since I've been this long without a drink.

"He coached the ball team, but you couldn't make much of a living doing that back then, so my daddy worked for Beau Berkey full-time. Him and them other boys cleared out thousands of acres below the lake, fighting off moccasins and gators and gar the size of pirogues. Then they went back through and replanted all of it with them trees that made Beau his billions."

"Billons?"

"After some choice investments," Coach smirks. "How else you think Beau could afford to chase off them oil and gas companies what wanted to come in and drill the county dry? That's how rich that motherfucker was. I mean, we're talking the biggest business in Texas kicked out of one whole corner of the state by one onery-ass man. And nobody could say shit to Beau about it. Anyway, like I was saying, after he built the mills and processing plant and all that, Beau gave my daddy and them first pick of new jobs, and my daddy worked his ass off in there for years, coaching football on the side. I can still recall the smell of that mill on him… resin, motor oil, Old Gold tobacco… all of it mixed with sweat. It was a good job. Dangerous, but good. Same as now. And then one day I come home from school—eighth grade—and there was two men in suits in our house, had ties on. I remember that because we didn't have AC at the time and their attire was opposite of what you'd wear in that kind of heat."

I remember the story now. It's not something you want to hear more than once.

"My mama was balled up on the floor, crying like a baby. Howling, really. I'd heard that sound blocks away, didn't know what it was. Thought maybe it was somebody beating a dog."

"I'm sorry, Coach."

"I can see it in my head like it happened this morning," Coach continues, his voice getting further away. "I see that scene every time one of those smells hits me. Back in them days, you wouldn't think to pass up a job because it was unsafe—you were just thankful, you know? Considered yourself lucky. I don't think my daddy fell in that machine on purpose, but me and mama were a hell of a lot better off after it happened."

"How's that?"

"Oh…" Coach says, shaking the scene from his head. "Insurance. Lawsuit prevention, really. Them suits had come over to write mama a fat-ass check. Right away. Like anybody would ever try to sue Beau Berkey. Maybe it was just his way of… shit, I don't know."

Coach pulls into the Best Western parking lot and cuts the engine. There are only three cars on this side of the building.

"My daddy wasn't much more than cat food when they pulled him out of there," he says.

The two of us look out on the hotel's manicured trees in silence. Both of my hands are trembling.

"I'm sorry," I say.

"You already said that," Coach replies, acres away.

"Maybe I should—"

"You should be proud of Steve," Coach clears his throat and looks at me as if just then remembering I was sitting there. "Steve made changes in there that should've been done a long-ass time ago. Beau always was more about dollar signs and just paying out whenever accidental shit invariably happened. No sweat off his balls. Used to have all these dropouts driving Camaros around here because they stuck a finger or two in one of them machines on purpose. Not worth the gamble, you ask me, but Beau always did pay out. But your boyfriend put a stop to all that. Installed cameras everywhere, updated the machinery… new-fangled safety measures all over the place. That's what made it extra stupid when ole what's-his-name went and tried to sue the BI recently. Judge took one look at that security tape and laughed that one-handed boy's ass right out of court."

"What?"

"You remember," Coach laughs, shaking his head. "What a dumb mother—"

"Who tried to sue Berkey International?"

Coach looks at me, genuinely confused. For a second, I almost stop thinking about that fifth of tequila I'm about to swallow. "You know, the guy who stuck his hand in there? Last year?"

I shake my head harder than necessary.

"Okay..." he sighs. "Well, like I said, Steve put them new cameras everywhere. Caught this pretty boy on tape trying to stick his thumb in one of those choppers. Just his thumb, but still. I mean, folks have been doing shit like that on purpose for years, but I think this sumbitch is the first to get televised for it. Then he's got the cajones to take the BI to court, and when it's evident his big payday ain't forthcoming, this motherfucker throws a hissy, shouting all this stuff—in court, mind you—in front of the judge, mind you—about how he's gonna get Steve and his faggoty ass and all that. Like, boy, you already done fucked up! Now you gonna threaten a Berkey? In public? The fuck's wrong with you?"

I can't swallow. My throat feels packed with glass.

"You seriously didn't know?" Coach asks. "I just thought..."

I look straight ahead and try to summon up enough moisture for my mouth to start working again.

"Ain't nothing come of it," Coach says. "In the end, that boy should be grateful. If it weren't for them new safety measures Steve put in, he'd a bled out right there on the floor."

"Ain't nothing come of it?"

"Yeah, like I said—"

"Were you at the same funeral I was?"

"Well, yeah, but—"

"You read the paper?"

"Sports section."

I summarize the headline for him: "Steve Berkey, beloved of Atlantis, goes out and kills himself in a lake he was too terrified to even cross a bridge over. Others suggest he may have drowned on accident while out on a midnight swim, which he notably could not do. By which I mean *swim*. Meanwhile, nobody look over here at that very fucking obvious large curtain, behind which the CC and all of their goddamn issues with the new gay boss man are. Oh, and also? Apparently, there's a redneck with cut-off hands threatening to get Steve in public. But yeah, you know, probably a suicide..."

"It's just one cut-off hand," Coach frowns. "And like I told you—"

"What's his name?"

Coach shakes his head and squints. "Shit, I can't even remember your name right."

"Why the fuck am I just now hearing about this? Did the cops take him in? Question him?"

"You see a police scanner up in here?" Coach waves his hand at the dashboard. "Go back to county and ask yourself. Rick something. That's it. Or maybe Richard or… you know this guy. Grew up around here. One of these fellas goes around quoting movies ain't nobody seen."

I get out of Coach's truck, my head feeling like it's been held under muddy water.

"Hey," Coach calls, rolling down his window. "Hey! You gonna get me that money?"

"Yeah," I say, both of us knowing it's unlikely.

"Maybe I don't think it was suicide," Coach says. "Believe it or not, I'm sorry about Steve dying. I know he was special to you and everybody else around here, but that don't mean… Just give it time, Bobby. Go back to Austin, fuck your groupies or whatever you got down there and let it be."

"Or what?"

Coach shakes his head and looks away. "Just give it time, Bobby."

"It's Sam," I say. "The name's Sam."

LEFT BLANK FOR YOUR BRILLIANCE

I wake up somewhere else on the calendar. My skull feels like it was jumped by indignant cacti, which it was. It's sometime early the next day and I'm back to normal, by which I mean hungover, recently showered, and on the hunt for coffee.

The young woman at the front desk looks up when I come in and then goes back to her phone. She's like a young Venus Williams, in her twenties, with expensive teeth and sepia skin. I give her a smile she doesn't see and splash some of the lobby's gratis coffee into a Styrofoam cup.

"Good morning," I squint.

"Not if you're drinking that."

It's true. Despite this Best Western (*The Bestern*) being the only four-star in Caddo County, the coffee is absolute diapers.

"Room service will make you something strong if you ask nice," she looks up. "And then there's the soda machine in the lounge."

"Y'all still have Karaoke in there?" I toss the cup in the trash.

"Used to on Wednesdays, but now it's open mic," she says. "Why? Feel like doing a set?"

There's something familiar about her. Not Atlantis-familiar, but something else.

"Do I know you?"

"Depends," she says.

"You know me?"

"That depends, too."

"You look sort of familiar."

"I get that a lot," she rolls her eyes. "Let me guess—Serena Williams?"

"Serena? You ain't five-nine."

"Some would say Venus."

"Personally, I don't see it."

"We wondered if you'd left us, Mr. Sorrow," she says. "Haven't seen you in a couple of days."

"Yeah, well... I was away on business."

"That what you call it?" She uses a remote to turn off the TV above my head I didn't know was on or above my head.

"Word still travels fast around here."

"Like you wouldn't believe," she says. "I'm Octavia, by the way."

"Like, *Kindred* Octavia?"

"He reads," she says, smiling to no one in particular.

"Some," I say, approaching the desk. "So did your parents, apparently."

"One of them."

I hold out my hand to shake. "Call me Sam."

"This where I ask for an autograph?"

"You could. Or I could just take you out to dinner instead. How about Gil's?"

"Sadly, Gil's has shut down," Octavia replies. "And then there's the part about me not being interested."

"Well, that's unfortunate. Still want that autograph?"

"Please," she grins, handing me a pen and a small paper pad with the hotel's insignia at the top. The bottom of the page says LEFT BLANK FOR YOUR BRILLIANCE. I sign my name.

"Anyway," she says, folding the paper away into her shirt. "Mother wouldn't approve."

"Haven't heard that one in a while."

"You haven't talked to her in a while, either."

Had she not gone and spelled it out for me, I'd still be trying to get in the pants of my former girlfriend's daughter. "Holy shit," I say.

"Took you long enough."

"Gonna pull the tequila card on that one. How is Sonya these days?"

"Sonya? Try calling her that in public. It's Ms. Tyson, especially if you're nasty. And Ms. Tyson didn't let on at the funeral, but I'm pretty sure you hurt her feelings," Octavia mock-wags a finger at me. "Could've at least stopped by to say hi."

"I was otherwise occupied."

"As was noticeable."

"I can't even count how long it's been since I talked to her. She tell you about me? How we used to be pretty close?"

"Is that what you old folks call it these days?"

"You're certainly funnier than she ever was," I say. "I'm guessing you knew Steve."

"Who didn't?"

"Your mom was always his favorite."

"So she keeps telling me. You gave her a thrill, you know?"

"That's nice of her to say."

"I'm talking about the funeral," Octavia makes a yuck face. "You calling out the Cracker Club like that. That's folk hero level shit around here. What's your encore?"

"You trying to ruin my day?"

"Not especially," she says. "I'm a big fan."

"Might still have a career after all."

"A short one if you keep at the CC like that."

"I've been warned."

Octavia closes her eyes for a second as if remembering something and then leans back around the corner to rummage through a cabinet. "About that," she says. "The CC being responsible for Steve's death. A little obvious, don't you think?"

"Most times obvious is what it is. Why, you got other ideas?"

"I might," Octavia mumbles, still digging around for whatever she's searching for back there. "Depends."

"On what?"

"On whether you're gonna stick around and do something about it." She returns to the front desk with a small envelope in hand.

"Yeah, well..." I say. "Too late for that. Supposed to head back today."

"You're already past check out." She points at the clock behind her on the corduroy wall. It's 12:13 pm. "Gonna have to charge you for an extra day."

"You're shitting me."

"Take it up with Ms. Tyson," she shrugs, handing me the envelope. "Her policy, not mine."

"What's this?" I open the unsealed envelope and remove two rectangles of brown plastic.

"Gift cards," Octavia says. "There's a Starbucks over there in Walmart."

NOT UNLESS FAT IS GOOD

The Walmart housing the promised Starbucks is a quick walk across the highway. I had every intention of driving there, but that was before I realized that Blue was still back at Hillcrest. Blue's my truck. And the half hour it'll take to walk back to the cemetery has just increased coffee's relevance by the power of twelve.

It's not a *Starbucks*-Starbucks. It's one of those mini-Starbucks with a roped-off courtyard of green Astroturf with plastic tables and chairs situated just so. The espresso machine is busted and all they have is blonde roast on drip. I order two ventis and try not to look around Walmart at the death of America—people wearing pajamas in public, ass cracks you could keep a pair of boots in, flag shirts with eagles and guns on them, fake plants everywhere, *Don't Tread on Me* trucker caps and the treaded-on people who wear them.

There's only one chair open in the courtyard, but somebody else has the table. Like me, he doesn't belong in Atlantis, albeit for other reasons than decades of stark antagonism. The dude is bald and tan all over, with flip-flops, cargo shorts, and an off-white, long sleeve Hawaiian shirt with red and brown fronds on it. The sleeves are rolled up. He looks like he fell out of a Key West wormhole, like maybe he's somebody who listens to Jimmy Buffett, but classy about it.

"Okay if I sit?" I ask. The man is reading *The Atlantis Advocate,* our local rag—the same one that just published that bullshit story about Steve committing suicide. He doesn't reply.

"Okay if I sit?" I ask again, but louder. The man lowers the newspaper long enough to nod at the empty chair and get right back to his reading. The nod is absent of friendliness or unfriendliness. It simply recognizes my existence, as well as the chair's.

I set my two coffees down as the man's long, manicured fingers turn the pages of the *Advocate* as if it were medieval parchment. His posture is immaculate, like he's a misplaced Pilates instructor. His scalp is shiny and polished, as if he just got out of a barber's chair, and that brief flash of crystal gray eyes also revealed a set of insanely long eyelashes. It was like being blinked at by two Mesozoic butterflies.

He lowers the paper and clears his throat. I've been staring.

"Thanks," I say. "For the seat."

Wasn't all that long ago that I'd be the one getting stared at. Autographs and handshakes and smiles for pictures with fans just about everywhere I went. Drove my introvert ex-wife crazy. I look around the Walmart now to see if anybody lets on that they recognize me. They don't.

I try the coffee. It's not bad. The guy sits across from me with his head in the *Advocate* like it was the *New Yorker.* Can't tell how old he is—could be 40, could be Abe Vigoda.

"Beats the hell out of what they were calling coffee back at the hotel," I say. "Tasted like somebody took a piss on some coffee beans and left em outside in a moldy oatmeal cannister for a couple of weeks."

The man recrosses his legs and lifts the paper another inch higher and does not laugh. Maybe it's his silent dismissal or maybe I just don't want to sit there quiet with the *Advocate's* follow-up story about Steve just feet from my face, but I feel compelled—no, *doomed*—to prompt this poor guy into a conversation that neither of us wants to have.

"Say," I continue, "you ever eat one of them egg bite things they sell here? Not *here* here, but in an actual Starbucks? Way better than you'd think, especially the bacon ones. Got cottage cheese in em. Real filling. Unfortunately, all they got here to eat are those little Larabars, and only the Peanut Butter & Jelly ones at that. Wouldn't you know it, but I'm allergic to peanuts. Not like they'll actually kill me—I just get jittery and itchy. I don't like being itchy, do you? Ever have crabs? Well, if you haven't had crabs, don't. Zero stars. I hate itchiness. Poison ivy, poison oak, all that. Mosquitoes! Why do mosquitoes have to make you itchy, anyway? Why can't they just suck out a little blood and fly off and that be it? Wouldn't that make more sense, evolutionarily speaking, than inspiring people to want to squish you out of hatred? Shit, I'd walk a mile to kill a mosquito right now. Two if it was sitting on a peanut."

Beach boy's demeanor doesn't let on that we share the same Walmart, let alone the same crappy plastic table. It's embarrassing. At some point, the coffee starts to hit, and the urgency of finding the men's room begins to override our shared conversational shitshow. He doesn't even look up when I thank him for the seat and bid him a good day.

I'm maybe twenty steps away from the restroom entrance when somebody grabs my arm from behind, and hard.

"You gonna have to come with me, sir," the man grunts.

I yank my arm back to my body and glare at the security guard. He's short, with a pot belly that looks like it came off a pregnant javelina. "I saw you touch that lady's booty back there," he whispers gravely, and then the whisper falls apart into an all-out, backwoods cackle. He slaps me on the shoulder and points at my face, laughing. It's Bobby Butz, a friend of mine from high school.

"How you doing, old timer?" he grins. "Got you good, huh? Maybe you did grab somebody's booty, guilty as you look!"

I say *friend of mine*, but it's more that Butz was a small-town classmate I sometimes got drunk with on the weekends. Having the same first name, he and I enjoyed the noble bond shared by Roberts everywhere, but the particulars of his last name rendered *Bobby* meaningless. He was always just *Butz* or some ass-related spinoff.

"What you doing here, man?" he asks. "I ain't seen you in a long-ass time!"

"You look good, Butz."

"Not unless fat is good." He pats his spherical middle with a grin, throwing a glance back at the coffee stand where Hawaiian shirt Pilates guy still sits in his perfectly unbroken silence. "How you been?" Butz asks. "You playing around here somewhere? Some gig or something?"

I point to my throat and try to leave it at that.

"Oh, shit. I heard about that. What happened again?" It's a question that comes up far more often than I'd prefer. What I'd prefer is never.

"Dysphonia," I say. "Stress-related."

"Like Tom Waits," Butz nods knowingly. "Like Tom Fucking Waits."

"Yeah," I say, but no. Tom can still sing.

"Yours is more Keith Richards, though. You ever listen to *Talk Is Cheap?* That shit is underrated, you ask me. Maybe you could—"

"Butz, how you doing? You been here long? Working, I mean?"

"Here?" he glances back over at the Starbucks. "Nah... Couple of months. Just part-time."

"I thought you were police."

"I am police. I just got that child support is all. Denise got the house, you know."

"Denise..."

"Benton," he coughs. "Ex-wife. Hey, I got one for you: What's fat, got two thumbs, and three jobs just to pay child support?"

"You?"

"Me!" Butz laughs, both thumbs up, a slight wince in the delivery. "I made that shit up, man! Anyway, it's all good..." Butz's eyes move back to the Starbucks, back to the bald man again, and then return to me. "All my kids are grown now but one, and he's a senior now, if you believe that. Second-string Merfoot, like his daddy," Butz says proudly. "Just spent the weekend with him out at my daddy's cabin near Deer Point. Remember that place? That one time my daddy caught us out there—you, me, Red, a couple of nasty D'Ville girls, ole what's-his-name... You know, the one who died? Remember how my daddy busted us, popped in there about three in the morning with a lady friend that weren't my mom and..."

Butz's reverie melts into his jowls. He puts a solemn hand on my shoulder.

"Steve's funeral. That's why you're here," he says. "Here I am rambling on about good times with fathers and yours has just tragically died."

"It's okay, man. I'm—"

Then, like an irate cobra, Butz's other arm shoots out horizontally and latches onto the sleeve of a young woman's oversized hoodie. She was on her way out of the store.

"Forgot something," Butz tells her, still looking at me.

"Let go, you fucking perv," the girl sneers, jerking her arm away. She's what it would look like if Depeche Mode and a construction worker had a baby—a multi-colored mullet and oversized Carhartts, all black.

"Reedie Morris," Butz chides. "Watch that language. And what do you want with three bottles of Manic Panic, anyway? What you gonna do? Start a goth farm?"

"I'm not a goth, moron."

"Look, I don't care. You and your girlfriend can go paint the whole school black or purple or teal or all other sorts of nonbinary rainbow colors, and more power to you. But you still gotta pay for the merchandise, Reedie. Either that or put it back on aisle twelve where you just pulled it from."

She's fourteen or fifteen, going on juvie. She throws a quick look at the exit.

"Please don't," Butz sighs. "I really, really don't want to run today, but I will. And I'm way faster than I look. I'm like a fat cheetah."

"Second-string Merfoot," I confirm.

She rolls her eyes at us and turns back to the store with a snort that enunciates the persecution of teenagers everywhere.

"Good kid," Butz says.

"Morris? Like, Orv Morris?"

"The same."

"Think I saw her at Steve's funeral."

"Probably," Butz replies. "Probably all of Orv's kids were there. Got four of them, but Reedie's the only one worth a shit. Speaking of that funeral… Sorry I couldn't make it, bud. Them three jobs don't leave a lot of daylight."

"I appreciate the thought."

"Of course, man, of course," he nods. "Everybody loved that guy. Everybody. It's just a goddamn shame. Sorry I can't say more about, you know, the investigation and all."

"I understand. Good to know there is one."

A look passes over Butz's face like the shadow from a chubby cloud. His eyes roll down one of the aisles, scanning all the way back to the rear of the store.

"What I should say," Butz clears his throat, "is that I'm not *supposed* to say anything about it. Not that there's much to talk about. Them assholes have pretty much closed the books on it."

"That's what it sounds like. From the paper, at least."

"Yeah," he whispers. "Exactly. And in keeping with my not supposed to be saying anything, I won't. However," Butz looks down a different aisle this time, "in my opinion? The aforementioned assholes in question? Not exactly the brains squad we're talking about."

"What assholes?"

"Two loser detectives they brought in from Dallas a couple years ago. One is this lanky, shiny shoe smart-ass thinks he hung the moon with his own pecker and the other's got about as much brains as a Fanta can, which I ain't even sure they make anymore. These two choads roll around town in a smoked-out Explorer like they're G men or something, like they're Tango and Cash, but without the cool hair. Why they sent them boys here is anybody's guess, and they don't seem particularly happy about it themselves. Won't shut up about how much they hate it here. Only come into the station when they absolutely have to. Most days they're out chewing Cubans on the back 9 with them CC boys."

Butz breaks into a welcoming smile and waves at an old woman entering the Walmart in a XXXL t-shirt covered with cartoon Dachshunds with googly eyes. She mutters and shakes her head.

"You're saying these new detectives work for the CC?"

"Hell," he snorts. "Half the department works for the CC."

"Coach says they're on the run. Says the CC has unwelcome competition from Sonya and all this meth business going on around here."

"Ain't no secret there," Butz nods. "Meth, man… That shit's terrible. You seen these kids around here? It's like *The Walking Dead* up in this bitch, but worse teeth. When'd you talk to Coach?"

"Yesterday. He bailed me out."

"How's that old cuss doing?"

"Meaner with age."

"Motherfucker can still coach, though," Butz says.

"Coach also says there's a one-armed dickhead out walking free who said he was gonna kill Steve."

"Ain't his whole arm. Just his hand," Butz says. "Name's Lefty."

"Lefty?"

"On account of him only having a left arm now? Or maybe it's the right… You remember him. Goes by Bill. Younger than us, ten years or so. The ladies love that dude."

"Bill Roberts?"

"Naw, not him. Bill ain't his real name. Just goes by Lefty now, anyway. Guess that's what happens when you rip off one of your paws."

"They bring him in for questioning?"

"That whole scene in court was a good ways back. Didn't nobody take it serious, least of all Steve. Hell, he even gave Lefty a job out at the Lodge. Even better than the job that sumbitch had at the BI. You believe that?"

"Lodge? What Lodge?"

"You know, Steve's rehab place?"

"What the fuck are you talking about?"

"Berkey Foundation? Up on Lake Atlantis, man. North side. One part's the Lodge, other's this church them Baptists got all bunched up about. You know, that big city preacher Steve brought in? Feisty queer fella? Big hair?"

It's exactly like Butz has been reading off a breakfast menu in Aramaic for the past twenty seconds.

"Dude," Butz says with a look of off-brand pity. "You really got no idea what I'm talking about…"

MAGISTER TEMPLI

I know I called Steve when I heard that Beau died. At least I did that. Told him I'd drive in for the funeral, even though I had no intention of doing so and Steve had no intention of believing that I would. Beau wouldn't want it, anyway. After Steve took me in, his dad always eyed me funny and once told me I'd never be a Berkey, as if the adoption was my idea, some scheme to backdoor my way into family money.

If I talked to Steve after that, I don't remember. Even if I did, it's unlikely he would've told me about his charitable doings. Steve was one of those expert listeners who make you forget how one-sided the conversational equation is, who allow you to ramble and blab about the most trivial bullshit imaginable while off-line they're occupied with saving the world without ever mentioning it.

According to Butz, Steve had been working on the non-profit (the Berkey Foundation) years before the old man dropped. It was supposed to be an umbrella org—mostly social improvement stuff for Atlantis proper and greater Caddo County, starting with the rehab facility (the Lodge) and a church next door. Helping druggies, I get—that's exactly the type of thing Steve would get himself involved with. But the church? Hard to see. The Steve I knew never had much good to say about religion, especially of the Jesus type.

The least I can do is go check the place out on my drive back to Austin. Maybe have some choice words with a one-handed man.

Butz offers to tote me to the cemetery to grab my truck, but he doesn't get off shift for nearly two more hours, so I start the long meander up into the Blacklantis highlands on foot. The road immediately south of the Bestern feels like the steepest climb in elevation in the whole goddamn county. The unwelcome exercise and the two cups of fair-haired coffee are almost enough to bend me sober. I have to stop twice to lean over and catch my breath, like it's the first morning of two-a-days again after sitting around all summer in the AC watching *General Hospital* and eating discount cheesy poofs on the sofa. I'm not even sure how to get to Hillcrest from here; I just know to keep going up. Small town cemeteries are always at the apex of town so Christians can get themselves buried that much closer to a God who lives in the sky.

At the top of the first road—a couple of Kilimanjaros up from the Bestern—I take a left. Hill Street—a short-cut I know. Per the name, you'd think it would have something to do with the incline that just tried to kill me, but in fact it's another one of those Civil War tributes, this one to a general who got court-martialed for trying to undermine Stonewall Jackson. Most of the homes I remember on this street are gone, which isn't to say that Hill is barren. There's a handful of newish custom builds— your standard 3/2 jobs—along with some HUD-style 2/1s, all built in the decades since my last visit to the street. There's a new neighborhood park up on the right. Multicolored climbing structures, a public bathroom that looks locked, a single hoop court, and six chain swings on a blue metal set. The street is empty and quiet. And even though it's October and cool by Texas standards, Hill Street still transmits that suffocating, quilt-like stillness of summer.

I don't know all the streets in Blacklantis like this one. I only know Hill Street because it's where Sonya's uncle, Tonkawa Tyson, lived. By most local accounts, the man was what's called *touched*, although my memories of him—at his house here and at Steve's—were that Tonk was just too outrageous and educated and brilliant for Atlantis. In Austin, he'd fit right in.

Like Steve, Tonk had made the specious decision to remain in the area, even after he'd traveled abroad for much of the 70s and 80s, come home with a JD, and set up shop as the town's best lawyer. Even the crackers wouldn't disagree that Tonk was probably the best in the county; it's just that very few locals could afford him, so Tonk came and went throughout the state and beyond, returning to Atlantis from time to time to his home on Hill Street—a three-story pyramid per his own design. Ever since he was an exceptional child, Tonk had been our regional expert in all things pyramid—he'd even spent time in Egypt and Mesopotamia studying the damn things. So when Tonk came back to Atlantis with money, what else was he supposed to build? A fucking pyramid, on a ley line, reportedly to scale.

That alone would've been enough to outcast the man, but there was also something about a newfound religion Tonk had brought back from Egypt, so the whole neighborhood (including his own family, including Sonya's mother, Miss Ida) denounced him as a Satanist, not that it seemed to bother him too much. Miss Ida forbade Sonya from visiting her uncle, but, then again, Miss Ida threatened to disown her for dating *that cracker-ass, powhite, Jewish boy* and look how that turned out. Which is all to say that if me and Sonya spent time together, it was usually at her uncle's groovy pyramid house, or Steve's, or alone in the somber grasses of Hillcrest Cemetery down the hill from where Sonya and Miss Ida lived. Because it was the 80s in a small town in the South. There were only so many places we could go.

Tonk's house looks much as it did back then, only overgrown by a tangled chaos of junipers and myrtles. The yard still doesn't have much grass to speak of, overshadowed as it is with towering pecans. Nobody has lived here in some time. Even so, Tonk's official hand-chiseled, hand-painted sign lives on, albeit cracked and warped and grayed from the sun:

Dr. Tonkawa Tyson, Esquire
Magister Templi, Naturopath, Attorney at Law

There's a less cracked and more unofficial-looking cat lounging in the bramble that hides the front of the house. The cat is dirty and orange, with a chewed-up left ear and a black patch over its right eye. It looks like a disreputable feline pirate.

"Meow," I say.

"Meow," it says back.

"Meow," I say back. "Meow, meow."

"Meow," it meows back. Just once.

I bend down and hold my hand out and the cat just stays where it is, blinking. The sun is hot on my back and my shirt is spritzed with sweat.

"Ole Tonk is gone, huh?" I ask, looking at the upper broken window. "Finally kicked it?"

"Meow."

"This your place now?"

No answer, just more blinking.

"Seems right. Left his pyramid to the cats."

I turn at the sound of a car pulling away from the curb about one block up. It's an off-colored Taurus.

"Meow," the cat opines.

"Yessir," I reply. "Meow, meow, meow…"

I stand up and keep walking and the cat stays there.

THE JAMMIE DODGERS

I pass more government homes, more pecans and bramble, more boarded-up shops and run-down churches, and more double-takes from the residents of Blacklantis from their cars, porches, and living room windows. Eventually I find Hanson Street, which borders the cemetery on its western edge. A couple of blocks up is where Sonya once lived.

Unlike elsewhere in the neighborhood, nothing on Hanson is new or rebuilt. It's just one shack after another—dozens in a staggered line, a cavalcade of just getting by. One of them on the right has fallen over in the front like a drunk passed out on the bar, its roof rotted and collapsed and slowly becoming the yard itself. The sky is cool and bright, like damp glass. There's the smell in the air of something being burned on purpose.

I squeeze through a gap in the obsolete chain-link and enter the labyrinth of gravestones on the black side of Hillcrest. Even the dead are segregated here. *Segregated.* That word always felt so benign to me, something intentionally neutral. Steve wouldn't want to be buried here, sectioned off in the pigmentally-favored section of Hillcrest, but who asked me? The cemetery is a charnel divide between the hills of Blacklantis and the less elevated neighborhoods to the north and east where we powhites were directed to dwell—a nebulous buffer betwixt the blacks and proper honkeys of Atlantis.

Blue is still where I left it—diagonally parked over the lines in elite douche fashion, not but thirty yards from Steve's grave. There's a fancier ride a couple of spaces over—a newish, pearl-tinted Caddy that's recently been waxed—only its operator had the decency to park normally. From this elevation, I have a clear line of sight over both vehicles and down Hickory Creek Drive to the empty lot where the trailer park used to be—Creekview, where I lived with my mom until she died. Hard to believe what an overgrown, mismanaged spot of nothing it is now. When I was a kid, Creekview was its own redneck city-state, serving as the residential-and-sketchy business center of the poorest part of the white part of town. It was two congested acres of entry-level mobile homes, travel trailers, refitted school busses, immobile 70s-era vans, and the factory workers, dishwashers, itinerant truckers, and assorted derelicts who lived and conducted questionable transactions therein—a horde of downtrodden who came and went with such fanfare and booze-fueled racket it's a wonder that any of us ever slept.

This is the Atlantis I know best. This is where Red and me ran around for years, terrorizing neighborhood animals and any child stupid enough to look our way, as if all of them together belonged to one inferior species of life form. This was our turf, and we even laid a wild-haired claim to the graveyard—the white part, at least. We never dreamed of adding any portion of Blacklantis to it. There were bands of older black boys who lived atop that hill, fearless and magnificent, and although we knew each other from school (where we played together on our own free will—laughing, rooting each other on, trading locker room pranks), out here the world was regulated by parents and the irrefutable wisdom of adults. And so we kept apart, as if held back by an invisible and benevolent hand, and were informed that like kept with like, that the division was of natural decree. And maybe I would've believed that had I not met Sonya.

Even by Blacklantis standards, her family was poor. They were, in fact, the black equivalent of my own. We were drawn together because our mothers worked in the same diner, and it was our not-entirely-clandestine encounters in that restaurant restroom that ended up costing our moms their jobs. After that, Sonya and I began meeting here in the cemetery—night after ball-bulging night—which is why, decades later, I can still find my way around Hillcrest in my sleep without tripping over a pebble.

I round my way over the last rise between me and Blue. There's the fresh mound that covers Steve. There's a woman there, too.

My first thought is Meredith. My second thought is I've been back for three days without calling Meredith, which would be a record. But the woman isn't Meredith at all. I hunch down about thirty feet away beside a four-foot-tall, probably misspelled tombstone (HOBRATSCHK) and watch whoever the lady is, because there's absolutely no way I can get to Blue without her seeing me. After my graveside performance the other day, being noticed is pretty low on my list of desirable outcomes for the day.

There's a black braid a third of the way down the woman's back. She's wearing one of those form-enhancing velvety vintage dresses, hunter green. She's on the small side, muttering lowly as she sits on the earth. This is where that smoke smell is coming from—sage, maybe, or some kind of herb people put on chicken. Then I see the smoke. There's a small fire on Steve's grave.

"Hey!" I yell, jumping out from behind HOBRATSCHK.

The woman spaz-jumps in the air like I just set off a bull horn. Stuff flies everywhere—feathers, candles, cookies, plant matter, coals, and a tiny bowl that must have held it all together.

"What the fuck?" I point at the shambles on the ground. "What the absolute fuck are you—"

The woman slaps at imaginary coals on her dress in a panicked squeal. Full mouth, cute face framed with bangs. "You scared me," she says, looking around helplessly.

She's younger than I thought, braless and doe eyed. Probably one of Steve's students. She picks up the scattered objects, putting some back into the bowl and others into a beaded drawstring.

"You scared me," she says again, this time with a shy laugh. Now that I have a better look at her face, it's clear she's not a student. Still young, but one of those women in her early 30s who can pass for a teenager in the right light. Maybe not technically pretty, but charming in a girlish way, with huge brown eyes done up Bollywood-style. Her nipples poke through the thick fabric of her dress.

"You burnt?" I ask, trying not to stare.

"Don't think so," she says, checking herself again. She straightens her dress, throws me a smile, and gets back to arranging the feathers and cookies just so.

I point at the ground. "Thought you'd caught the grave on fire or something."

"Oh, no… I'd never do that. It was in this bowl, see?"

She shows me the bowl and wipes her hands on some nearby grass. Her fingers are lean and tipped in taupe that's just one shade away from Steve's dirt.

"You're Sam, right?"

I touch my hat. "Yes, ma'am. Sorry about the other day."

"What other day?" she asks, putting her hand over her eyes, squinting at the sun behind me.

"The funeral. Wasn't exactly at my best out here."

She shakes her head and looks down. "I couldn't make it."

"Then nevermind," I say. "But you know Steve, huh?"

She nods.

"And me?"

"Red's got pictures of y'all back at the house."

I don't mean for my spine to tighten up like a rusty spring, but it does. "Red?"

"Yeah," she says. "We're... you know, together and stuff?" The woman's face is warm and open and tied down with a set of dimples that would normally make my knees go funny. Even so, there's something tilted or askew about her eyes that I have to wade through an inch of mascara to identify. It's not so much that she's been squinting every time she looks at me; it's more that she's just... squinty. Her eyes are set just a tad closer together than you'd expect—not in a *pet-a-puppy-to-death-on-accident* kind of way, but more like just one step up from the short bus. As we say in the South, *Bless her heart.*

"Well, I'll be," I say. "You're Red's old lady."

"I'm not that old..."

It's impossible to picture them together. It's not the close-together-eyes thing, it's that Red is a foot-and-a-half taller and outweighs her by several head of cattle. I wonder what Red's told her. I wonder if she knows what I did to his life.

"Red's got pictures of y'all," she says again. "Plays your music all the time, too."

"At least somebody still does."

"You got a real nice voice. Used to, I mean," she smiles, but then corrects herself. "Oh, I'm sorry... I'm not supposed to say that, huh?"

"It's fine," I lie. A crow squawks at something from the top of a dogwood up the hill. "Thought I might see Red at the funeral."

"He wasn't sure he should come."

"Hope it wasn't on account of me."

She looks confused. "No, it's just... Red wanted to, he really, really did, but..." She turns and looks over at the Caddy. "I should probably go," she says, touching her face.

"Something wrong?"

"Nothing's wrong," she says, shaking her head and trying not to cry. "It's almost lunch time, and..." She turns away, hand on her eyes, shoulders shaking. I go to put my hand on her back, but then don't.

I just stand there and pretend to care and let her have it out. Pretty sure I left a flask in the truck. Pretty sure I'd like to drink it.

After a minute, she turns back my way with a face that looks like Priyanka Chopra crossed with a sad raccoon.

"Can I... can I tell you something?" she sniffs, wiping her runny face.

"Sure," I say, pretty sure I don't want to hear it. There's a thin thread of snot hanging out of her right nostril.

"Because you're Red's friend?"

"Uh..."

"He's gotten worse. Lots worse."

I don't say anything. I just stand there trying not to stare at her boogers or nipples.

"Pretty much anything makes it worse," she says. "Like, can't-get-out-of-bed worse. So, I think with Steve's dying... Red wanted to come, but... You know how when you can't do something you want to do it just makes everything worse? Red wanted to be here for Steve, but he couldn't get out of bed, and I can't leave him too long when he's like that. So I didn't come, either. That's why..." she sniffs and waves a mascara-stained hand at the re-arrangement on Steve's grave, "why I came here today. I wanted to make these offerings and... I didn't expect anybody out here," she inhales deeply. "I was just gonna come and say these prayers and get right back to Red. He don't like me being gone too long."

I point to the feathers and candles and everything else. "You're native, right?"

She wipes her nose and nods. "My grannie's full and my mom's half. Caddo. Up in Oklahoma."

"Out near Anadarko, right?"

"You know the Rez?" she smiles.

"Just because of Steve. He was kind of an expert on your people, I guess..."

"Part of why we got to be friends," she says. "I didn't come up on the Rez. My mom moved us to the city when I was little. Oklahoma City. You part native, too?"

"Couldn't say. Probably not."

I recall Chuck's obsession with her. It's justified.

"Met somebody the other day who knows you," I say. "He said you were some kind of medicine woman."

She shakes her head. "Who said that?"

"Old buddy of mine. Red's, too. Chuck Tender."

"Oh, Chuckie," she says. "Wow... we haven't seen Chuckie in a while. He was helping us out at the house. You know, on account of Red not being able to do stuff sometimes? Red pays him. Gave him a place to stay down there, too. But I'm not a medicine woman. Where'd you see Chuckie?"

"County jail."

A blank look crosses her face, which then shadows over with concern.

"Oh no... why's he in jail for?"

"Long story."

"Is he okay?"

"Oh, yeah. Can't hurt folks like Chuck. He's like a human cockroach, but fatter."

"That's not a nice thing to say," she frowns, looking down.

"I just meant in a post-nuclear survival sort of way. Like, it's a good thing."

"I don't think he likes being so heavy, it's just... Well, what did he do this time?"

I don't feel like giving her the PG version of Chuck's X-rated story. What I feel like is more tequila and getting the fuck out of Atlantis.

"Is that booze?" I point at a Dixie Cup leaning against Steve's headstone that survived the earlier disruption.

"Just water. For Steve's passage? I put out those cookies, too." There are three circular, biscuit-looking cookies centered with a red heart in a line in front of the cup that doesn't contain booze. "They were his favorite," she says.

The cookies don't look like anything I remember Steve liking. Other than pecan pie in the fall, Steve was never one for sweets.

"Jammie Dodgers," she says.

"Jammie Dodgers?"

"Yeah, Jammie Dodgers."

"What is that, some new hipster band?"

"Jammie Dodgers?" she says. "It's what they're called. The cookies. Funny name, right? Hey, you know what else is funny? Guess what they call cookies in England?"

"Biscuits."

"Oh," she says. "You knew that already…"

"I've been over there," I say, almost apologetically. "Got any more Jammie Dodgers on you?"

"That's all I brought."

"There's three. Have one with me?"

"Oh no," she says solemnly. "They're for Steve's journey. Supposed to take six days for a soul to leave the body and get to the other side."

"Six days? What's he doing, walking there?"

"I guess so. Anyway, six days is a while, so they need food and stuff." She watches the array on Steve's grave approvingly, as if Steve were right there, munching away, full of appreciation for some pre-journey nourishment. Then she giggles and sticks out her hand to shake.

"I'm Rain! I forgot to tell you that!"

"Rain," I say, shaking her hand. It's stronger and warmer than expected.

"Little Rain Moon, but everybody calls me Rain. Except Red. He's got, like, hundreds of nicknames for me."

"I bet he does."

"Yeah," she laughs again, a wine-ish color rising in her cheeks.

"Hey," I say. "I'm really sorry, Rain. About Red. I know he isn't doing so good and..."

Her face quickly turns from Cab Franc to Blanc. "I shouldn't have said anything," she says quietly. "I was just... upset, you know? He wouldn't like me telling folks. Red's... well, he's sensitive."

That's one way of putting it. Even before the deterioration started to set in, Red was famous for flying off the handle at the most random slight or insult.

Rain picks a stray feather out of the dirt and puts it in her bag thoughtfully. "You know what? I just thought... Boy, it would really cheer him up to see you, you know?"

I almost take a step backwards. "Yeah, well, thing is... I got to get back to Austin, you know? That's my truck right there. And I was..."

"He'll probably be up pretty soon," she says, looking up at me with those baby seal peepers.

"Tell you what: I'll give you my number and you give me a ring when that ole rascal gets his big-ass out of bed—"

"Or you could just follow me there," Rain says hopefully. "He'll probably be up pretty soon..."

In the battle of desperations, it ain't mine that's gonna lose out. I point to Steve's grave and give Rain some nonsense about spending some time alone with him and then I walk her over to the custom XTS Caddy. I have every intention of getting in Blue as soon as she drives off, but I just stand there and close my eyes and feel the smells of an East Texas October enter and exit my body without complaint or repair. It's not like I feel Steve behind me in a ghost-watching-you sort of way, it's more that he's just there. Like how you can feel somebody in another room in a different part of the same house, just two or three doorways away, maybe reading or drinking tea or writing encouraging comments on your history report, the one you tried your absolute best on, because you wanted him to see that in you, because you knew he would, because his recognition and kindness were some of the few decent things you had going for you, and it wasn't just you who felt that way. It wasn't just you.

I lean back against Steve's stone, muddying the ass on my jeans. I pick up a small black feather Rain left and tuck it behind my ear and talk to Steve for a while. He doesn't say anything, and nothing I say makes sense. Somewhere in there I eat his Jammie Dodgers cookies, all three of them.

LOOK WHAT THEY DID TO PBR

When my mother died, social services didn't even try to look for my father. I was fifteen. They shipped me off to Arlington to live with my mom's older brother—Uncle Randy—who worked nights at the railroad and either drank or slept off his drinking in the day. His wife was hands-down the worst person I've ever met, and it was her contempt that kept me out of their house as much as was legally possible. As long as I showed up to school most of the time and didn't land in juvie, my uncle's wife allowed me to crash in their garage and fend for myself on the streets of greater DFW. Which is where I learned to sing.

I first met Johnny Blue in Deep Ellum, but he and his crew also hit Sundance Square in Fort Worth every other week or so. Eventually, Blue took me in, taught me all he knew about performing, and baptized me in the acoustic fire of the busker scene. He showed me how to sing in the old ways, before amplification and TC Helicon pedals and autotune, because making your living as a street performer requires the type of volume, projection, and charisma that inspires curiosity blocks away. Blue called it *harmonious hollering*. Most folks think it was me singing like that for decades that sizzled my voice, and I just let them. Sure beats sharing the truth.

Anyway, that's how I came to name my pickup *Blue*.

Blue the Truck is a 1970 C10 "custom sports truck" with top-of-the-line trim, an 8-foot bed, and a rebuilt 307 that can still punch a Chevy-shaped logo through the horizon. The paint is the most 70s thing about it—something on the unsavory continuum between sea-foam and teal. An off-green Chevy truck is a feeble tribute to what the man gave me, but it's one Johnny Blue would appreciate.

The first thing I notice after getting into Blue is that there's no flask of tequila. The second thing is a card under the windshield wipers—a Tarot card. It's a naked woman and man, both with hands held out and down as if asking each other, *Well, what do we do now?* There's an angel behind them, backdropped against a giant sun, who doesn't have the answer. The card says THE LOVERS. I'm all out of reasons not to call her.

"Mere," I say. I crank Blue up and start down the potholed road where Creekview used to be.

"Nice of you to call," she says smoothly. Meredith says everything smoothly.

"Got your card."

"How'd you know it was me?"

"Lucky guess," I say.

"I've got a work thing in a little bit. Why don't you swing by the house before I leave?"

"That a request?"

"More like a suggestion with a question mark at the end," she says.

I'm approaching the junction of Dewey now, where I'll have to choose left or right. Either way will lead me to tequila, but not necessarily to Meredith.

"Thought you might've moved away by now," I say.

"Why would I do that?"

"For about a hundred different reasons, beginning with the fact that Atlantis sucks."

"Everywhere sucks," she says. "In its own way."

"Austin doesn't suck."

"Says you."

"What sucks about Austin?"

"Bad shit happens there."

"Bad shit happens everywhere," I counter. Both of us are right.

"The rent's too damn high."

"Okay, Jimmy..."

"Traffic's out of control, they screwed up the aquifer, South by Southwest and ACL have become a fucking joke, you can't throw a piece of avocado toast down Congress without hitting about twenty hipsters—"

"Hipsters are everywhere," I say.

"Not in Atlantis."

"Yeah, because it sucks. Give em time. Look what they did to PBR."

"I've got about two hours. Can't say when I'll be free after that."

Now I'm sitting at the stop sign at Dewey. There's an oddly colored car behind me, waiting for me to go. I make a quick right without thinking it through, instantly regretting it, because it's the most obvious way to Meredith's house. The guy behind me does the same, and we both head south through the wretched downtown—me in Blue, him in his yellow-pinkish Taurus. The car stays exactly two lengths behind me the whole time.

"Hello?" she says.

"I think I'm being followed."

"Probably you aren't."

I speed up and so does the Taurus. I slow down and it's the same. I try to make out the driver through the glare in my rearview.

"Are you still fucking McCarthy?" I ask.

The quiet on the other end is Meredith reminding me it's none of my business.

"Part of our arrangement, you'll recall, is avoiding questions like the one you just asked."

"Well, send my regards. How's Melody Boy doing, anyway?"

"Who knows... Last I heard he was on tour and getting more famous by the day."

"So, who you screwing now? Tweedy?"

"Ugh. Give me a break."

"Sturgill?"

"Now, Sturgill I might," she says. "Got his number?"

Right after I drive past the county jail and Steve's house, the man in the Taurus takes the next right.

"I'm not being followed anymore," I say.

"That's a relief. You coming over?"

"Depends," I say. "What are you wearing?" I pull Blue over into the parking lot of a run-down laundry mat with nobody inside. There's a little boy hanging out beneath the yellow-roofed awning with a crawdad in one hand and a purple BIC in the other.

"That's not why I'm asking you over," she says.

"Okay. So, what are you wearing?"

On the other end of the line, Meredith blows air out of her shapely nostrils.

"A burlap sack with wool socks on my hands," she says.

"Now we're talking."

"My hands are getting sweaty."

"Wetness is good."

"There's kale in my teeth."

"I'll be right over."

"Finally."

"Right after I hit the Line," I say. "I'm fresh out of tequila."

"Goddammit, Sam. It'll take you an hour to get there and back. By the time you show up, I'll have to leave."

"I need my juice," I say.

"I've got some juice."

"How horned up are you?"

"Not that kind of juice."

Predictably, the crawdad latches onto the boy's thumb and the kid hot-drops the lighter with a squeal and runs off shaking his arm, *Hey Ya*-style.

"Look, Mere... I'll come over, but if it's about money..."

"When's the last time I asked you for money?"

"I don't know," I say. "I'm just saying it's all gone, if you were. I don't want to waste your time, is what it is. Royalties are shit nowadays. Can barely pay rent. If it weren't for Blue and this worthless voice, I wouldn't have a pot to piss in."

Meredith's side of the phone goes quiet for a while. I play what I just said over in my head and cringe.

"Mere?"

Meredith Lee, nee Meredith Taylor. How many versions of Meredith have I known over the years? Meredith the student, Meredith the fortune teller. Meredith the stripper, massage therapist, artist, nanny, maid, eco-terrorist (alleged), drug runner (acquitted). Meredith my on-and-off-and-on-again paramour, the closest thing I'll ever have to true love. Calling our relationship complicated is like saying Padre Island is sorta sandy.

"I don't need your money," she says. "And your voice isn't worthless. You coming over, or what?"

It's not like Meredith to push like this, and both of us know it. No matter the configuration or agreement, I've always been the chaser.

"What's wrong?"

"Steve," she says after a pause. "It's about his murder."

ETIOLOGIES

The day Steve swooped in to save my 17-year-old ass from certain homelessness and anonymity was the day immediately after I first met Meredith. It was a late-80s, mid-August in East Texas, when the heat comes at you from all directions like an inexplicable fuck-off from God. I'd earned enough cash from busking with Johnny Blue to ditch my pretend family and bus back to Atlantis, paying for a month of camping fees at Deer Point up front, where I had little more in mind than playing music and resuming my romance with one Sonya Tyson.

I'd been gone for just over a year. Sonya's letters had crapped out to nothing about halfway through my absence, and it took about a dozen calls to Miss Ida's house from the camp payphone to finally get I was being sabotaged. Sonya's mother had no intention of allowing or abetting my woo. Who knows how many of my letters got through to Sonya's hands before Miss Ida found a way to stop them entirely. And now Sonya was never home when I rang.

It was a Sunday. Deer Point was popular with regional tourists in the summer, but more so with day-tripping locals, including families popping in for afternoon shenanigans after church. Meredith's was one of those families. I'd likely seen her several times before this particular Sunday, because I was classmates with her older sister, Marie. We all grew up together in Atlantis, and me and Marie shared the same smallish circle of friends and had done so since middle school. The sisters also had a pair of orangutan-like cousins I knew from football: Darwin and Derwin, twins. One of them had disparaged Sonya out at Nirvana once and I had to take it out on his racist little face.

On this Deer Point Sunday, I had just toweled off and put on my best (shortest) cutoffs as the afternoon partiers rolled in to lay claim to the communal cement tables. I didn't realize how hungry I was until they commenced to cooking, transforming shiny cylinders of mechanically separated mystery meat into the delicious tubes we call hot dogs. I was probably as close to starving as I'd ever been. I walked down to the beach about thirty yards away from them and sat down in the muddy grass and looked out upon the water in the well-rehearsed, nonchalant manner I'd picked up from Johnny Blue. First on my set list was "Everybody Wants to Rule the World," followed with "Raspberry Beret," and I was just about to slide into a bitchin Night Ranger rendition when one of Marie's uncles rambled over, Schlitz in one hand, half-gnawed hot dog in the other.

He downed the remainder of both, tossed the can in the grass, and wiped his fingers on a ripped-up Panama Jack t-shirt, hands hanging off his arms like warty squashes. I'd seen him around town before. Nobody liked him.

"You sing nice," the man said, mushy bun squished in his teeth.

"Much obliged."

"Real pretty like."

"Thank you kindly."

"You know lots of songs?" he asked, scratching the side of his swollen belly.

"Yessir. If it plays on the radio, I either know it or can figure it out."

"I don't listen to that new shit they got out there these days. Too much poofy hair and dudes dressed like chicks. Give me that old shit any day. You know any old shit, boy?"

"I know some old country. George Jones... Stuff like that."

"Well, what I was wondering," he grinned, "is if maybe you know any of them nigger songs."

I looked over at the growing piles of food. There was grilled corn now and burgers and chips in more flavors and shapes than I knew existed, along with an armada of icy beer and soda and flavored tea in frosty cans. I was too hungry to understand the man was sticking it to me about Sonya.

"I know some Prince," I said.

"Not that little faggot," he spat. "I'm talking old stuff. How about Ray Charles? That's the type of nigger stuff I grew up with."

As it happened, Johnny Blue had been a huge fan of Ray Charles and I'd picked up a couple of hits along the way.

"How bout 'I Got a Woman'?" I smiled, trying it out in A.

"That's a good one, but I was more thinking... 'Hit the Road Jack.' You know that one?"

"Oh, for sure. I know every Percy Mayfield—"

"Good for you, Coonass boy. I'm sure you do," and with that he dug a piece of chewed up hot dog from his mouth and flicked it at my chest. "Now get back to your fucking trailer or whatever piece of shit structure you crawled out of. This is supposed to be a decent picnic at a decent fucking park for decent-ass white people. *Real* white people, you hear? Who said you could be here? Go on, now. Get your Cajun trash-ass out of here."

It stung me like I'd never been stung, but I did it. I sulked off to my tent, playing it up as best I could. I let that fat cracker bask in his moment in front of the others and all their diabetes-promoting bounty while my belly and pride hurt something fierce, but under that I was celebrating a hard-earned victory and laughing at the man, laughing at all of them, because I knew the game was about to play out.

I remembered that Marie was a sucker for English pop (hence the Tears for Fears). I'd positioned myself on the beach so that she'd just happen to see me, and my brief encounter with her uncle had only amplified my presence at their picnic. It took an hour longer than expected, but Marie eventually snuck over to my tent, and with her a plate arrayed with Cool Ranch Doritos and a bacon-wrapped hotdog topped with relish and the yellowest mustard I'd ever seen.

"You smell," she said, watching with maternal pleasure as I wolfed it down.

"Incorrect, ma'am. *You* smell. *I* stink."

She looked around and squinched her nose in disgust. The inside of my tent was a spatial and olfactory wreck—lake-washed clothes that stayed damp, assorted food scraps I'd scavenged from other campers, my Epiphone in its battered case, an open sleeping bag that was more mildew than polyester, and my current pile of old paperbacks.

"Thanks for the chow. You're uncle's a real asshole, by the way."

"No duh," she grunted. "He left, though. You got skinny."

"Did I?"

"Must've happened when you were in prison, huh?"

I almost choked on my Doritos. "Is that what they been saying?"

"Where'd you go, then?"

"Well, there was that whole thing about my mom dying?"

"Oh, my gosh. I'm so sorry..."

"Had to go live with my uncle out near Dallas."

"Anybody know you're back?"

"You're the first," I lied.

"Really?"

"Sure."

"I hear Dallas has rad malls. I love Six Flags."

"That's in Arlington. Closer to Fort Worth."

"I went on the Shock Wave one time. Almost barfed."

"People die on that thing all the time. Get stuck upside down, fall out, break their necks, and just die."

"That's not true," she said.

I raised my eyebrows and fingered up the last of the mustard.

"You haven't changed at all," she shook her head. "Got skinnier is all."

"Well, you've changed," I pointed at her chest. "Filled out real nice."

We both looked down at her boobs, which were straining to climb out of her one-piece swimsuit.

"This one's bigger than the other," she said.

"Look the same to me."

"No, look," she cupped each breast in turn, weighing them. They both appeared equally firm and full. "Mom says it'll catch up eventually. Even out."

"They're exactly the same size."

"They're not. See?"

"Let me feel for myself."

"No way, Jose!"

"Come on, I'm an expert. I'm like a boob scientist or something."

"That's not a real thing," Marie blushed.

"Who's gonna know?"

"Uh… God?"

"Your loss," I shrugged. "Y'all got any beer over there? I need a wash down."

"I can't bring you any beer!"

I pointed to my throat. "Think I got some hot dog stuck in my throat… hard to… swallow…"

"Shouldn't've ate so fast."

"Might have to give me mouth-to-mouth…"

Marie rolled her eyes and got up. "Oh, fine..." she said. "I'll get you some Pepsi."

She came back exactly two minutes later with a lukewarm liter of Cherry RC and somebody else with her.

By the standards instilled in me by the 1980s, Marie was by far the more attractive of the sisters. She was the type who'd look right at home on a red sports car in a White Snake video. She had blonde, teased out hair that poofed up in front, and she was noticeably curvy in that baby fat, country girl sort of way. Her eyes were a happy blue, and her lips perpetually sparkled with pink gloss, and I'd even kissed them once at an 8th grade church lock-in, but that's as far as it went. Everybody knew Marie wouldn't put out. She was one of the good girls at Atlantis High—cursed with Christian niceness, good cheer, and a pure-heartedness about her that almost made you feel terrible for the fantasies of what you'd do to her.

Meredith was otherwise. At the time, she was just weeks away from entering Atlantis High as a freshman. It would take a couple more years for her body to assume full womanhood, but even then Meredith would look much as she does today—streamlined and muscular, like a collegiate pole vaulter or Linda Hamilton in *Terminator 2*. Her hair was a dark chestnut with a touch of red, and her eyes were like umber coals from another planet. She had full lips that stood out on her angular, pale face, and there was something stark and Paleolithic about her gaze that engendered disquiet wherever it landed. No one would call Meredith beautiful—at least, not at that point in her life—but when she slipped into my tent that day, my lungs stopped working for a full five seconds.

"Meredith wanted to come," Marie waved. "Here's some RC."

Meredith looked around the tent blankly while Marie poured out precise servings of the soda into three plastic cups.

"None for me," Meredith said.

"I'll take hers," I said. Meredith sat down on my sleeping bag and I tried not to stare at her. "Ain't y'all gonna get in trouble over here?"

"I told you my uncle left. Nobody else cares," Marie said.

"That's not true," said Meredith, picking up one of my paperbacks.

"Well, if nobody cares, how about a couple more of them dogs?" I suggested.

"Rude," Marie replied.

"You said yourself I'm getting skinny."

"Could at least say *please*," she said, tilting her voice and head to the side.

"Pleaassse!" I made an exaggerated supplication that lasted half a minute. The sisters laughed, Marie more so.

"Okay," Marie said. "We'll be right back."

"She can stay here," I said, looking at Meredith. "I won't bite."

Meredith shrugged. I grinned at Marie, who smiled back—the portrait of teenaged, Jesus-loving cluelessness.

"Okay," she said, ducking out of the tent.

Meredith picked up my torn-up copy of *The Unbearable Lightness of Being*. I slid exactly four inches closer to her.

"That one's in Czechoslovakia," I said. "The main guy used to be a doctor and he's got these two girlfriends. Well, later on he ends up—"

"I know," Meredith said. "I read it last year. Very grown up stuff," she said.

I was thinking about all the sex in the book and hoping that Meredith was also thinking about all the sex in the book.

"She lied," Meredith said, leaning back on her elbows.

"Who?"

She pointed her chin in the direction of the picnic outside that neither of us could see.

"Doesn't sound like her," I said.

"Marie said that nobody cares, but our parents definitely do."

Meredith looked at her toes and wiggled them in the light that came in sideways through the flap in the tent. I looked at them, too.

"She's taking her time," I said, adjusting my shorts. So far it was still on the stealth side of boners.

"She gets distracted."

"Maybe that pyramid got her."

"Probably not," Meredith laughed. "You can't see the pyramid unless you believe in it. Marie definitely doesn't believe in that pyramid."

"Why don't your parents like me?"

"Seriously?"

"Well, yeah."

"Marie had a boyfriend last year—well, she tried to have a boyfriend last year—but he was Lutheran. They made her stop talking to him."

"I'm not Lutheran."

"Well, you're not First Baptist, are you?"

"No," I said.

"And then there's that talk about you being half-nigger."

"Don't say that," I scooted away and sat up. "That's... Don't say stuff like that."

"I'm just telling you what they say," Meredith said, hurt and a little surprised. "I don't talk like that."

"You just did, though."

Meredith went quiet for a moment, inhaled through her nose, and nodded to herself with fierce, fourteen-year-old resolution. "I won't say it anymore."

I looked at her toes again and felt the blood run back to my dong and got over it.

"I don't care what you are," she said quietly.

"Look, if that's what your parents are saying about me, why'd they let y'all come over?"

"Marie told them we're gonna get you to come to church with us. Like, Jesus loves everybody, hung around with the hookers… stuff like that."

"You want me to go to church with y'all?"

"Not me. Her."

"I might go if you wanted me to."

"I don't see why," she responded flatly. "It's hypocritical and stupid. Not to mention boring."

"Doesn't sound very Christian of you."

Meredith looked at me sideways. "That's the kind of thing you hear adults say," she said. "Are you an adult?"

The question startled me. No, it wasn't the question—it was the boldness of somebody her age asking it. I didn't know how to answer.

"I'm almost eighteen," I said.

"Eighteen isn't adult," Meredith said. "Adult isn't any kind of number."

"How old are you?"

Meredith rolled her eyes and tossed the Kundera down in disappointment. And without intending to, I asked, "You have a boyfriend?"

She shook her head slowly and studied me with interest.

"How about we go to the movies sometime?" I asked.

"What?"

I slid closer to her, unable to stop myself. It was like watching your own foot disappear into quickmud. I reached out slowly and put a hand on her thigh. Something turned up in her eyes like a burst of brown fire.

"Are you a virgin?" I asked.

"That's none of your business," she said, pushing my hand away slowly. Her touch was hot and damp.

"Just trying to get to know you," I said, looking at my hand as if it belonged to somebody else.

"Does the movie depend on whether I'm a virgin or not?"

"Of course not."

"Then why ask the question?"

"I'm sorry," I replied, and all of the momentum had vanished. I could breathe normal again and remembered I was just some kid in a horrible smelling tent on an impossibly hot day with a weird girl I'd just met. I shook my head and poured myself more Cherry RC. Meredith lay back on my sleeping bag and considered the patches on the ceiling of the tent.

"I've never been on a date," she said after a while. "What's supposed to happen? You pick me up in your Camaro, we go to the movies, and I let you feel me up in the balcony?"

I snorted warm soda out of my nose. "I don't have a Camaro," I said, wiping my face.

Marie threw the tent flap open and I nearly jumped out of my bulging cutoffs. Meredith sat up slowly, like a cat waking up from a nap. She smirked at Marie. It was one of those smirks you give somebody you don't think all that much about.

"Not much food left," Marie said breathlessly. She sat down and held out a paper plate with three hot dogs on it—one without a bun, and all three without mustard or relish. In their stead, a giant mound of ketchup tilted the plate dangerously to one side. "Ran out of mustard," she said.

"Ketchup's good," I replied. "And thank you."

"You're welcome," Marie beamed.

"Good news," Meredith said. "He's joining Club Jesus with us."

"What?" Marie asked, clearly embarrassed. "I don't—"

"Don't do that," Meredith glared at her. "Do you how stupid you look when you do that?"

"I don't know what you're talking about," Marie lied, looking down at the hot dogs.

"Church," I said. "Apparently, I'm going with y'all next Sunday."

"Oh?" Marie smiled. "That's... good. That'd be nice. Won't that be nice, Meredith?"

But I never did go. Because the remaining events of that day and the next and the one after that rerouted my life in several unexpected, church-averse directions at once. It would only be a matter of hours until everybody in the county knew I was back. Red squealed into the park the next day in a brand-new Bronco, courtesy of under-the-table college funds, lifting me four feet off the ground in a rib-cracking hug that made my teeth hurt. We hooked up with a Nitro Fish & Ski packed with friends and enough booze to kill off a field of buffalo, and Steve found me hours later passed out face-down on a concrete table wearing somebody else's pants.

But before all that it was still that fated Sunday when Meredith, Marie, and I climbed out of my tent smelling like grilled meat and teen salacity. Meredith peeled off on her own as Marie led me over to the table where her parents, their adult friends, a frizzy-headed youth pastor, and somebody else—somebody I knew quite well—awaited. It was Coach.

Coach jumped up when he saw me and messed up my prodigal, tangled hair with such happiness you'd think I'd just come out of a coma. He told me I was too skinny. He said two-a-days started next week. He said maybe I could work my way into the 2nd string rotation, though, hinting I might be back to a starting position by mid-season. He introduced me to his new wife, who looked like she'd stepped right off the nose of WWII bomber, and then he introduced me to Meredith's and Marie's parents and extended family, as if the whole encounter had been his own genius idea. All they could do was shake my hand and nod with compelled approval and clear a seat for me at the imperial end of that big-ass cement table.

There've been times when I've wanted that afternoon back. Had I not done what I did, I could've gone on to do just about any middle-class, hick-town anything. I could have rejoined the Merfeet squad, gone to that church, never been adopted by Steve, never kept up my music and become famous, never lost my beautiful voice. I could've earned a scholarship to play D-II football, married Meredith, gone to work for her dad, bought a two-story brick house in Caddo Hills, popped out a couple of pups, hung out with my Caddo Club buddies playing golf on the weekends, got a pony for the kids... All of it and more. So much more.

My organs shiver when I remember what happened next. I can't even remember who asked the question, which was something like, "So, what are your plans after high school, young man?" And I was stupid enough to tell them.

As a matter of fact, I'm gonna be a star. I'm a singer now. Sam Sorrow. That's what I go by. Y'all hear me singing earlier? Those were just covers, but I've got plenty of my own. How about I play some for y'all? How about I go get my guitar and...

And even that cringy, utterly-misreading-the-room blunder would've been alright. In time, I could have recovered. Sure, I would've been made fun of for years, but it wouldn't've prohibited the unfurlage of the fantasies listed above. Because with football front and center and with those Baptists and Coach on my side, everything would've been alright.

What stopped them laughing that day was the same thing that slammed and locked the door on that sunny back porch of the multiverse. Because I pushed back. I told them that I meant it. I was serious. More serious than anything. And since fame only comes at a price (how little did I know), I wasn't coming back to football. I'd have to swear it off. I wouldn't have the time, because I'd be too busy practicing and rehearsing and traveling around to perform and... *I'm sorry, Coach, but I'm just gonna have to say no.*

PERIWINKLE BLUE

I pull up to the security gate of the Caddo Estates—the walled-in, camera'd community where Meredith lives, tucked off 59 west of town like a bashful child. Like Creekview—the place where Red and me once called home—all bona fide trailer parks in Atlantis were disposed of in the early 2000s in the name of communal uplift. Anybody who calls Caddo Estates a trailer park couldn't tell the difference between a baguette and a buttermilk biscuit.

Caddo Estates is what's known as a *manufactured home community*. It's the kind of place people willingly retire to in a sensible grid of largish, newish, and no-longer-mobilish homes kept in proper alignment and code. There are rules aplenty—rules about pets, parking, visiting hours, sub-leasing, the upkeep of yards and exteriors, noise levels, and so on. All of this is enforced by a semi-retired staff (usually a couple, sometimes siblings) whom you're meant to know. They live there; they're like you. In actuality, they're employees of an out-of-state corporation who owns dozens of these places scattered throughout the sub-rural and almost-middle-class landscape of the South and West.

In contrast, if your parents or grandparents live in an actual *trailer park*, someone's American Dream done died. You don't visit a trailer park to see Nana; you go there to fuck somebody's spouse while they're off pulling a double or to procure something illicit from shirtless dudes known only by their initials or with names like Nashville and Waco Tony. A trailer park lacks official perimeters. There's no central intelligence to monitor your visit. The only noise regulations are those enforced with violent threats and extemporized projectiles. And when it comes to pets, when they're not chained to something grimy and immobile, ungoverned dogs roam the trailer park with abandon, shitting over garbage-strewn yards and humping each other with wanton indifference. The humans are not substantively different.

That's where I grew up. That's a fucking trailer park.

Meredith buzzes me in and a security camera records my passage into the guarded interior of matching homes fabricated in the same factory in one of five pastel colors. Meredith's is periwinkle blue. I bought it for her three or four years ago, at a time when I still had the cash and was still subject to the mistaken belief that my voice would someday return (or, more notably, my record label believed so). Although the corporate decrees of the Caddo Estates require uniformity regarding the homes' external forms, they can't say shit about their innards, because, you know, America. And so inside is where Meredith stands out like an anarcho-heathen, former drug-running stripper in church. There are convocations of candles, incense, sage and cedar smudge sticks, prayer beads, charms, essential oils, dried herbs and mushrooms, tapestries, Tarot decks of all sorts, rune sets in wood and stone, statues of deities in sexual arrangements, shells from the Gulf, antlers and bones from the Hill Country, jewelry, gems, drums in various sizes and skins, charcoal sketches, unframed paintings in watercolor and acrylic, antique mirrors and lamps, pine cones and bird nests, and enough books to fill one of the larger rooms at BookPeople in Austin. That's just the living room.

"What this about Steve?" I ask, stepping in.

"Have a seat," she says.

I plop down on her oversized blue sofa and take off my boots. The house smells like a celestial, fur-lined cave where shamans gather to fuck and impose their will upon the rest of our causal streams.

"Something to drink?" Meredith asks. "Water, tea…"

"What do you have in the way of tequila?"

"Nothing."

"What do you have in the way of booze?"

"How about juice? Cran-grape, cran-apple, cran-straw… That's with strawberry."

"What's with all the cranberry?"

"Proanthocyanidins. Want some?"

"Cran-grape," I say. Legendary for her straightforwardness, this around-the-bush-beating by Meredith is suspiciously atypical. She rolls her shoulders and pours out two cups of juice on the kitchen counter.

"You're wondering why I'm not getting to the point," she tells the fridge.

"No, I'm wondering what's the hold up with that cran-grape."

She hands me a green plastic cup full of purple juice. I drink some. It's pretty good. Meredith looks at the clock hanging over the front door and sighs through her nose.

"When'd you get that TV?" I ask. It's substantial.

"Few years back," she says, sitting down on the other side of the sofa facing me, the small of her back against the far arm, cross-legged in black jeans and a burgundy sweater.

"You've had a seventy-five-inch Samsung for years?"

"Eighty-five, actually."

"Bullshit," I say. "Eighty at best."

"Interesting. You don't usually underestimate the size of things."

"I see what you did there."

"You're thinking the old TV. You haven't been here in three years."

I snort. "Woman, I came by a year ago."

"When was that, exactly?"

"Okay… Well, year and a half ago. Two tops."

"It was three. I should know."

"What's that supposed to mean?"

Other than the growing streak of silver above her right ear, Meredith doesn't look a day over thirty-five, and a smoking hot thirty-five, at that. She glances out at the street through the big bay window and says, "It means your memory is shit."

"Why does everybody say that?"

"Well, to begin with, because it's true," she says, sipping her juice.

"If we're not going to fuck and we're not going to talk about who killed Steve, why am I here?"

"As opposed to…"

"You know what I mean."

Her eyes are watching me, but her face is still facing that window.

"Give me a minute," she says. "Who bailed you out?"

"Not you."

"Was I supposed to?"

I look out of the window, too. The juice is feisty and tart.

"On policy, I avoid the authorities whenever possible."

Meredith has what you'd call a history of run-ins with the law.

"Coach got me out."

"That's interesting."

"Not really."

"How's Coach doing these days?"

"Mellowing with age," I say.

"I doubt that."

"Speaking of Coach and my so-called shit memory and us sitting around bullshitting about bullshit and things and stuff, I was just thinking about that one time at Deer Point on my way over here."

"Which one time?"

"*The* one time," I say. "The day we first met. In my tent."

The slightest of smiles touches Meredith's mouth. She says, "That was a Sunday, mid-August, 1986... I was about to start high school. I wasn't there for the Coach part, though."

"Yeah, you were."

"Not really," she replies. "I was barely nearby. You and Marie were talking to Coach and them; I'd gone off by myself. I heard Coach yelling at you, but I didn't know what it was about until later."

"Same difference."

"In your version, maybe," she says. "I might as well be right there with you in your version, because I'm just an object in the background. One you can move around to fit the retelling."

I puff my cheeks with air and take off my hat. One of these days, I'll make it through a conversation with Meredith without being reminded of my self-centeredness.

"Uh huh," I say.

"Would you like to hear my version?"

"More than just two things shy of anything."

She pauses with a tilt of her neck and then says, "I went to sit under a big willow close to the water, and I looked out through its branches and leaves at the lake. There were two kids swimming out there—two girls. I didn't know them; they weren't part of our group. It was hot and humid and I wanted to take off my clothes, at least wear a bikini, but my father insisted I wear jean shorts and a baggy t-shirt—an Amy Grant t-shirt, as I recall. So I just sat there sweltering and feeling sticky and out of place and confused... All sorts of unfamiliar things were turning over in me. The only thing I was sure of was that I wanted you to forget about Marie and those stupid adults and come find me and sit with me under that tree and look at me the way you'd looked at me earlier in your tent."

"Like this?" I try it out.

"No. You'll never look at me that way again. It's funny... I can remember exactly what you looked like that day."

"Like something out of a Dexy's Midnight Runners video, probably."

"Close. But mostly I remember your smell. It was like... an unknown animal den in the woods, or the first time you get a whiff of a rare spice from India. Something that totally rearranges your previous sense of what's pleasant or unpleasant."

Meredith takes a break to sip her juice and search my face for something. "I remember the jealousy, too."

It's an all-too-familiar topic between us, and not one I want to get into right now.

"I'd never felt that until that day," she says.

"Is that what you want to talk about?"

"No," she says. "I believe that subject has finally been talked to death. Speaking of, Steve... What do you know so far?"

"I don't know anything so far," I say. "I thought you invited me over here to tell me shit."

"You at least know what the paper says."

"That he killed himself? Sure. Clearly bullshit, but so what?"

Meredith shakes her head. "You didn't feel *so what* at the funeral. You basically put it on the Caddo Club in front of everybody. Beau's death, too. I'm surprised you can still walk."

"What can I say? I live a charmed life."

"What did Coach tell you?"

"What's there for him to say?"

One of Meredith's perfectly plucked eyebrows tries to high-five the ceiling.

"Okay," I sigh. "There's this guy who tried to sue the BI and threatened Steve in court. Then I find out later it's all cool between them, because Steve gives ole Lefty or Bill or whatever his name is a job out at his charity, get-off-drugs place up at the lake."

"Guy," she says.

"Guy?"

"That's his name."

"The guy's name is Guy?"

"Guy Polder," she nods. "I used to work with him out at the *Sirens*. He did security for a while. Handsome man. Smart, too. Reads books, always talking about movies... you'd like him."

"Great. He single?"

"But I wouldn't start looking there," she says thoughtfully. "A little on-the-nose."

"Well, I'm not looking," I tell her, "but if I were, seems like on-the-nose is exactly where a person is supposed to start looking."

"Why would Guy knock off Steve after Steve gave him the cushiest job he could hope to find in the county? Guy knew what he had. That whole blowup in court was reactionary. It was simply Guy trying to save face."

"Maybe he was as good at saving face as he was at saving his hand. Maybe he went a little too far, you know? Things got out of control. That's how it happens in the books and movies."

"Books and movies?"

"Yeah, books and movies. TV shows. Detectives," I say. "Shit like that."

"This is real life, Sam."

"How's it different?"

Meredith stands and walks over to the kitchen. "That's probably the most Sam Sorrowinest thing I've ever heard you say."

"Thank you."

In a minute, she comes back to join me on the couch, her cup freshly full of cranberry mystery juice.

"It's auspicious you bring up Deer Point," she says. I only know what *auspicious* means because my ex—my *other* ex, that is—liked to use that word a lot. "I had a dream of that place the other night."

Out of habit, I bite the side of my tongue. Meredith's always had these elaborate dreams. For her, they're revelatory—instructional, prophetic, pregnant with meaning. I've always considered dreams to be little more than sleep trash, but a man learns to shut his mouth about such things.

"I get it now," I say. "This whole thing is about one of your dreams."

"Partially, yes. You take issue with that?"

Meredith asks the question with the unblinking confidence of a hijacker who's finally got the jet in the air. What am I supposed to do now—leave? If I stay and listen, there's still enough time for some action. At least, that's what I'm meant to believe.

"Get on with it," I say, pointing at the clock.

Meredith looks down at her hands and clears her throat. "I'll keep it short. In my dream, Steve's at the beach at Deer Point. He's in the water, about waist high. He's looking out toward the middle of the lake and it's raining a little bit... More mist than rain, really. It's foggy, too. And there's a man standing out there, almost like he's perched on something. An island you can't see from shore, maybe, or some sort of rock. He's waving to Steve. Beckoning. And even though I can see Steve clearly in the dream, the man is... It's like looking through a veil. A wet veil. And Steve starts walking further out. The water gets deeper and deeper, and he's afraid. Really afraid. Even so, he keeps walking out toward the man."

"He was terrified of water," I say. The result of him being thrown into the deep end as a boy—the favored Texan method for teaching kids how to swim.

Meredith shakes her head. "I don't think so. Steve loved the beach."

"Only from a distance," I say. "Like, the Mexico beach. Crystal clear water, fruity drinks, tan dudes in Speedos. But that haunted, murky-ass lake water? He'd never come anywhere near it."

"Except when he came to get you," she says. "That day at Deer Point, right?"

"Right," I say. The day Steve saved my life, which must have taken some doing on his part. "So, what about this dream are you wanting to leave me with? Somebody invited Steve out there and... what, killed him?"

"It's not just the dream," she says, looking at the clock again. "Look... There's a reason I'm taking so long to tell you."

"I should fucking hope—"

"Just listen, okay?" Meredith's eyes are blinking more than usual. "But I only have time to tell you some of it now. Can you wait here while I'm at this meeting? Or come back later?"

"Why?" I laugh. "So you can vanish on me again?"

Meredith's eyes drop to the floor and stay there. "That's not fair," she says.

She's right—it's not fair. We've both stepped out of each other's lives without warning with roughly the same frequency over the years. I don't tell her that I'll stay to wait for her or that I'll come back later, and neither do I tell her why, because my hands are starting to shake again, even though I'm keeping them out of sight. As soon as Meredith leaves, I'll be off to the nearest booze purveyor, and I know better than to make promises that a liquored-up Sam Sorrow can't keep.

But shame's a funny thing. In this case, it'll make a man listen and put on his best take-something-serious face, even when he knows that what's being said isn't worth taking serious. Meredith buns up her hair and blacklines her eyes in the mirror as she tells me the rest. This after changing into some ass-fitting slacks and a no-frills cardigan.

A couple of weeks back, she tells me, Steve invited her over for dinner. He hadn't done that in almost a year. Steve had a new boyfriend (Meredith hadn't met him yet—actually, nobody she knew had met his boyfriend yet) and Meredith assumed that's where Steve had been spending all his time when he wasn't teaching or working at the BI or the Foundation. At first, Meredith thought Steve's house smelled different—not off or pungent, but more alert. Wary, even. Over dinner, Meredith understood that the scent was coming from Steve himself, that it was the smell of something bothering him—something he was reluctant to talk about, something Steve didn't want to burden her with. So she found another way.

Then she tells me how. "Are you fucking kidding me?" I ask.

Meredith stops applying her Chanel le Crayon Yeux Precision Eye Definer Eyeliner in Noir and shakes her head at herself and the person standing behind her in the mirror, which is me.

"Tarot?"

"I did it casually," she says, resuming the eye job. "Made him feel like he was humoring me."

Which he was. As much attention and sincerity as Steve paid to Caddo legends about Bigfoot and our submerged pyramid and all sorts of other superstitious Lake Atlantis hoo-ha, Steve was just about the least woo-woo person I'd ever met. Even so, per Meredith, she gave Steve several Tarot readings over the next couple of hours that night, aided in no small part by a bottle of white Burgundy. In the first reading, she says, Steve inquired about his boyfriend, and the cards were unilaterally good.

"The Sun, the Hierophant, Ten of Cups… You couldn't ask for a better set when it comes to love. Steve was blushing. But the next reading was all downhill."

Clearly, the boyfriend thing wasn't what was bothering Steve. But another glass of wine or two loosened him up enough to try the cards again, only this time the questions were more serious. They were all about business stuff, specifically people he was doing business with. That's when Meredith noticed the smell again—minty concern with peppery notes of mistrust.

"Justice, Page of Swords, Ace of Pentacles… but all reverses, mind you," she says.

"What's that, like, three of a kind?"

"Three of a bad kind," Meredith says, frowning in the mirror. "Deception, manipulation, bad investments... Not exactly what Steve wanted to hear."

"Okay... Sort of brings us back to Lefty, doesn't it? Steve trusts him enough to give Lefty that job even after he tried that hand bullshit out at the BI."

"Stop saying Lefty," Meredith says. "It's offensive."

"What do you want me to say?"

"Guy," she sighs.

"You mean Bill?"

"It wasn't Guy. Steve's questions were about somebody else, somebody with... how do I say it... power? That wasn't Guy. Steve was asking about somebody with leverage. I'm thinking a major shareholder in the company or somebody in upper management. Somebody who was giving Steve trouble. Or had the power to."

"Somebody who'd gain from getting him out of the way," I say, balling up my hand again.

"Yeah," she nods, putting her fancy eyeliner back in its zippered pouch. "If by out of the way you mean dead. Shit!" she says, looking out of the horizontal blinds. "My ride's here."

"Hold on a second," I say, grabbing her shoulder. "You can't just leave me hanging at that. How long's this fucking meeting?"

"Two hours," she says, removing my hand. "Three, tops. Wait here. There's more."

"Goddammit—"

"The part about somebody with influence or power... That's important, Sam."

"That could be anybody in the Caddo Club, Mere! Could be the Mayor, could be some kind of regulatory bullshit, could be a judge or any number of businessmen around here—"

"Business*people*," she says.

"There you go. Including Sonya Tyson."

Meredith stifles a laugh and grabs her keys.

"How's that funny?" I ask. "Coach says Sonya owns half the damn county these days. If anybody has a huge share of Berkey International, Sonya does."

"Sonya Tyson," Meredith shakes her head, checking her hair one last time in the mirror. "The CC would love it if you thought that, Sam. They've been after your girlfriend for years."

"She's not my girlfriend."

"Whatever."

Sonya's another long-running sore subject between us.

"You haven't been around in long time," she says, looking down at her naked feet. "Oh, I forgot the boots."

Meredith quickly picks out a pair of tall black boots near the front door and zips them up to her knees, where they disappear beneath the bottoms of her ass-hugging slacks.

"Sonya and Steve were close," Meredith says, standing up. "You remember that, at least. And they've been working together on all sorts of stuff for years—charities, safety measures at BI, social services for lower income folks… Additionally, whoever killed Steve is a man. That's what the dream reveals. Whoever was with Steve at the lake that night was a man."

"Right," I mumble. "The dream."

"Don't be an asshole."

"Why not?"

"Are you sticking around, or what?" Meredith asks, examining her boots. "There's still something major I have to tell you."

"Tell me now."

Meredith opens the door. She puts her keys and phone into her bag—a leather satchel I gave her years ago in Austin. On it are two embroidered owls, who are not what they seem.

"I'm past late already," she says. "Wait for me here and we'll figure it out together."

I put my trembling fingers in my pockets. "Mere, look... I have to—"

"I know," she says, nodding at my pocketed hands. "You don't think I saw? It's okay, Sam. There's half a bottle of Tito's in the pantry. Help yourself."

THE TWO SENJOS

Through the louvred blinds, I watch Meredith trot-walk past the common house and wave to a septuagenarian who's weed-eating the sidewalk in front of the Caddo Estates mailboxes. He smiles and watches Meredith's ass hurry out through the pedestrian gate and climb into the back of an enormous, platinum white Lincoln Navigator—the kind that cost more than Meredith's periwinkle blue house. Then the old man turns back to his job, shins splattered with crabgrass and veins that don't work, as the SUV pulls away slowly toward the highway.

I snatch the Tito's from the pantry and splash some cran-grape into the top of the bottle. Vodka's not my favorite lady, but she'll do in a pinch as a side chick. I dig around the fridge, munch on stale plantain chips, and walk around the house wondering what else Meredith has to tell me until I gradually return to my unwondering and somewhat operationally tipsy self.

Meredith's bedroom's been upgraded. Now she has one of those beds that adjusts to your personal curvature and temperature, along with another giant flat screen TV on the far wall. There's a multi-nubbed, brightly colored dildo on her nightstand that looks like it was designed in space, as well as a four-foot tall safe in the corner of the room that, for the absolute fuck of it, I try to crack and fail. I rummage through her walk-in closet—dozens more boots and shoes, pricey business attire, three wigs (two blonde, one black), a locked suitcase that must weight seventy pounds, lingerie with the tags still on... I've never been one for lingerie and Meredith has never once worn it for me.

There's a new painting in the bathroom I don't recognize, but I know it's Meredith's work as soon as I see it. A watercolor—gray with other earth tones and highlights of ochre and burgundy (her favorite color). I back away to straighten my eyes and take a good look at the two women featured in the painting. They face each other and hold hands by a creek or perhaps a river and there's a light rain falling through broad shafts of faded, diagonal light across their nude, lean bodies. They're identical, the women, and both of them are Meredith. They dance around each other, twirling and merging into one. Then it hits me. It's from a story she told me when we were kids.

Back in the grungy haze of the early 90s, when she was 20 and I was just a stretch older, I was just starting out in Austin and Meredith was out in the mountains near Asheville on some sort of back-to-the-land commune thing. We hadn't seen each other for more than a year, but time warps in inexpressible ways when you're that age, and so at the same time it felt like a decade had passed it could've easily been no more than a handful of minutes since we'd last met. Out of the blue, I received a weird letter from her, freaked out about it for possessive reasons, and decided to drive my crappy LTD out to North Carolina to change her mind or rescue her or some-such. This was back before I was famous and was still pretending to go to college on Steve's dime. In other words, I had the time.

The LTD made it as far as an I-40 off-ramp just west of Knoxville. That's where my car died and where Meredith told me the story.

The off-ramp was just a truck-stop diner, a gas station/repair shop, and a pull-in L-shaped motel named after a noble, mythical beast—*The Centaur* or *The Pegasus* or *The Griffin*. Something like that. That place is probably a full-blown city these days, but back then it was just a run-down impediment between me and Meredith, in addition to being an advert for every Tennessee stereotype imaginable. The first person I met was a mechanic with all of five teeth in his mouth who looked as if he'd breakfasted on nicotine and coal. The second person was a newly pregnant diner waitress with sunken eyes and scars crossing the insides of her forearms who couldn't have been more than seventeen. Everybody in the place looked like they'd stepped right out of a Loretta Lynn song.

The mechanic said the LTD needed a new timing belt, and the part would take at least a week to arrive. I had twenty-seven dollars. Even with the car up and running, I wouldn't have enough for the gas it would take to find Meredith and the hippies she was living with. I would've called Steve, and no doubt he would have wired me the funds, but he'd just found out that I'd lied about being in college again and I just couldn't face how horrible I felt about it. Steve had given me everything—money for that car, a house in Austin to rent out the extra rooms, cash for living expenses, and tuition to UT on top of that. I'd taken his generosity for granted again and covered it over with the shame and tar of another half-truth it took him a surprisingly long time to see through. After I got busted, I stopped cashing his checks. I just couldn't take his money anymore. That's why twenty-seven dollars.

I can't remember how I convinced Meredith to meet me at that motel. I can't remember how I got ahold of her. It took the rest of the day for her to get there, and in the meanwhile I sold off the extraneous components of the LTD to the mechanic for seventy bucks more. I told him to order the timing belt, install it when it arrived, and I'd be back in a couple of weeks, payment in full. He knew I'd never be back, even if I didn't.

I burnt through that cash over the next two days and nights with Meredith in that diner and lousy motel. I didn't find out about the bedbugs until my way back to Austin. While I waited for Meredith to show up, I drank diner coffee the color of chicken stock and flirted with Deena, the knocked-up teenage waitress. They had a special on all-you-can eat hoecakes and Deena kept em coming. She was as sassy as a twice-divorced waitress three times her age and not bad to look at when you got past the scars and baby bump. It gave me something to do. By the time Meredith got there, I was hopped up on hoecake syrup and weak coffee and half a Mountain Dew. I was buzzing so hard that the nerves in my fingers were like crazed and horny bees.

As was the case at that age, not four or five words passed between us before Meredith and me were fucking like randy, short-lived forest creatures. And that's all we did for the next three plus hours, only stopping when she appeared to pass out beneath me, with me still huffing away like a chain-smoking werewolf. I collapsed off to one side and held her hand and watched her legs twitch in post-orgasmic recovery. It was raining.

When I woke up, it was still raining. Meredith was sitting naked in a chair next to the window looking outside at Tennessee becoming progressively wetter. I got up to piss and rinse my mouth out with the rest of that Mountain Dew and my dick felt worked over and sore. I went back to bed and tried to fluff up the pillows so I could lean back on them, but they were flaccid and mushy and kept flattening out in a useless pile just above my crack.

"Come here," I said.

Meredith didn't do anything. She just sat there looking outside.

"I think you broke my dick," I said. "It's bent all weird."

"It's always like that," she said, still facing away. The rain chased versions of itself down the smudged window and she placed her palm upon the pane as if to comfort some ache beyond the glass.

"No one fucks me the way you do," she said.

"Don't say that."

"*Fuck?*"

"You know what I mean."

"Why shouldn't I say it? It's true," she grinned. "You should take pride in it."

"I do, it's just I don't like the comparative aspect."

"Me fucking other men?"

"Something like that."

"How about other women?"

"*Other* women?"

"Me fucking women," she said. "You know."

"I don't mind that much. Is that even called fucking?"

"What else would you call it? And why wouldn't you mind?"

"I don't know. I just... that's not the kind of thing that makes me jealous. And I'm not one of those guys who get off thinking about that stuff, either. Why, is that your thing now?"

"I don't have a thing," Meredith said.

"Well, I have a thing. Why don't you come over here and sit on it?"

"Thought it was broke."

"I need you to bend it back the other way." I showed her my cock. It really did look bent to me.

"You're too much."

"Thank you," I grinned.

"Not how I meant it."

"Well."

"I like thinking about it."

"My cock?"

"You and other women."

"You like thinking about me with other women."

"I do. Always have. Ever since we first met," she said.

"You were a kid when we first met."

"Fourteen."

"Fourteen's a kid," I said.

"I'd already lost my virginity by then. Did you know that?"

"I don't like thinking about that, either."

"Makes two of us," she said.

"But I do like thinking about you thinking about me with other women. Tell me about that."

The light from outside haloed her hair and shoulders and flashed through the reddish-brown mound where her inner thighs met together like an agreement from heaven. She came back to the bed, put a pillow under her butt, and sat facing me, cross-legged. Her breasts were small and bright and blotched with stubble burns and bite marks. Every now and then she turned to look at the rain, like she was checking on it. The room was stuffed with the fog of our sex.

"There's two of them," Meredith said. "Two fantasies."

"Go on."

"The first involves what's-her-name. The one you were seeing before me."

"Jenna?"

"No, the black one," Meredith frowned. "Who's Jenna?"

"Nobody," I said quickly. "Your fantasy is about me and Sonya?"

She nodded. "Nothing elaborate, but it is kind of romantic, now that I think about it. Y'all are in the bathroom at Martin's. You're doing it standing up against the wall. Facing each other."

"That bathroom ain't romantic."

"You're going slow, looking into each other's eyes, touching each other's faces... stuff like that."

"Sounds like a Harlequin Romance."

"That's what y'all used to do in there, right? Rumor was you two used to fuck in that bathroom. Like, nobody could put a stop to it."

"Jesus Christ, we were, like, thirteen or something."

"Is it true?"

"No, we just made out in there. Until some old redneck busted us and told the whole damn world about it. That's how my mom got fired from Martin's. Hers, too."

"Did you love her?" Meredith asked suddenly.

"I plead the Fifth," I threw my palms into the air dramatically.

"I'm not jealous, I'm just asking. Did you love her?"

"I don't know."

"You're lying," she said. Even back then, Meredith always knew when I was lying.

"Then yes, but…"

"There's no buts when it comes to love."

"Butts have everything to do with love. If you're an ass man like myself."

"Ha fucking ha."

"Okay, then. Sure, I loved her," I said. "*But*... I loved her in a childish way. We were just childs. Children."

"It wasn't that long ago."

"It was."

"A couple of years isn't anything to the cosmos. Not even a finger snap."

"It's not comparable. To the way I feel about you, I mean."

"You mean *felt*," Meredith said.

"No, I mean the word I just used."

"I'm not asking you to compare."

"You're sitting right here asking me about somebody else. You know how I feel about you."

"Nobody knows how anybody feels about anything," she said to the rain.

"That's just philosophical yoo-hoo. For example, I'm pretty sure I know how your dad felt when he walked in on you sucking my dick in his own house."

"Jesus Christ," she blushed.

"That's what he said."

"Yeah, like over and over again," she laughed, covering her mouth. "I'll never forget that."

"Neither will he."

"Do you think it's the same love?" she asked.

"What?"

"The love you had for Sonya and the love you had for me. Is it the same love?"

"I still have it for you. Past tense ain't nothing to do with it. And me and her have been over for years."

"Answer the question. Is it the same?"

"No. Not even close."

"Think about it, though," Meredith said. "Really think about it."

"I don't have to. I already know."

"Come on…"

"Okay," I closed my eyes and inhaled and pretended to contemplate the mysteries of young love. "There," I said. "I did it."

"And?"

"And it's not the same. By the time you and me got together, I was a completely different person than when me and her were doing our thing. So we're talking about two different versions of me who felt two different versions of love for two different versions of women. Hence, unidentical love."

"What if a version is just another way of looking at the same thing?"

"I don't know about that."

"Like the two Senjos," she suggested.

"Well, I don't know what the fuck a Senjo is, but it ain't like that, either."

"Yeah, you do. Steve told us the story. *The Two Senjos?*"

"You think I remember every damn story Steve told us? Must be a million of em. Two million."

"You'll remember when I tell you."

"I'd rather hear about this other fantasy of yours."

"Now I feel embarrassed about it."

"I doubt that," I said.

"Used to keep me up at night," she blushed again. "Made me hornier than what-all."

"Holy shit, will you just get on with it?"

"It's about my sister."

"Your sister?"

"Yeah, my sister," Meredith said to the rain on the window again. "Ever since she told me about y'all making out that one time—I mean, this was even before you and me met—it was kind of a... I don't know. An anchor of some sort. Like, the first coherent sexual fantasy I ever had."

"When did I make out with your sister?"

"Some church lock-in thing."

"Oh, yeah," I remembered. "I tried to feel her up, too."

"She didn't include that part."

"She's got great tits, or used to. Wouldn't let me, though. Y'all being good Christian girls."

"Exactly," she smirked. "You want to hear about it or what?"

"Does it involve romantic bathrooms?"

"No, the setting is kinda vague. Maybe it's in that church, though."

"Nice," I said.

"And it's kinda rapey."

"What?"

"Yeah," she nodded. "I told you it was embarrassing."

"I don't think…"

"It's just a fantasy."

"Yeah, but I don't think… you know, that your sister would be into that?"

"What's that have to do with anything? It's my fantasy. Anyway, she might be. What would you know?"

"I know she kissed like a dead frog."

"Might be different now."

"Maybe I ought to give it another try."

"Good luck with that," she laughed. "She's off in Amarillo now. Started a church with her husband."

"Sounds about right."

"He's gay."

"Really?"

"She's got no idea, of course," Meredith shook her head. "As usual."

"Huh."

"It'll come out one of these days."

"*He'll* come out one of these days."

"Want to hear the fantasy or what?"

We spent the rest of the afternoon eating more hoecakes at the diner, watching *Simon & Simon*, and fucking several more times until we were thoroughly disgusted with the human body. It was always like that with us. We'd just go and go until we were sick of each other. At some point, I must have stuck something in the wrong place or said something at the wrong time and her feelings turned dark, because Meredith sat away from me on her side of the bed in a sweaty, wordless gloom, and she didn't come out of it until it began to get dark outside and both of us started giggling at the TV at the Simon brothers, who were engaged in undercover hijinks at a loony bin. When the episode ended, we tried to take a shower together, but the stall was too small, so we just rinsed off, each on our own, and then got back into that funky, sticky, sex-saucy bed.

"What are you going to do now?" she asked.

"Fall asleep."

"I mean tomorrow and after that."

"Didn't you once tell me the future doesn't exist? Like, it's a figment or something?"

"Don't be a dick," she said.

"Why not?"

She turned on her back and stared at the ceiling and didn't say anything for a full five minutes.

"Remember when my parents sent me off to that Jesus school in Virginia?" she asked quietly. I did. It happened a couple of days after her dad busted up that fellatio.

"Yeah," I said, half-assedly attempting to rise out of slumber.

"And you said you'd come rescue me?"

I didn't want to nod off. It was important that I didn't nod off. Meredith was awake, asking me things in an unfamiliar tone I didn't have the answers to, and beneath the incoming tide of sleep I heard the low mumble of the TV, and Meredith's voice rolled over me like the wind-pushed waves on a lake, and then it was Steve talking, or Steve sounding like another man with an unusual accent who was telling me about a girl from long ago—a girl named Senjo. Senjo grew up with her best friend, a boy from the village, the two of them in love. And they wanted to marry each other more than anything, but they couldn't, because her father became ill, and the boy was poor, and there was another suitor for Senjo who was rich and could take care of the family, and the boy ran off because he couldn't take the hurt of seeing Senjo with another man. And as he was departing downstream, the boy saw Senjo running after him along the banks of the river, and he pulled over so she could hop into his boat, and the two of them ran away together. They traveled for days downstream, found a place to start a farm and family, and only years later did they even think about returning to their old village. When they did, it was decided that the boy—the boy who was now a man—would go to Senjo's father first and make amends, to apologize for what they'd done, and then he'd call up Senjo and their children. But when he knocked on the door and told the old man his story, Senjo's father looked at him with joy and awe and incomprehension. *What do you mean Senjo is with you? Ever since you left our village that day, Senjo took to her bed here in our house, heartbroken and sick, and she has rarely left it since. Just wait until she hears of your return! Perhaps you can revive her, perhaps now she will be well and...* and then the old man went back into the house to tell his daughter, the Senjo inside the house who'd been in bed for several years, and, just as the father expected, the girl was overjoyed. She miraculously got out of bed and walked outside to greet the boy, and at the very same time the other Senjo—the one who had left with the boy those many years ago—was hurrying up the hill toward her old father's house. And when the two women saw each other, they wept with laughter. They embraced and danced together, twirling around and around each other, their hands enjoined, swirling until the two of them became one. So, which is the true Senjo? Are they two, or are they one?

*

When I woke up the next morning in that motel, Meredith was gone and the TV was off. Other than her smell and a handprint on the window, it was like she'd never been there at all. I had just enough money for coffee and an omelet at the diner and a Greyhound ticket back to Austin. The bus was mostly empty until Memphis, but by then I'd already claimed the back seat, and I watched the sad lineage of Little Rock and Texarkana and Dallas and Waxahachie and Waco roll by in an itchy, insomniacal, bed-bugged blur. When I got back to my house in South Austin, I slathered myself with cortisone and passed out on the living room floor as if I'd been shot in the back of the head and left to rot face down in an alley, except the alley was carpeted with nasty shag carpet that had never been cleaned.

Meredith didn't write me after that. Somewhere in the fuck-fugue of those couple of days together, I'd promised to visit her at that farm or commune or whatever it was, and maybe even spend next summer there, and then we'd ditch those hippies and go travel, just the two of us. I told her I'd line up some gigs in Europe to pay our way, that we'd hit Amsterdam and France and Spain and Ireland and Wales... Meredith had always wanted to see Wales.

We both knew none of it would happen. It was just me talking, back in the days when my talking sounded melodious and true. I used to love the sound of my own voice. It was another ten years before I saw Meredith again.

THE DREAM OF MARTIN'S

Hand to a God I have never believed in, I have every intention of coming back to Meredith's place before she returns from whatever suspect SUV business adventure she's on. The only reason I leave is that vodka gets me snacky, and all Meredith has in her fridge is overpriced Whole Foods nonsense—organic chard, herbed-up goat cheese, and a quinoa salad that smells like rope if rope smelled like feet... The nearest Whole Foods has to be fifty miles away.

It's not until I hit the highway that I realize I won't be able to get back into the Caddo Estates, what with the security gate and all. I'll have to wait outside the off-pearly gates for Meredith to return. Either that or break in. The most obvious thing to do now would be to go back to the Bestern, dial room service, cozy up with some decent liquor, and sack out for a couple of hours. Instead, I head to Martin's.

The diner has been a fixture of the old downtown since before Coach got face fuzz. If there's a heart and soul of Atlantis worth mentioning, it's Stanley Ave, where Martin's sits along with the town's antediluvian movie theater (enterprisingly called *The Stanley*) and other establishments that made a Caddo County childhood in the 70s and 80s somewhat worth living. My mom ran the register at Martin's and worked as a server for years, while the black ladies

(Misses Ida, Rose, Evie, and others) flipped burgers, chopped hash browns, and frothed out shakes and malts from a pink Hamilton Beach machine in the back. Martin's was a working-class joint and as racially mixed as it came in Atlantis—an uncommon salad of multicultural mirth. I'm not talking your Walmart variety of transient nods across the aisle; I'm talking people of varying tones actually rubbing shoulders, shaking hands, and sitting at adjacent tables. It's the only place I can think of from that time in which people always seemed happy to be there. Even the old school, white-haired crackers super-glued to their counter stools seemed happy to be there.

Before we got busted for making out in the bathroom, Sonya and me were core members of the pack of kids with moms on shift, all of us congregated in the back corner booth to read, play salvaged board games with absent components, and consume more cheeseburgers, onion rings, and French fries than the digestive system of any human child should be able to handle. We weren't allowed up front at the long Formica counter, but if we behaved we were permitted to free range the main room and visit with the folks at the communal gingham-covered tables or the four-tops that lined the walls and front window. That included Steve.

Steve was the exception to the working-class clientele, although his name might as well have been engraved on one particular table—the far corner window booth. It was like nobody else was permitted to sit there, even in his absence. In his presence, that booth is where we spent a good amount of our time, because Steve was our philanthropist and patron. Every comic, every well-used chess set or game of *Clue*, every paperback (*Anne of Green Gables, The Witch of Blackbird Pond,* the original *Shannara* stuff) came from him. And for Sonya and me and the rest of the kids, Steve was as much a part of Martin's as our moms and the burgers and those impossibly delicious butterscotch milkshakes. It wasn't until much later that I understood how much the place meant to Steve, too.

Before he came out as gay, Steve and my mom had dated until 10th grade. She'd known the whole time, of course, because years before, Steve had admitted his forbidden feelings for Mack Clayton, their mutual and, sadly, homophobic friend. Nobody was surprised when Steve and my mom called off the masquerade and Steve morphed into her gay best friend as if single-handedly inventing the cliché. Their bond survived well beyond high school, and it would still be going strong today if it weren't for the cancer that melted my mother down to nothing and Steve also being dead.

Steve was with my mom when she died. By then, she was nothing but a collection of right angles, horrible breath, and skin like a mottled banana. Air clacking in the back of her throat. I was a sophomore—wrapped up in football and Sonya and mischief with Red and fistfights at Nirvana and anything that kept me out of that trailer. I couldn't be around her anymore. But Steve could.

I park Blue in front of Martin's, which is gone. Even the diner's sign is gone. The double doors are chained with a lock the size of a bear paw. Broken glass. Crappy, small-town graffiti. Overlapping plywood on the inside of the translucent front that I used to clean for spare pennies and nickels and the occasional dime. I check up and down Stanley Ave just in case, but all I see are ghosts who don't know what to feel. Almost the entire street is like this now. No letters on the movie marquee, no display in the shoe store with all the sneakers I could never afford, no patriotic barber's pole in the tiny room that smelled like talc and blue water and dirty jokes. Even our legendary sporting goods store is gone—Squirrely's Sport-N-Shoot, with its rows and rows of rifles and shotguns and bows and fishing rods and water skis and an eight-foot-long case up front packed with arrowheads, pottery shards, and one identifiably human jaw accompanied with a random assemblage of bone—all for sale, all reportedly Caddo, all of them found at the lake.

WARSIES

The Denny's out on the highway is the apotheosis of everything Martin's was not, but it's open. I can only imagine what Steve would say about Denny's "America's Diner" rebrand after it got sued for being obnoxiously racist.

The shift host is a large white lady in her thirties in black Dickies and a powder blue polo with the company label surfing atop of her substantial left breast. The right one's big, too. She gives me the corner window booth with a wink and a sway. I look past the parking lot full of idiot trucks and across the highway where Falway exits the western edge of Blacklantis. There once was a sprawling frame house on that side of the intersection guarded by a mean-as-fuck goose who would assault passers-by on sight. To avoid it, we had to cross the highway in a panicked dash across the northbound rush of traffic that rightly should have killed more than half of us. Even in the 80s, truckers and the like blew through that intersection (with no light, and at a curve in the highway, no less) in both directions at over 60 mph, but not getting nipped by Satan's goose on the back of your knee or your butthole seemed more than worth it. That bird and its house are gone too, replaced on one corner of Falway with a Pep Boys and the newest E-Z Mart in town. On the other corner is one of those KFC/Taco Bell marriages that works out to everybody's surprise. There's still no light at the intersection.

"Ready, hon?"

It's the server. She wears the same pants as our host, but with a powder pink polo and a nametag that says *Tammy*. Tammy has an upturned nose, chipped nails, and eyes that dart around the room like marsupials. A faux-gold, cross-shaped ring almost hides a graying tattoo on her right hand, and she's sporting a twelve-week baby bump that ain't no baby. I order a plate of fries and two pieces of caramel apple pie crisp. A couple of minutes later, Tammy brings me a mug of coffee I didn't order and spills a good portion of it on the table when she sets it down too quickly, hurrying off without the slightest notion of wiping it up.

There's a hefty-looking guy standing outside the E-Z Mart across the way. He leans against the paned glass of the convenience store, laughing into his cellphone. In his other hand, he holds a cigarette and a Styrofoam cup large enough to accommodate a small pond of soda. By the looks of it, his Cowboys jersey has been washed since our recent rendezvous. It's my recent cellie, Chuck Tender.

"Matthew 10:34," somebody chirps nearby. It ain't Tammy.

The first thing I see are buffed Red Wings and cuffed-up jeans. My gaze climbs to a black leather belt, an ironed white t-shirt, horn-rimmed glasses, a Colgate smile, and a head piled high with magnificent hair. It's the preacher from Steve's funeral.

"Jesus," I say.

"Not quite. Just his reluctant agent here on this patch of forsaken earth. May I?" the preacher asks, sliding into the other side of the booth before I can answer. He's smaller than I remember—slight, even.

"Knock yourself out," I say. "I'm leaving shortly."

"Luke 12:51, too," he continues, "but there's no sword in that one. But that's my favorite part! As they say, a picture is worth a thousand words."

"Depends on the picture," I say, pushing the mug of so-called coffee away from me. "Also depends on what the fuck you're talking about."

"*Do not suppose that I have come to bring peace to the earth. I did not come to bring peace, but the sword* and blah blah and so forth. Referenced in the rousing finale of your speech at Steve's service. You know your scripture, Mr. Sorrow!" There's an extended lift at the end of his sentences, infused with an unmistakably urban umlaut.

"It's just Sam," I say, looking back across the highway at Chuck Tender, who's now simultaneously lighting up a fresh smoke, slurping carbonated syrup, and cackling into his phone. "And you're from Dallas."

"Now, what gave that away?"

"That loopy accent, for one."

"Arlington, actually."

"Near Six Flags?"

"Oh, hell no," the preacher wrinkles his nose. "More like Pantego—Pioneer and Bowen? You know it?"

"Unfortunately. What can I do you for, Padre? I know an accidental encounter when I see one."

"Padre! Oh, I like that," he says with genuine pleasure. "Padre Mike, *Padre Miguel*... Everything sounds better in Spanish, don't you agree?"

"Claro."

"Bueno! Padre's way better than most things I'm called around here. And to answer your question, I popped in solo for pie when I saw you over here sitting by your lonesome and thought I'd come by to express my heartfelt *thank yous* for what you did the other day. Didn't get the chance at the time, seeing as how you were a little tied up."

"Is that an attempt at humor or assholery?"

"Sometimes hard to tell myself."

"Your commentary on my performance is unnecessary," I tell him. "I'm perfectly capable of punishing myself without you and Jesus jumping in."

"Smells like it," the Padre says.

"That'd be the tequila."

"More like vodka," he shakes his head. "And some kind of weird juice."

"Cran-grape."

"Proanthocyanidins are all the rage. How's the coffee here?"

"Most of mine is on the table. And you're welcome to order some with your pie up there at the counter, Padre. What with me being about to leave and all."

"Oh, I know you can do better than that," he smiles. "You're a truth-teller, ain't you? That's what I heard the other day. That's why you're out of favor in these parts."

"Trying to be polite. You being a man of God and all..."

"Don't let that stop you."

I pick up the ridiculously oversized menu and pretend to read it. "In case you haven't heard, Padre, this out of favor sinner is beyond salvation. So save your sermon for Sunday."

"Consonantly, I will."

"Alliteration, actually."

"Do I seem the sort to surreptitiously sermonize?"

"Did a fine job of it the other day," I say, nodding toward the general geography of the cemetery.

"Well, that's just... Were you even listening?" he pouts. "Of course you weren't. Had you been, you'd already be in on the secret."

"The secret... Like the book?"

"The fact that I'm very much also out of favor and not one of *them*," he gestures at the room behind him.

"Who them?"

"*They* them!" he flaps his hands dismissively. "Baptist, Pentecostal, Jehovah's Witness, Mormon, or whatever other kind of thumpers y'all got around here."

"What are you, some kind of Quaker?"

"Shit, that'd be nice," he says. "No, Sam, I'm Unity. Born and raised."

"What's that? Like, the church of believe-whatever-the-fuck-you-want?"

"Pretty much, but we're mostly progressive Jesus types. Universal truths, meditation, love over hate, LBGTQ, brunch, shit like that."

I breathe out in relief. "Know what would help your case here, Padre?"

"A rainbow pin? Purple scarf from H&M?"

"The hair," I point. "You look like Eddie Cochran fucked a Billy Graham."

"Oh no, you didn't!" he gasps. "And who is Billy Graham?"

"Seriously, you should shave it or something."

"No way. Hairs are your aerials."

"Maybe a crewcut. Or a Mohawk."

"Anything else about me say butch to you?"

"Since when has there been a Unity in Atlantis?" I ask, puzzled by the sheer improbability of it.

"Technically," he sighs, looking around the restaurant, "we're outside city limits. And it's been a little over a year now."

"Oh," I say, because that's what you say when your own personal idiocy dawns on you. "It was Steve. Steve brought you here."

"Invited is more like it."

"And y'all were... friends?"

"On the books, I work for Steve and the Foundation. Off the books, yeah, we're friends. Were. You know..."

"I'm sorry," I say, wishing I'd kept my mouth shut earlier. "I didn't know who you were."

"Shit, that's okay... Don't know myself half the time."

Tammy materializes with cigarette breath and a plate of dejected French fries and two pieces of pie crisp thingies. The dessert looks like somebody jizzed low-grade corn syrup on some freezer-burned vanilla and dressed it up with clammy apples.

"Anything else for you, sugar?" she asks, turning her back to the Padre. "More coffee?"

"No thank you," I reply. "How about you, Preacher?"

"He ain't no preacher," Tammy says, stink-eyeing him as she struts off.

"Coulda fooled me," I say. "Padre, didn't you want to order?"

He points at my food. "Them pears look soaked in dog piss."

"Supposed to be apples."

"Nuh uh... Those there are d'Anjou pears," he replies. "And about the stink eye, it's either the heathen church issue or the say-no-to-drugs or perhaps my militant homosexual agenda."

"Can't imagine what it was like for you and Steve," I say, very much regretting trying the pears. "I mean..."

"Sure, but... In what way?"

"You know," I shrug, and then I touch the points of my index fingers together repeatedly.

"What's that?" he asks. "Skinny dicks bumping heads? Is that what you think it looks like?"

I shrug and fart out some ketchup on the soggy mass of fries.

"Listen," he says. "You... You do know we don't all sleep together, right?"

"I don't know shit. Especially about Steve's love life. Y'all are both gay, so..."

"Do you sleep with every straight woman you know?"

"Of course not."

"Okay, then."

"Unless they're hot," I say. "And, you know, willing. You want some fries?"

"For your information..." he says, looking out of the window perturbedly. "Steve and I weren't compatible. Yeah, we were friends and all, but... I guess you could say we both fished out of the same pond."

"I don't know what that means."

"Are you planning on going around the county asking every gay man you meet whether or not him and Steve..." The Padre repeats my finger touching gesture, but more vigorously.

"No," I say. "I'm leaving soon."

"So you've said. Several times now."

"I mean this whole fucking shitville of a town."

"It has its charms."

"Wait," I say. "You work at that Foundation for Steve? Not just the churchy part?"

"That's right."

"So, you know Lefty?"

"Who?" The preacher asks, turning to locate Tammy, who is three booths away and chatting up an equivalent number of meatheads in trucker caps. The Padre waves at her.

"Uh... Bill, you know? Chopped his hand off, said he was gonna murder Steve or something."

"Oh," he says. "You mean Guy. Sure, I know Guy. Used to work for us out at the Lodge." The Padre *pssts* Tammy's way to zero effect.

"What do you mean *used to*? When'd he stop?"

"Couple days back," the Padre thinks. "Had to fire his lazy ass. Excuse me a second?"

The Padre turns toward Tammy and absolutely yells out her name.

Tammy throws him a Febreezy glare and then replaces her undelicate hand on the closest guy's shoulder and laughs with the men at her table who all have matching beards that Sasquatch most of the way down their necks. They look like the type of guys who'd fix the wrong thing on your car.

My voice being what it is, I can't match the Padre's volume, but when I shout Tammy's name, all of America's Diner goes hush. The sound of my voice at volume is horrible. It's like a tone-deaf Death Metal vocalist mid-vomit.

After an alarmed pause, Tammy snorts and shakes her head. Of the three Bubbas at her table, there's one facing our way. He gives me a grin and a wink.

"You might want to leave now, Padre," I say, standing up. "Things are about to get devilish."

It's not uncommon for me to be on the losing end of a fistfight when I come back through Atlantis. What's uncommon this time around is that it's taken so long to happen. I walk over to where Tammy is obliviously yacking away with her back to me. The guy who just winked at me sees what's coming and nods at his buddies, who both turn to look.

"Uh oh," one snickers.

Tammy turns and takes a half-step back. "I'll be right with you, sir," she says.

"No," I say. "You won't."

"Excuse me?"

"I won't excuse you, either," I say. "Besides, we no longer require your services, because we'll be leaving."

"Well, Suzy will ring you up at the counter, then," Tammy fake smiles. "You have a nice day."

"Suzy will do no such thing," I fake smile back, sharing it with the three guys in the booth, who appear three times larger than they did back at my table. "Here's the thing, Tammy… My meal is going to be on the house today, on account of you inconveniencing me and my new religious friend. Furthermore—and this is way, way worse, Tammy—you have besmirched the good name of diner waitresses everywhere, including my late mother, and that will not fucking stand."

Tammy looks like a ghost just pissed on her leg.

"So," I continue. "Either you or one of your boyfriends here will be treating me today. Boys, be sure to leave a nice tip," I say, winking back at Dude One.

He lets out a laugh that's louder than he intended. Despite their Skoal-stained grins, none of the three look prepared for an actual scuffle amidst all these pancakes. The whole restaurant has gone quiet now, even more than before, such that everybody has stopped feigning interest in whatever culinary failure lies in front of them. Several smartphones are out, most of them filming. Tammy flaps away like a disgraced pheasant.

"Got some balls on you, Bobby," nods Dude One.

"You know me?"

"Don't everybody?" he laughs, looking around the room. "What happened to your pretty voice, partner?"

"You sound like a shitty Darth Vader," adds Three. "*You know it to be true...*" he says in his best James Earl Jones. It's not bad.

"More like the Emperor," suggests Two. "*Become my apprentice!*"

"Or Chewie!" Three antes, trying out his Chewbacca, which is not nearly up to snuff.

"Seriously?" I ask. "Is that the best you Trekkies got?"

That makes them stand up in their seats, or try to. Only Dude One succeeds, because I'm blocking the other two in their booth with the right side of my body.

"Warsies," growls Dude Two, pinned in. "*Trekkies* are for Star Trek. The term you're looking for is *Warsies*."

Dude One slides out and squares up with me. I'm taller by a couple of inches, so I've got the reach, but he's built like somebody who throws engine blocks over fences for a living. He's got at least sixty pounds of beef on me.

"That was rude of you," he says, inches from my face. "My little bros here take their nerd-dom seriously. Can't say I understand it myself, but it's clear you've insulted them and should apologize. And to Miss Tammy, as well, for trying to gyp her out of what you owe."

"Good one!" snorts Three. "Cause he's a Gypsy," he explains loudly to the rest of the diner.

"I thought he was Kike," Dude Two adds quietly.

"Fellas..." says somebody new. It's the Padre, immediately to my left. "Y'all know we don't say any of them words anymore, right?"

"Go sit your little fairy ass down, Pastor," says Dude One. "Ain't no need for you to get hurt, too."

"Oh, I'm good," the Padre smiles, working his neck from side to side.

"I ain't asking," warns One.

"Wait..." Two tells One. "It ain't cool to hit a cleric."

"A what?" asks One. "Look," he sighs at me. "Tell your girlfriend to go home and powder her asshole or something. Ain't nobody but you needs to get hurt."

"Listen here, neckbeard," the Padre says, elbowing his way between me and the big guy. "You've clearly misread the situation, so why don't *you* apologize and pay for Sam's meal as he kindly suggested."

Dude One roars at that, looking down at the Padre like he was a Pomeranian.

"Okay," One shrugs happily. "Have it your way."

The Padre gestures at the enrapt crowd of diners. "You do know this is being filmed, right?"

"So much the better," One turns to look. "You're both overdue for an ass-whuppin. The CC will probably give me a—"

"No, no, no, no, no, no, no, no...." the Padre tsks in the big man's face. "Here's what's gonna happen now: All the CC are gonna do once they see this on camera is laugh their cracker asses off. Because this little fairy? I'm about to choke your Bigfoot-looking ass out and leave you jerking around on the floor of Denny's here like a runned-over squirrel who done pissed itself. Rear naked choke, motherfucker. The *Mata Leon*, the lion killer, only you ain't exactly what I'd call a lion, bitch. Look more like a kitten to me, bitch. Look like some not-knowing-Jiu-Jitsu, lapping-up-buttermilk, one-eye-barely-open, no-neck-shaving, little-bitch-ass kitten, bitch!"

For a brief moment in time, all thought is suspended in the entire East Texas universe.

"What?" Dude One stutters.

"What?" I ask for everybody else in attendance.

"He knows Jiu-Jitsu?" Dude Two asks me.

"Viral!" the Padre shouts. "Viral, Bubba! On the floor, resuming consciousness only to discover you've wet your Wranglers, or—as sometimes happens—shit yourself. Now, does that sound like what you had in mind today? That something you want out there on the Interwebs, Bubba? You havin to walk out of here in shitty piss britches?"

"You don't..." Dude One says, "I mean... y'all heard me give preacher here an out, right?" he asks the room tentatively. It's not lost on the room that he's backed away from the Padre a good five or six inches. Then the Padre jams a finger into the man's keg of a chest.

"Too late, kitty kitty," the Padre purrs. "I'm about to make you a star, Bubba."

Dude One looks like he's trying to swallow a short stack in one go. "My name isn't Bubba," he says. "It's Brad. Bradley Swa—"

"Your name is Bubba now, Bubba," whispers the Padre menacingly. "Now, can we get the fuck on with this, or what?"

*

I wish I could say what happened next went down as the Padre prophesied. But just as Dude One/Bubba/Bradley was approaching peak waver, realizing too late the position the Padre had pushed him into (either back down in publicized shame or run the risk of getting choked out and souring his trousers on camera), a couple of white-haired old timers left their stools at the counter to break things up, much to the displeasure of nearly everybody in attendance. Even so, every word of the Padre's homily had been captured on film. It hit the Internet within minutes, gathering flocks of thumbs-up and pulsing red hearts and yellow-faced laughing emojis from around the globe, but mostly from Caddo County where it mattered. Among other unforeseen consequences of a beatdown that never happened, the Padre saw his congregation triple overnight. To twelve.

COLLISION COURSE

That legendary day should have ended right then. I should've put my ass in Blue, bid the Padre adieu, and either driven to Caddo Estates to wait for Meredith or gone to the Bestern to grab my shit and hit the road back to Austin. But that's nothing like what happened.

As noted, the Padre's elocution was televised. Word of the fight that never came to be spread on the Internet like a 5G grease fire and alerted folks in the vicinity (namely those across 59 at the aforementioned E-Z Mart, KFC/Taco Bell, and Pep Boys), who rushed over to Denny's to see two of the town's great undesirables (i.e., the Padre and me) get what was coming to them. People sprinted across to catch it, either in bunches or solo, at the curve in the highway with no light. It's a miracle only one of them got hit.

A southbound driver struck the man's body and launched it more than ten feet in the air. Witnesses said he twisted gracefully ("like a fat Craig Mouganis," one said) before belly flopping on the trashy median with an inelegant thud. The collision snapped his spine in two places, fractured nearly all of his ribs, broke both arms, and severed his right leg mid-thigh as cleanly as an owl pops the head off a rabbit. Even so, that XXXL Cowboys jersey came out intact. The driver sped off, leaving Chuck Tender forever late for a party he'd never arrive at.

By then, me and the Padre were already gone. He wanted to tell me more, he said. Something about Steve. And why the hell not. In my post-almost-fight adrenalization, I told him to follow me back to the Bestern, with the plan of refueling with the Julio before deciding what came next, and when I hit the hotel lobby for ice, Octavia was there to deliver the news: Chuck Tender had checked out.

The news dropped the Padre and me into an irredeemable funk. Before that, we'd been passing the tequila back and forth like jubilant hobos, reliving the high points of the Padre's oratory with a glee I hadn't felt in years.

"Wish I'd been nicer to him," the Padre mumbles at the floor. "People always say that, don't they?"

I can't get Chuck out of my head. It's not his runned-over corpse I'm seeing and it's not even how he looked in our cell; it's him as a child in Steve's class, up there in front of us all. Stammering, terrified, and absolutely no one on his side.

"Can we talk about something else?" I ask.

"Probably not," says the Padre, handing me the bottle. I take a swig that's the equivalent of three or four shots and hand it back.

"How'd you know him?" I ask.

"He was one of our odd jobs guys," the Padre drinks. "Did stuff here and there out at the Lodge. The rehab side, mostly. Yard work and the like."

I hear what sounds like the hotel door room click, but then I realize the click isn't outside my head.

"What?" I sit up and try to shake out the sound.

"You know... mowing, raking pine needles, painting the dock—"

"Did he know Lefty?"

"You gotta stop saying that," the Padre frowns. "It's really, really—"

"Bill. Did Chuck know Bill?"

"Everybody knows everybody around here, remember? And his name is Guy."

"Right, Guy. So, Guy and Chuck..."

"Yeah," the Padre burps. "Here and there they worked together. Because, like I said, Chuck was there just here and there, whereas Bill was—"

"Guy?"

"Whereas Guy was there full-time. Not that he did a lick of work, which accounts for my firing his ass. Only thing that rascal had going for him were cheekbones and a bubble butt for miles. Anyway, that's a dead-end, like I said, unless you like listening to people yap about obscure movies that nobody—"

"When?" I ask.

"Fuck, all the time," the Padre replies. "Jodorowsky this, Gaspar Noe that. Yap, yap, yap... Wouldn't shut up—"

"No, when'd you fire him?"

"The other day," he says, handing me the tequila. "Why are we talking about Guy?"

At some point after hearing that click in my head, I hop off the bed and start pacing a twelve-foot rectangular track in the carpet.

"Wait a minute..." I say, taking another swig. "What was I saying?" The tequila is finally starting to do what tequila is supposed to do.

"I'm telling you, Guy ain't worth the paper your submission is... the paper your *suspicion* is printed on. Because, like, why?"

"Steve's dead, Chuck's dead, Guy's alive..."

"Probably," he says. "Two out of three, at least."

"All three at the Lodge, all three..."

"Three lemons don't make a banana tree," the Padre says, closing his eyes and leaning his head sagely against the wall.

"You fired Guy..." I take another drink. "So, I don't know... Like, he gets pissed? Kills Steve? Maybe Chuck sees something he shouldn't... You see where I'm going with this?"

"Yeah," the Padre says. "Nowhere. I fired him the *other* day. *After* Steve died, see? Gimme that bottle."

The Padre takes a quick swig and wipes his mouth with his sleeve.

"Ain't trying to poop on your parade or anything," he says, "but if Guy was gonna do anybody harm? It'd been me. That job was the best thing ever happened to him and I removed it. Subtracted it from his sad little life. And not kindly, by the way," he frowns. "*Get your ass out of here*, I told him. *Put a hook on that stump and a patch on your eye and go work for Disney with all the other pirates!* I said. You believe that? My exact words..."

"Shoulda just choked him out."

"Woulda been the Christian thing to do," he sighs.

"You really know Jiu Jitsu?"

"Well, I ain't no Buck Sweet, but you should hope to never find out," he winks. "The name's Mike, by the way. Mike Menry. Either that or Pastor Mike."

"Just gonna go with Padre."

"I was sorta hoping so."

I stagger toward the bathroom and pause to balance myself with one hand on the wobbly TV. "Gotta hug close to the toilet for, well..."

"Bueno," he yanks off his Red Wings and snags a pillow off the bed. "Barf away.... Gonna hafta crash here tonight," he burps again. "Don't get any ideas, Ennis."

"You were gonna tell me something," I say from the bathroom. "What was it?"

"Repent!" he cackles, going almost all the way horizontal on the floor. "No, what I was gonna... Shit, I was supposed to be back at the church by now."

This is the point where Meredith should come to mind, but she doesn't. I stumble-weave back into the main room with my zipper still down.

"No thank you," he points.

I zip myself back up with as much care as I can muster.

"Didn't want to get you in danger," he shakes his head.

"Danger?"

"You know who," he says. "You know..."

I think back to Coach's warning. When was that? Yesterday?

"Fuck the CC," I say. "Let em come."

The Padre snorts. "Man, I ain't talking no Cracker Club Caddo Club! Why would they... Hand me back that hoochie juice."

I toss him the bottle. To my surprise, the Padre catches it one-handed, ninja-style. He grins the most tequilaest of grins and take another drink.

"Stop backwashing," I say. "You're drinking like a two-year-old."

The Padre gives the bottle the sloppiest backwash imaginable and puts it back on the floor, slobber and all.

"Gave millions to the Foundation..." he shakes his head. "Like Steve needed a dime, you know? All on board. Helping grandkids and nieces and nephews and—"

"What in the Don Julio are you on about?"

"The CC! Goddamn, keep up! I'm tryna tell you stuff and you keep talking about... Look, weren't Guy who killed Steve and it definitely weren't no CC. They been so grateful this whole damn time they gave the Foundation money it don't even need! Like, at all. You got any idea how much money's in the bank? Shit, I don't. But it's... Well, it's a lot of goddamn money. CC might not care for the whole Unity church thing, but rehab? Shit... they got all kinda kin in there. New ones every week. Half our clientele is their grandkids or something... Why they gonna fuck with that? Bout the only damn thing functionable in the whole county is the Lodge! You got to look... to think... Man, like, *cui bono*? Cui bono, get it?"

I lean my weight into the frame of the exterior door and try to hold the spins off long enough to make heads or tails out of the drunken pile of loose change I just heard from the Padre.

"Bono?"

"That meth lord, man..." the Padre nods sleepily. "What I was gonna..."

I close my eyes and the variegated darkness slides from top left to bottom right. I open them up again and inhale quickly through my mouth and try to focus on the light next to the bed. For somebody who openly professes to hate barfing, I sure do it enough.

"Teisenberg..." the Padre mutters from across the room. "Fucking Teisenberg..."

RISEN

It's probably me and the Padre hobbling into the Bestern's continental breakfast together late the next morning that releases the come-stained doves of rumor that a once-famous singer from Atlantis has officially turned homo with one heretical, shit-talking, big-haired, ectomorphic Jiu-Jitsu preacher from Dallas. The stink of Jaliscan moonshine follows us into the hotel lounge like a flatulent phantom.

It's the tail end of sanctioned breakfast and most of the edible contents are gone. The only other people in the room are the two white biddies whose job it is to wipe down tables and gradually die from fluorescence. They look at us with pinched smiles. I can read their judgment in bold print between the saggy lines that web out from their eyes and trickle down their soft necks like uppity rain.

We load up on the remains—a pair of flabby croissants, a watery loaf of scrambled eggs, insufficiently cooked bacon, and three boiled eggs that have smelled like butt for days. Then we squirt out the last of the coffee—almost half a cup each—and slump into a freshly wiped booth on the far wall. The old ladies keep popping in and out of the room with no discernible purpose other than to pretend to check on the cereal dispensers and stab us with their eyeballs.

"Want some?" the Padre asks, indicating the pile of bacon on his plate.

"I think I'm still drunk."

"Pig will help that."

At some point in last night's Pyrrhic victory against vomiting, I sent an incoherent chain of texts to Meredith that she still hasn't answered. I put my phone away with a moan.

"Did we finish that whole bottle of anejo?" I ask.

"It was reposado," replies the Padre, "and no. *We* didn't finish it; *I* finished it. *You* mostly watched."

One of the ladies walks back into the room for some other fake reason.

"Excuse me, dear," the Padre calls out to her. "Would you mind making up some more coffee for us?"

"I'm sorry, sir," she smiles, bending over at the Padre like he's a child. "We're just about to close up."

"Just one teensy pot of coffee?" he matches her smile with an even faker, flirtier one.

"I'd love to," she shrugs, "but we done washed the pots and put em up, you see."

"No problem," he replies, nodding at me. "We'll wait. We'll even take it to go, if that helps."

"I'm afraid I can't make a fresh pot just for you, Hon," she says, strained to her wattle with condescension. "Why don't you try the Starbucks over there at the Walmarts?"

"And miss out on your delicious brew? No thank you, ma'am."

"I'm sorry, sir, I just can't," she huffs. "That's all there is to it."

"Is it, though?" The Padre's voice tilts, angular and dark. I recognize the tone from his oratory yesterday at Denny's. "Please tell me, ma'am... What are your hours of operation?"

"You're talking breakfast times?"

"I am," he nods solemnly.

She looks away stiffly. "6 to 9 in the AM."

"And—forgive me, ma'am, but I seem to have misplaced my timepiece—what time do you have now?"

"It's 8:52. 8:53, actually."

"Goodness me and praise the Lord!" he claps. "I was so hoping we were still within the technical confines of serving hours and that my request was not unreasonable. Now, can you make that coffee extra strong, *Hon*? My boyfriend likes it that way."

She stomps off into the back room, stiff-arming the door like she's Marshawn Lynch.

"Making friends," I say.

"Everywhere I go," smiles the Padre, eating one piece of bacon after another as if every part of him were fully functional.

"Hey, what was that name you kept saying last night?"

"Menry," he points to himself. "Mike Menry. And then you were like—"

"No, not you... Something about *Bono*..."

"His real name's Paul Hewson," he chews. "In case you didn't know."

"It was a T-something... Tyger? Tiberius? Tyrell?"

"Androids or dragons?" he swallows the last of his coffee.

"Teisenberg!" I snap my fingers. "That's what it was—Teisenberg!"

The Padre's eyes instantly go plate-sized and he shushes my mouth with a full, greasy palm that still holds a strip of floppy bacon. He hushes me while checking around the room. No sign of the biddies.

"Lower your voice," he whispers. I wipe the bacon grease off my face. "Did I really say that?"

"What's the big deal?" I whisper back. "Why can't I say Teisenberg?"

"I wouldn't say it too loudly," Octavia says, seemingly out of nowhere. It's like she Fay Presto'd herself to the next table over. The Padre and me jump in our seats like we just pissed on the wrong kind of fence.

Octavia pulls up a chair next to the Padre. "Minister," she nods.

"Octavia," he grins. "How nice to see you."

"No intros needed, I guess," I say.

"I've been to a couple of Mike's services."

"Didn't take?" I ask.

"A little conservative for my tastes."

"Now that's just hurtful," he frowns, offering her a piece of bacon.

"No thanks," Octavia grimaces. "So, gentlemen... I just received a report from trusted sources that the two of you are in here swapping slobber and touching dicks and getting your grody gay all over my breakfast room. And, I quote, *chasing off our Christian clientele.*"

"Is that what that old bat said?" the Padre asks.

"Her name is Miss Ballard."

"Miss Ballard was immune to the Padre's charms," I inform her.

"Sounds about right," she replies. "Well, it's after 9 anyway. If it's coffee you're after, I can make it up to you."

"Wait. Can we go back a minute?" I ask. "Who's this He-Who-Must-Not-Be Teisenberged?"

They glance at each other briefly. The Padre looks down at his bacon while Octavia looks at him looking at his bacon.

"Y'all..."

"Teisenberg..." Octavia says quietly, checking around for Miss Ballard. "Not sure where to start."

"That's the new meth lord around here," the Padre adds. "He's the whole reason Steve built the facility. Had to, I mean. Wouldn't need rehab in these parts if it weren't for kids needing rehabbing. That's on Teisenberg."

"I wouldn't go that far," Octavia says.

"Wait... *Teisenberg* is the meth lord around here?" I chuckle.

"What's funny?" asks Octavia.

"The name? Teisenberg? Meth? You know..."

They both give me a harmonized shrug of cluelessness.

"*Breaking Bad?* Walter White? Mr. White? Heisenberg?"

"Oh..." says the Padre. "Never seen it."

"Me, either," Octavia says, standing from her chair.

"Are you fucking—"

"Just don't go saying Teisenberg around here like that," Octavia checks the room again. "Or anywhere, for that matter. Word is he's supposed to have folks working for him everywhere. I wouldn't be surprised if Miss Ballard's on the take."

"I'd believe it," says the Padre.

"Yeah..." I say. "But Teisenberg?"

"Look," Octavia replies. "I've got to get back out there. Y'all want some Starbucks cards, or what?"

"Does the Pope shit in the woods?" the Padre asks.

"Give me a minute," Octavia says, halting at the door to the lobby. "But hey, good news, huh?"

"How's that?" I ask.

"Your buddy, Chuck Tender? Turns out he didn't die after all."

AIN'T NOBODY CARE ABOUT THAT STORY

We rush to the hospital in the Padre's spitfire orange Fiat ("supposed to look spicy," he says). As we fly down 59 without any sort of Starbucks, the Padre unpacks the whole Teisenberg thing for me. Turns out Steve's plans for the Foundation went way beyond one measly rehab place tucked away at the lake with an affiliated, underattended, unevangelical church. No wonder Steve kicked up so many hornets. The Berkey Foundation was built to change the world—or at least one East Texas corner of it—in three carefully mapped-out phases. Only the first was up and running when Steve got killed.

He called Phase One *Alternatives,* and it was meant to redress Caddo County's lack of same. Steve assembled a quality staff (including the Padre), built the facility (the Lodge), got local players on board (mostly the CC), and threw enough cash at the two-headed Cerberus of addiction and spiritual vacuity (hence, the affiliated church) to make it all stick. Steve wasn't one for religion, but he was familiar with its powerful role in southern communities. All that Bible-thumping and finger-pointing and threats of hellfire wouldn't push anybody, let alone teenagers, one inch closer to recovery. Unity was supposed to offer something different.

The Padre doesn't know much about Phase Two, only that it was called *Restoration* and was mostly about native species, wilderness preserves, and connecting with the Caddo Nation (long since pushed into Oklahoma). There was a Phase Three rumored, about which the Padre knows zilch. Steve was waiting to see how One and Two went first.

Phase One started out about as you'd expect. Berkey International was demanding way too much of Steve's time for him to focus on the Foundation, and the local evangelicals freaked out when they learned that a gay minister was coming in to preach some limp-wristed, Commie-hugging, Kumbaya gospel. They spread word that Satan was afoot and convinced their congregants that the Padre and Steve were going to convert the county's substance-addled children to faggotry. It took months for the Lodge's success to trickle out and silence that nonsense, aided in no small part by unexpected allies within the CC, because unlike most rehab courses available in the region, Steve's plan worked. Phase One grew legs. Kids started coming in from neighboring counties, and before they knew it the Lodge was getting overflow from Dallas, Little Rock, Shreveport, and beyond. That's when Steve decided to build another facility or two and double their outreach. According to the Padre, that's what did it—that's what got Steve killed.

"It was never about money," the Padre says flatly. "Teisenberg's operation is huge... Hell, we could've had ten facilities going and it wouldn't have made a dent. It was about reputation and power, all that testicular bullshit. Teisenberg said he'd let us have one place, but that was all."

"Y'all were negotiating with a meth lord?"

"Not me, Steve," the Padre inhales. "And I wouldn't call it negotiating." He pulls up to a red light on the south side of town, where traffic might as well be an endangered species. The Padre looks both ways and runs the light.

"It was a little ways back. Months ago," he continues. "Teisenberg's goons picked Steve up from the Lodge and took him off to some secret location. Steve wouldn't let me go with him. He knew what it meant, actually meeting Teisenberg. Nobody knows what he looks like, see. So, Steve... shit, I don't know. Maybe he just wanted to see the man's face, talk to him in person, work some of that Steve magic on him."

I look out of the Fiat's window at the numbness of trees and grass and roadside filth. I know exactly why Steve did it. If there was going to be a target in the days to come, Steve made sure to pin it on his own back. I'm guessing he also offered Teisenberg a shit-ton of cash to quit the business and split town.

"I don't get it," I say. "We both know Steve wouldn't agree to any drug lord's terms, so why does Teisenberg let Steve go? Why not just kill him then and there?"

The Padre shrugs. "I don't know. Steve wouldn't give any details. Maybe he told Teisenberg he'd think about it?"

"Doubt that."

"Me, too."

"Did he go to the cops?"

"The cops?" the Padre scoffs. "Shit, they knew all about it before that meeting. All of them are either scared shitless or on the take or both. Two detectives came out to the Lodge to quote-unquote investigate. Give me a fucking break. Came out to sleepwalk is more like it. Only cop I met who seemed to give a damn and look into it was this droopy little bear boy who came by to check on us a couple of times."

"Believe I know who you're referring to."

"Good guy," he says. "But what's one overworked police supposed to do about it? Can't beat meth lords with good intentions."

Two crows peck at the swollen belly of an unidentified roadkill on the side of the road. They don't even flap when we speed by.

"Here's something to keep in mind," the Padre says heavily. "Corresponding with Teisenberg's arrival, Caddo County now has the greatest number of disappeared people per capita. I'm talking vanished without a trace. I'm talking more than any other county in this whole stupidly large fucking state. Think about that. What that means is Teisenberg is out-performing those Cartel-run counties on the border in the making-people-disappear contest."

"Steve wasn't disappeared," I point out. "They found his body."

"I've put some thought into that. Here's what I think: snitches, dealers who dip into Teisenberg's pockets, wannabe competitors… Nobody gives a shit about them, see? But Steve Berkey? He was like a superhero around here—Superman, you know? Teisenberg knew that. You can't just make Superman go poof. The whole world takes notice. It would mean camera crews and news reporters and all kinds of media shit everywhere for weeks, and that's the last thing Teisenberg wants. So, what's he do instead? Makes it look like an accident, a suicide, but, you know… also leaves it in doubt. So we'll all know. See what I'm saying? Teisenberg took our Superman and turned him into some aging, wealthy queen who offs himself in Lake Atlantis for some unknown, gay reason. Same result, different story. And ain't nobody care about that story."

We're getting close to the hospital now. We cross the Greenridge viaduct, heading east and uphill, passing the old WWII ammunitions plant that's still falling apart into rusty indistinction next to the railroad tracks where Red and me spent a couple of summers leading unofficial tours through the dilapidated maze of multi-leveled structures and strange machinery straight out of a steampunk's wet dream, exposing ourselves and younger friends to God-only-knows what cocktail of contaminants and toxins.

"See that?" I point.

"Looks like a theme park for tetanus," the Padre says.

"Old weapons factory. Steve's dad owned it until after Vietnam when it shut down. It was already boarded up when we discovered it as kids. Me and my best friend took other kids through there, told ghost stories, built forts... But then one time a kid snuck in there by himself—younger than us, somebody's kid brother, can't remember who... Nine, maybe ten years old. He'd been in there with us before, so he knew how to get in. Fell down this long chute and couldn't get out. Broke his leg, I think. Was stuck there for days."

"And a great lesson was learned that day," the Padre says.

"Not really. He died."

"Oh, Lord..."

"Whole town blamed us," I say, straining to see if anything's changed about the place. "Kid couldn't climb out, nobody could hear him yell... Didn't find him until a couple of weeks later when me and Red went in there. We knew something was off by the smell. Everybody thought the kid had run off or got abducted or something, but then... It was summer, so, dehydration..."

The Padre pulls the Fiat into the parking lot of Atlantis Memorial—the last functioning hospital in the county. As he backs into a spot, a champagne-colored Taurus pulls by slowly in front of us, heading for the exit. It's the same car that was behind me the other day when I left the cemetery on my way to Meredith's. The driver is bald. He's wearing a Hawaiian shirt.

"What the... Did you see that?" I ask.

The Padre looks to where I'm pointing, shielding his eyes from the morning sun, but the Taurus is already out of the lot. The Padre shakes his head.

"I think we're being followed," I say as we get out of the car. "I saw that guy the other day. Hawaiian shirt. Great posture. Crazy eyelashes."

"Huh," the Padre says, looking down the street. As we hit the steps to the hospital's front door, he urks the Fiat and says, "Flowers. Now, what kind of flowers do you suppose somebody like Chuck Tender would like?"

AN UNRECOGNIZABLE LUMP OF A MAN

We wait in a small room just outside the front doors of the ICU. To our surprise, the nurse informs us that Chuck is full with visitors at the moment, so the Padre and me putz around the 150 square feet of contrived coziness—him holding Chuck's hydrangeas, me rummaging through what's left of the Keurig. Medical personnel come and go through the double-doored entry with the remote air of people whose livelihoods are appended to trauma. The TV volume is stuck on low.

"Want some coffee?" I ask, digging through the pods. "Sumatra, decaf, French Roast, Dark Magic…"

"Magick with a K?" he asks.

"No, just regular."

"Might as well," he sighs. I bring over two Styrofoam cups of suspiciously good, planet-destroying coffee and sit down on the beige couch next to the Padre.

"How long between that special Teisenberg meeting and Steve's death?" I ask.

The Padre blows heat off the coffee and frowns at the TV. "Seven, eight weeks? I could check."

"Still doesn't make sense. Why not kill him sooner?"

The Padre unsuccessfully tries to click off the television, where three suit-wearing dudes on Fox News are all trying to out-smug each other.

"Like I said, too much attention." He hops off the couch and goes over to the far wall to unplug the TV with an unpastoral yank.

"Teisenberg's got a reputation to keep," I say. "You telling me he's gonna wait two months to pull the trigger? Nobody knows what he looks like except his crew, right? But now Steve knows, can describe him, and—"

The ICU doors bang open and Coach struts by, passing so quickly he doesn't see us.

"Coach!" I shout.

Three seconds later, Coach pokes his whistle-wearing head back inside the frame with a puzzled look that rolls over on its side with a knowing smirk.

"Well, well, well..." Coach says, entering the doorway. "If it ain't the Von Erich boys! Word is you two legends clotheslined a whole pack of mouth-breathers at Denny's yesterday. Way I hear it, pancakes went everywhere."

"How's Chuck?" I ask.

"Undead," he says, picking up a copy of *Good Housekeeping* and frowning at the cover. "Word around town also has it that you two unfavorables have made it official! I guess congratulations are in order. So, felicitations on your sexual union, or whatever y'all call it..."

"Why, thank you," the Padre beams. "What'd you get us?"

"Twin butt-plugs and a doily set to match," Coach says.

"You shouldn't have," the Padre replies sweetly.

"Thought you didn't care for Chuck," I say.

"Well, factually, I don't," Coach says, dropping the magazine on the coffee table. "But that don't stop the hospital from calling me every goddamn time one of y'all catches a cold or stubs his toe or—in this case—goes and gets himself runt over and momentarily deceased."

"One of y'all?" asks the Padre.

"Merfeet," I tell him. "Coach has been running football in Atlantis ever since Teddy Roosevelt was in office."

"Gonna let that slide, Kim Carnes," Coach says. "But only on account of you referencing my favorite president of all time. Oh, speaking of Merfeet... Red's in there."

"Red?" My old friend's name comes out of my mouth with a fuzzy squeak.

"Him and that voodoo woman of his—Sprinkles or Drizzle or something."

"Rain," says the Padre. "Ain't that sweet?"

"You know what else would be sweet?" Coach points at me. "You paying me back that bail money. Got it on you?"

Considering I just had to pay for an extra night's stay at the Bestern and failed to check out this morning, I've never been more broke in my entire adult life. The Padre sees the shadow on my face and tells Coach to buzz off.

"Know what? Not a good time for us, Teddy," the Padre smiles, but there's that threatening turn in his voice again. "We're here on urgent Chuck-related matters, so you can just go run along now."

The two of them cordially fake grin at each other for a full five seconds. Coach finally breaks it off with a chuckle. He pats the wall and turns to go.

"Good to see you got yourself a new daddy, Bobby," he says. "Be sure to get me that money soon, you hear?"

A minute later, a nurse gives us the all-clear. We follow her through the swinging doors into a long hall that smells like feces, disinfectant, and open wounds. The nurse makes sure we Purell our paws before entering Chuck's room and I take twice as long as the Padre to survey the scene inside. Red doesn't know I'm here. I hang back on the off chance he's mobile.

Chuck's room is twice as large as the one we were just in. Other than the Padre and me, it contains an unrecognizable lump of a man in a body cast plugged with wires and transparent tubes, but also Rain and a gigantic figure passed out on a cot in the far corner, pillow over his head, legs hanging off like a pair of diagonal trees. Eric "The Red" Ravning. At the peak of his career with the Oilers and aptly named Titans, Red stood just over six-foot-six in the jumbo neighborhood of 340 pounds.

Rain's awake. She faces Chuck, cross-legged in a chair, and doesn't turn when we come in. Her small body rocks and hums quietly, almost in harmony with the room's machinery. There's an adjustable tray to her right—the kind used to serve food to patients in bed—covered with the same collection of feathers and Native American what-all I saw a couple of days ago at the cemetery. Except for the Jammie Dodgers.

Rain pivots our way with a face full of unbrushed hair and eyes that look like they've been underwater for a week.

"Hi, minister," Rain whispers, trying to smile. "Hi, Sam. Oh, you brought flowers..."

The Padre hands her the hydrangeas, staring at Chuck's body. Then he nods sideways at Red. "How's Tiny?"

"That's what he calls Red," she tells me, as if I, too, were missing fries from my Happy Meal. "He's sleeping," she says.

"What are y'all doing here?" I ask.

"Oh," Rain says, confused. "Chuck had an accident."

"We heard," the Padre looks at me.

"We came by to help," she sniffs. "He almost died."

I review Chuck's improbably bloated face, the tubes, his cast, his missing lower leg...

"I guess we were the only people they could get ahold of," she says, sitting up in the chair. "Last night."

"Y'all been here since last night?" asks the Padre.

"It was hard to get Red here by myself, but I did it. When we got here, they were still operating," she says, looking back at Chuck.

"We heard he died," I say.

"Yeah, a couple of times," she smiles weakly, "but then they brought him back with that electric shocker thing. Didn't think he was gonna make it through the night. I've been here praying. Didn't know what else to do," Rain says, tearing up. The Padre puts a comforting hand on her shoulder.

"It's going to snow," says a new voice in the cold room.

With his size, you'd guess Red would have one of those booming, Michael Duncan *Green Mile* voices. You're expecting something like Andre the Giant when out slides Bobby Hill, breathy and tenor. How Rain got him to the hospital is a wonder of physics. His CTE (brain degeneration from years of concussions) has become so bad he can rarely get out of bed anymore. But Red sure as shit was out of bed the last time I saw him. In fact, he was sprinting. After me. With a tire iron. I'd been nailing his girlfriend while he was out of town.

"It's going to snow," Red repeats, sitting up. He rubs his massive eyeballs with knuckles gnarled up like a live oak.

"That'd be a first," I say. "Been a while since it snowed in Atlantis."

He jerks his head up. "Bobby?"

"It's Sam now," Rain says. "Remember, baby?"

"Sam..." Red replies absently. "Yeah," he points at Chuck's hooked-up body, then looks at the floor. "He make it?"

Rain nods at Chuck and smiles. We all ponder the unlikelihood of Chuck's survival in itchy silence. Red stands up and I back one step closer to the exit. He looks absolutely terrible. The Red I grew up with was a good hundred pounds heavier, even as a teen. This Red has hollowed-out eyes, sagging flesh, and a messy braid that dangles down his back like a frazzled gym rope.

"I'm starving," he says.

TANGO AND CASH

After his seventh slice of pepperoni, Red's head is almost clear, almost normal, almost the Red of old, only way more talkative than I recall, and most of what he wants to talk about is Denny's. Not Steve's murder, not Chuck's near demise, and not Red's failed attempt to end me with an automotive tool a few years back, but the now widely publicized encounter me and the Padre had at Denny's.

"Man, I wish I coulda been there!"

"Would never have happened if you were," the Padre says. "So, yeah... me too. Chuck wouldn't be in his current condition if it weren't for me having to—"

"Hold on," I tell him. "It wasn't you who—"

"Y'all both know better than that," Red interrupts.

"It was me," I tell the Padre. "You just joined in on the fun. Chuck was on his way already, was already about to get run over because of me."

"No, no, no," the Padre says. "I'm the one in the first place who had to—"

"Fucking cause and effect!" Red says. "How far y'all gonna take it? Go a little further back, and y'all gonna have to lay blame on me and Rain!"

"What did I do?" she asks weakly.

"Precisely," Red says. "Nothing. Everything. Maybe something. Who knows? Everything webs out in all directions is the point, baby. So, as a matter of practicality, if y'all are so hell-bent on attributing responsibility, probably best start with our dear friend, Chuck. Sumbitch should already know he can't walk through cars."

Rain shakes her head. "Yeah, but—"

"Nonsense!" Red says, loud enough for Rain to go wide-eyed and jerk a good foot away from him.

The Padre holds up a hand and Red takes a deep breath in.

"I'm sorry," he says softly. "Look, everybody knows there should be a goddamn light at that intersection with a crosswalk and everything. Only reason there ain't is because it's Blacklantis. So, any of y'all want to lay blame, put it on the city for not giving a shit about black folks. And that's the last I want to hear about it."

He stands up and shuffles away from us. Rain looks down at her hands. The Padre gives me one of those looks that asks about forty questions at the same time.

"Okay," I say, getting up to follow Red.

I trail him to the pizza counter and clear my throat when I get close. It's bad enough waiting for the hammer to drop. It's worse knowing that the hammer belongs to Thor and that he's probably going to drop it on your skull and that your hammer-crushed head is going to be put on display on some torchlit wall in Asgard.

"Hey, bud," I say.

Red turns from the hair-netted teen behind the cafeteria counter with whom he'd been discussing the finer points of jalapeno placement on another extra-large pizza. He looks at me as if trying to figure out if I'm actually there.

"You okay?" I ask.

"Don't do that," he says, looking back and forth from one of my eyes to the other.

"Do what?"

"Ask stupid questions," he replies. He points back at our table, where the Padre inclines his head toward Rain with palpable compassion. "See that? *That's* what they want. They put up with the likes of you and me, but when it comes down to it? It's archetypal. Parental. Grandparental, even. Transcending sexuality and time. What was missing shall always be sought."

"Red," I say.

"You're wincing."

"I'm not wincing."

"Boy, if that ain't a wince, I don't know my pecker from a tree trunk."

"I just... Look, can we just go ahead and address the elephant in the room?"

"That's offensive," Red frowns. "For your information, I've lost close to a hundred pounds in the past year and change."

"I wasn't talking—"

"I know, dipshit," he laughs. "Take a fucking joke, will you?"

"Well, I just wanted to—"

"Say," he stops me. "You ever seen them nature programs about big cats? Lions and such? Nature Channel? National Geographic? They don't all show it, of course, but when it's mating time? Them big cats will pair off and fuck, like, every half hour over a twenty-four-hour period. You believe that? That's nearly fifty times a day. You'd think somebody's big cat dick would fall off, but it don't. Which, you know, is fortunate. Anyway, that's all offered in explanation as to my current state of leanness. That little thing over there?" Red nods at Rain. "There's a cowgirl who likes to ride, buddy. T-I-G-E-R. Animalistic. Bestial. Fucking primal. That woman loves her some D."

Red tells me how they met. A little over a year ago, he noticed a plume of smoke coming from the river bottoms a mile or so behind his house. He didn't think much of it—probably a couple of hicks out there on a duck hunt—but then he saw the same smoke the next morning and more over the course of the next two days. Then a bad storm jumped up from the Gulf. Red knew the high winds and heavy rain would doom whoever it was out there. The water level in the river bottoms can rise several feet in just a couple of hours—slough beds are overrun, entire islands disappear, and currents start to roil where the water normally sits flat and shallow as your knees. That fire-builder was about to get washed down to Arkansas, so Red trolled out in his Jon boat to warn them, taking his twelve gauge and a scimitar he'd picked up at a flea market just in case. Neither was necessary, because it was just Rain. She was shivering next to a dying fire with one eye swollen shut, clothes in tatters, and scratched-up, welted skin. Per Red, she smelled like something from the ass of a channel cat.

"What the fuck was she doing down there?" I ask.

That stretch of the river is as remote as it comes—uncharted, desolate, and downright unfriendly. Red says she was searching for Caddo mounds. Even though the natives were all dead or chased out of East Texas nearly two hundred years ago, there were rumors into the early 1900s that a rogue band of Caddo still lived out in the swamps, refusing to leave, protecting a village that had been there for millennia, savaging nearby farms and plucking off random Christian children for scalps. It was all paranoid bullshit, of course, but even some of the Caddo in Oklahoma believed the rumors held some truth. Somewhere in the unpeopled expanse between Lake Atlantis and the Red River was said to be the overgrown remains of a Caddo center that rivaled the one just west of Nacogdoches. No one had ever found it, though, even generations of researchers with Lidar technology and grants on the line. Even so, a couple of Caddo families had devoted themselves to finding the place. This is where Rain came in.

It was her grandmother's idea. Because Rain was mixed, she could pass in the white world. No one would suspect her if she were caught exploring the bottoms; Rain could always play the lost, naively adventurous college kid who got turned around. But Rain wasn't exactly what you'd call *intrepid*, Red says. On her first attempt, she lost her map, managed to sink a virtually unsinkable kayak, ate through her supplies two days early, and became irrevocably lost along the way.

"Bless her heart," Red says. "Sweeter than molasses and great in the sack, but we ain't talking Marie Curie here. Keeps wanting to go back out to look. If it weren't for me saving her ass that day, that ass would've been inside a gator by nightfall."

"For nothing but a legend," I say.

Red snorts. "That's what people think, but whatever... She said I could tell you, so I did. But you got to keep your mouth shut. Who knows how many folks have died out there looking for the place. And some would kill to find out what she knows."

"I don't—"

"She figures you'll be on board like Steve was," Red says, turning to check on the pizza. "They had some stuff in the works with the Caddo back in Oklahoma. Now that Steve's gone, well... I told her you care two runny shits about this place or anybody else but yourself, but she wouldn't hear it."

It doesn't hurt because it's true; it hurts because he says it.

"Anyways," he says, clutching the back of my neck with one of his Yeti paws. "How about we catch up on all this later? Among other topics."

"Let's just go ahead and get it over with."

"Not now, good buddy," he points back to our table. "We got bigger concerns."

Two detectives in tailored casual wear have added themselves to the cafeteria. One sits next to Rain with his back to the table, long legs extended in a creased show of nonchalance; the other—short and balding—paces back and forth about ten feet away on the other side of them, mumbling into his cell, looking around the room and pinching up his nose as if the place were a poorly serviced outhouse. Both wear shoulder holsters under their sports coats and badges clipped to their belts, just like in the movies. The short cop's badge is upside down. These must be the two assholes Butz was talking about.

Red shuffles back to the table, picking up steam as we approach. The fingers on his right hand are starting to twitch.

"Can I help you boys?" Red demands, not sounding at all interested in helping.

"Oh," says the tall cop, "there you are!"

The cop stands up to full length—all six-three of him—and extends a manicured hand Red's way. You can tell he's unaccustomed to looking up at people taller than he is, and his hand floats out there in space like an abandoned canoe. It's three seconds before Red finally shakes it. Even diminished, Red remains a bona fide giant. His hand swallows the cop's as if it were a prop in a kid's play.

"Detective Wetch," the cop introduces himself cheerfully. "Like Witch, but with an E. And that's Detective Smith there on his phone, probably speaking to his mother, and I say that as loudly as I do in another futile attempt to shame him."

"It's not mom," Smith whispers back with a frown.

"It's mom," Wetch tells Red. "Anyway, huge fan of yours. I don't imagine you still get asked for autographs much, but..." He pulls out a pen and small flip pad with an almost convincing childlike smile.

"I get asked all the time," Red replies flatly.

Detective Wetch tries to hold his smile steady as he waits for Red to do something, but the pad and his stupid smug face start to waver.

"Looks like a no," I tell him.

Wetch squints at me. "And you are?"

"Big in Japan," I say. "What are you two Dicks doing here?"

"Excuse me?"

"Dicks—you know, slang for detective? I would've said Sherlocks, but by the looks of it you two took the short bus here."

"That's funny," Wetch laughs, looking over at Rain and the Padre. "And, personally, I don't take offense. But my retard partner over there might."

"Might what?" Smith asks, strutting back over as he tucks his phone away.

"I'll handle this, Bobby," Red says. "What's the problem, detective?"

"Who says there's a problem?" asks Smith.

"Well," Wetch says to his partner, "You do, for one. All you've done since we got here is bitch about how much you hate hospitals."

"Who likes hospitals?" Smith complains.

"People who need them? Like, citizens in need of medical assistance?" Wetch counters.

"Yeah, but that don't mean they *like* them. Needing and liking ain't the same thing, Wetch."

"Profound, Smith, and point taken," Wetch turns back to Red. "You'll have to forgive my partner here. As the evidence shows, he's a retard."

"Am not," Smith retorts. "Besides, you're not supposed to say that word anymore. It's offensive."

"So it is, Smith," nods Wetch. "My apologies to you and your people... Now, to follow up with your question, Mr. Ravning, we are here to investigate the hit-and-run case of one Charles Tender, recently sent airborne by a yet-to-be identified vehicle and subsequently rendered... Well, as you yourself have already seen," Wetch chuckles, "He's pretty fucked up."

"And what's that have to do with us?" Red asks.

"Really?" inserts Smith.

"Smith," Wetch holds out a hand. "What my illustrious partner means to say is that we know that Charles was in your employ, that he was living on your land, and that, frankly, no one else in this godforsaken county seems to give a shit about him. We're simply collecting information at this point, and you and the missus are all we've got. May we sit?"

Red grunts and sits down. I grunt and remain standing. The Padre clears his throat and pats Rain's hand reassuringly.

"It's not serious," he tells her. "Otherwise they'd ask y'all to the station."

Wetch nods. "Correct. Although, serious or otherwise, we don't typically operate out of there."

"We don't like it there," adds Smith.

"And then there's that," Wetch confirms. "Sadly, the locals don't seem overly fond of us."

"Wonder why," I say.

"Exhibit A," Wetch waves a hand at me and turns back to Red. "So, can you confirm that Chuck was your employee and also your tenant?"

Red looks at the detectives. He doesn't say anything; he just stares at them blankly and breathes through his nose.

"Oh, don't worry about all that," Wetch holds his hand up. "We don't give a shit about how little you paid Chuck, or with what form of currency, or under what table, or the conditions of his lodging, or whether or not you provided dental coverage for those outrageously beautiful teeth of his. All we're trying to do is place the victim in space and time and hope to catch the turd who drove off with his leg."

"He drove off with his leg?" Smith asks.

"Smith!" Wetch barks.

"Yeah," Red says, glancing at Rain. "Chuck works for me off and on, under the table."

"Why off and on?" Wetch asks, jotting in his notepad.

"He travels a lot," Rain adds.

"He fucks off a lot is the truth of it," Red tells Wetch. "He ain't exactly made of reliable material."

"But he lives at your place… with you two?" Wetch throws Rain a smile.

"Fuck no," Red says. "I let him use an old travel trailer to keep his stuff in and crash when he needs to, but I can't say whether he does, nor how often, because it's down in the sticks behind the house. Can't see it from where we are, thankfully. But I know he hasn't been around in a while, because I ran him off."

"Ran him off?" Wetch asks, still writing.

"Red caught him peeping," Rain says quietly.

Red holds up a hand and flashes her a dark look. "On multiple occasions. I warned him the first time it happened, but the poor boy's in love. Couldn't help himself. So I had a more convincing conversation with Chuck, you could say, and he sort of tucked tail after that."

"How convincing?" Wetch asks.

"Look," Red sighs, glancing back over at the pizza counter. "If I were gonna kill Chuck, you think I'd leave a body behind?"

"Baby…" Rain says with concern.

"And y'all already know I can't drive," Red says. "So what's this all about?"

"Why can't you drive?" Smith asks.

"He's got a… condition, right?" Wetch checks with Red. "But, you know, after seeing you up and at em like this, Mr. Ravning, I'd actually forgotten. And I'm sorry to give off any sense that you're under suspicion, which, of course, a man in your condition is not. If Chuck ever wakes up from his situation, we'll just confirm all that and call it good."

"He ain't waking up," Smith opines.

"Ah, but miracles have been known to happen, my challenged friend," Wetch tell him. "As the Lord Jesus has shown us. Ain't that right, Preacher?"

The Padre looks at Wetch as if Wetch were a fart in the shape of a person.

"I talked to Chuckie yesterday," Rain blurts.

All heads within earshot turn to stare at her.

"What?" Red and Wetch ask together.

"You mean...." Wetch says. "Here? At the hospital?"

Rain shakes her head and looks at Red warily. "On the phone. We talked on the phone."

"You didn't tell me that," Red says.

"You were asleep, baby," Rain tells him. "And I only woke you up yesterday because the hospital called."

"What time was that, ma'am? The conversation with the victim?" Wetch asks, pulling his pad out quickly.

"Gosh, I don't know," Rain says, straining to focus. "In the afternoon?"

"That's before he got runt over," Smith calculates.

Wetch sighs. "And what were the contents of your discourse?"

"That means what y'all talked about," Smith translates.

"Well..." Rain thinks. "A lot. Chuckie always talks a lot. Said he was boat shopping... talked about the Cowboys... Talked about some weird guy following him around town."

"Following him?" Wetch scribbles.

"Really, I should say that Chuckie said he *thought* somebody was following him around town," Rain adds with a decisive nod.

"Why *thought*?" asks Wetch.

"Active imagination," Red says. "Chuck makes up these stories."

"That's what I'm saying," Rain says with relief. "Red knows. Because, like, you never know for sure? Chuckie tells these stories and you just never know what's what. This one was about some weird guy following him around town."

"He give a description?" Wetch asks.

"Said he was weird," Rain shrugs. "And following him? Oh, and kinda funny looking. And, well..." Rain looks over at the Padre shyly.

"What is it, girlfriend?" the Padre asks.

"I don't want to say, pastor," she tells him. "Not in front of you."

"It ain't nothing I haven't heard before," the Padre says. "Go on and say it."

"Okay, well…" she blushes. "Chuckie said… he said the guy dressed like a… a faggot. I'm sorry, but that's what he said. Said the guy wore these flower shirts and had long eyelashes and sat up straight and the guy was interested in Chuckie. You know, for sexual reasons? Chuckie said he kept seeing this guy around town—at a football game, at E-Z Mart, one time at Walmart…"

"Hawaiian shirt and flip flops," I say.

"That's right!" Rain exclaims. "That's what Chuckie said! Like the guy was dressed for the beach or something…"

"And what do you know about it, Mr. Big in Japan?" Wetch asks me.

"Real Hawaiian-made, by the looks of it," I reply, and Wetch jots it down with reluctance. "Expensive looking—not a cheap knockoff. Cargo shorts. Great posture. Bald, nice eyelashes, drives a Taurus…"

"And how exactly," Wetch looks up at me with three-fourths of a smile, "do you know so much about this peculiarly dressed mystery person?"

"I've seen him twice recently," I say. "Three times, actually. Once at the Walmart, then following me around town, I think. And then just a couple of hours ago leaving the hospital parking lot, as the Padre will confirm."

"That so, Preacher?" Wetch turns to ask him.

The Padre shakes his head slowly, looking down at Rain's hands. "Well, technically no."

"We just saw him in the parking lot," I say.

"No, you said that *you* saw him. And I can confirm that, detective," the Padre says. "But I didn't see anybody who fit that description, Sam, and—"

"Hold on," Wetch interrupts, turning to me. "Your name is Sam?"

"Like, Sam Sorrow?" asks Smith, his mouth opening three inches wider than normal.

I confirm with a grunt and a nod.

"Well, I'll be... You don't look anything like the picture we have of you."

"Don't sound like it, either," Smith adds. "You kinda sound like Beetlejuice."

"This day just keeps getting better and better!" Wetch laughs.

"Ain't he supposed to be half Mexican or something?" Smith asks Wetch. "This one don't even look one eighth Mexican to me."

Wetch ignores his partner, eyes wide with glee. "I'm so sorry, Mr. Sorrow! You see, for the last couple of days, my partner and I have been trying to locate you, driving all over this shit-hole tracking you down. We'd lost all hope you were still in the vicinity!"

"Well, here I am," I confirm. "Let me guess—y'all are big fans?"

"Huge fans!" Wetch says as he pulls out the handcuffs. "Now, Mr. Sorrow, may we have the honor of your company down at the station? It seems you are under arrest for the murder of Steve Berkey."

THE MAN WHO TALKS TO CATS

What the cops have on me is so damning I almost believe it myself. A couple of anonymous somebodies had seen me driving around Atlantis in my truck the night of Steve's murder. In addition, Smith and Wetch let it slip that there was a certain unnamed and credible witness who'd put his one remaining good hand to Bible that he'd seen my truck in Steve's driveway just hours before he was drowned. My assertions to the contrary aren't worth hog balls until my lawyer shows up. Thing is, I didn't ask for a lawyer.

"The man who talks to cats," he says, entering the station's interview room with gloved hands clasped behind his back.

"Tonk?"

"Please," Tonkawa Tyson says, "Mr. Tyson."

His mustache is still bushy and dignified, but much grayer than it was over thirty years prior. Sonya's uncle is thankfully still alive and still the best attorney money can buy in the county. He kicks up his black cherry alligator boots on the table, adjusts the crotch of his burgundy suit, and interlaces his turquoise gloved fingers upon his vested lap.

"I didn't do it," I tell him.

"Clearly," Tonk replies. He looks around the room disapprovingly and then back at me as if I'm responsible for the wretchedness surrounding us.

"You say something about cats?"

"No time," he says. "Tell me everything."

I do. And less than two hours later, Tonkawa Tyson returns with the DA, a tech guy, one pair of aforementioned asshole detectives, and video footage confirming that at the time of the crime in question, Sam Sorrow was indeed at Antone's on 5th Street in downtown Austin, Texas. I'd been catching an old friend's acoustic set, putting a dent in the bar's Casa Noble stock, and trying to hang on to my waning musical relevance. In other words, I was 300 miles away on the night of Steve's murder.

Dr. Tonkawa Tyson, Esquire—Magister Templi, Naturopath, and Still the Most Feared Attorney at Law in All of East Texas—lays out his plan to sue Caddo County back to the Paleozoic on my wounded behalf. I can hear the DA's mouth go dry as he says it. Three minutes later, I'm a free man.

CONVERSION

Had I known that Steve had named me his sole heir, I'm not saying I would've killed him for the money, but nobody would've faulted me for having it cross my mind. Other than my fondness for premium tequila and decent coffee, I've been living on the edge of lean for over a year, so lean that I recently moved into a friend's garage apartment just to afford my fondness for premium tequila and decent coffee. The garage was supposed to be temporary. I'm maybe months away from asking my ex for cash.

Tonkawa Tyson was Steve's lawyer and fiduciary. With unmasked reluctance, Tonk has me sign the papers that give me the keys to Steve's house, access to millions in checking, a 60% majority of Berkey International, and a labyrinth of incomprehensible stocks that even Tonk can't make sense of. Technically, Steve left more money to the Berkey Foundation, but those funds are stashed away in a trust so secure that nobody—not even Tonk—can catch a whiff of it.

I can understand Steve leaving me the house. After all, it was my home for a spell, but the mindfuck bounty of the rest of my inheritance leaves me gazing at the walls of Tonk's office (downtown now; he abandoned that old pyramid house years ago) for what might be eight hours straight. I can't make words with my mouth. I can't even make words with my brain.

When my head finally does jump back online, my first thought is how atypically stupid it was for Steve to make me his sole beneficiary. And then, as if to confirm a point nobody asked me to substantiate, I set out to prove it.

My first impulse is to grab Meredith, slap her ass with a wad of hundreds, and buy the first aircraft I come across, pilot included. We'll fly to some exotic island and spend the rest of our days with our toes in the sand and tacos in our bellies, along with an endless conga line of alcoholic fruit drinks adorned with tiny umbrellas.

Thing is, I can't find Meredith anywhere and she still isn't returning my voicemails or texts. Her neighbors haven't seen her and I can't locate anybody in the whole damn town who knows where she is. The best thing would be to wait around for a couple of days, but I don't have it in me—I'm higher than I've ever been on Mexican cactus and cash and the burning urge to do something undeniably epic, so that's what I do.

Like I said, Smith and Wetch hadn't exactly kept my accuser's identity secret. With Tonk's assistance, I find out that Lefty/Bill/Guy (aka *Motherfucking Liar Who Tried to Frame Me with the Cops*) split for Houston. The whole drive down there, I convince myself that showing up on his doorstep is an Inigo Montoya-level maneuver that's righteous and worthy and good. Truth is, the other suspects in Steve's murder—the Caddo Club and some lowlife who calls himself Teisenberg—are too amorphous for my hopped-up, hammered, *nouveau riche* brain. Lefty, on the other hand, is real. He had it out for me. He's traceable. Plus, he'll never see it coming.

A day later, I track him down at a joint in Montrose called Ripcord. If somebody asked you to draw your best guess at what a gay leather bar in Houston looks like, Ripcord is exactly what you'd draw. Guy is working the patio bar, shirtless, every bit as attractive as Meredith and the Padre indicated. He's also followed up with the latter's advice to dress up his mangled stump, fitting it out with a black leather cuff with a brass ring where his fingers used to be. It takes Guy pouring my third shot of Villa Lobos before he recognizes who I am. I don't know what I was expecting, but it's not him chatting me up like we're redneck chums and very much not acting like he'd just accused me of killing Steve.

After buying a couple of rounds for the patio, I'm surrounded by shirtless and expressively gay McConaughey clones who all keep calling me Harvey for some damn reason. By the time it comes to put up the tables, I've laid down four grand, a good chunk of it in Guy's tip jar. Which is how I get him back to my hotel.

It's a top-end suite looking out over the grounds of the Houston Zoo, where the only animals I see are either drugged or sleeping. I stagger into the hotel bathroom while Guy waits for me on the bed, and when I stagger back out a couple minutes later, he's stretched out on top of the comforter with nothing on but that leather cuff and a grin.

"Just so we're clear," he says, "I ain't gay or nothing."

"For the record," I confide, "neither am I."

I hook a pair of seductive fingers through his cuff ring and gently pull his stump onto my lap. I try to picture Steve in my mind, try to imagine his arms thrashing around in the filthy water of Lake Atlantis as he drowns with a panicked animal look in his eyes. For a moment, the picture almost comes to me, but all I end up seeing is blurry wallpaper and the spins. Even so, I know what I have to do.

The scene that follows is like watching somebody else act it out on TV, somebody who calls himself Sam Sorrow—a Sam Sorrow who grabs an overly ornate bedside lamp, wraps the cord around his fist, and holds it aloft over a naked man's confused face, pausing right before hammering it down with a skull-crushing thud. But that's not how it goes. The picture sticks right before all that, frozen as if jammed in the VCR, and then I come back to a different version of myself who knows it isn't right, because I've got the wrong guy.

Guy sobs loudly, intact hand over his exposed junk, leathered nub between his face and my almost-weaponized lamp. I probably knew it wasn't him as soon as I saw him with that dressed-up stump at Ripcord. He didn't kill Steve. And he wasn't the one who framed me.

Guy says the reason he split Atlantis was because he was scared out of his head. He didn't leave because of Steve's murder; Guy ditched because of certain events occurring just prior and after. The cops came by the Lodge to check his alibi, but they didn't seem the least bit interested in trying to pin Steve's murder on him. It was like they were going through the motions, Guy says, just covering their ass. And they certainly didn't want to hear what he and Chuck had seen just days before.

The two had been out in the Lodge's driveway pretending to rake up pine needles when they heard raised voices behind the church. Thinking it was some rehab kids having a fight or lovers' spat, Chuck and Guy snuck around the far side of the church to get a better look. It was Steve; his back was to them. The fuss was between him and another man, but it was clearly a one-sided affair, because Steve was chewing this other fellow out, pacing, pointing, his voice almost in tears. And the other man just looked down into the dirt and took it like a whipped dog, arms crossed over his chest, not even attempting a reply. The man was bald. He was wearing a Hawaiian shirt.

Then, a couple of days after they found Steve bobbing in the lake, Guy saw the Hawaiian shirt dude again. He was talking with the Padre. Well, not talking, exactly. The two were down at the docks below the Lodge where the canoes and boats are kept, and the two men were looking out over the surface of the lake, not saying a word or even seeming to acknowledge the presence of the other. They just stood there in utter silence for what seemed like hours, with Guy watching from behind a patch of crepe myrtles up the hill. And then the Hawaiian shirt man turned and caught Guy staring.

After that, he popped up everywhere Guy went—the gym, down the street from his house, the E-Z Mart gas pump... But the freaky thing was that the man always seemed to be there before Guy arrived, as if Guy himself was the one doing the following. The man always had on a pressed Hawaiian shirt—a different one each time—and he always wore the same blank expression, the same freshly shaved head, the same freakishly long eyelashes. Guy says he was like the Mystery Man in *Lost Highway*—the one played by Robert Blake—or even Monty Montgomery's Cowboy in *Mulholland Drive*. Guy also believes that these are two versions of the same David Lynch movie, when you really think about it.

When I wake up on the hotel floor the next morning, the door to my room is wide open and so is my mouth. An arroyo of drool crusts up on one side of my face. I sit up against the bed and attempt to massage the tequila out of my temples when a flash of color appears in the open doorway—a Hawaiian shirt.

I spring to my feet like a hungover cat—shouting, hands in front of me like a useless set of claws. The cleaning lady jumps about four feet up in the air with a chirp. She pats the floral-patterned shirt above her heart, takes a deep breath, shakes her head, and frowns over to the next room. Guy is still in bed, ass up and passed out. I take the rest of my cash, fold it lengthwise, and loop it through the brass ring of his cuff.

I know everything I need to know to drive straight back to Atlantis. Either the Padre was lying to me or straight-up keeping me in the dark, and I don't like either option one bit. There's a glaring, dangling thread just asking to be yanked, and all I have to do to unravel Steve's murder is point Blue north and start pulling. Atlantis is only four hours away.

But Austin's only three.

INTERLUDICROUS

My stated intention is to grab some fresh gear and maybe Gatsby it up a couple of days before heading back to Atlantis. In the weeks that follow, the only place I go is everywhere around Austin, but by the way I make it rain, you'd swear it was Seattle.

It's not like I can blow it all. Arguably, most of the shit I buy could be categorized as a *safe investment*. There's the house in Travis Heights (a rambling Victorian on a double lot with a rickety, three-story turret), the dive bar on South Congress (where I'd played my first gigs decades back), the 40-foot yacht on Lake Travis, and the *Torchy's Tacos* in East Austin (in the end, actually profitable, as it turns out).

But the crown jewel of all has to be *The Pearl*—far and away the greatest strip club known to humankind, or at least the greatest known to me in Austin—which I rename *Sam's*. Surprisingly, it's where I spend my time, awash in tequila and strippers. Getting engaged to one of the star dancers—a curvy blonde who calls herself Sativa (nee Velvet)—is a poor surrogate for making good on my repeated vow to bring Steve's killer to justice, but I keep telling myself I'm getting around to it, I'm recharging, refueling, and that when I finally do pull the trigger (tomorrow? next week?), nobody in Atlantis will see me coming.

And that's how I die. Well, temporarily, at least. Sativa's first impulse is to let me pull a Bon Scott and choke on my own hurl. A couple of days prior, she walked in on me getting a blowie from one of the other dancers, and my betrothed had every right to let me die on *Sam's* sticky floor and thereby inherit the club, the castle/house, the boat, and a lifetime's supply of tacos. Only, not. Because we're not yet officially hitched, so Sativa makes the smart business move and calls the paramedics. By the time they arrive, my skin is the color of a Dutch girl's eyes.

What happens next isn't any sort of roadmap or prediction about *what comes next*. In truth, I'm not even sure how much of it occurs or which parts I puzzle together in one of those post-dream assemblies to wrangle bewilderment.

It starts with me getting up from the glutinous carpet of *Sam's* and wiping off a face full of barf. At a neighboring barstool, Tonkawa Tyson laughs and points at my crotch—that is, the crotch of a dying version of me who remains on the floor.

"Well," he says, "you done gone and pissed yourself."

"Huh," a standing me replies.

"What's that smell?"

"Cash and poon," I sniff. "Beer, probably."

"No," Tonk tilts his head. "Smells like... smells like it does when it's about to snow."

"Shit..." I say. "Ain't never no—" but the rest of it never comes out. A black EMT with a shaved head and bushy mustache stabs my left arm and digs his fingers into my mouth, shouting over his shoulder at somebody I can't see. Somebody else rushes up and rips my shirt open, but then Tonk and me are in the shallows of Lake Atlantis in a tiny canoe, beached in a horizonless expanse of mud. At the same time, I'm also at Deer Point overlooking us, feet in the grass, as Tonk plunks out a song on my old Martin guitar. Then I look to the far shore where a large figure holds up an enormous hand, palm facing me as if saying *stop* or *hold up* or *don't*. And when I zoom in on the hand there are three interlocking triangles moving clockwise around each other, the shapes branded into the palm.

"Who told you I was here?" I ask, sitting up in a hospital bed.

"I work here," she says. "It's my job, Bobby." It's my ex-wife, Marie. She's put on a little weight since I've last seen her. She looks great.

"You look great," I say.

"You keep saying that."

"I miss you."

"You keep saying that, too," Marie says. "And you keep not meaning it."

I'm not sure which one says it. There are two Maries sitting parallel to each other in identical hospital chairs.

"My throat hurts." I try to swallow.

One of the women stands up, holds her face, and weeps out of the room.

"What's that about?" I ask the Marie who's still there.

"Don't do that," she says, disappointed.

"Do what?"

"Don't ask stupid questions."

"Time heals all wounds," I say. "You'll see."

The nurse rubs my shoulder. "What's that, sweetie? What were you saying?" Her dark hair waves behind her like a banner of crows.

"It doesn't go away," I say.

"Time heals all wounds," she smiles.

I start to heave again. My stomach lurches up into my mouth, but nothing comes up, but that nothing keeps trying. There's a cup of water on the bedside tray. I fumble for it and finally hold it still enough to take a sip through the straw, but it isn't water. It's tequila. The shock of it turns my mouth to liquid fire and tosses a bolt of pain down me like an arrow of acid, and that arrow shoots out of my asshole, tearing through the bed. I shit myself. Somebody giggles nearby.

"Ain't funny," I moan.

It's a little girl—two or three-years-old. There are playground swings where the walls recently were, a couple of slides, and other kids in the background falling off a merry-go-round as their parents clap in tandem. The little girl runs off and hides behind a slide.

"Over here," she sings, peeking through her hands.

"You're not supposed to tell me," I laugh. "The whole purpose of—"

"What's that, sweetie?" the nurse asks, patting my arm. "What were you saying?" Her hair lies flat and black on her shoulders like a flag of dark feathers. I start to heave again.

"Give it time," she says. "Give it wounds."

This whole procession (me on the floor of my club to the girl in the playground and back to the nurse again) does a *Groundhog Day* at least three more times, but it might be thirty. I begin to anticipate each reiteration a second before it happens, trying to say the words before anybody else, hoping that will reroute the series or just make it stop, but it doesn't. I just keep going around and around until, eventually, I'm just off the loop. And then I slide into the final part, which only happens once.

I'm on a marshy trail. There are moss-covered trees and an upright circle of stones in the distance. In the middle is a wagon like the kind once pulled by miserable horses across prairies, and there's music coming from it. I recognize the song and it hurts to hear it. It hurts so much I have to turn and go back the way I came. I walk and walk, but every path I take away from the music leads me back to that circle, and the music gets louder from inside the wagon, so I finally just sit down with my back to one of the stones and try to shout or cry, but I can't.

"What you doing that for?" a voice asks.

"For you," I say.

"Bullshit," says Steve. He steps out of the wagon and sits against another stone about ten feet away, grinning like a cat who just said the funniest thing ever. He lights a cigarette and sniffs the sky.

"You smell that?"

"Don't say it," I shake my head. "Don't you dare fucking say it. And when did you ever smoke?"

"Always smoked," he says, but it's not Steve anymore. I've never even seen a photo of my bio father, but it's him.

"Oh," I said. "Great."

"There was this Royston rook," he says, inhaling the smoke as deep as it will go. "That's the kind that's black and white. Both colors, both worlds."

"Shut up."

"And this Royston boy," he continues, "was hanging out with the crows one day. *Where'd you get that shiny white on your coat?* they asked him. *That look nice,* they said. And he go, *Oh, that? That there I stole from a pigeon man I met.* Later on, this Royston rook was off playing dice with the pigeons, see. And they ask him, *Hey boy, where'd you get them sharp black trousers and sleeves you got on?* And he say, *Oh, that? Won em in cards off them crow fellas!*"

My father slaps his knee and laughs and laughs. "You hear what I'm sayin, son?"

"Don't call me that," I say, and I stand up and walk away. And I keep walking away from that circle and past paths that fork off toward rivers and lakes and forgotten little towns and then I see a building in the distance and then I'm in it and then I wake up.

TWO GIRLS

Before our baby died, my ex-wife put up with me for the better part of a decade. Our marriage was one of those well-intentioned fuckups that adults are prone to make, insisting at some point in their 30s that it's high time for the round peg to grow up and find itself a properly contoured hole. I knew better, even if Marie didn't.

I named our tiny girl Adelia. She was born with a heart defect and not enough weight on her to make it in the onerous world. She died two weeks later. They say it happens. They say you'd be surprised how much it happens. And, in time (they say this, too), couples make it through, emerging on the other side of the nightmare stronger than ever, hand in heartbroken hand, gradually winding their way out into a mutual light.

That's when I lost my voice. Adelia died and when I woke up the next morning my beautiful baritone was gone.

You'd think that'd be enough to keep me spiraling down, but only one of those losses felt permanent. The docs told me to take it easy, said I was in shock, said most cases of dysphonia fix themselves in a week or two. They were wrong. That happens, too.

Adelia dying was terrible enough, but what ruined me in the end was worse. Despite knowing how unreasonable and cruel it was, I couldn't stop from blaming Marie for Adelia's death. I never said it out loud; it was just evident in how I wouldn't look her in the eyes and how I sat under my favorite tree in our front yard for hours while leveling up to day-drinking. And because of that mysterious and fundamental whatever that was missing between us—that binding essence I'd waved off as insignificant before we did the *I Dos*—I didn't have it in me to turn the torment into something better. And because there wasn't enough despair at home, I took to the road—unceasingly hammered and still celebrated wherever I went, shit voice and all. And it wasn't me screwing groupies and star-fuckers that put an end to it all, because getting hitched to Marie had never been an obstacle to that. It was Meredith. Only Meredith could make Marie finally cut herself free.

"You're heading back?" Marie asks now, sitting across a new table in my old house.

I'm one day out of rehab. Marie and her new husband have asked me over. Don's over in the open-windowed kitchen, prepping breakfast tacos and screwing up the words to one of my favorite songs—"Two Girls" by Townes.

"Tonight," I say, looking out into a yard I used to call mine.

"Tonight?" she asks with surprise, looking over at Don.

"I'm fine."

"You're fine."

"I'm fine."

"Don, does he look fine?"

Don assesses. Being as he was my agent for most of my career, Don's qualified to opine.

"He's fine," Don says, going back to the tortillas. "Mighty fine."

Funny thing is, I'm the one who introduced them years ago, and in this damn house. They're good together. They fit. But what I don't get this morning is why invite me here. We meet up from time to time, but never here.

"What's wrong?" Marie asks, fingers fidgeting in her lap.

"You tell me."

"I knew you'd be upset," she says.

"Why would I be upset?"

"Look, we really wanted to come, but... I just—"

"It was my fault," Don says.

"It wasn't his fault," she shakes her head. "How was it, anyway?"

"Rehab? Piece of cake," I say. A piece of cake stabbed through the ass with a cattle prod.

Marie's confused. "Steve's funeral," she says.

"About what you'd expect. What kind of tacos we having?"

We've stayed friends, I guess. If you don't look too hard at it, we're friends. Although it's still weird to me how she took Don's name. Never occurred to me to ask her to change it to Sorrow, especially after what she'd been through with her first husband. So: Marie Anne Beis, born Taylor. Meredith's older sister.

"What are you staring at?" she asks.

What I'm staring at is the empty spot in the front yard where the old pecan was, the tree that reminded me of the ones at Steve's house, so much so that I might've bought the house on account of it. It was over two hundred years old and every couple of years it dropped so many nuts on the roof I had to pay a neighbor boy to sweep them off in a cascade of shells that sounded like a stampede of geese.

"I appreciate the visits, Marie," I say, turning back to her. "Was nice to have somebody I knew when I was going through all that."

They probably paged her to the hospital as soon as they wheeled my almost-dead, blue ass in. She's worked there as a chaplain for years.

Marie moves her head slowly from side to side. "I only came by once," she says.

"Not to me, you didn't."

She doesn't say anything. She just tries to read something in my eyes she never learned the language for.

"Nevermind," I smile. "Just, you know, thanks."

I inhale the barbacoa smoke and look around the living room until my eyes catch something missing on the wall behind her. "Where's my fireplace?"

"Not yours anymore. And it's been gone for a while now."

"What'd it do, run off with the pecan tree?"

"That tree dropped a branch the size of a telephone pole," she says quickly. "Crushed one whole corner of our porch. Could've killed somebody!"

"Okay."

"And it's not like we ever need a fireplace in Austin," she says, looking at Don, who is doing everything possible to stay in a different part of the house than the two of us.

"I apologize," I say, and I mean it. "Things are just sort of weird for me right now."

"See?" she throws out her hands. "You can't drive back tonight! You're not fine, like I said."

"I am fine," I say. "I'm just... sensitive."

"Sensitive?"

"More sensitive. Even these colors," I wave at the birthday-cake-colored walls. "It's disorienting. All these changes, the brightness..."

"They were gray, Bobby," she says. "You'd painted the walls gray."

"Said *slate blue* on the can."

"Never comes out like it looks on the can," Don adds.

"We needed another bookcase," Marie leans back in her chair. "That's why the fireplace... That's all there was to it, and—"

I hold up my hands and smile and Don clears his throat and Marie stops. It's a different house now; it's their house now. But I really did love that tree. And that fireplace, too, even if I never did use it. The other changes don't bother me so much—the locking gate and new fence outside, a living room arranged by Ethan Allen himself, new fixtures and appliances, security locks on the windows, plastic plugs on the unused outlets, the enormous Christmas tree...

"That's a lot of fucking presents," I say. There must be a hundred of them.

"Don?" she calls.

"Just a minute!" he lies.

"We're having company," Marie stands and checks the hospital pager on top of the bookshelf. "For Christmas. Lots of company. Lots of guests, lots of presents."

Don shoos us away from the table and throws on a brightly colored Mexican tablecloth with matching napkins. It was my wedding gift to them—a wedding to which I wasn't invited. We never talked about that, either. I load up a pair of tacos. The barbacoa's overdone. We're all busy with our plates, wordlessly passing onions, cilantro, pico, tortillas, salsa, cheddar, and when I glance up, Don has his arm around Marie and she's doing a terrible job of trying not to cry. She shoves her face into his rumpled shirt and two seconds later finally gives way to an all-out bawl. Don pulls her tight and holds her shaking head close with both hands. I remember that sound. Except whenever I used to hear Marie cry like that, I'd leave the house.

"Hey," I say. "Hey, is everything..."

"It's nothing," Don tells me over the sobs. "I mean, it's something. It's about Meredith."

"Mere?"

"I mean, it's probably nothing," he says.

And then he tells me the *probably nothing* that's most definitely something.

ESTRANGED

Long before me and Marie began our unlikely courtship, Meredith had been out of both of our lives for nearly a decade. After our last encounter in Tennessee, I just assumed Meredith had shacked up with somebody from that farm in North Carolina, although I'd get selective word here and there from Steve about her movements and travels across the country. I was too busy making my bones in the scene and enjoying the slow rush of fame to follow up, but I never forgot Meredith was out there. I just assumed she'd pop up unannounced at one of my shows one day and then I'd take it from there.

My first couple of albums did okay. I started opening for the likes of Uncle Tupelo (and later Wilco), Steve Earle, Emmylou, the Jayhawks, and even Willie a time or two, but it wasn't until I wrote my first hit ("If You Die, Can I Have Your Shit?"—an offhand joke I'd thought up while stuck in Denver during a blizzard) that all hell broke loose. That's what brought in the bigger record deal and interviews in *The Wire* and *No Depression* (the latter rag being the one who called me ATX's answer to Elvis Costello, who I'm told didn't take kindly to the comparison). Attendance at my shows went up tenfold, the royalty checks started coming in with extra digits, and I was thoroughly enjoying the hell out of a seemingly continuous uphill ride. And (with no small help from Don) that's how it was for a few years there. I surfed the apex of the bell-curved wave of my career, and for a couple of standard deviations, I was happy.

But it wasn't long until I was cooked. Being on the road in your 20s is one thing; getting up night after night for gigs you don't particularly want to play in your 30s is another beast entirely. I'd always hated the promotion side of things, and now that aspect of my career was in peak-rut overdrive. Add that to constant touring and my label's scheme to milk me of goofy hits until the Alt-Country well ran dry. I didn't mind the dollar signs; what I minded was seeing somebody else chalk out my future on the blackboard.

I'd seen some of my Austin peers do better. I'd seen them pull back into that Goldilocks Zone between shitty weeknight slots and six-digit, sold-out arenas. They toured sparingly, remained respectable with cherry gigs in town, recorded whatever they wished in home studios, and settled down with a good woman and an anthology of genius, feral children. I wanted that, too. More than anything. At least, that's what I told myself. And it didn't take long until the power of that desire set something talismanic in the field that made it so.

It happened in Dallas, of all places, at a club called Trees. I recognized her the second I walked out onstage. As soon as our eyes met, Marie broke out in an enormous, toothy smile that was so genuine it felt like I was being pierced with cartoon heart arrows by a little chunky flying boy. I played one of the best sets of my entire life that night. I sang with gratitude and heartbreak and humor and raw loss—an unlikely gumbo I hadn't accessed in years. And when the set was over, I wrapped Marie up in the biggest hug I'd given anybody in ages. She smelled like mountain laurel and porch swings and home-made biscuits.

"You smell," I said.

"Au contraire," she smirked. "I stink."

We hung out in the green room on a saggy red couch and told each other the stories that constituted our lives since leaving Caddo

County. She'd walked in on her first husband—a certain Minister Charles—unsuccessfully trying to convert a young man with his pastoral penis. Her parents back in Atlantis were hardline evangelicals. Not only would they not accept the divorce, they blamed Marie for turning her preacher husband homo in the first place. So she split for Colorado, took up yoga and meditation, crossed over into Buddhaland, and became an interfaith chaplain, of all things. She was wrapping up a residency at a Dallas hospital and shopping around for longer term work. Talk about leaving Atlantis in the rearview.

"Well," I said, looking down at her once-mismatched boobs. "You filled out nicely."

"You're gonna try that stunt again?" she smiled. "Still can't touch em."

"Why?" I scooted closer. "They belong to somebody?"

"They belong to me, thank you."

"Yeah, but... you with anybody?"

"Bobby Soreau, are you hitting on me?"

"It's Sam Sorrow now," I said. "And if you'll look down, you'll see we're already holding hands."

There's a type of magic that only happens on backstage couches—the more suspiciously stained, the better. Marie would tell a different story later, but for me it was clear—she was it. I could have proposed right then and there, and I might as well have for how it worked out in the end. But at that moment I knew beyond a doubt that Marie was the beautiful and supportive bride I'd invoked with my longing, the one who held the golden keys to that middle-way bliss I'd been dreaming and chasing, despite there being one outrageously obvious problem.

Marie didn't know about me and Meredith. The sisters had never been close, and they hadn't spoken since Marie left the house, and somehow nobody—not Steve, not Marie's parents, nor any cousins or friends or gabby church members or apparently her own damn sister—had ever informed Marie that Meredith and me had been a thing. Sure, it had been an off and on thing, and a thing relegated to an increasingly distant past, but it had been a special thing and it had been her one and only sister. Marie not knowing didn't sit right, even for somebody with my suspect morality. But I'd be goddamned if I was gonna tell her.

In the coming months, Marie moved in with me into that Hyde Park house, she landed a job downtown, we got married, and everything was peachier than a Hill Country summer. As with many mismatched couples, we brought out qualities missing in each other—aspects that were underfed or lacking. Marie always said that our union was karmic—that we were something *meant to be*—but for me it was even better than that. If I was meant to be with anybody, it was probably Meredith, wherever the fuck she was, but that didn't mean shit anymore. With Marie, I had attained something better—something practical, sane, evolved, and thoroughly adult. I had accomplished what *should be*—something beyond the heartbreak and co-emergent misery of youthful passion. The time in my life for Meredith was long gone. But it wasn't the same for Marie.

Despite our demanding careers and us not having much of a supportive village to speak of, we both wanted kids. Oh, we had friends aplenty, but something felt misaligned or missing in our straggled path to parenthood. I had Steve, but that was it, and he was hundreds of miles away. Marie was irreparably cut off from her parents, but she was instinctually drawn to reconnect with her sister. If we were going to have babies, she wanted Meredith in the picture.

To my credit, I told her it was a bad idea. We'd both heard the rumors. That Meredith had overdosed. That she'd been busted for trafficking across state lines. That she'd worked as a stripper. That she'd been involved in some plot to blow up a ski resort in Wyoming. I told Marie that even if a quarter of the rumors were true, Meredith had always been unreliable and moody, and that was no influence to have around forthcoming children.

Who knows how she tracked Meredith down. I'm guessing Steve had a hand in it. Before I knew it, the sisters were chatting regularly on the phone, conversations I was encouraged to participate in on speakerphone, holding my breath each time. And despite how anxious and wrong it made me feel, I couldn't bring myself to douse Marie's growing happiness. There was a new glow about her that was organic and restorative and, frankly, catching. And it turned out that Marie was glowing so organically and restoratively because she was two months pregnant.

I was about to head out on a short Southwest tour the night Meredith landed in Austin. In exchange for helping us with the baby, we leased her a studio apartment on North Loop about a mile from the house and paid for her massage school in exchange. I was in a bad state about her arrival. It was clear Meredith hadn't told Marie about us, but that didn't mean she wouldn't. She never was one to leave cats in a bag.

I tried to make the best of it. I was at my extra loving best as me and Marie prepped Meredith's welcome dinner—mashed potatoes, gravy, and one of my favorite chickens that up until earlier that day had been pecking the shit out of our backyard. Meredith was walking over from North Loop as we cooked, and we awaited her arrival with disparate jitters and an open bottle of Malbec. Then Marie's pager went off.

"Shit," she said, "shit, shit, shit…"

The chaplains took turns with the pager at night. If it was an emergency, they were required at the hospital ASAP. This was one of those times.

"Can't wait til you don't have to carry that thing anymore," I said. Marie was supposed to take a month off after the baby was born. Maybe longer.

Marie sighed, holding her belly. "Makes three of us." Then she huffed around the room looking for her keys and hospital badge.

"Well," I said. "Call your sister and reschedule. She'll understand. We can do it tomorrow morning before I go."

"No way," Marie frowned. That baby weight made her cute as hell, and also out of breath. "I won't be long—an hour, tops."

"That's what you always say."

"It's always true," she replied.

"I don't want to fight, baby, but that shit always takes longer than you think it does."

"That shit is my job, Bobby."

"Okay," I said. "Okay."

"I'll cut it short," she smiled. "I promise. Just... I don't know, make her feel welcome. Tell her jokes, get started on dinner... You'll do fine without me for a bit. She thinks the world of you, you know. She's always asking about you."

Then Marie pecked me on the cheek, rushed out the door, and I watched myself say goodbye to my wife in the hallway mirror and almost melt into the floor with regret. I was tired of trying to stop what had been so long in coming.

Six minutes later, Meredith knocked on our front door. I waited for as long as I could before I opened it. Maybe she'd go away.

"Sam," Meredith said, looking at me evenly.

"Mere."

"I'm standing here on your lovely porch," she glanced into the yard and smiled, "wondering if you're going to invite me in."

I moved out of the doorway and bit my lip behind her as she passed. I'd hoped the years had taken their toll, that she'd show up hollow-faced and scarred and gaunt from drugs, but she was even more beautiful and magnetic than I remembered.

"Marie texted," Meredith said. "Says she'll be back in an hour or so."

"She won't."

"I know."

"Welcome to Austin. Been before?"

Meredith looked around the living room, amused. "These walls supposed to be gray?"

"Slate blue."

"A couple of winters back I lived off Oltorf and South First," she said, as offhandedly as possible. "It was just for six, seven weeks. What, Marie never told you?"

"Are you—"

"Just joking," she said. "I didn't tell Marie I was here or anyone else, for that matter. May I sit?"

I gestured at a chair and tried to steady my legs. I'd forgotten how much Meredith enjoyed throwing people for loops just for the absolute rush of it.

"So, now I'm sitting," she said, "and you're standing."

"Would you like some wine?"

"Don't drink anymore," Meredith replied. "But a glass of water or juice would be nice."

"I think there's cranberry."

"Too tart," she said. "Water's fine."

I came back from the kitchen with a glass full of water and a heart flopping around in my chest like two-and-a-half Charlie Sheens.

"You okay?" she asked.

"Never better."

"You know," Meredith said, sipping her water, "You look exactly as I imagined you'd look."

"Distinguished? Striking? You know they make us wear makeup in those videos."

"Guilty. You look guilty."

"Oh, that."

"You didn't tell her," Meredith said, setting the glass down with noticeable focus.

"Never got around to it. Too late now."

"It isn't too late. She should know. She should know tonight."

"You're right," I nodded. "Tell you what... As soon as she gets back from the hospital, fresh from—oh, I don't know—trying to comfort the parents of a dying child or something like that, you and me will sit my pregnant wife down—your pregnant sister down, that is—and inform her that we used to be in love, or whatever you call it when you're obsessed and can't get enough of fucking each other's brains out for years on end. Sound good?"

Meredith moved the glass of water away from her another inch or two and then she moved it back.

"And then I'll tell her the bad news," I said.

"I don't think any of this is funny."

"The bad news is that I still think about you. I still dream about you, I still love you, I still wake up from time to time and wish it were you next to me in bed. See, Mere, a half-ass truth ain't gonna cut it this time. It's all or nothing."

I didn't mean to say any of it. I didn't even know it was true until I said it.

"That has nothing to do with anything," Meredith glared.

"Your eyes say different."

"Your eyes say bullshit, you arrogant prick. You really think I'm here for you?"

I shrugged and poured myself another glass of wine. I was starting to feel warm inside and unshaky at last.

"I'm here because my sister asked for help. No other reason."

"Good to have you on board," I laughed.

"Whatever your present feelings are, they have nothing to do with me. Nothing at all. And they aren't reciprocated, by the way..."

I just stood there and laughed some more, because it was all just suddenly so fucking funny.

"And, frankly," Meredith added. "I don't care if you tell Marie all that stuff or not, seeing as it has nothing to do with me. But I do care about the past—our past. Me, you, her... And that's what my sister has to know. And that's what you're going to tell her."

"Those mind powers won't work on me, girl," I said, waving a Jedi-deflecting hand her way.

"You can't not tell her, Sam."

"Oh, I don't know. I've been pretty good at not telling her for years now."

"And you want me to go along with the lie, is that it?"

I poured the rest of the Malbec into my glass and swished the deep red around in a circle and watched the legs slide down like languid rain.

"Withholding the truth and lying ain't the same thing," I said after a while. "As you should know."

"Sam..."

"I'm going out on tour tomorrow," I said, downing the rest of the wine, and I knew right then it was over. It was entirely out of my hands, and I was glad—relieved, even. "So go ahead and do what you have to do, Mere. Make sure you feel good about yourself, okay? Full of integrity or whatever it is you need to walk away from the explosion with. Just do me the favor and text me when it's done. Imagine I'll need to move out, which is kinda too bad. I really like this house..."

It was the time to say something better than that, something sharp and memorable. It was the time to give in and agree with her and make a plan to come clean with Marie. Or maybe it was the time to pull Meredith close and kiss her full-mouthed sloppy and fuck her right there on the dining room table next to the gravy and getting-cold chicken. But none of that's what happened. What happened was me breaking off one of the chicken legs in a napkin and grabbing the first bottle of red I could find. I wanted to look at Meredith one last time as I walked out of the house, but her face was turned away, dark hair on her neck like a shawl, so I left without a look and not another word between us.

Marie called an hour and a half later. Meredith was laughing in the background. Marie teased me for taking so long on my errand. Meredith had told her I'd run over to Central Market for dessert and a couple more bottles of celebratory wine.

It was the first in the oncoming cavalcade of lies.

GIFT SHOP

Meredith's gone missing. That's the *probably nothing* that Don and Marie have to tell me. Meredith's out of touch, vanished, dropped off radar.

"Two weeks and a day," Marie says, blowing her nose. "No calls, no texts, no emails, nothing."

Not technically *missing*, but abnormal, considering the sisters have been in touch daily for years, even after our affair in the booze-fugue that followed Adelia's death. Marie never held it against her.

I try to remember the last time I saw Meredith. My mind vaults from one picture to another: Meredith across a table from Steve, Tarot cards in hand; me drinking cran-grape on her sofa; the watercolor in her bathroom; us in bed together that night in Tennessee nearly thirty years back; Meredith climbing into the back of a polished Lincoln Navigator...

"What do the cops say?" I ask, pacing a room that isn't mine anymore. Don shakes his head and tries to sneak a look at Marie, who tries not to sneak one back. "Tell me y'all called the cops."

"There are some… complications," Don says hesitantly.

"Complications? Is she fucking missing or not?"

"The complications I'm referring to," Don continues, "might involve a certain level of illegality. A certain, maybe, act of illegality. Acts, even. Like, many of them. Probably."

"Illegality?"

"Well, see, the thing is…"

"Just tell me, Don! Jesus!"

"Okay," he says, checking with Marie. "So, here's the thing…. Meredith has been… sending us money."

"Money," I repeat.

"Yeah," he nods. "Lots of it. For safekeeping. I set up a security box to keep it in. She asked me to, and it's all in there—the money. And whenever it comes in, I just go to the bank, put the money in the box and—"

"I know how it fucking works, man. How much are we talking about?"

"See, nobody knows but us. And you, now. And we didn't want to involve you, because—"

"How much?"

"Lots," he replies. "Well, maybe not a lot for somebody like you, but for us… I mean, me and Marie—"

"How. Fucking. Much."

"Ten grand," he says. "In cash."

I don't mean to laugh; it just sort of pounces out of my mouth. I plop down onto one of their uncomfortable chairs and start to breathe normally again.

"Okay," I say, "ten grand. Not exactly nothing, but—"

"Per month," Don clarifies.

"Per month?"

"Per month for the last ten months," Don says.

"Eleven," Marie corrects him. "This last one was eleven."

I blink and try to do the math. "Are you… That's over…"

"Yeah," Marie says. "We know."

Of all of Meredith's challenges over the years, earning money has never been one of them. Even so, 110K is a lot of dough for somebody who purports to read Tarot cards for a living. Years before Meredith turned the corner and reentered our lives, she'd been making rent by showing her tits at *Seven Sirens*, but at some point it dawned on her that there was more to gain in the hierarchy of illicit enterprise than what she was making from letting the Chuck Tenders of the world grope her yams and hooha. She'd stopped shooting up by then, and dealing was never her style, but Meredith was a perfect fit for the transport division, and she must have escorted hundreds of loads in and out of Caddo County before she was finally busted. Per the amount of smack the cops found in her trunk, it should have been ten years minimum, but Meredith was mysteriously repped by a top-dollar lawyer from Houston. She was also young and beautiful and white. She walked out of the courtroom without so much as a timeout.

As the story goes, the whole ordeal scared her straight. Meredith ditched the drug trade and East Texas for a few years, traveling who-knows-where before landing at a permaculture farm in Washington state, growing shitakes and hugging trees. What happened in those middle years is anybody's guess, but that farm is where Marie found Meredith and convinced her to come to Austin and help with the baby.

"Ten grand each month in the mail?" I can't fathom Meredith doing something so stupid.

"UPS," Don says. "Wrapped up in women's clothes. Dresses for Marie. Things like that."

"Why?" I ask.

"Why what?" Marie replies.

"Why y'all? Why the mail?"

"For safekeeping," Don says. "I put it in the security box when it comes in."

"As you've already said," I reply. There's something reverberant in the way he says it, though. "What's the money for?"

Most people believe that lying is a straightforward thing, that it's simply a matter of uttering a believable untruth and repeating it, and that all you have to do is keep your distorted facts straight long enough until the more honest parts of you just die off or forget. But lying's more than that. It's a way of being—an art. It's a whole approach to life that requires disconnecting yourself from mutual reality and viewing your fellow humans either as implements or inferior forms of intelligence. Which is why few people are made for it.

"We don't know," Marie lies.

These two couldn't call in sick to work without breaking out into hives.

"Bullshit," I say.

"We've told you everything we know," Marie says.

"You ever notice how her eyes squinch up in the middle when she lies?" I ask Don.

Don examines the tell. She scowls at him and then scowls at me.

"I think we're done here," Marie mutters, standing up and pretending to clean up our breakfast.

"Might as well tell me, Don," I say. "You know I'm going to find out anyway."

Don gets up to follow her and swallows. Hard.

"Don..."

"We're not supposed to," he says, almost in a whisper.

"He doesn't know anything!" Marie says, very much not in a whisper.

"Marie," he says with his hands on her shoulders. "We have to..."

If I knew what they were about to tell me, I wouldn't be wearing such a victorious smirk. As I listen, my feet go numb from the outside in. My boots might as well be glued to the floor.

The money is for a little girl. A little girl born just over two years ago. Meredith gave her up for adoption not long after she was born. I'm the father.

The money is supposed to be for our daughter's private school, her pony, her first car, her college, her whatever else her heart desires. The adoptive parents don't know about the money, they say, but it's there, and when the time is right, Don and Marie are to deliver the funds per Meredith's instructions. They don't know where Meredith's getting it. About that, I believe them. What I don't believe is them telling me they don't know anything about the girl—where she lives, the names of her new parents, not even if the girl's still in Texas. Meredith never told them, they say. They're just supposed to handle the cash.

I call them fucking liars. The fucking liars respond by telling me they're not fucking lying. It's a pointless exchange that doesn't net me anything but more rage, so I apply said rage to the remaining buffet of fixings, flipping over their shitty new table and sending diced onions and cheddar and charred barbacoa everywhere. And when they just sit there with their stupid mouths hanging open refusing to tell me where my daughter is, I scream. I scream as loud as I can, forgetting that my voice can't scream anymore. I do it anyway. I kick bowls across the room. I throw a plate that shatters on the bookcase where my fireplace used to be. And when these and other acts of tantrum still don't get them talking, I yank their Christmas tree out of its holder, throw it across the room, and stomp on it. Stupidly, Don tries to stop me.

I toss him to the floor like he was a corn tortilla. Maybe I punch him in the face, I don't know. I remember leaving the house and kicking the door on my way out and looking back once upon the anarchy of smushed Christmas presents and Marie's broken, stunned face. And then I'm miles away, downtown, trying to hail a cab. I must have walked the whole way.

I stand on the sidewalk outside the Mexicarte museum on 5th and Congress, heels blistered and bloody from the hike, trying to slow my breath. A young woman comes out of the museum and asks me if I'm okay. Her eyes are the color of syrup.

"Sam?"

"Yeah," I say. I've met her before. Where have I met her before?

"Want some water or something?"

"No," I say. "I want a cab."

"Don't have one of those," she smiles. "Fresh out."

We look at each other. And then I remember.

"Good to see you again," the woman says, walking back inside. A few seconds later, I see her looking out at me from her spot behind the counter in the gift shop. When my cab pulls over, I wave goodbye. She doesn't wave back.

The cabbie takes me to the airport, where I charter a private plane to Atlantis.

PART TWO

RED FLAGS

The rental place appended to the Atlantis airport has all of six cars and all of them are Tauruses. I hit Meredith's house first. The bed's made up and all the dishes are washed and put away. No sign of theft or forced entry. There's a single Tarot card leaning up against a mushy avocado on the kitchen counter—a blindfolded woman holding two swords.

I hop back over the security gate, drive to the Sheriff's, and—to my good fortune—catch Smith and Wetch during unlikely office hours.

"You motherfuckers lied to me," I say.

"You're back," Wetch says, shoes up on his desk. "Yay."

"We're not supposed to talk to you," Smith adds loudly. He's squinting at a curved computer monitor with a headset on, jerking sideways and jabbing a game controller with his thumbs.

"Don't mind him," Wetch says. "Christmas came early—new *Call of Duty*."

"Shitballs!" Smith shouts at the screen.

"And he's right," Wetch adds. "We're under orders of the most direct sort to not even gaze upon your haggard face. And yet, here you are—haggard, with your face."

Smith rips off the headset. "Fucking Russians," he says. "We're not supposed to talk to him," Smith reminds Wetch.

"Yes, Smith," Wetch sighs, "I know." He flaps his right hand at me and gets back to reading his *Maxim*. "Back to the front with you."

"Teisenberg," I say.

Smith throws his headset back on and turns away. "Never heard of her," Wetch coughs behind his magazine. There's a busty young woman on the cover pretending to talk into an old push-button phone in her underwear.

"Hawaiian shirt man," I add.

"Never heard of her, either."

"We're not supposed to talk to him," Smith warns his monitor.

Wetch dips the *Maxim*, grins, and mimes zipping his mouth.

"I'm not going anywhere. We're gonna have a conversation about y'all trying to set me up, believe me, but first we've got more urgent matters to attend to."

Wetch puts the mag down, checks the room, and keeps his voice low. "What we told you is what someone told us. How is that setting you up? And the urgent matter you're here for is the least fucking urgent thing on my list today. They'll help you with that up front."

"You know why I'm here?"

"Of course we know why you're here," Wetch scoffs. "We're detectives. Not that it was much of a challenge. I mean, there were *red flags* everywhere."

"Good one," Smith snickers, rejoining the party. "That's a good one."

"I don't... what?"

"*Red? Flags?*" Wetch throws me one of those smirks that expects you to bow to its brilliance. "Come on... It's not like it was a surprise or anything."

"Are you... Is she... Are you talking about her priors?" I ask.

"*Her* priors?" Wetch asks. "What priors? What her?"

"Her Meredith."

"Who Meredith?" Smith asks. "Your special lady friend Meredith?"

"Why are we talking about your special lady friend Meredith?" Wetch asks. "I was—"

"Would y'all stop calling her... Look, man, that's why I'm here! Do you two dipshits even know she's gone missing?"

"That's terrible," Smith says with absolute sincerity.

"Yeah, that's... No, see, I was talking about Red," Wetch says. "Your friend? You're not here for him?"

"Why would I be here for Red?"

"That's why he didn't get the flags joke," Smith tells Wetch.

Eight people witnessed the hit-and-run that transformed Chuck Tender into barely sentient dog meat. Accounts varied, but there were enough overlapping statements to narrow the number of offending vehicles down to four, and only two were a match with anything registered in county. Neither checked out. Well, not until an anonymous call came in about the submerged tail of a 90s van peeking out of a slough a couple of miles downstream from the lake. The van was registered to Red—in fact, it was the same Chevy he'd reported missing months earlier. Red's oversized prints were all over the wheel, the windshield had been recently shattered, and there were chunks of human leg—Chuck Tender's human leg—still embedded in the grill.

Smith and Wetch escort me back to the cells to see him. We can hear Red on the other side of the outer door. I can't make out a word—it's mostly howling and addled ranting. Red won't look at me; he won't look at any of us. He's too busy clutching his head as if it were on fire and pacing like a giant, red-headed possum trapped in a flaming box.

"Been like this since yesterday," Wetch says, leaning against the wall and examining his fingers.

"What the fuck's wrong with him?" Smith asks me.

"He needs his medicine," I say. "Call his wife, for fuck's sake. She's got it."

"Not his wife," Wetch says. "She just lives with him. Or did."

"What the fuck difference does it make? He's got brain damage, man! Call her!"

"We gave him aspirins," Smith says.

"We did call her," Wetch acknowledges. "Thing is, she won't come down. Won't have anything to do with him. Sounds pretty upset, to tell the truth. So much so that she's thinking about filing a restraining order—not that he's ever getting out, mind you."

"Punched her in the face," Smith adds.

"Orbital fracture," Wetch says, studying my eyes. "Knocked her out cold. So, Rockefeller," he nods at Red. "You're all caught up with the latest gossip. You gonna spring the beast free, or what?"

Red's bail is a record—the largest ever in county. Makes sense. A human of Red's size with his history of violence who's in for murder. And slugging your tiny girlfriend after running her would-be Romeo over in a Chevy van and gibbering in tongues in court doesn't exactly say recognizance. What it says is discernible danger, that the world would benefit from having you locked up for a long-ass and likely forever time, and that maybe there's even more to where this misbehavior came from. What else could Red have taken too far?

I leave him there. On my way out, I file a missing person's report with the new deskie up front who's never heard of Meredith who tells me they can't expedite the search.

"What do you mean *can't expedite*?"

"Like, can't make it go faster—"

"Are you fucking serious?"

"Well, yeah, because see…" he reviews the form I just filled out. "Like, do you actually know she's in danger? Ain't nothing here says it. Maybe she's on vacation or something. I mean, you didn't even check this box about whether you talked with her kin. Maybe she's with kin for the Happy Holidays."

"Happy Holidays?"

"That's how you're supposed to say it now," he tells me. "On account of all the different ones? I don't know, like what we call Christmas your people call Kwanzaa? Or maybe Hanukkah or something?"

The possibility of Meredith being somewhere off-line with her family hadn't occurred to me, and it hadn't occurred to me because the last time I saw her dad was thirty plus years ago when he walked in on me and Meredith being physically attached, by which I mean her mouth being attached to my penis. Her father chased me out with a 12-gauge and shipped Meredith off two days later to the evangelical equivalent of a nunnery outside of Roanoke, Virginia. Meredith ran away a month later and never talked to her parents again. If her old bastard father is still alive, he wouldn't know shit, and if he did, I'd be the last person he'd tell.

Marie is all the family Meredith has left. Other than our daughter, that is.

I've wasted an hour and now there's Red to deal with. I tell the cop to let Butz know, to give Butz a copy of the form when he comes in next, and I get out of there fast. The Sheriff's lobby is cornered with a celebratory pagan tree with brightly wrapped presents that are just ripe for smashing.

FOR UNTO YOU IS BORN

There's only one way Meredith could make that kind of money on a regular basis. Officially or not, it would have to involve drugs, which in these parts would have to involve Teisenberg. I haul rented Taurus ass up to Steve's rehab place—the only spot I know to look for the Padre and find out more. Red's house is supposed to be an ancillary detour: grab his meds, check on Rain, find that lying-ass preacher.

Red's place is close to the Lodge, but in the uncharted bog-world downstream from the lake and just east of the highway. Unless the county has found some fucks to give about the condition of its throughways to nowhere, the roads out near Red's are still a bunch of potholes strung together in a patchwork of trails that twist around and wither into meandering tracks that peter out into one suspicious body of water or another, like something from *Children of the Corn*, except without Linda Hamilton and there ain't no corn. It's an ideal situation for a man whose priorities don't include being easily found. Pre-retirement, Red bought a thousand-plus acres of used-up scrabble from Beau Berkey, nearly all of it mowed down and logged a half century back, which is why it's an absolute vegetive mess of shaggy second-growth trees. No wonder this is where our version of Bigfoot is said to live.

Red's house is tucked into a grotto of loblollies and slash pines, and I wouldn't be able to see the damn thing through them if it weren't for the lights being on and the house being so ludicrously enormous. The square footage is normal, but Red had the house designed to fit his personally oversized proportions. Everything's a good foot and a half higher than where you'd expect—windows, light switches, outlets, kitchen and bathroom counters. The front door must be twelve feet high to the top.

Rain opens the door and I nearly gag when I see her face. The upper left is a swollen wreck, that eye all the way shut. The colors are splotched and unusual, like a preschooler's fingerpaint. Rain turns away blankly and waves me in. The inside of the house smells like sage, tobacco, and sex. She shuffles out of the room, turning the corner into the bedroom. I stay where I am a couple of feet inside the cavernous entryway. What used to be a citadel of bachelorhood has been transformed into a postmodern fuckery of coziness. There's nary a pizza box in sight, and no indication of Red's signature boulder-sized beanbag. Instead, there's a chocolate-colored Italian sectional, brushed metal tops on the counters, custom table and chairs made of polished cypress, cork and stained concrete for the floors, and Native American appurtenances everywhere: footlong feathers, bleached bones, drums, multi-pronged antlers and horns, paintings of braves on horseback and deer and buffalo and tranquil, pastel villages...

"I'm here for his meds," I call to Rain.

"I know," she says. The words come out muffled, probably because part of her face is broken.

I wait on the leather sectional. Centered on the coffee table is a framed black-and-white of two straight-faced Native women in traditional dress with sad, inscrutable eyes. The younger one cradles an intricate hand-woven basket. The elder has a jagged scar down her neck.

"My Eeka and her Eena," Rain sniffles, shuffling back into the room. She plops down next to me with a bulging paper bag.

"Your mom's people. Out near Anadarko, right?"

"Red tell you that?" she asks, picking up the photo. I try not to look at her face.

"You did. That day at Steve's grave."

"That right," she nods, and sets the picture down like it were an egg made of glass. "I've been having a hard time... remembering stuff." She picks up a Topomatic roller from the table and pulls out a baggie of loose tobacco from a pocket in her even looser skirt.

"Want one?" she asks, rolling a smoke.

I shake my head. "Can't stay."

"That's my grandma there, and that's her mom—my great-grannie," Rain says while she rolls the cigarette. "Never got to meet her. She's the one who started the quest. You know, for our village—the Caddo one out there? The one I never found. That I was supposed to."

"Red told me."

"I asked him to."

"Rain, I'm sorry about..." I don't know what to say, but apparently it involves gesturing at her messed-up, puffy face. She turns away.

"Me, too," she says. "Me and Red were trying to find a way to bail you out, but Red's money is tied up all weird and... But we were trying. He kept telling them they had the wrong man, but they wouldn't listen. I'm glad you got out quick anyway," she says, squinting her good eye around the room. "Red didn't like me smoking in here."

"Probably don't have to worry about that no more."

"Probably not."

I point to the bag. "Meds?"

She opens it to show me. Orange bottles with white lids and barely legible labels, Ziplocs marked in cursive sharpie—some with dried leaves and berries, others with earth-tone powders and skinny twigs.

"Instructions are on that," Rain points to a piece of folded-up yellow paper. "The detective says they probably can't give Red the herbs, though, on account of them not being, you know, official. But he's gonna see what he can do. Red needs all that stuff. He goes sorta bonkers without it."

"What detective?"

"The nice one from the hospital," Rain says, tucking a clump of hair behind her right ear. She closes the bag and places it on the table in front of us."

"He told you I was coming?"

"Called a half hour ago. Been checking on me regular since, you know..."

"Is that right?" I ask, not thinking to hide my wariness.

"Is something wrong?"

"No, I was just talking to him at the station. He's who told me about Red and Chuck. And you... I didn't know, Rain."

Rain looks away and takes another long drag on her smoke. "I was gonna file one of those restraining orders, but then that detective said maybe there's, you know, no need and stuff. Said the only person who could afford to bail him out is you and... You ain't gonna bail Red out, are you?"

I can't bear the way she looks when she asks it. "Of course not. I mean... Hell, even if I wanted to, I wouldn't. I probably couldn't afford it, anyway. But he does need those meds, so..."

"Yeah," she says curtly.

I stand up. "And I should probably get back there before it gets too late..."

"Okay," Rain says, looking down. "Sure." She doesn't hand me the meds.

"So, I should probably..." I say, pointing at the bag. Then I realize it isn't that Rain is ignoring me, it's that she can't see anything out of that beat-up eye.

"Everybody thinks I'm stupid," she says, looking at the photo of her family.

"I don't think that."

"I knew what I was getting into," Rain waves absently at the room and turns her good eye to face me. "I'm not dumb. People think I am, but I'm not. I mean, maybe I didn't know what I was getting into at first, but there were signs, even in those first weeks I was with him. Early enough to do something about it. But I stayed anyway, not because I didn't know better, but because… by the time I knew it, I was already in love. Folks told me I was crazy to shack up with him. Even Steve warned me."

"Warned you how?"

"He'd been looking after Red before I showed up," Rain says, holding her skirt as she recrosses her legs. "I mean, Steve didn't actually do it himself, but he made sure these home health people came by a couple times a week to take care of him and then Steve would come by, too, to visit. So, he knew. About Red's waves. Like, sometimes the waves are big and far apart, other times Red goes from happy to angry in minutes. Crazy angry. You ever been around when he's like that?"

I nod. It's not on accident I haven't seen him in so long.

"You get used it," she says quietly. "Because if you weather the storm? On the other side is the sweetest, calmest man you'd ever meet. Smart, too. Thoughtful. So you just have to… just have to know when it's okay to let him sleep and when to wake him up, make him eat something, all that. When to push, when to pull. When to keep quiet…" She stares at the smoke from her cigarette, which struggles up into the rafters like an anxious ghost.

"Did Red ever… do anything like this before?"

She shakes her head. "Just yelling. But more, recently. Been getting worse. Pushed me around a couple times, but not as rough as this time."

Red could just about throw me through a wall and I've got a good hundred pounds on Rain. I sit back down and go to put a comforting hand on her shoulder. Rain doesn't catch sight of it until the last moment. She jerks away in animal fear.

"Hey..." I say, scooting back with my hands up. "You're okay, Rain. It's okay..."

She grabs her ruined face with both hands and shakes her head and weeps into her palms and shivers—a whole body shiver from her cute nose to her sockless, diminutive toes. And that's how it is for a long time, with me trying to keep the right amount of distance and struggling to say something tender and unstupid.

I check the clock. "Can I get you something before I go?" If I stay any longer, I'll have to look for the Padre tomorrow.

She wipes her face and doesn't reply.

"Glass of water, maybe?" I suggest, walking to the side of the room that serves as their kitchen. The counter is salvaged teak and four feet off the floor. German appliances everywhere.

"Maybe some tea?" she replies quietly. "I like tea at night."

"Sure," I say, and put the kettle on. "Got any coffee? Maybe I can take some for the road."

She shakes her head. "Red didn't like it. Might have some caffeinated tea, though…" She comes over to the cavernous pantry and digs around, emerging a minute later with a transparent bag of dark green leaves.

"This is from India," she says. "Steve got it for me."

We make a pot of it. It tastes like bark and cloves and black pepper and it doesn't do shit to wake me up.

"You look tired," Rain says.

"I'll go after this cup," I say, not wanting to go anywhere. The last couple of days run together in a vague, backwards processional, each muddy scene more exhausting than the last. Me and Rain head to the sectional, which grows less uncomfortable by the second.

"I'm tired, too," she says, going cross-legged and blowing on her tea. "Been packing all day. It's back to Oklahoma for me…"

"Oklahoma?"

"Can't stay here. Can't even take that car Red got me. He said it was mine, but he never did put it in my name…"

"Just take it, Rain. Nobody'll fault you for it."

She shakes her head. "I'll just take the bus or something. Mail some stuff back to my mom's."

"Oh, for fuck's sake," I say. "I'll get you a car."

She looks over her tea distrustfully. "I wasn't... You don't have to do that."

"Well, I want to. I haven't done shit for anybody yet. Will you let me get you something before I'm all the way broke again?"

She thinks about it and gives me the slightest of nods.

"Thank you," I say, downing the tea and standing to go. "What you want? Camaro? A truck? Another Caddy? Just give me a call and tell me what you want."

"Wow," she says, looking up at me. "That would help so, so much. Then it wouldn't be like I'm going home a failure. Not as much, anyway."

"Don't say that."

"It's okay. It's true," Rain says without any charge whatsoever. "Only reason they sent me down here was to find that place out there and I failed. Most of em thought I'd mess it up, but my grandma said *No. Rain's the one. She can do it.* Well, she was wrong."

"Tell em Red stopped you. Which he did, right? Come back next year. Try again."

Her smile is grateful and also sad.

"Doesn't have to be over, Rain."

"Maybe I would try again," she says, looking down. "If that was all there was to it. That village is one thing, but they'll never forgive me for messing the thing up with Steve."

It's 7:55 and my legs are feeling the strain. "What thing with Steve?"

"I told them too early. Got their hopes up before we worked it out. But that's how I am sometimes—talk, talk, talk—especially when I'm excited. Used to drive Red crazy."

"What, that thing with the Berkey Foundation? Native species and stuff? I heard Steve was working with the Caddo Nation. Or wanted to."

"He was—through me. Like, I was kinda this middle person, you know? One of my cousins is a rep for the Nation—Anadarko region. It doesn't matter now. The whole thing fell apart because I had this plan lined up with Steve, but I didn't double check with Red before I told my people, and when Red found out... Well, like I said, the plan just sort of blew up in my face. Steve's, too."

"I still don't know what you're talking about," I say. "Or what Red had to do with it."

"The land," she says, looking at me funny. "I'm talking about the land. You know, the donation? Steve and Red's land donation?"

"They were gonna give land to the Caddo?"

"Well, Steve was all set on it. It's the Red part that went wrong."

"Land for what? Like that place outside of Nacogdoches?"

Steve took students there on a field trip every spring—a reconstructed Caddo village of a hundred or so acres with actual mounds, thatched huts, a giftshop, everything.

"I guess, but... Steve didn't tell you?" Rain asks. "Or Red? I thought he was..."

I shake my head heavily as Rain tucks her skirt under her legs. A seriousness comes over her face now, although it's hard to tell on the pulpy side.

"Sam... The thing I messed up wasn't just a little bit of land. Steve was gonna donate it all."

It feels like somebody just switched my brain off and forgot how to turn it back on. Other than what Red owns, this whole corner of the state is mostly BI land—Steve's land. Over five thousand acres. Probably closer to ten.

"Steve was going to donate all the BI land," I say. "To the Caddo. To your people."

"Well, he wanted to."

"And Red... Steve wanted Red to give all of his land, too?"

"All but five or so acres right here where the house is," she clarifies. "Like, from the road you came in on back down to the closest slough. That's because Red wanted access to the water so he could fish whenever he wanted—you know Red and his fishing... But, like I said, the deal fell apart. It was that dang ole mineral rights thing. You know how there's supposed to be all this oil around here? Down in the ground? Red was distrustful, see. Said we had a responsibility to keep it down there, make sure there wasn't any drilling, keep the land pure and stuff. And I saw his point. Really, I did... I mean, you never know with tribe politics and everything, so much in-fighting and different camps... But I think Steve had a better point, honestly."

"What did he say?"

"Like, you can't exactly say you're giving people their land back if you make all these rules about what they can do with it. It's got to be all or nothing, Steve said. Especially since it was the Caddo's land in the first place. Our land, I mean."

It feels like all of the electrons in the room have gone still. Phase Two wasn't just about removing kudzu and putting up some memorial plaques along the highway. Phase Two was earth-shatteringly ambitious. If something like that was in the works, it would affect everything around here—tourism, business, jobs, drugs, you name it. Returning that much land to the Caddo would toss shockwaves across the state and over into Oklahoma, Arkansas, Louisiana, and beyond. Mineral rights for the oil and gas deposits would just be the beginning—a transaction of that size would be a matter of national concern. How could it even happen? All the Caddo had to gain, all the parties who'd be against them gaining it. Billions of dollars at stake. Toll roads, lumber, fishing, shopping malls, outlets, not to mention casinos. Casinos would probably mean billions more in annual traffic that now crosses over into Louisiana—a distinctly non-*bons temps rouler* for our friends to the east. And what was Steve planning for Berkey International? Shut it down? No wonder the CC has been pitching a fit. Talk about the end of Caddo County as we know it...

This is what Meredith was talking about with Steve and the Tarot cards. All that stuff about his business, about worries about his business... it wasn't woo-woo, it was real. And the more I try to box my mind around the possibilities, the more dangerous it sounds.

"Fuck," I say.

"I just thought you knew," Rain says. "You okay? You look..."

I kick off my boots and lean back on the sectional and close my eyes for a second. "I'm just gonna..."

"Sure," Rain says. "Go ahead. It's a lot to take in, huh?"

"You remember that day we were with the Padre?" I ask. "At the hospital... and..."

It was in the cafeteria, all of us together, the detectives taking me away, and did I see Red and the Padre share a look, or—

WHITE FLOWERS AND FERNS

Rain's curled up next to me on the sofa, or just was. She squints around the room through one operable eye and a dark wreck of hair. On instinct, I check my zipper. Everything crotch-related seems in non-coital order and Rain's still in the same clothes she had on last night, thankfully. It's 10:37am the next morning.

"Shit!" I yank my boots on and check my cell. Still no word from Meredith or Butz or anyone else.

"What's wrong?" Rain asks, pulling back her hair. "Are you..."

"I was supposed to... Look, I've got to split."

"You crashed out," she smiles sheepishly. "Right there in the middle of us talking. I turned out the lights so you could sleep. You must've needed it bad cause you just zonked out on me."

"We shouldn't've..." I point archaically at the sofa.

"Nothing happened. I just... well, I started out on that end and I guess I just kinda made my way over to you when I was asleep. That's kinda weird, huh?"

"Well," I say, considering my past involvement with Red's girlfriends.

"Want some tea for the road? Some eggs or something?"

It's too late to catch the Padre off guard now, but it's not like burning more time is going to help anything.

"No thanks," I say. "Hey, I meant what I said about the car last night... You let me know, huh?"

She nods distantly and clutches her hands. "I'm just... what if he comes back?"

"Red's not getting out, Rain. You don't have to—"

"Not him. That other guy—the one I was talking about last night."

"Huh?"

"You don't remember? That guy in the Hawaiian shirt?"

You never know how much hair you have on your back until every last one of them decides to stand up at once. Feels like somebody rubbed a balloon on a gorilla back there.

"The one Chuckie said was following him," Rain says, wringing her hands. "The one you told the detectives about at the hospital. I saw him after that. I was telling you last night, but you must've been asleep already. Driving a Taurus, like you said. Like yours, but different colored."

"When?"

"Four or five days ago? I was coming back from shopping and he was leaving here, driving away from the house."

Red's driveway isn't wide enough for two vehicles to pass. Rain says she pulled over to let the Taurus by, and in so doing got a clear look at the driver. Hawaiian shirt with white flowers and ferns on it. Shaved head. Sitting up straighter than you'd think a person could. There was something about him that felt wrong, that made Rain's skin itch, and seeing him leave the house threw her into a panic that something terrible had happened to Red, who never wanted visitors, much less visitors he didn't know. Rain sprinted into the house to find Red watching TV in bed like normal. He said he didn't know anything about any strange man in their driveway, but the way he said it didn't feel right to Rain. Red would have known, because even on his worst days, there was a part of him that was always watchful and protective, like a sleeping animal in its den, and more than once Red had hopped out of bed in the middle of the night with his shotgun to investigate some outside sound beyond the range of Rain's detection—usually a racoon or something. That's how she knew he was lying. Red was fully awake and the stranger's car had been no more than thirty feet away from the bedroom window. So Rain pressed him on it, but the more questions she asked, the more agitated Red got, and the more irritated Red became, the more anxious and frantic Rain felt, and the two of them kept spiraling tighter and tighter like that until the last thing Rain saw was Red's arm lashing out from under the covers like a copperhead—too quick to track—and everything exploded in a flash of sharp light. When Rain regained consciousness, Red was gone.

"That's the last I saw him," she says.

"What did your detective friend say about the Hawaiian shirt man?"

"Not much. Just to let him know if he shows up again. They seemed more interested in arresting Red for what he'd done."

I look at the driveway from the open door. If Rain ever had to call for help out here by herself, she was as good as dead. It would take the cops over half an hour to arrive, and that's if they didn't get lost along the way.

"Okay," I tell her. "Grab some stuff. Let's get you out of here."

"What? But…"

"You need to get out of here, Rain. Drive down to the Sheriff's and stay there. I'll wait here for you to get your things, but then we have to go. Take the Caddy for now and I'll follow you out to the highway. From there, you drive straight to the station and don't stop for anything or anybody. You hear?"

"Yeah, but—"

"When you get there, ask for Bobby Butz. Then you tell Butz everything you just told me. Not those other guys, okay? Only Butz."

"But I was gonna—"

"Well, you ain't gonna no more. I don't know who this Hawaiian shirt dude is, but I'm pretty sure he doesn't have your best interests in mind. Now, grab a bag and let's get out of here."

Ten minutes later, we're out of the house and heading back to 59. At the intersection, Rain throws me a gawky backwards wave as she turns south toward Atlantis. I make a right and head for the Lodge.

DUBSTEP

The ample signage makes it easy to find. Both the Lodge and the Padre's church are on the same campus, a mile or two west of the highway and on the north side of Lake Atlantis with a view facing the multihued brilliance of the noon-shy sun.

I stop by the church first. It's locked. All the lights are out and there's nary a Padre in sight. I try the side door and give each portal I come across a peaceful, non-threatening knock. No answer at any of them. No hint of movement or perjury. The sign says next service is tonight at seven.

The Lodge is maybe a hundred yards across a manicured and trimmed and appropriately bushed lawn. It's a two-storied A-frame with a front face of paned glass thick enough to stop a bazooka. Inside, natural light crashes into the main room over an array of sofas, salvaged wormwood, and a stone hearth that looks pulled from a Colorado ski lodge. Two rectangular wings extend out from the primary building—one medical, one housing. The whole facility sits on top of a gradual slope maybe a hundred feet above the lake, with well-maintained trails that wind down through the pines to the waterfront beach and a newly built dock. There's a swimming area down there, too, with buoys, canoes, and decent-sized boat. That's where Guy saw the Padre and Hawaiian shirt man.

"Yo!" somebody says. It's a gangly white kid close to twenty with stringy hair hanging in his face on purpose. He's behind the front counter with a crazy sweater on—Santa riding a unicorn in space while swinging a light saber.

"Oh, snap! It's you!" he beams. "What up, Rumblefish? Steve's boy, yeah?"

"Well, not—"

"Condolences," the kid bows, solemn hands yoga'd together. "I heard you pissed on a lady cop after that funeral," he grins. "Sorry: female police officer person."

"What? No..."

"You sure?" He punches the air in front of my left shoulder. "You were tore up!"

"I'm sure, man. So, look, I'm wondering—"

"Woulda been a lot cooler if you did, am I right? I mean, not on account of it being a woman, which would not be cool. Like, not at all. I'm just talking the po po part, because, you know, fuck the po-lice! Am I right?"

"You work here?"

"In a manner of speaking," he nods proudly. "Allow me to introduce myself—I'm Dubs. At your service."

"Sam," I say. "So, Dubs—"

"Dubs is just my initials, which are WW. William Wetch, if you can believe it, but around here I go by Dubs. Either that or Dos Dubs, Dub-Dub, or just Dos. Sometimes Dubbies. Mostly Dubs, though."

"Wetch is your last name?"

"I know! Sounds like vomit, right? Which is why I'd prefer it if—"

"Dubs—"

"Correct, Dubs is the preference, but—"

"Is the Padre in?"

"Padre? Minister Menry? Pastor Eminem? We don't call him that to his face, though, on account of the real one's homophobiacal comments in the past."

"Yeah, so, where is he?"

"Shit," Dubs laughs. "He ain't here!"

"Gonna be in today?"

"Naw, man—Pastor M is gone. Not *gone* gone or *dead* gone, but gone in like what them ecclesiastical types call a sabbatical. You know, like on a long-ass sabbath?"

I try to breathe and think at the same time. "How long are we talking here?"

"Two or three months? I don't right remember, to be honest," Dubs grins. "The time part of my brain ain't what it used to be."

I feel my hopes of ever finding Meredith sneak out of the room behind me. The Padre was my best shot. My only shot. Unless Butz knows something, my leads have gone sub-zero.

"But look," Dubs whispers, glancing around the empty room. "I know y'all was friends, so I don't think he'd mind me telling you about him Mexico way. Some little town on the beach. Chocka-something. Chocka Locka? Chocka Khan, I think. Yeah, that's it."

"Who said we're friends?"

"I assumed it on account of that video of y'all at Denny's. Shiiiit... Y'all got, like, 8 million views or something! But also, like, in addition? The Minister himself told me y'all was friends before he went off and sabbaticalled. Said give you a big ole hug and this letter he wrote just for you. You know, in case you come by."

"In case I come by?"

"What he said," Dubs replies. "Want that hug now?"

"No, but I'll take that letter."

Dubs snaps his fingers. "You know, I was keeping it right up here at the desk in the event of your appearance, but seeing as how you didn't appear after a while and I myself ain't always exactly present? That letter is currently in the care of our interim manager, the one we—"

"Dubs," I clear my throat and try to keep my hands in a non-strangling position. "Look, I should have made this clear before, but I'm here for something important. Like, really important. A woman's life is probably in danger. Two women, actually. Hell, as far as I know, a whole bunch of lives are in danger. Mine included."

"Dang! For reals?"

"Yeah, so can you get me Mr. Interim Manager man up here right away, or what?"

Dubs sucks in through his teeth and looks down at the floor and shakes his head. "Oh, man," he says, disappointed. "I don't... See, that right there? You just assuming it's a man?"

"Fuck, I don't care—where is *she,* then?"

Dub places a hand on my shoulder. "When in doubt, see, it's best to say *they.* That's how it is now, you know? *They, theirs, them...* Plural, gender flexy and shit. We're all—"

I remove his hand and bite my teeth. "Them!" I say. "Where. Are. Them."

"They?"

"William..."

Dubs breathes in through his nose and looks at his watch and then double-checks the wall clock above the counter and then triple-checks the time on his phone. "Well, this boss in question don't typically come in today, but if womens are in danger and all, I should probably ring them up, huh?"

"Yes," I say. "You should."

We both stand there nodding at each other. I point to the office behind Dubs and then Dubs nods once more, tells me to hang tight, and disappears into the back. There's a quiver of incoherent mumbles followed by a minute of inexplicable silence and then Dubs returns, victorious. The boss-them is en route, he says. They'll have the Padre's letter in hand.

NO FUNNY STUFF

The dock where Guy saw the Padre and Mystery Hawaiian Shirt Man together is currently about four feet above the mud-beige surface of the lake. In Meredith's dream, Steve was a couple of miles away on the opposite shore walking into the water in this direction. You can see the conspicuous bluff of Deer Point from here and just about anywhere else on the eastern half of this miserable lake, although the adverse wouldn't be true. This cove is secluded with willows, white oak, and dogwood past flower. If you wanted to sneak out onto the lake for the purposes of dispensing with a human body, say, a place like this is where you'd set out. I look back up the trail to the Lodge when my phone starts to buzz:

> *Dont no bout car yet* [hands folded emoji, winky kiss emoji]
> *TY still thinkin*
> *That Butt guy not here???*
> *Coudnt go inside so talkd to nice one told U bout* [police officer emoji, arms held out in the "what are you gonna do about it?" emoji]
> *Detectiv*
> *Dont wanna see Red* [two eyeballs looking sideways, broken heart]

Detctev gonna put me in hotel for safe [arms held out in the "what are you gonna do about it?" again, high-five]
On hiway near Walmart
That western one its nice
I tell you room when I no and U come over? [hands folded, tongue out and one eye closed, water drops, vibrating heart, and three winky kisses]

I flew in yesterday with the ridiculous notion that me and Meredith would be on a flight back to Austin by now. Tomorrow at the latest. That she'd tell me everything—where she'd been hiding out and why, how she earned the money, and, most importantly—all about our daughter. We'd explain our situation to the adoptive parents and probably have to liquidate most of my recently acquired assets to get our daughter back. Then our new family unit—Meredith, me, and little girl makes three—would jet off to resume my beach and tacos forever fantasy, minus the girlie drinks. An aboveboard, vigorous, sober plan. No Reds, Rains, Padres, or Teisenbergs required.

When the text buzzes become an actual phone call, I know it's Rain without checking. But I'm wrong; it's an unlisted number. I almost don't pick up until I realize it's probably Butz.

"Yo," I say hopefully.

The garbled response sounds like it's swimming through a filthy rag.

"Butz? Call back! Sounds like you got a mouthful of seaweed."

Louder mumbling, but clearer. Sounds like *eyesehtihmihyuhmuh-fuh*.

"I'm out at the lake, man! I can't understand a goddamn—"

There's a burst of instantly coherent cursing. "Motherfuckin goddamn told you, man! That shit ain't work. Bitch can't hear me through this thing. Yo!" says a man who isn't Butz. "You hear me now?"

"Yeah, who's this?"

"Sam Sorrow?" the guy asks.

"Yeah! Who the fuck is this?"

"Don't worry bout that. You worry bout ten million dollars! Worry bout ten million dollars or your bitch gets got, you hear?"

My face turns cold. Out in the lake, even the fish have stopped swimming.

"Uh… I think you got the wrong number, buddy."

"Ain't no…" he pauses. "You said you was Sam Sorrow?"

"Yeah, but—"

"The half-Canadian one?"

"What?"

"Man, you know Meredith or what? Like, know-know, you know?"

I swallow so hard my lungs hurt.

"Yeah, I know Meredith."

"Okay, then. Then I got—Wait a sec, what's up with your voice, cuz?"

"Who gave you this number?" I ask, looking up at the Lodge for the answer.

"Never mind that! What you need to mind is ten million, you hear?"

"And why's that?" I don't know why I'm stalling; it's just something I inherited from TV. Clues in the background, the chance he'll give something away…

"Boy, we got yo witch," he laughs. "You can't talk right and listen good, too?"

"You mean Meredith?" There's a quiet clang and mumbles passed back and forth on the other end. There's definitely more than one person involved.

"I'm done playin, yo. She worth that money or not?"

"Sure. Of course…"

"Alright then."

"No problem, man. Just tell me how to spell it, okay?"

"Spell... what you mean—"

"Like, with a Z or an S or what? And is *burg* with a *u* or an *e*? I mean, a name like Teisenberg could go all sorts of ways, and if I'm gonna cut this check—"

"Man, fuck you! Ain't nobody say nothing bout no Teisenberg!"

"Quadruple negatives aside, I'm gonna have to post-date anyway, because I don't get paid until—"

"Ah, you funnin now," the man snorts. "I see, I see... You think this is fun-n-games. How bout I send you one of her lil fingers? How'd you like that, Mr. Fun?"

"I wouldn't like that at all."

"Keep on funnin and see. Might make it two fingers for you, Mr. Half-Ass Canadian. Might make it a whole finger basket if'n you don't deliver that cash tomorrow."

Either this is the real deal or it's amateur hour here at the Berkey Foundation. If it's Teisenberg or one of his flunkies, I should probably stop fucking around. On the other hand, I'm getting amateur vibes here, which means it's a scam.

"Cash?"

"Now you listenin," he replies. "Cash. That's right. Ten million American goddamn cash in dollars. And tomorrow. We good?"

"Yeah, we good. So, you want 1000s? 5000s?"

"You stupid? They don't make them no more! Bring them hunnerts, son—ones with Rich Franklin on em."

"100s? Are you... What am I supposed to do, roll it in on a schoolbus or something? That's like... a hundred thousand of them. Even if I—"

"Man, ain't no hundred thousand—"

"Dude, have you actually seen ten million dollars cash in person? It's not exactly portable."

"That ain't my problem, son! That ain't—"

"Yeah, but maybe it is? Like, I can bring it, but you gotta be able to haul it out, right?"

"Hold on a sec," he says. Background mumbles ensue. "Goddammit," he says after a long, math-filled pause. "God-shittin-dammit. That's a hunnert thousand of them bitches. How is we supposed to... Yo, we gonna hafta call you back, son. I gotta... You better pick up, hear?"

After he hangs up, I discover I've walked all the way back up to the parking lot without remembering one inch of the beautiful trail behind and below me. I'm standing next to my rented Taurus, catching my breath from the climb and waiting for imperatives to follow.

But something's off. First of all, I'm not standing where I parked. Second, the Taurus I rented was teal, I think, so it must be that one over there. The Taurus I'm next to right now is champagne-colored and way, way cleaner. I can't put it together. Not even when I hear him behind me.

TEISENBERG

It's all the way dark, the kind of dark that makes it difficult to remember what color was like, the kind that makes you wonder if maybe you're blind. The back of my head feels like it was hit with something medieval and spiky. My mouth is gagged and partially open. My wrists are pinched together in my lap with zip ties.

As my eyes adjust, I see him outside the car—thirty feet away, standing perfectly erect, bald, and in a recently pressed shirt ornamented with giant oranges and alligator heads, their sizes nonsensically relative to each other—the oranges are three times the size of the gator heads. The more I try to focus, the more it feels like somebody's stabbing me in the eyes with a fork. Mystery Man is looking down at the ground, maybe at a tombstone. We're at the Hillcrest Cemetery.

This part of the graveyard hasn't changed much since my Visigoth days with Red. I know it like my proverbial hand parts, mostly from those gropey nights with Sonya a little ways up the hill. Even with my hands bound like they are, I could ghost any flip-flop wearing pursuant in under a minute. If only I could slip out of the car.

Surprisingly, the door opens with a muted click. No sign he's heard a thing. The wind is up a little bit in the trees, which helps. I edge my right boot out until I feel the damp smoosh of grass beneath the heel, but even that worm slow movement makes my skull feel like somebody's ratcheting it with a come-along. I bite the side of my tongue and tighten my core, gradually turning my left leg to join its twin outside. I ease the door a little wider, take a big breath, get ready to Usain Bolt my ass downhill, and—

The seatbelt snaps me back with a yelp. No, not quite a yelp—it's more like the falsetto a kid might make if grabbed from beneath the bed by a clown. Hawaiian shirt man turns to look at me with disappointed eyebrows. I wave.

He walks over to the driver's side, gets in, and hands me a bottled water from behind his seat. It's Dasani. Then he loosens my gag, holds the bottle out in front of me, makes the *shh* gesture with his index finger, and nods for me to take the Dasani and drink. I show him my zip-tied hands and shrug. He exhales through his nose, twists off the cap, and fits the bottle just so into my cupped, pinched hands. I guzzle it down like a parched gerbil.

"Dasani is tap water," I hold up the bottle. "From Atlanta, Georgia."

He looks out on the cemetery in composed silence. The water tastes better than water.

"Just, you know, FYI," I tell him.

He glances at his watch and turns his face away. There aren't too many places in this part of the cemetery to covertly park a vehicle without somebody noticing. We're somewhere close to Steve's grave and only spaces away from where I douche-parked Blue at Steve's funeral. I try to feel the back of my head over my right shoulder with my tied-up hands. It doesn't work.

"What'd you hit me with—a halberd? Can't open my eyes all the way."

He examines my eyes with something resembling concern if concern was purely academic and adorned with magic frond eyelashes. I can almost feel a breeze when he blinks. He tilts my head and probes the back of my skull with his fingers—gently, he probably thinks, but it feels like a rhino is stomping my head in football cleats. Then he inhales and turns once more to look outside.

His cellphone buzzes from the heart pocket of his Hawaiian shirt. He pulls it out and thumbs back a brief response. Five seconds later, a pair of lights flash on about a hundred yards away on the other side of the cemetery and then lurch toward us in a roundabout manner. It takes me a while to understand that the lights are the kind designed to assist motor vehicles through darkness. The headlights bob along the rough track that perimeters Hillcrest on its eastern edge, and only when the car gets to about fifty feet away can I tell it's an SUV—a polished, off-white, giant SUV. A Lincoln Navigator. Like the one that picked up Meredith from the Caddo Estates.

The SUV shuts off in front of us, but the high beams stay on. Whoever's inside wants a good look at us. My chauffeur gets out and stands next to his door, facing the SUV in silhouette like a tropical deity haloed with light. After a second or two, he bends back into the car and squints at me.

"You want me to get out?"

His left eyebrow raises. Translation: *Yes, stupid.*

I get out, unbuckling my seatbelt this time. My body feels unusually alert and I almost forget about the pain in my head. Maybe this is what happens right before the end. You climb the gallows, look out over the crowd, nod to the hangman, and your mind goes calm and perfectly clear, like a samurai. At the same time, I feel like a samurai who might shit himself.

One of the back doors of the SUV slowly opens. And then, as natural as rain falls from the East Texas sky, an angel descends.

I don't recognize her at first. She's older, but the essentials are all there. Her once soft-around-the-edges, Rubenesque figure has evolved into a more potent version of itself, advanced in feminine power. The same exquisite skin. The same intelligent eyes that used to turn me upside down. The same curves that turned me right-side up again. It's my first love, Sonya Tyson.

She gives the driver a casual backward wave and the SUV lights shut off, leaving all of us to adjust in the charnel dark. Then she points at my hands and Hawaiian shirt guy pulls a large knife and cuts the zip ties away so quickly that I hear the click of the plastic hit the ground before I can flinch. Then he walks over to the SUV and climbs into the front passenger seat.

Sonya approaches slowly, looking me up and down with a short, perplexed smile. Then she opens her arms to embrace me. The hug feels warm and familiar and dangerous.

"I could kill you," she laughs in my ear.

"Please don't."

"Not what I meant," she replies, patting me on the chest and looking me in the eyes. "Octavia was supposed to give you my number and you were supposed to call that number."

"Octavia..."

"My daughter? Runs the Bestern?"

"Oh. That Octavia."

"What's with the voice?" People usually look at my throat when they ask that question, but Sonya's gaze stays with my eyes. She's dressed for business: knee-high leather boots and an off-white, ruffle-cuff, wool sweater dress. Her whole ensemble oozes money and professionalism and class. I look like an extra from *Hee Haw*.

"I underdressed," I say.

"You haven't changed a bit."

"Neither have you. Still smell like oranges and vanilla."

"You don't."

"Stinky Sam... Isn't that what you used to call me?"

"No," she says. "You were always Bobby to me."

I move my wrists around until they start to feel in working order. Hawaiian shirt guy and Sonya's driver just sit there watching us like a pair of sleepy, disinterested detectives. Sonya walks over to a nearby grave and I follow her. She kneels down and places a palm on the mud.

"We didn't end on the best terms," she says.

"That's putting it mildly," I say behind her. Our breakup wasn't half as ugly as the one I had with Marie, but that's not saying much.

"I was talking me and Steve," she points to his tombstone.

"Oh, him," I say. "Sonya, where's Meredith?"

"Nice segue."

"I'm sorry... *Hey, how's it going? Yeah, me too.* Where's Mere?"

"How should I know?"

"No use lying if you're gonna kill me."

"Bobby..." she stands up. "Really?"

I show her my recently tied hands and point to the back of my still aching skull and then to the guys in the SUV.

"Don't mind them," she sighs and gives the driver another wave. "Walk with me."

Sonya leads us up the cemetery hill, stepping around the stones and the suspect indentations that separate them. We wind our way up the slope until we reach a spot of flat grass. We're deep in the Blacklantis portion of the graveyard now, surrounded by markers with illegible inscriptions packed with lichen and moss. A couple of lights are on in nearby houses, yellow from decades of smoke. Most of the houses are just shanties or cabins in various stages of disrepair, attached to tiny yards supplemented with rusting cars and abandoned appliances. I don't remember it being this run-down. Then again, whatever time I spent here as a teen didn't involve me paying much attention to anything else other than Sonya. I only came here then for Sonya, and she's the reason I'm here now.

"Don't get the wrong idea," she says, sitting down and crossing her legs.

"We're not going to make out? Not going to let me feel you up under your Sade t-shirt?" She loved the shirt from that concert and I loved what was under it.

Sonya rolls her eyes and holds out the ring for me to appreciate. It's more like a finger belt attached to a ten-carat rock—a rock with its own supporting cast of diamonds.

"Not bad," I say, sitting down next to her. "I used to have one of those."

"So I heard," Sonya says to a neighboring stone. "And to Marie Taylor, no less."

"Marie Beis now. New husband and all."

"I've always been curious about your thinking with that, Bobby. I mean, getting married to Meredith's sister. You know, like, I'd think you'd marry the sister you fucked around on me with, as opposed, say, to her goody-two-shoes, Jesus-loving big sister…"

"Not exactly how it went."

"You didn't marry the girl you cheated on me with's sister?"

"No, I… You're the one who left me, as you made perfectly—"

"I'm the one who—"

"I know you're Teisenberg, okay?"

At first, she laughs. Then she feigns disbelief and then mock offense. Then she waves it away like it were nothing more than a gnat between us.

"I'm glad you think it's funny," I say.

"Way to spoil the reveal, asshole."

"A meth lord? Really?"

"Oh, don't believe everything you hear."

"You're not a meth lord?"

"I'm no more a meth lord than you are a…" she looks at me, "a somebody who takes baths."

"I take baths. Occasionally."

"Exactly."

"Original name, by the way."

"Wasn't my idea. That show is so overrated—"

"You know what that shit does to kids, right?"

"What I know," she says, "is that nobody ever talks about what drugs do to kids until those kids have names like Chad and Becky and Joe Bob."

"Don't pull that—"

"Where was your outrage when the government was feeding crack to black folks, Bobby?"

"It's not like I'm pro-crack, Sonya!"

"As if your hands are so fucking clean..."

"Hold on, now," I say. "I'm an alcoholic who can't keep his dick in his pants. I'm not some murderous drug dealer. I'm not a..."

"Neither am I. Never murdered a person in my life."

"Oh? What do you call it? Murder-adjacent?"

"Kind of like all that money you just inherited?"

"Money? What money?"

"Steve's money. You know every last penny of it's dirty, right?"

"Bullshit," I say. "Steve would never—"

"You're right," she says, dusting her hands off. "Steve would never. Never, never, never. But don't kid yourself. He knew how Beau made his fortune. Not that he had the balls to do anything about it."

"Nice," I say, standing up. "Real nice, Sonya. Well, good seeing you. You look great. Good luck with the whole meth thing, okay? And don't mind walking me out. I know the way."

"Sit down," she says softly. "I've got something to tell you."

"That you know where Mere is..."

"No, I don't," she says, looking away. "Yet. That's why you're here. So we can find her. Together."

"You kidnapped me to—"

"I didn't kidnap you—"

"No, you just had nightmare Magnum PI do it!"

"Look, do you want to hear my proposal, or not?"

"Proposal?" I squawk. "Proposal? Wait... Teisenberg, meth scourge of Caddo County, has a proposal for me? Let me guess... Uh, Mere's been transporting for you again and she, oh, I don't know... disappeared with a shipment or something? Millions of dollars? And I'm supposed to help bring her back so you can give her a talking to?"

"It's not like that."

"Right. Which part?"

Sonya inhales quickly and looks up the hill. "You know, with your help, in three years all the drug trade in Caddo County will cease to exist. Every last bit of it. Meth, heroin, oxy, you name it."

"Marijuana?"

"Fuck no. Life's hard enough as it is."

"You're telling me the Tyson family is going legit? That this is what the whole meth thing is about?"

"Something like that, yeah."

"And you've consolidated enough power to make a multi-million-dollar business just... what, go poof?"

"You haven't heard the stories?"

I look back down the hill toward the SUV and Steve's grave. I can't see either from here.

"I heard about your meeting with Steve," I say. "That's why you killed him, huh? Steve found out it was you and you just fucking had him killed..."

"No," she says, focused intently on one of the nearby shacks. "I didn't."

The back porch of the house has fallen away into a heap of rotting lumber, cinder blocks spilled out into the yard like cheap dice. The door is boarded up and missing its knob. There's not a window that isn't broken or covered up with plywood or cardboard, and yet there's a light on inside. A thin stream of smoke rises out of the partially tarped roof.

"Steve didn't find out about the drugs," she says. "I told him. And, believe it or not, he was on board with my plan. And you're a bigger fool than I remember if you think I had anything to do with his death."

"Holy shit," I say, finally recognizing what she's looking at. "That's your house."

"No."

"I used to wait for you..." I look at the piece of earth all around us. "Somewhere around here, right? Sometimes for over an hour. You'd have to wait til your mom fell asleep and then you'd crawl out of that window in slow-mo, right there, butt first."

"That's not my house, Bobby," she says. "My house is a five-thousand square foot villa on over a hundred fenced acres up at the lake. Just up the shore from where Steve built the Lodge, in fact."

"Well done. Miss Ida must be proud."

She keeps her eyes on the shack in front of us. No, not *at*, but somewhere inside, as if reading something written there in the wobbly gelatin of time. "I think she is," Sonya says.

"And I doubt she lives in a shanty anymore."

"She doesn't live anywhere. She's dead."

"Shit, I'm sorry."

"Me too," she says, turning back to me quickly. "Look, I get it. From the outside, why wouldn't you think I had something to do with Steve's murder? And Meredith disappearing. But it wasn't me or my people, I can promise you that."

"Great," I say.

"And we were getting so close to finding out who killed him, and now—"

"We? Who we?"

"Never mind that part. Just listen: Steve and I were close. Me and Meredith are close, too. She's not just an employee. She's... Look, I shouldn't have said that about Steve not having the balls to do what it took. We just had different approaches, is all. But we were both working for the same goals. And all the things Steve was trying to do to make it better around here, well, I was trying to do them, too. Help him, even. We were always close, you know. But he just couldn't..."

"Why'd you say that about his money?"

"Beau's money? What, you think he made his fortune turning trees into toilet paper?"

"What's that have to do with Mere?"

"I didn't say it did," Sonya replies with a heavy breath.

"Okay, I'll play... If it's not Teisenberg who kidnapped Mere, who did?"

"Who said anything about kidnapped?"

"Some loser who called me yesterday," I say. "Demanded ten big ones in cash or else—"

"What?" Sonya stops me with alarm. "Why didn't you tell me?"

"Tell you what? And when? You just now—"

"When did this happen?" she asks. "Kidnapping?"

"Yesterday, like I said! Right before your Boogaloo Boy knocked me out and—"

"Why would I have a Boogaloo Boy working for me?"

"I don't—"

"How much did they ask for?"

"Ten big! And in cash, if you can—"

"Ten thousand?" she laughs. "What kind of shit ransom is that?"

"I didn't say ten thousand! Ten million!"

"You said ten big, Bobby. *Big* means a thousand. Jesus Christ, you're like the walking definition of new money."

"What's a million, then?"

"*Rocks* or *Ms*," she says. "Like, *ten rocks* or *ten Ms*..."

"Okay, ten Ms."

"Ten million in cash? What do they want you to do? Bring it in on a bus?"

"That's what I said!"

A car tries to start up in a nearby driveway. We both turn toward the sound. The motor sputters and dies a couple of times before eventually laboring off in a steady chug. It's almost first light now and the world is struggling to wake up for work.

"Okay," Sonya thinks. "What did they sound like? Did you recognize their voices?"

"Why would I—"

"Right," she says quickly. "You haven't been around much."

"No, but... Maybe one of those white kids who tries to sound black? What's that called, a wigg—"

"Nope," Sonya holds up a hand. "We don't even say that."

"Well, they were supposed to call back, when... Hey!" I pat my body down for a cellphone that isn't there. "My phone!"

Sonya has her hand on her mouth, trying to think.

"My phone's gone!"

"It's not gone," she says, waving for me to follow her down the hill. "Vajzh has it. Come on."

VAJZH

Down at Steve's grave, the sun labors up indifferently. Sonya walks back over from the SUV, outfitted now in a pair of cat eyed DGs that would make Eartha Kitt bust out a meow.

"Vajzh?" I ask her.

"Vajzh," she says, handing me my phone.

"What kind of name is that?"

"Who knows. Look at that text thread."

My phone has never been as clean as it is right now, not even when I pulled it from the box. I open the thread. It's full of the man named Vajzh pretending to be me and misspelled mandates from the kidnappers, as well as photos of Meredith: Meredith tied to an office chair, Meredith's hands bound behind her, Meredith with a t-shirt pulled across her mouth...

"Fuck!" I yell, kicking the bumper on Vajzh's champagne Taurus.

"It's okay, Bobby! Vajzh set it up and—"

"Fuck!" I yell again, because I might've broken half of my toes.

"Bobby, she's okay, she's—"

"Fucking okay? Is tied to a fucking chair okay?"

"No," she insists, grabbing my arm. "Look! Look what he showed me..."

These are the details that an amateur would miss: the normal color of Meredith's wrists and hands, the absence of tension on the shirt around her face, the bold look in her eyes...

"See that look?" Sonya asks. "What does that tell you?"

"That she doesn't like being tied up? What the fuck, Sonya?"

"No. *Look...*"

I've been in love with those eyes for two-thirds of my life. I'd know Meredith's icy pissed-off glare from three miles off in a fog.

"So fucking what? Why wouldn't she be pissed?"

"As opposed to being afraid. That's the point," Sonya says, scrolling to one of the other pics. "And here: she's hydrated. Look at that skin."

"So she fucking moisturizes, Sonya, I don't see—"

"Don't you get it? They're going out of their way not to hurt her. Extra careful, even. Meredith's barely tied to that chair!"

Vajzh has a theory, Sonya tells me, and it goes like this: The kidnappers found out about me and Meredith and they went for an easy score. What they didn't know was who Meredith worked for, but at some point she must have told them.

"And?"

Sonya laughs. "And let's just say that Teisenberg has a reputation. He's a butcher. Specifically, he likes to cut off heads."

"You cut off heads?"

"Of course not," she says impatiently. "Bobby—"

"I don't... If they're so fucking worried about Teisenberg, why wouldn't they just let Mere go?"

Sonya looks back over at her driver and takes a long breath in. "Pondering the criminal mind is a waste of time, but here's my guess: Meredith told them she works for me and they realized just how bad they'd fucked up. But that doesn't mean they can just let her go. The heads thing is just a rumor we spread to illustrate just how not-fucking-around Teisenberg is, so these guys know how much worse it'll be if they hurt her. You see? Even so, these bozos *need* that money now just to get out of Dodge safe, and they need it quick before I find them."

"Before Teisenberg removes their heads."

"Right."

"That's a lot of guesswork."

"Maybe. Point is that Meredith is safe and we need to do this trade quick before that changes. Vajzh set it up for early tomorrow morning. In with the cash, out with the girl."

"One problem," I say.

"Oh?"

"I don't have anything close to ten million dollars. I sorta... spent some of it back in Austin."

"The strip club," she says.

"That and the... Wait, how'd you—"

"Don't worry about the cash," Sonya says. "I got you."

"You're giving me ten million dollars?"

"I'm not giving you shit," she raises her DGs. "Like I said, I've got a proposal."

"This should be good."

"It's very good. For both of us."

"And for Mere?"

"Maybe especially for Meredith."

"And could this proposal somehow involve Vajzh negotiating these guys down to, I don't know, like only a million dollars or something?"

"That part doesn't matter," she says.

"It fucking matters to me, Sonya. I mean, was bargaining even on the table?"

"You've got to remember that these losers think they're dealing with you. To them, you're just some lovesick sucker with too much cash on hand. Cash they need, remember? What with Teisenberg after them and all."

"Same Teisenberg I'll owe ten million dollars to after I hand it over to these fuckers," I say. "That's my issue."

"Ah," she smiles. "But you're getting it all back. And I'll ensure that you do as part of our deal."

"How?"

"Vajzh," she points.

"What's that mean?"

"He'll retrieve it for you."

"And what happens to whoever these mouth-breathers are when he does?"

Sonya looks up into the bruising sky and purses her mouth. "Slap on the wrist," she says.

"I was hoping for worse."

"Didn't say what we'd slap them with."

"That's more like it. But I need to add a condition."

"Too late. Deal's already set."

"Not with them. With you."

"You're not exactly in the position—"

"Mere isn't going back to work for you. Ever. Whoever she is in your empire of sketchiness, whatever she does... Find somebody else. Deal?"

Sonya checks her watch—a mother-of-pearl Cartier, swaddled in a duvet of diamonds. She looks back over at the SUV.

"Deal?" I repeat.

"You should probably find out what she does for me first. You should ask her."

"I don't care."

"You might care if you knew. And you might also do better with Meredith in the long run if you don't try to make decisions for her. Our girl doesn't like that, in case you haven't noticed."

"Our girl—"

"But fine," she holds up a hand. "I'll add a condition of my own."

"I'm listening."

Sonya points to the phone in my hand. "That chick sending you those thirsty texts is bad news, Bobby. Keep away from her."

I look at my phone again. In addition to the thread with the kidnappers, there's dozens of one-sided, emoji-filled texts from Rain that get more suggestive and desperate by the page.

"It's not what you think," I frown. Holy shit, am I stupid...

"It's exactly what I think. Like you said, you're an alcoholic who can't keep his dick in his pants, and I'm going to need you to amend both attributes if we're going to be partners."

"I stopped drinking."

"Halfway there."

"We're going to be partners?"

"That's the idea," she says. "That's my proposal."

"So what's the catch?"

"Who says there's a catch?"

LYNN SWANN

Oh, there's a catch. It's me signing over 23% of my share of Berkey International to Sonya, which, when tallied to what she already holds in the company, will give Sonya majority control. Not to worry, she says. If I stay out of her way and agree to sign off on her decisions, my remaining portion of BI should be good for two or three million in profits every year.

I don't know much, but I know that anything that sounds too good to be true probably isn't. I'm getting fleeced, and Sonya's holding the clippers. Ten million's a lot of fucking dough, but 23% of the BI? An official cash out for those shares would double or triple that. But I've never been one to haggle. Plus: PowerPoints and windowless offices... conferences and signing paychecks... Italian suits and Neiman ties... golfing with Asian investors and taking them bass fishing at the lake... No fucking thank you. If Steve couldn't break free of that office, how the hell would I? Sonya can have it. One day of that bullshit would be a year too long.

"And what are you gonna do when you're in the big seat?" I ask, trying to sound like I care.

"Exactly what I told Steve I'd do," Sonya replies. "Start by firing every cracker in there, including those CC chumps in upper management, and replace every damn one of them with hardworking folks of the more melanated sort."

"Wait—what?"

"You heard me," she grins. "Reparations, Bobby. The blacks and browns of this county have it coming. I'm even gonna help out mulattos like yourself."

"Now there's a term you don't hear every day."

"Healthcare for families," she continues, "afterschool programs for kids, tutors, laptops, college placement programs. You dig? The BI employs close to 1000 people, and right now exactly 17 of them are black. Now you understand?" But it's not a question. It's the triumphant interrogative of a woman who isn't fucking around.

"That's what you and Steve were up to," I say. The scope of it is almost impossible to imagine. What would Caddo County be like with so many empowered black folks?

"Sort of... Steve was behind the plan, he just... Well, he wanted to take a more gradual approach. That's what we argued about."

"That and the drugs."

"The drugs were part of it," she says. "But that gradual approach? Taking all those preventative measures and calculating delays? That might've been what got Steve killed. And we're getting closer to finding out all about it..."

"Again with this *we*. Is that some Teisenberg royal we, or..."

"First things first," she says. "Be at Steve's house—your house, I mean—at 9 o'clock tonight. Vajzh will meet you there with the cash and paperwork. If we've still got a deal, that is..."

"Yeah," I say. "We've still got a deal."

"Alright, then. Get a good night's sleep. And do it at your house. I don't want to hear anything about you going over to the Bestern."

"Yeah, whatever. But look, I don't even know where this whole Mere thing is supposed to go down and what—"

"Jesus Christ, did you even read that text thread. Handoff is at Nirvana, bright and early."

A decade before anybody had heard of the band, what we called Nirvana was a clearing in the woods that had once been a functioning sulfur and gravel mine about five miles south of town. In truth, Nirvana was a death trap, and it was rumored to be the site of an old Caddo burial ground, to boot. When Cobain and company blew the lid off the early 90s, it was as if their music had been created with our weekend parties in mind—open pits and boarded-up mine shafts, spray-painted vehicles of yore, charred circles from bonfires of implausible size, machinery rusted over with tetanus, and—most notably—a ramshackle trailer packed full of discarded pillows and filthy fishing coolers stuffed with Bartles & James and Schlitz. In short, for teens with nowhere to go, Nirvana was a kind of heaven.

"That's fucking perfect," I say. "What could go wrong? Place is right out of the final scene of an 80s movie."

"Wouldn't know. My kind was never welcome there."

"Right," I say, recalling a fight we'd had about it as teens. *It ain't just for white kids,* I'd argued, because I'd been that stupid.

"And technically? Nirvana is more like something from the climax of those movies," Sonya says. "Denouements always go down in happy places—arcades, skating rinks, burger joints... Anyway, them wanting to make the exchange at Nirvana is a clue."

"To what, them not watching 80s movies?"

"They're locals," Sonya says. "Only locals know Nirvana's out there."

THAT'S HOW YOU END UP WITH YOUR HEAD CUT OFF

An hour or so later, I'm back at Steve's house, but I don't go in. I sit for a while in the cold, dead grass with my boots off and look up through the canopy of shivering pecans and let myself stop trying to figure it all out for a while. Something doesn't feel right, and it ain't just the cartoon knot Vajzh gave me on the back of my head. At some point, I lie down. When I wake up a little while later my toes are nearly numb from the December air and my rented Taurus is back in the driveway. Somebody returned it while I was asleep. Keys are in the ignition.

My phone starts ringing. It's another strange number—different from the kidnappers and Rain. Maybe it's actually Butz this time.

"Where you been, shitbird?" It's Coach, an extra dose of put-out in his voice. "Must've called you ten times yesterday!"

"Really? I—"

"I need that money!"

"Yeah, you and everybody else."

"Oh?" Coach says. "And did all of them bail your ass out? I told you I needed that cash before you split town, and then you done split town!"

"Well, I'm back."

"Good. Bring it to Martin's in ten. I'll be waiting."

"Can we maybe... I'm sorta busy right now."

"Goddammit, Bobby!" he says, his old voice straining. "Look, I got some..." His volume drops 40 decibels. "I got what you'd call a little bit of trouble. I know that kinda cash don't mean shit to you nowadays, but it would go a long, long way to getting some bad news off my ass, you hear? Help an old man out, would you? It's... it's pretty damn important."

Twenty-two minutes later, I pull up in front of what used to be Martin's. I do it not so much to alleviate Coach's distress, but mostly to delay stepping into Steve's house and because I've got hours to kill before Vajzh shows up and helps me sign over a fortune to Sonya. There's also the matter of withdrawing twenty grand from the local credit union. It's not the sort of transaction they see that often in Atlantis, which necessitates a visit to the manager's office and me having to fill out a Homeland Security document and everything. Coach is pacing outside his truck when I finally get there.

"Fucking late-ass..." he spits, checking one end of Stanley Ave and then the other. "You bring that cash?"

"What are you looking for?" I ask, checking down the street, too.

"Stop looking," he whispers tightly. And then, back at volume: "You've got the cash I asked you to bring? That you owed me?" He's enunciating way more than usual.

I hand over the wad of bills and look behind me in case Coach missed something. He throws me an agitated *shh* gesture and points to his phone, exaggerating the movements required for turning it off.

"I'll see you later, Bobby!" he shouts, wide-eyed and nodding obnoxiously.

"You too!" I shout back, going nowhere.

Coach mouths something I can't make out and moves his hands like he's twisting an invisible, greasy knob. I reply with my best *what knob?* gesture. He shakes his head in frustration, and then—in a mime not half-bad for a crotchety non-thespian—Coach conveys that it's crucial that I turn my phone off, too.

Why? I mouth.

Just do what I tell you, you stupid shit, he mouths back.

You're the stupid shit, you stupid—

Coach places his phone face-down on the driver seat of his truck and shuts the door, backing away with his hands up, as if retreating from an open box of cobras. He indicates for me to do the same.

No.

Bobby...

Why the fuck... Fine.

I turn off my phone and leave it on the dash of the Taurus, much to Coach's relief. Then he waves for me to follow him across the street.

We scramble up the cracked stairs to the raised sidewalk under the awning of what used to be Squirrely's Sport-N-Shoot, then hook left on the boarded-up corner onto Willis Street. Coach checks over his shoulder again. "You're lucky to be alive," he says, still whispering.

"Why are you whispering?"

"Jesus Christ, are you stupid!" Coach says at normal, angry volume.

"Did you even count that?" I point to the cash in his pocket.

He digs the bills out and shoves them back at me. "I didn't call you for that, dipshit!" He paces the elevated walkway and runs a wrinkled hand through his hair. "I just said that to... I just said it because... Shit, Bobby! Your phone is bugged!"

I turn back to look at the phone I can't see around the corner.

"Mine, too! I don't know how, but they did it. They can hear everything through em, even when they're turned off, which is why we gotta..." Coach waves his arms back in the direction of our vehicles as if shooing back a horde of invisible chickens.

"The fuck are you talking about?"

"Teisenberg, shit-ass! Teisenberg!"

"I don't—"

"I know, okay? I was leaving up there early this morning, getting in my truck, pulling away from my lady's house, when I hear talking just down the hill there in the cemetery. One of them voices? Unmistakably yours. Sound like a goddamn crow with emphysema. I take a look and who the fuck do I see you talking to? Holy shit, Bobby!"

"How the fuck would you—"

"I got a lady friend, okay?" Coach holds up a hand in protest. "I ain't gonna lie. She lives up there on the ridge, edge of the graveyard. Purple house with that broke-ass swing in the backyard? Shit, y'all were only, like, a hundred feet away. Why you looking at me like that?"

"You've got a black lady friend?"

"Now who's being racist? Thought you of all people would understand."

"Well, thanks for fucking telling me in time, Coach."

"I don't see how my love life is—"

"About Sonya being Teisenberg! Her being the new drug lord in Atlantis?"

Coach stops pacing for a moment and shakes his head at the sidewalk. "It ain't drugs. It's meth. Big difference. And it ain't just Atlantis, Bobby. It's the whole goddamn Ark-La-Tex. And why would I fucking tell you? Like you fucking care about us. How's I supposed to know you're gonna stick around long enough for all that other shit to happen?"

"What other shit?"

"Them trying to pin Steve on you!" Coach shouts. "Okay? And them stupid crank twins getting me involved with this bull mess! And Meredith getting herself kidnapped, and you and Teisenberg, and who the fuck knows what else!"

Coach saying Meredith's name hits me like an anvil in the mouth. Now he's chewing at least three of his fingernails at the same time.

"Meredith what?"

"I don't—"

"What," I say, index finger in his face, "Do you. Fucking. Know."

"Everything," Coach rasps. "The ransom, who's got her, everything!"

The sensation of lifting up that old bastard by his jean jacket collar and tossing him into a plate glass window happens way too fast for me to enjoy it. I go for his throat with one hand and snag his crotch with the other.

"The next words out of your mouth…"

"Let go… of my balls," Coach squeaks.

I let go but keep the hand close by.

"And throat…" he gasps.

I release his throat and move my grip back to his jacket collar. Coach heaves in and out in a high-pitched rasp.

"You've got five seconds until I put your head through this window!"

"Easy, Bobby. Easy…" he protests, holding up his hands. "Trying to help out here. I'm trying to help!"

"Doubtful. Real fucking doubtful."

"Who got you out of jail, huh?"

"Yeah, out of the goodness of your heart."

"More goodness than anybody else had! Ain't I always helped you out? Even after you quit the team, I was always there for you. Always! And that's what I'm trying—"

"One second left, Coach."

"Let go first, will you? You're messing up my jacket. I can't tell you where Meredith—"

I hit him with an uppercut. Right in his old man dick.

"I was gonna say… I can't…" he wheezes, bent over, "because… Jesus, Bobby, what's with you and my junk today?"

"It's Sam, asshole."

"Sam. Right. I don't know where they have her, not exactly. But I can tell you who and why and all of that, okay? And then you and me got to figure how to get out of this mess with our heads still connected to our bodies."

"Just fucking talk," I say.

Coach says there were plenty of people who knew I'd inherited a fortune from Steve way before I found out myself. The CC were probably the first to know. Some of them wanted to approach me straightaway to get me to sell my portion of the BI before Sonya got to me, but then Steve's funeral happened, and me publicly wiping the CC's noses in their own collective shit didn't sit well with some of the old timers. They're the ones who came up with the plan to have me take the fall for Steve's murder.

"You telling me the CC have Mere? That they killed Steve?"

"I didn't say any of that," Coach says. "Why would they do that? Steve was the only thing standing between them and Sonya! And they ain't who's got Meredith, either."

Coach says word of my multi-millions trickled down the evolutionary ladder of local ne'er-do-wells. Two knuckle-draggers in particular—Darwin and Derwin, meth-dealing cousins of Meredith and residents just over the border in Arkansas—came up with the genius plan to fake a kidnapping with Meredith's cooperation, certain she'd go along with it for a cut of the action. The possibility of her turning them down had not arisen anywhere in their collection of hopped-up, toxic synapses. Thinking Meredith was after a bigger chunk of the profits, they offered two million, then three. At some point, the boys had their Mensa moment to go ahead with the plan, Meredith's compliance bedamned. So they gagged her and stashed her in a travel trailer, promising to throw her a couple of 100k when it was all said and done. After all, she was family.

But then she worked her gag off and relayed the unpleasant news. However much Darwin and Derwin ended up scamming me for wouldn't be worth the trouble. Meredith was a made woman with Teisenberg, who'd be more than a little disappointed to discover that Mere had been detained by bit meth players that Teisenberg was already trying to run off. So if Darwin and Derwin enjoyed having their heads attached to their respective torsos, the rational choice would be to release her immediately and leave Texas forever. That would've been the smart play (in addition to ample groveling and apologies), but the boys had already made plans with the money, and it wasn't exactly what you'd call a brains operation to begin with. Additionally, like most small-timers in the region, Darwin and Derwin had been running scared from Teisenberg for over a year already, trying to fly under the swampy radar and having to cook meth in the most remote shithole, out-of-the-way spots they could find. Not only was Teisenberg terrifying; Teisenberg had ruined business for everybody else in the known multiverse of meth. Insignificant players like them were vanishing by the dozen. Learning that their cousin was in cahoots with the infamous drug lord threw them into a panic. It was like hearing Keyser Soze chuckling in your pantry.

"How you know all this?" I ask.

"Shit, boy," Coach shakes his head. "I wish to God I didn't. I wish I didn't know half the shit that gets dumped on me in this town. Like I told you with Chuck—everybody and their mama thinks I keep up with every Merfoot there ever was, like I got some kinda lifetime responsibility for em, especially the ones with shit for brains. Ain't a week goes by I don't get a call from the Sheriff or the hospital or the goddamned FBI. I've bailed these ugly sumbitchin brothers out more times than I can remember, and look where it's got me! Stank-ass, snaggle-tooth motherfuckers! Just had to tell me all about this Einstein idea of theirs, to which I rightfully inquired, *Is it y'all are fucking stupid or is it y'all are fucking crazy?* Trick question, it's both! I told em, Bobby, I told em! *Y'all want to end up with your heads cut off? Cause this is how y'all end up with your heads cut off!* And now I'm gonna end up with mine off, too! And, you know... I don't want that, Bobby!"

"Sam."

"Sam!"

"What the fuck is with this head stuff?"

"You ain't heard?" Coach grins, his face contorted in skeletal fear. "Teisenberg's got this decapitation fetish. Keeps a pile of heads like a treasure. A pile. Of heads. Even mounts special ones on a wall somewhere!"

I can't help but laugh.

"Oh, it's funny? Hahaha, yeah... Enjoy your head while you have it, motherfucker."

"Come on... You actually believe Sonya cuts off heads and—"

"She don't do it herself! She gets that ex-Mossad Hawaiian shirt-wearing freakshow to do it for her!" Coach slides down the grubby glass into an exhausted squat and grips his head, out of breath, sweating like a rat in a sock in August.

"Mossad?"

"You ain't met him? Smooth head, beachwear, got these eyelashes..."

A car rolls by. It's not a Taurus. The driver waves at Coach and Coach strains a half-smile and a half-wave back.

Another course to this whole thing starts to unfold before me. "I tell you what," I say. "Bring me Mere by 8:30 tonight... no, by 8. You do that and I'll make sure you keep your head and your balls. Deal?"

Coach spits to the side and groans. "You're an idiot."

"Right now, Sonya still doesn't know. I can make sure Mere doesn't tell her."

"Oh, can you, now?"

"Take it or leave it, Coach."

"You know what your problem is?" Coach stands up and dusts his ass off. "You've got old fashioned notions about women. You're still looking at these two like they're the same lovestruck teenyboppers who got damp every time you walked by or sang one of your songs to em. What you got now they don't already have? Money? Give me a fucking break. I bet you Sonya is already three times as rich as Beau Berkey ever was."

"I've still got something she wants."

"Yeah? Well, it ain't your looks or your voice or your pecker, I can tell you that."

"Don't you worry what it is."

"I sure as shit hope you ain't talking about the BI!"

I look at Coach like he just swapped faces with Miss Cleo.

"Don't tell me you're thinking about giving her that!"

"I'm not giving her shit," I say. "I'm trading it for something I want more."

Coach shakes his head in disbelief. "You already made a deal."

"Not officially."

"Well, let me tell you something about your former lady friend, son," he says, his eyes shadowed heavily. "I'd like you to recall the state of things in Caddo County when Sonya moved back here with those business degrees in the mid-90s. Think about who was still running the show around here at that time. Think about how nobody else could do dick without the CC okaying it. Nobody. I want you to ponder that word. I want you to consider who the word *nobody* includes and who it most certainly does not."

"Is this fucking history lesson going somewhere?"

"You don't get it? How about this... How many of them Caddo Club boys do you think's got Black Lives Matter signs up in their yards? How many you gonna see participating in the MLK parade? You think for one stinking second that Beau Berkey or any of his CC doormats would let a black woman get one inch of power in a place like Atlantis? Like, real power?"

"Yeah, well, she has it now, so..."

"That's right," Coach says coldly. "And why do you think that is? You think she got what she has by playing by the CC's rules?"

"Good for her! Good for fucking her! I don't give a shit, Coach. All I give a shit about is getting Mere back. Help me with that, and I'll use this deal with Sonya to help save your ass."

"Tell me something," Coach says. "You ever hear any story where the devil keeps his side of the deal?"

"Sonya's no devil to me, buddy. From where I'm standing, she's looking pretty angelic."

"Steve thought so, too," Coach says, looking away. "Look what happened to him."

The chill I get bypasses my spine and goes straight to my gut and just sits there, unwilling to move anywhere, as if it, too, can't believe what Coach has implied. Reluctantly, Coach tells me the rest. It took Sonya nearly twenty years (including seven blood-smeared years to finally control the drug trade) to amass a quarter ownership of Berkey International. But no matter what she tried or who she threatened, Beau made sure it stopped right there. Even on the far side of his dead body, Beau swore that Sonya would remain a minority partner forever. By the time Beau finally kicked it, Sonya had already secured pretty much everything else Atlantis had to offer—more property and businesses than she knew what to do with, a meth goldmine, and more cops and judges in her fur-lined pockets than Beau and the CC ever had. But Sonya wanted Berkey International, and bad. It's long been the crown jewel of legit business in the region, not to mention that the BI land sits on top of untold billions of untapped oil and natural gas. From day one, Beau wouldn't hear of selling it off or having it drilled, and the old man enjoyed nothing better than flipping off Big Oil for no other reason than the sheer nut-clutching pleasure of bragging that he'd done it.

But other players in the region resented him for it. Even granting off a third of the land's mineral rights would be a mother lode of golden geese, not to mention the jobs and retail boom it would bring to Atlantis. So, without Beau's knowledge, several investors and shareholders began regular convos with Chevron, Exxon, Halliburton, and the like. And then the old man croaked, leaving everything to Steve.

It was the shot Sonya had been waiting for. Understandably, Steve's mind was on other things than running the BI. He'd already launched the Foundation and kicked off Phase One at the time of Beau's death. To Steve, the BI was just a necessary evil to fund the non-profit, so when Sonya came wooing with plans for a company-wide reorg, a minority-hiring strategy, and a shift to more sustainability, Steve happily handed her the keys to the Porshe and took off to Mexico for an overdue vacation.

Unfortunately, Steve didn't get any of it in writing. While he was off the grid in Margaritaville, Sonya made changes, alright, but every one of them was way more drastic than advertised. To start, she laid off close to 80% of the workforce and replaced them with a crew of Central Americans who somehow managed to freely cross the border and make the 600-mile trip all the way up to Atlantis. She set the new workers up in a tent village behind the factory, but the conditions were terrible even by Central American standards, and after a couple of weeks the workers began to grumble and talk of moving on or striking. Sonya met with their reps, listened to their complaints, and explained to them in fluent Spanish that improvements to the camp were sadly not in the works, but that they were all welcome to leave at any time, no questions asked. In fact, she'd just been on the phone with ICE to make sure she clearly understood deportation proceedings. And that was the end of that.

"Bullshit," I say.

"We got pictures. That'll make a believer out of you. Seeing all that raw sewage in the camp, eight Guatemalans per one little-ass tent... Three of em lost arms in the factory their very first week. A couple got chewed up in machinery just like my daddy..."

The chill in my gut turns over backwards and stars to look for an exit. I shake my head.

"That's not Sonya," I say. "And ICE? Sounds more like something you and your right-wing CC buddies would pull."

"Don't lump me in with them Cheeto Jesus motherfuckers!" Coach hisses. "I voted Gary Johnson! And tell me how it makes one lick of sense the CC would be responsible for any of that? Firing off hundreds of lily-white kin? Shit, boy... they wouldn't live to see breakfast."

"How's Sonya supposed to get away with it, then?"

"She didn't," Coach says. "Somebody got word to Steve."

When Steve found out, he flew back and relieved Sonya from her position the very next day. But he couldn't do anything about her shares in the BI, and the damage was already done. Most of the Central Americans ended up in ICE warehouses across the Southwest, despite Steve donating a fortune for legal battles, and Sonya's gamble had temporarily sent the BI's profits higher than they'd been in over a decade. That meant instant boners for the other BI players, as well as Big Oil and Gas, who were always keeping tabs. Coach wasn't implying that Sonya killed Steve. Coach was saying that somebody else would've killed Steve just to put her in charge.

"Now you get it?" he says. "I don't know what she told you, Bobby, but—"

I hold my hand up for him to stop. I walk back around the corner to my car slowly, my heart full of tar. Across the street is the spot that used to be Martin's. I try to imagine what it looked like decades ago. I try to see my mother through the plywood that covers the windows. I try to find Steve in his place, always with his paper, kids running around with soggy fries and milkshakes and the suspect promise of summer pulling them forward through childhood. Somewhere in there are two kids—one black, one white—both as poor as cemetery clay.

Coach shuffles up behind me.

"We gotta work together, Bobby. I know it's... Well, probably a lot to take in."

I can't say I'm surprised. It's just that the treachery runs way deeper than I thought possible. Currents and currents of it, crossing each other and doubling back to form whirlpools and squalls and doldrums of fuckery.

"How does Red fit into all this?" I turn to Coach, on the off chance he's the owner of a feasible answer.

"Listen, I don't..." Coach scratches his head. "Bobby, I don't think that's related. Red punched that little gal in the face all on his own, and I'm guessing he ran over Chuck like they say, too. I don't know... The man always did tend to violence."

I sit down on the sidewalk across from Martin's and feel the back of my head. The lump Vajzh the ex-Mossad man gave me still doesn't like being touched.

"Forget Red," he says. "We gotta come up with a plan."

"Too late. It's way too late..."

"Maybe," he says hopefully. "Maybe not. But it's definitely too late if we don't put our heads together. Tell me about this deal y'all have. Can't stop an offense from scoring if you don't know who has the ball."

It's the first in an increasingly excitable string of football references and cliches to come my way over the next hour. *Late in the 4th... Down by 6... 2-minute drill... When the going gets tough... This one time I called a double reverse with 37 seconds to go... Onside kick...*

I tell Coach the details and all about Vajzh coming over tonight with a truckload of cash and all that paperwork and how I, like an idiot, fell for it and told her I'd show up early tomorrow morning at Nirvana like the dangled bait I'm intended to be. Coach listens solemnly and writes everything down on the chalkboard inside his old-ass brain that nobody but Coach can see, desperate Xs and Os and arrows every which way. A wet wind lifts up from the west that makes me shiver like a cottonwood in for a twister, but Coach keeps at it (*Statue of Liberty? Nah, overplayed. Hook-and-Ladder? When has that shit ever worked?*) until he lands on the gadget play he's convinced just might do it.

It's not that trick plays don't work. It's that they never work if the other team sees them coming.

HAIL MARY

On my way back to Steve's, I park across from the Sheriff's. My visit here isn't part of Coach's gadget play; it's to scratch an itch I can't shake. The rookie up front is different from the one who didn't know Meredith a couple of days back. I tell him I want to see Red. He points at the clock behind me on the wall. It's 8 minutes until 5.

"So?"

"So 5 is cut off," the deskie says. "Visits got to be over by 5."

"I'll make it snappy."

"Cut off to begin said visits is a quarter til. It look like quarter til to you?" He still hasn't looked up from his cell.

"What it looks like is you having a stick up your ass." That gets him to look.

Just then, Bobby Butz strolls in with a cup of E-Z Mart coffee in one hand and a slice of pepperoni pizza in the other.

"Sam Sorrow!" Butz beams. "To what do we owe the pleasure?"

"This'n wants to see A-11," the young officer snorts. "Past cutoff."

"Look, buddy," I tell him. "I don't intend to spend too much time in here, I just—"

"Hey…" Butz interrupts. "Sam, come on back to my office," he waves the slice of pizza for me to follow and winks back over the kid's head in my direction.

"We got to sign in everybody!" the kid grumbles.

"Put him down and I'll sign later," Bobby commands.

I follow a humming Butz through a maze of beige cubicles with desks sprouting paperwork, dingy take-out boxes, and refurbished Dell computers with ten-year-old keyboards that are more crumbs than functioning keys. There's nobody else in the office. Butz plops down in a window cube beneath the fluorescent hum. Pictures of his kids and an autographed 8x11 of Red in an Oilers uniform are taped to the concrete wall, which is also beige. Butz pulls up a stool for me.

"Those were the days, huh?" I point to the photo of Red.

"Fuckin A," Butz mumbles through the pepperoni. "Just signed it for me."

"He awake?"

"Manner of speaking."

The ceiling is too low and the room smells like a convention of feet. "Where's Smith and Wetch?"

"Probably on the back nine being assholes," he says. "Hey, soon as that rookie clocks out, we'll slip on back and see Red."

"Thanks, bud. But I'm actually here to see what you found out about Mere."

Butz clears his throat. "Mere?"

"Don't fuck with me, Butz."

"Look," he whispers and looks around the room. "This ain't the place to be talking about—"

"About her getting kidnapped?"

"Meredith?" Butz asks loudly. "Meredith *Lee* has been kidnapped?"

"Are you... Man, I filed the damn report! Told them to get you a copy! You didn't know?"

"Hell no!" Butz yanks his keyboard close and flips on the monitor with a squint. He types fervently. "Ain't nothing in here... You filled out a TPS report?"

"Filled out something two days back."

"Ah," Butz nods. "There you go. Probably still up front and ain't in the system yet. Unless you asked them to expedite it."

"Expedite it?"

"You know, make it go faster? Holy moly... kidnapped," he whistles. "Well, what do you know about it? Who did it? Where is she?"

I shake my head, which still feels full of malicious glass. "I was sorta hoping you... Well, there goes that idea."

"I'm sorry, Sam, I didn't... Shit, man. How can I help?"

"There is something else," I say, sitting up.

Butz looks at me warily, like somebody who's just beginning to suspect that he's been set up, which he has.

"Just information, really," I say. "Something I'm guessing you already know."

"Well, like I told you, I don't know shit about—"

"I'll give you a description to help: Hawaiian shirt, bald head, goes by the name of Vajzh..."

Butz's eyes go bright and then they go dull. "Huh."

"Works for Sonya in some capacity. Might be ex-Mossad..."

Butz swallows hard and turns to his monitor. "Huh," he says again. "Hawaiian shirt, you say?"

"Quit fucking around. You know exactly who I'm talking about. He was there that day I ran into you at Walmart, and you could barely keep your eyes off him."

"Nope. I sure don't recall that!" He stands up quickly and looks to the front of the office. "Rookie's gone now," he says. "So, you know... you can go back to see Red if you—"

"Cut it, Butz. This is about Mere and me and Steve and... Shit, man. I need your help."

Butz pulls in an extended breath through his nose and then breathes out at twice the length. Then he turns off his monitor and looks at his watch.

"No," he says, staring at the glossies of his kids on the wall.

"What do you mean *no*?"

"I mean *no* as in stop asking me about somebody I clearly shouldn't be talking about." Butz pushes his pizza crust to the edge of his desk and swigs down the rest of the E-Z Mart coffee and shakes his head. Then he closes the blinds to his window.

"You got no idea," he says. "No idea."

"Maybe I do."

"Maybe you don't. Maybe you been gone since forever and ain't seen what's happened around here and don't give a fuck anyway. Maybe you got other places to go and I don't."

"Butz..."

"Believe it or not, used to be that being police around here meant something," he continues. "You could make a difference. A decent wage, too. Sure, kids would talk shit about you—*oink oink* and all that—but every now and then you'd get somebody locked up that woulda done them or their mama wrong, you know? Stop a beating in progress. Keep an apple from spoiling the basket. You got to do something right here and there, and you got to feel right doing it. But now?" Butz looks up at the ceiling as if it were trying to crush both of us with its sadness.

"You're talking Teisenberg," I say.

"Teisenberg?" he laughs. "You kidding me?"

"You know, don't you?"

"Look, you want to see Red, or what?"

"I want your help."

"Well, find another way."

"Look, Butz... I'm pretty sure I just fucked up and I... I might've made a deal with somebody I shouldn't have."

"I'm sorry to hear that," he sniffs. "Really, I am. And, for the record? If that deal involves a certain former girlfriend of yours not named Meredith? I wish you all the best. Furthermore, I wish you all the best by you getting the fuck out of here and not involving me no more. Door's up front," he points. "Same way you came in."

"You tell me what I need to know and I'm gone. And I'll help you out. Like, in a big way."

"Yeah," he snorts. "How?"

"I got money."

"Is that right? Well, I got kids," he points at the photos. "Kids I want to stay alive, thank you. Kids who need me to stay alive to pay for iPhones and braces and community college and shit like that. You know how hard that is to do in this town and still feel upright? Still be able to look at yourself in the mirror? Every goddamn day it's getting harder. Every goddamn day there's a new landmine. It's like *Minesweeper*, the hard version with more bombs and the big map and the countdown clock."

"That ain't no way to live."

"You don't say."

"I'm not asking you to help me with Sonya," I say. "I'm asking you to help me with Vajzh. It could save my life, Bobby. Mere's too, if I'm right about something. Tell me what you've found out about him. I know you've been looking. All you got to do is let me in on it, and I promise you'll never have to work two shit jobs again for the rest of your life."

"It's three," Butz stares at me, thinking. "I work three jobs just to get by and take care of my kids. Three shit jobs, and I'm lucky to have em."

"How about we make it just one?"

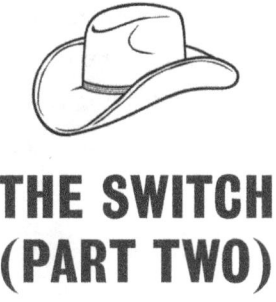

THE SWITCH
(PART TWO)

In freshly pressed beachwear, a newly shaved scalp, and posture that would make Baryshnikov give way on stage, Vajzh backs into Steve's driveway at precisely nine o'clock in a white Econoline van, the same kind I spent hundreds of hours touring in before making my way up to air-conditioned buses with my own toilet, bunk, and PlayStation. How times change.

"What, no Taurus?" I ask, wasting a perfectly nervous smile on him.

Vajzh opens the back of the vehicle without comment and stands to one side to allow me to regard the promised monetary units with awe. I'm opening the first case to check the cash when a truck identical to Coach's drives by on Dewey heavy-thumping some Doja Cat. My back goes stiff until I notice the truck is silver, so it can't be Coach. Plus, there's the Doja Cat.

I breathe normally again and return to the five rolling cases, the hard plastic kind used to transport sensitive gear—IMAX cameras, sniper rifles, cold hard cash. Vajzh pops another open while I flip through the bundled stacks of hundreds in the first and do precisely what you're supposed to do when a fortune displays itself so blithely before you: I whistle. Then Vajzh and I roll the cases to the front door, one at a time. When the last is parked at the entry, Vajzh hands me a green document bag, locks the van, and pauses to sniff the air. He looks up into the pecan trees and across the street at the county jail and then up into the window of the attic. I guess whatever he sees or smells or doesn't smell is good enough. We bring the cash inside.

So far, so good. The plan only works if he's alone.

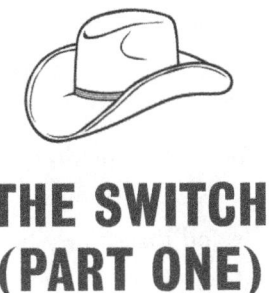

THE SWITCH
(PART ONE)

After Butz spilled what he knew, I went back to check on Red. Butz said they had to call the EMTs yesterday. Red had been shivering on the floor for hours and at some point he'd stopped shaking or moving at all, going stiff as a post with his mouth grimaced open. Nobody was willing to get into the cell to check if he was alive. The EMTs shone a flashlight into Red's eyes, hooked him up to a saline drip, and finally got him sitting up and conscious again. Dehydration, they said. Dehydration and withdrawal. I never brought him his meds.

I watched Red stretched out under two blankets on the smutched-up floor—skinny, feral, and weak—an emaciated, bog-man version of his former self. He was nowhere close to the Red who terrorized AFC defensive ends for almost a decade, although his hands looked the same—knobby and stump-like. Hands that could crush a bowling ball without trying.

When I walked out of the Sheriff's, I left my rental where it was and crossed Dewey on foot and stood in Steve's yard beneath the pecans and stared at the exterior of what was supposed to be mine. I couldn't remember the last time I'd been in the house. I still didn't want to go in.

I'd been calling Austin home for a long, long time, but the truth was that ever since that late 80s afternoon when Steve retrieved my stinky, tent-living, teen body back to this house and offered me the attic (fulfilling his promise to my dying mother), this has been my true home. Not Atlantis, but this noble house. This manse amidst all the redneck madness.

The front door was a portal to something sophisticated, pure, and impervious. It's stupidly large, not unlike Red's, although for older reasons. Made of a hardwood that's likely been wiped from the face of the earth by now and standing almost ten feet tall, entering the house this way never failed to flood me with tranquility and relief. Even when Steve and me went through our requisite clashes, I still felt uplifted any time I was in this house—like I was actually okay and that I had a purpose in life and that it was right that I should endeavor to fulfill it. That was all Steve.

Marie used to talk about this Buddhist idea of *basic goodness*. It's this fundamental quality of a person's psyche or soul, something pure and kind beneath all the horseshit and selfishness that's typically more than evident. I can't say that I've seen basic goodness in many people, but Steve was one of the few, and it was Steve who first saw it in me, and Steve who kept seeing it, no matter what, and I could feel that he saw it, because he spoke directly to that part of me, and because he conversed freely with that essence I would occasionally remember it myself. That was Steve. That's how he was with everybody.

I opened the front door and felt the shame slide off me like a cloak. I felt strong again and intelligent and young. Everything inside the house was as I remembered it—exquisite and just so. On your right immediately upon entry was the intricate armoire Steve's grandmother had custom built and shipped from Italy, the four polychrome panels depicting birds and tropical flowers her own design. When I first moved in, Steve asked me to repair one of the doors that wasn't shutting properly, and I couldn't figure it out. Not because I'm not handy (I'm not handy), but because I couldn't find a single nail or screw anywhere. The armoire was held together—is still held together—with hand-carved pegs, some no larger than a toothpick.

The whole house is like that. I don't mean packed with expensive stuff from Europe; I mean everything perfectly situated to manifest the genius of its craft and presence. There's a gilded mirror when you come in that must weigh two hundred pounds, and its reflective power is almost extra-dimensional. Steve placed it on the wall facing you as you come into the house, which means that you see yourself and at the same time the exterior world behind you in backdrop until the latter recedes as you close the door and there's only you looking back upon yourself, and whatever's in that mirror makes you look highbrow and gorgeous and fucking great. Nobody ever looked bad in that mirror.

On the left when you come in is what we called the *sitting room*. Nobody ever sat there. The same cream-colored Chesterfield, same navy blue Persian rug, same fireplace with the brass grate and tools that nobody ever touched. Same bay window looking out on the front yard with drapes I just assumed never opened, although I pulled them back when I came in this time. I still had a couple of hours before Vajzh arrived.

I crossed through the foyer to the main part of the first floor into what I always thought of as *Steve's Room*, but was actually our 20' x 30' dining area adjoining the open-bar kitchen. I considered the room Steve's because it's where he always was, parked at the longest cypress table I've ever seen—the top still covered in his sublimity of books, photos, scribbled papers, coffee mugs, pens, pencils, notebooks, and everything else that kept him company no matter my presence or passage. Steve would only clean it off an hour or so before one of his *Moveable Feast* type parties, and even then the table would return to its natural state the following morning, as if the clutter had cultivated its own volition and magic.

I put my hand on Steve's chair. It was neither cold nor warm. The temperature of the house had vanished.

I went through the rest of the house like this—room by room, piece by piece. The living room in the back of the first floor with its leather sofa and 90s entertainment system (complete with VCR); the stairway up to the second story that housed Steve's bedroom, official study, and two immaculate guest rooms; claw-foot tubs in the bathrooms on each of the three floors; the narrow staircase up to my attic with my old twin bed looking recently made up, the remainder of the room a reliquary for random objects collected and stored there since my childhood. But there was something else.

On my bed—on top of a quilt I didn't recognize—was a row of maps. Professional maps—not the kind you pick up at Texaco, but the type that are so technical and detailed that it takes a while to understand what they're even maps of. These were all of Caddo County, specifically the vast expanse of acreage in the corner of the state between the lake and the Arkansas and Louisiana lines. I opened the maps side-by-side on the floor, but the only one I could even halfway read was topographical. The others were marked with indecipherable shapes and symbols over what looked like property lines, and the margins were covered with arrows and question marks and writing in multiple colors I couldn't understand. Most of the individual letters made sense to me, but their combinations and orientation in relationship to each other made the whole thing wonky and damn near hieroglyphic.

The only thing I could make out in common were two dots—one red, one green—in the same spot on each map. The red wasn't too difficult to figure out, because on one of the maps it was directly atop a tiny rendition of the various structures that make up the sprawling campus of Berkey International. The green dot took longer to decode. It was on top of Red's house.

I heard the van pull up outside. I looked at my watch—nine o'clock sharp. I walked down and met Vajzh in the driveway, checked out the cash, whistled, brought the cases to the doorstep, and watched Vajzh pause in the yard for what was probably no more than two or three seconds. And when he followed me into the house, I looked at his face in that beautifying, unmasking mirror as he shut the door softly behind us. And when he caught me looking at his reflection, I knew it was going to work. The new plan, I mean. And all because of what Butz told me.

FUMBLEROOSKI

Vajzh leaves the driveway in the now-empty Econoline, granting me sole custodianship of five gear cases packed with ten million cash. One minute after the van is out of sight, I flick on the light over the kitchen sink and turn it off again. Then I go to the door off the living room in the back of the house and do the same with the porch light.

Coach knocks on the back door twenty seconds later—three bumps and a slide. I forget the code I'm supposed to answer with, so I just open it up. Coach jumps three feet back and into the air like a cucumber-spooked cat, ripping one of the porch's screen windows out of its frame. He clutches his chest.

"The code?" Coach pants, peering inside the house. "The fucking code?"

"Hootie hoo?"

"We cool in there or what?"

"All cool, buddy," I say, patting his shoulder. "Now let's get the fuck out of here before they figure it out."

Ironically, Coach's plan depended on Sonya's trust in me. He said it all hung on her believing I'd fallen for her supposedly gracious deal and then me going through with the swap for Meredith tomorrow morning, but that trust would be her undoing. And it was the key to our getaway.

Coach's A game was straightforward: I'd pretend to sign away my share of the BI and kill Vajzh. *Leave the gun, take the cannoli.* In this case, our cannoli being ten million bucks. I was quick to point out Plan A's shortcomings: For starters, I'd never killed a man, so there was that. And even if I tried, there was a high probability of failure, because rendering a former Mossad assassin-type person dead, flip-flops notwithstanding, was likely not as easy as it sounded. Even if I managed it, I informed Coach, Sonya would be waiting nearby to receive the paperwork from Vajzh, and if he were somehow delayed or miraculously made dead, Sonya would put an APB of butchery out on us faster than a stripper's Chuck Tender dismount.

Our real problem was time. If Vajzh didn't show up with the goods, we'd be lucky to make it to one of those stupid billboards at city limits.

Hence, Coach assembled Plans B, C, and D, each branching off in multiple *If Then* Booleans and flowcharted with Xs and Os (external this time) for my reference, but it just looked like chicken-scratch versions of plays Coach had been running for fifty years—e.g., *Eagle Right Fifteen Ponies Left C Gap on Three.* In the end, it gave me enough to work with.

Getting out of the house alive with the money was the easy part. The trick was getting out of the house alive and undetected, making a new deal with the meth boys, grabbing Meredith, convincing her to go along with the rest of the plan, and every last one of us pulling a DB Cooper and vanishing before Teisenberg figured out anything was askew.

Coach knew that Darwin and Derwin had become increasingly hopped up and desperate. They knew their heads were unmetaphorically on the line and their terror regarding the matter enabled Coach to talk them down to a million flat, of which Coach would retain half for his troubles. That would leave 250k for each of the meth brothers—not a small score to escape the state with. They were, reportedly, satisfied.

As far as Sonya knew, everything was still on at Nirvana. Coach guessed that Vajzh would be there waiting for us when we arrived in the morning—Vajzh and a few unsavory, gun-toting others who'd mow us all down as soon as Meredith showed up safe. To avoid the overlap, Coach rerouted the switch to go down hours earlier at the Atlantis airport instead. Meredith would be waiting in a gassed-up Citation CJ1 with a pilot on hire (all brokered by Coach), and from there she and I would fly to Austin, pick up our daughter, and spend the rest of our lives with a stolen nine million dollars in our Mexican villa.

I kept the Austin-and-daughter-and-Mexico idea to myself. I didn't ask where Coach planned to go with his money. Maybe he'd have his own plane waiting. Maybe we'd see him in the tropics down the line.

Thanks to the sheer size of Steve's house and the hulking boxwood that separates it from Falway, it's a cinch for me and Coach to sneak the gear cases out the back door and around the block to where his truck awaits beneath a sky so fluffy and dark it might as well be constructed of black cotton. Then we hurriedly divide the stacks of bills into professional-grade lawn bags—the kind so tough you can't even poke a knife through—and leave the gear cases behind in somebody's yard. That was my idea. I guessed there'd be a transponder in at least one of the cases.

"You count this?" Coach looks up suddenly.

"Yeah," I snort, working as fast as I can. "Every damn dollar. You want a receipt or something?"

"Chill out," he grins. "Just want to know it's all here. I've already spent half of it!"

"Half your share."

"Half my share is a shit-ton of money, son," he laughs.

"You want to count out thousands of bills, be my guest. Should be a hundred of them in each band, so... Fuck, I don't know. What's it look like to you?"

"Like a lot of fucking money we just stole!" Coach hoots.

"Keep it down and shake a leg. We got maybe ten minutes until Sonya finds out."

"Teisenberg," he corrects me, shoveling the last of the cash into a gray bag. "That ain't Sonya no more. That's Teisenberg."

"Whatever," I say, and I hop in the truck.

"Which plan was it, anyway?" he grins, starting up the Ford. "Which one'd you go with?"

"What's it matter? Can we get the fuck to the airport or what?"

"We're going, we're going…" he says, pulling up to the sign at Falway and taking a left. "See? Nobody anywhere! I'm just asking so I know where we are on the flowchart."

"C2b," I say, rolling down my window. "Or maybe C2d."

"What's that one again?"

"The one where I sign all those documents as Turd Ferguson."

Once we hit the highway and start south and it's clear that nobody's tailing us, Coach yips and yaps like a cracked-out coyote and bangs on the steering wheel like Keith Moon. We're only two minutes from the airport and Coach has the windows down and the heat blasting and there's a smell outside like wet carboard and cold manure rolling in from lowland pastures miles away. I can't make out what Coach is chattering about, but he must think what he's saying is funny—between checking the rearview, he gesticulates and laughs at the air as it whirls inside the cab and throws his white hair around like a skydiving Christopher Lloyd. I only catch pieces of what he's shouting: *Daddy* and *Sirens* and *Wouldn't you know*. I just nod and look out as the lights of 59 fly by as I sit on my freezing hands.

There's not a soul at the airport entry when we squeal through the gate. It's a Homeland Security nightmare. Coach makes an unimpeded left at close to full speed and runs us out onto a single-track alley of a road that parallels the primary airstrip, the same one I bounced in on two days and change ago. Then Coach hooks a stiff right into an open-door hangar where the promised Citation awaits alongside one particularly hooptied Honda Prelude, adorned with an equally disputable driver sitting on the hood. It's Derwin—ladies' sunglasses, fur collar, vape cloud, and all.

When Coach jerks the truck to a stop, I jump out, run over to Derwin, and slap him in his ear, Stockton style. The pop of it ricochets around the metal hangar like a clap track.

"Fuck!" Derwin screeches. He grabs that side of his head with both hands. "What the fuck?"

There's ear blood everywhere, but mostly on Derwin—all over his multi-colored parka with the faux collar and splashed like a low-rent Pollock on his fake gold chains, baggy camo shorts, and recently unboxed pair of Yeezys. He looks up at me like I just kicked his dog. Like I just kicked his dog in its ear.

Coach snickers behind me and points at Derwin's head. "Damn!"

"Where's Mere?" I demand, looking over at the plane. Its lights are off.

"What?" Derwin asks, clutching his ear.

"Where's Meredith?" I shout.

"I ain't hear you, fool!" Derwin grumbles. "You done messed up my audio—you supposed to sound like Batman?"

"That's his voice now," Coach says, checking the plane. "But what the... What's up with the lights?"

"I's just about to tell you," Derwin replies. "But yo, my hearing ain't right. I feel all unbalanced and shit."

I take a step closer and clench my hand. "Where is she?"

Derwin looks down at the pavement and shakes his head, cussing.

"Listen, shithead..." Coach says, stepping closer to him, too.

"Ain't my fault, y'all," Derwin stands up, removing his blood-splattered parka and holding his arms out beatifically. "She ain't wanna come."

"What?" I growl.

"I said it ain't my fault," he repeats, backing away. "She ain't wanna come with us!"

"She ain't..." Coach looks at me sideways and then back to Derwin and then at the plane for good measure. "What?"

"We told her what was up and she ain't like it," he protests, trying to clean the blood off his rat-fur collar with spit. "I say, we got your man coming, tell her about the monies, got a plane going somewhere nice, like Fiji or Tuvalu or some shit, but she ain't like it. She don't trust us, man, I done told you. After I apologized and everything! She say she gonna wait in the Cobra for Teisenberg to roll in and smoke us. She laughin at us, man! Our own damn cousin. That bitch cold."

"Cobra?" I ask.

"Their shitty trailer," Coach explains.

"Ain't no trailer, man," Derwin spits. "That's our kitchen. Class C!"

"Where the fuck is it?" I demand.

"Maybe I ain't tell you now," he looks away, pouting. "You done wronged my ear."

"Why didn't you boneheads just take her?" Coach asks. "Like we planned."

"Like how?"

"Tape her hands, pick her up," Coach puts a finger into Derwin's blood-stained chest. "Put her in your shit-sled there and haul her immobile ass over here. Look, we've got—"

"She our cousin, man. She already tied up! But it's all wrapped around that swivelly Home Depot chair and... Look, man, she ain't wanna go! Aight? What's the big motherfucker up in here? Besides," he says, looking down at the ground, sniffing, "she bit Derwin the other day, right up on his arm."

"Derwin?" Coach says. "I thought you were Derwin."

"Naw, man!" he frowns. "I'm Darwin, bitches! How you gonna confuse me with that ugly motherfucker? You see a Merfoot tattoo up on this arm? With new witchy-mouth bite marks on it? That Merfoot tattoo was fresh, too…"

"Sweet," I mutter. "Real sweet."

"Ain't sweet no more, Deuce Wayne. Shit's getting tetanusy," Darwin says.

Coach puts his hands on top of his head, like he's trying to keep it from blasting off his neck. I take a deep breath and double check the hangar.

"None of you," I say, "are getting a fucking dime until you take me to Mere and we make the trade."

"I don't know," Darwin sniffs, glancing at Coach. "Maybe I just take me and Der's share now and y'all go on ahead. She just waitin there, man. You can surprise her and shit."

I look over at the hangar's office and up into the rafters and beams above. "Where's the pilot?"

"Shit," Darwin says. "Prolly drunk by now. I told him what was up and that motherfucker split."

"I count three security cameras," I say, pointing to each of them. "Y'all get any ideas, it's going on record. Somebody's gonna find out."

"Bobby," Coach replies, holding out his hands. "Come on…"

"I ain't see no…" Darwin double-takes the cameras. "Is them cameras?"

"Doesn't matter," Coach tells him. "Both of y'all just calm down with the paranoid bullshit. Last thing we need with Teisenberg after us. Look, the deal is still on, it's just…"

"Word," Darwin says, holding out his hand for me to slap or shake or tickle or something. "Ain't no Decepticons up in this bitch. I forgive you, son. We good, son."

I leave his hand hanging like a stuck kite. "Don't call me son," I say, looking at Coach. "What now? We didn't flowchart this."

"Nirvana, man!" Darwin beams. "Same place we had the Cobra for a week. Ain't nobody go to Nirvana no more!"

"Fucking what?" I say. "That's the last place..."

Coach winces and cusses at the floor of the hangar. He checks his watch and cusses some more—louder this time. The chances of us getting all the way out to Nirvana, making the trade, and leaving there undetected before Vajzh and Sonya's other goons show up are more than small—they're, like, Ant-Man small. Ant-Man's testicles small.

"Let's go," Coach claps, pointing to Darwin and hopping back into his truck. "Text your brother. Tell him we're there in ten!"

Under the best of conditions, Nirvana's a good fifteen minutes away from where we are, but the way Coach hits the farm road puts us there in twelve. It's a twelve that feels twelve times as long on account of Coach insisting on the windows staying down and it turning even colder now—way too cold for the Ford's heat to keep up. The truck floats over the dips and hills in the road like one of those speedboats in Miami Vice over blacktopped waves, only these waves feel made of ice.

"She's got to know by now!" I shout.

"What?"

"She knows! How are we supposed to..."

"Back way!" he yells, drawing something in the air with his free hand.

But there's only ever been one road in and out of Nirvana, and you can't even call it a road. It's barely a path—a path so crooked and scabbed with washboard ridges you can't make it around the first turn without your whole body going Lexy Panterra on you. Blue would never make it through that shaking. Meredith's cousins getting an RV back there must've taken a miracle of physics. But the good thing about the clearing is that you can hear folks coming in a good ten minutes off, if their vehicle can even make it there at all. Bad news is there's no other way out. It's the quintessential geography of a mutual trap. I shake my head pointlessly and say something I've been running over in my head for hours now.

"What?" Coach yells.

I bring my face closer to his and yell, "Fail to prepare, prepare to fail!" I can't tell how much of it he hears. My throat feels like I drank an ashtray full of gravel. I point to my neck and try to swallow.

Sure enough, the fucked-up trail back to Nirvana is the same ass-shattering experience it was decades ago when jarring your spine into numbness passed for fun. But the place itself is unrecognizable. Nirvana's nothing now but a bulldozed patch of earth in the sketchy middle of some even sketchier woods. The place looks smaller now, not much more than a flattened acre or two, with all the telling contents of the past (beer cans, bottles, blown out tires, stained mattresses, rusted metal) shoved to the periphery like a teenage nuisance. The brothers' RV is on the back side of the clearing, lights off. As advertised, it says COBRA on the side in faded 80s script.

Coach mumbles something, pulls up close to the RV, and cuts the engine. A flashlight pops on inside the Cobra as Darwin revs his shitty car in behind us, dragging something mechanical beneath it that isn't supposed to be dragging.

"Mother fuck," he says when he gets out and looks under the car.

"You lock that gate?" Coach asks him. Darwin nods and holds a key up in the air as he struts over, almost dancing. I don't remember seeing any gate.

"A gate isn't going to stop them," I say. "Let's get this over with and get out of here."

Derwin pops open the Cobra's door, dressed almost identical to his brother, only this brother is holding a shotgun and his ear still works.

"What's with the matching parkas?" I ask. "Walmart running a sale?"

"Man..." Derwin says. "This ain't no Walmart... You need to dress more appropriate to the season, son. It about to snow up in here."

"Whatever. Get Mere out here," I say. "Coach, I'll toss you an extra hundred big for that truck and then you and these flunkies can dangle."

"What's with that voice," Derwin laughs. "Christopher Bale or some shit?"

"Nah, man," Darwin scoffs. "He more like Ben Aflac tryna be Christopher Bale." Then he pulls a revolver with a cartoonishly long barrel from the waistband of his shorts and winks at me. Derwin whistles.

"Put the artillery away," Coach tells them. "I told you—nobody gets hurt."

"Somebody already done been got hurt!" Darwin points at his head. "In they ear!"

"And they arm!" Derwin points to his arm in kind.

"What the fuck's going on?" I turn to Coach.

"Drama class, bitch!" Darwin laughs.

"Rude Mechanicals up in here, motherfucker!" Derwin yaps.

"Master thespians and shit!" Darwin adds.

"Don't look surprised," Coach tells me. "You know what this is, Bobby. It ain't personal, it's just math."

"Yeah, son!" Darwin says. "Math! Like, three to one!"

Coach sighs, rubbing his eyes, "I was talking about the math of ten million dollars in the back of my truck. Now get in the Cobra, Bobby, and me and the boys will be on our way."

I look around the edge of the clearing and take a deep breath in. I'm not sure how much time I have left alive on this earth—Nirvana or elsewhere—but I'm pretty sure getting in that RV is going to chop it down to just minutes.

"How long you been planning this?" I ask Coach.

"Half-blood Prince don't listen so good," Darwin says, leveling the barrel of his revolver at me.

"Man, cap this Oreo and let's jet!" Derwin shouts.

"I don't know," Darwin leers. "Maybe we have a little Slither-in-styles fun with Bobby afore we go."

"You'd better take your cut and get the fuck out of here is what you better fucking do," Coach says. "Bobby, get in that goddamn trailer."

"Ain't a trailer," Darwin complains.

"Yeah, Coach," I say. "It ain't a trailer, and I ain't about to get inside."

"He say he ain't about to get inside..." Derwin snorts, pointing the shotgun at me.

"You're pushing it," Coach tells me. "These ain't my dogs, Bobby. I just feed em every now and then."

"Where is this on the flowchart, Coach?" I smile, trying to string it out as long as possible. "E3b2x? I don't remember going over any triple-cross."

"Get in there," he points to the RV. "Now."

"And Steve?" I ask him. "You have your dogs make Steve get in that boat? Maybe shove him overboard yourself?"

Coach looks down into the dust of Nirvana and runs a wrinkled hand through his wind-messed hair. "No," he sighs, finally meeting my eyes. "I didn't have anything to do with that. And you'll never find out who did unless you get in that shit-show of a meth-bucket there and watch us drive off with the cash."

"And Mere?" I ask.

"Man, fuck her!" Derwin shouts. "Bitch sucker bit me and got away!"

"What happened to her?" I ask them before turning to Coach. "I know where this is going, Coach, but you at least owe me that. What happened to Meredith?"

"I don't owe you shit," he spits. "I took you under my wing back when you still had peach fuzz. But then you came back to Atlantis with your nose in the air and shacked up with that fancy-ass faggot, the both of you too good for the rest of us. Made sense Steve would be that way—he was somebody; he was a Berkey. But you? Who the fuck are you? You ain't nobody. You ain't nothing but some changed-name, washed-up, some kinda mixed-blood, frog-voiced, powhite trash. And ain't no amount of money can change that, you hear? That being the case, I might as well take it from you and get mine, see? So, if anybody here owes anybody, it's you owing me, because in this moment right the fuck now? I'm the only thing between you and some buckshot to the teeth. You got me? Now get in that fucking trailer."

"Ain't no—" Derwin starts.

"You're right. I do owe you, Coach," I say, holding my hands high and making a calm show of not going anywhere. "And I owe you brothers, too," I nod to Darwin and Derwin, respectively. "Which is why I'm willing to renegotiate the terms of our deal. On one condition."

"Condition? Terms?" Derwin snorts. "I'm about to give you some terms!"

"We got ten million terms in the back of that truck, motherfucker," Darwin laughs. "You ain't—"

"Ah, that..." I point to the Ford. "Now, that's where you're mistaken."

"Fucking shoot him and let's get out of here," Coach says, turning away.

"I wouldn't do that, boys," I say, trying to keep my voice from shaking. "Not until you get a good look at those bills. I mean, genuine playas like yourself know funny money when you see it, right?"

"What the fuck he talking about?" Derwin asks Coach.

"He's bluffing," Coach says. "Shoot his ass."

"Security thread," I tell them. "Boys, ask Coach what color the security threads were on those hundreds when we double-checked them under the UV."

Coach chuckles. "Bobby, Bobby, Bobby... what do you think a couple of minutes are gonna buy you, huh? It's over, boy. Take the L."

"What color was they, Coach?" Derwin asks, a half octave higher than before.

"They'd be on the left," I tell Derwin. "Pink, I believe."

"Coach?" Darwin asks, looking over at his brother.

"He's lying," Coach tells them. "Calm down. He's just stalling."

"Was they pink, tho?" Derwin demands. "Was they—"

"You think I carry a goddamn black light everywhere I go?" Coach snaps at them. "I looked at the bills good enough! Trust me—they're real."

"Well," I say, "there you have it, boys. You've got Coach's professional word on the matter. He says they're clean, but what do I know?"

Coach grabs my neck with both hands and squeezes. "If those bills are bogus," he whispers so that only I can hear him, "I'll chain you and that bitch of yours together and feed you to the gators myself."

"Fail to prepare, prepare to fail," I whisper-laugh, but I'm losing air.

"What the fuck does that mean?" Coach demands. "What the—"

"Something... Steve..." I try to say, and my vision goes dark at the edges.

"Coach..." I hear Darwin squeak.

"Hand me that pistol!" Coach barks at him, letting go of my throat. The light rushes back and the air around me is full of swirls and upside-down stars.

"Coach..." Derwin says, his voice tight and panicked.

"No! Hand me that shotgun, you simple-ass, mouth-breathing—"

"Coach!" Darwin shouts. And the sheer, organic terror in his voice makes the old man freeze.

"I was trying to say... something Steve... used to tell me," I say, massaging my neck.

"You got red on you," Darwin points at Coach's chest.

Coach looks down at the steady red dot of light floating over his heart. He shifts one inch to the left and the dot follows suit. He tries two inches to the right, and the light stays where it is.

"That's a laser," Derwin says, looking at his brother.

"I know what it is," Coach says.

"That's a goddamn laser," Darwin says louder, gawking at the edge of the clearing.

"Attached to a sniper rifle," I confirm, waving at the sniper. "Austrian-made, I believe. And with his particular set of skills? He could nail a dime at three times the distance. Imagine the impact from here..."

Darwin kneels down, honey slow, facing the direction of the rifle. He makes an exaggerated show of placing his pistol in the dirt, as if offering up a sleeping child to a silent god. Then he puts his hands on the back of his bloody head and his face starts to shake.

Derwin chooses otherwise. He sprints off like a coked-up rabbit in a zig-zag pattern, somehow managing to shuck his bulky parka along the way, dropping his 12-guage in the process. It goes off and blasts a hole in the side of the Cobra the size of a regulation Frisbee. Something begins to hiss inside. The red dot leaves Coach's chest. A half second later, there's a muffled pop, and Derwin tumbles into the dirt and rolls around grabbing his right knee, screaming.

Coach looks at each of the brothers, open-mouthed and wide-eyed, as if the contents of a forgotten nightmare had just been called up and made public. He turns to me and points at my face. His fingers look feeble and embarrassed. Then he lowers his hand, shakes his head, and gradually starts to smile. The smile opens wider and wider until a sound comes out that's half gobble, half laugh.

"You sly motherfucker," Coach says. "You sly..." and he claps his hands in genuine appreciation. "Well, goddamn! I never woulda thought you had it in you, Bobby... You can come out now!" he shouts at the tree line. "I ain't runnin! You got me!"

If Vajzh hears him, he doesn't show it. Other than Darwin and Derwin and their snot-bubbled weeping, the sounds of Nirvana resemble a crypt.

"No?" Coach shouts into the night. "I had a suspicion that motherfucker was a little deaf," he tells me, taking a giant breath in. "Well…" he nods at the brothers. "Is that how you're gonna do the old man, Bobby? Is that how we gonna leave it?"

"Something like that," I say.

"Something like that…" he nods. "Can't say I blame you. Well, certainly not something you and me drew up on the flowchart, is it? I suppose this is the preparation you alluded to earlier…"

"Where's Mere, Coach?"

"Ah," he shakes his head. "Sorry, Bobby—can't help you there. I'm sure she's alive and well somewhere, though, having recently escaped the captivity of these short bussers. Unbeknownst to me, of course. They only recently owned up to the fact that they let her slip away."

"I don't believe you."

"Guess I wouldn't, either."

"Last chance," and I indicate to the red dot that's returned to his heart. "Not sure what grain he's using in that thing, but I bet the hole will be enough to stick one of my boots through. Tell me where Mere is and I'll call him off."

"And Sonya?" he asks. "You gonna call her off, too?"

"You mean Teisenberg?"

He gives me a sad little smile. "I got nothing left to hide, Bobby, and no reason to do it. I ain't gonna waste what's left of my time sending you off on some chicken-chase just to have that Hawaiian shirt-wearing bastard track me down anyway. I'm telling the truth. I got no idea where Meredith is, but if I had to guess? I'd say she's as far away from you and Sonya as she can get. Understandably. And you should probably think about that before you go looking. Now, go ahead," he nods toward Vajzh. "Get it over with."

Of all the things I'll remember about this night, it'll be Coach's face that keeps coming back to me—his skin collapsed and diaphanous, like an old scroll in faded script. All I have to do is give Vajzh the sign and in less than five seconds this scheming, wretched, shriveled-up bastard is dead. It would be an act of kindness to let him die.

But kindness isn't in me tonight.

"Nah," I say, "I've got something else in mind."

Vajzh stands up about a hundred yards away in the shadow of a longstraw pine and shoulders his rifle.

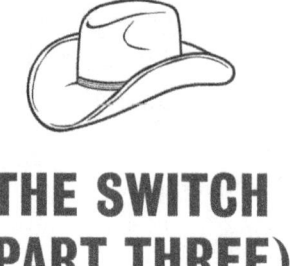

THE SWITCH
(PART THREE)

Earlier that evening—hours before Nirvana and Coach's predicted betrayal—I stood in the dining room next to Steve's chair as Vajzh laid out neat stacks of paperwork conveniently marked with *Sign Here* stickies. Then he unceremoniously handed me an expensive pen (a Cartier)—one large enough to hide the transponder inside. It was 9:13 pm. Vajzh stood on the kitchen side of the table looking straight ahead as if investigating the front wall for stationary vermin, wearing his typical outfit. Like a mannequin assassin, but also one who likes to party.

"Wanna sit?" I asked. "Gonna take a while."

Without looking down, Vajzh reached for the chair immediately in front of him.

"How about here?" I gestured at Steve's seat. "Best in the house."

Vajzh shook his head almost imperceptibly and sat down in the one he'd already pulled out and I took Steve's place with reluctance and twirled the pen in my fingers and began the cramp-inducing process of signing away a fortune to Sonya.

"My father loved sitting here," I said, feeling the armrests smoothed down over the years by Steve's arms and hands. "Not that I ever called him that when he was alive. Not even *dad* or *pop*. Would've been weird for both of us, so he was always just Steve to me." I tried to catch Vajzh's gaze, but it was no use. He was still examining the interior of the wall.

"He was more like an uncle," I continued. "Like a cool, gay uncle. The sophisticated kind, you know? He had to adopt me because of my mom. I mean, he had to adopt me because of what people would say otherwise, like, if he just let me move in. Even so... can't imagine a better father than him."

I looked around the room and it felt full of color and warmth again and I nodded at it, because, for a moment, Steve was back. Maybe upstairs or right outside, but he was back. Vajzh cleared his throat. I got back to signing.

"You know that inner voice that keeps reminding you what a piece of shit you are? The one that keeps the list? Like, no matter what good you do, that voice keeps bringing up every little shit thing or transgression you've ever committed. You might have other voices in there, good ones even, but there's this one that keeps coming back and shoving the others out of the way, saying they don't count, that they aren't the real you, that deep down you're just kinda irredeemable. Know what I'm saying?"

Vajzh stiffly gave absolutely no sign that he knew what I was saying.

"That voice I'm talking about... Other people can hear it, too. Not *hear it*, hear it, but underneath anything else you might say or profess about yourself, that's the voice that comes across. But Steve..." I stopped for a moment to uncramp my right fingers. "I don't think Steve ever heard it. And if he did, well... whenever I was with him, I couldn't hear that voice. It wasn't gone, just... rendered unimportant or something. A lesser message. When I was with Steve, I was something better, because I could hear those other good voices coming through. That's just how he was. Not just for me, but for everybody else, too."

Vajzh sighed and stared at me sleepily. Then he got up to turn the floor lamp on behind me and sat back down. I could see the documents and the table and everything else much better.

"Thanks," I said. I wasn't expecting him to nod back, but he did. I looked down at the remaining paperwork and shook my head.

"There's nothing a person could do with this company that wouldn't leave blood on their hands, is there?"

No response from his side. Unless breathing counts.

"Which is why I think Steve would understand me signing so much away. I wish he hadn't known himself, but I don't see how he couldn't. All this covert offshore stuff. Money tied up in defense contractors. This drug bullshit... And I know what knowing all that would've done to him. He would've felt complicit. Guilty. And not being able to get out from under it would've been torture on him. That's the only reason I think maybe he killed himself after all."

I hadn't wanted to say that last part, but I had to. I finished off the glass of water I'd been drinking and set it back down on that grand table without a coaster and watched as a wet ring began to form on the polished cypress. Steve's presence stiffened with disapproval.

"I'm parched," I said, standing up. "You want some water?"

Vajzh glanced at the documents. There were only a dozen or so pages left to sign and I was almost out of time. It was no secret to him or me that I'd been fishing for the past few minutes, but Vajzh wasn't biting, and I only had one idea left to confirm my suspicions, and that pretty much amounted to a coin flip. I walked over to the kitchen to refill my glass. Then I swallowed hard and grabbed the oversized mug I'd found earlier and filled that one up with water, too. From the kitchen area, Vajzh had his back to me, and his back was motionless and relaxed and perfectly balanced, like a stone placed just so on top of a cairn at the bottom of a lake. I started walking back to the table, that big mug in my good hand, and I tried not to pause. Even for somebody of Vajzh's skillset, it would take Marvel-grade reflexes to prevent me from bashing his skull in. I switched my grip on the mug.

"Here you go," I said, offering it to him.

It was the first time I'd seen him smile. It was crooked and a little on the shy side—a smile that was out of practice. The mug I'd handed him wasn't your typical beach souvenir—it was well-made and elegant. Classy, even. All around the side was an ornate Huichol tree of life in hand-painted design, with deer, birds, fish, snakes, flowers, and people all around the tree in colors so bright and alive that the mug itself looked like it was dancing. In blue cursive, the mug said *Mar de Jade*.

Vajzh took a sip of the water and set the mug down on a coaster in front of him as his eyes pooled up with sadness.

"*El Arbol de la Vida*," he enunciated. His voice was soft and smooth, like an audible latte. The voice was familiar, although I couldn't place the accent. He sounded like somebody who'd grown up in France to English-speaking parents originally from Germany saying something in Spanish.

"You're the one who called me," I said. "You're the one who told me Steve died."

"Yes."

I pointed to the mug. "Nice place, from what I could tell online. Small, out of the way, *tres romantique*."

"*En effet, ca l'est*," Vajzh nodded. "My favorite in Mexico. I wished to retire there."

"Mar de Jade?"

He shook his head. "Just down the beach in the village of *Chacala*, which means *Where There Are Shrimp*." Vajzh paused to straighten out the one vertebra that was undetectably out of place. "I purchased a small building there," he continued, "a restaurant with an apartment and patio above that faced the bay and the sunset over the bay. This is how I met him."

"Steve."

Vajzh nodded. "Someone referred him to my restaurant for the Tuscan Butter Shrimp," he smiled. "After dinner, Steve wanted to compliment the chef—*c'etait moi*. I have always wanted to do this in my life, you see. To be a chef. Ah, which reminds me. I have a letter for you, but not on me. I apologize."

"From Steve?"

"From Michael. The one you call Padre?"

I'd forgotten all about the letter Wetch had told me about.

"For Michael's safety, he is temporarily relocated to my restaurant," Vajzh clarified. "The one in Chacala. He tends bar there. Hopefully in a manner which does not bring too much attention to himself."

"Good luck with that."

"Indeed."

"You're the *they* Dubs was talking about at the Lodge. The boss while the Padre's away."

"Young Wetch, I feel, is overly concerned with pronouns," Vajzh said. "But who am I to say? And I am only involved with the Foundation in this capacity until Michael's return. Until it is clear for him to do so."

"Is he in danger?"

Vajzh took another sip from the mug. "We are all in danger. It is just that some of us are more prepared to face it. Accordingly, you and I should address the more pressing matter before us."

"Right," I said, checking the clock. "Coach will be in position soon."

"Very good. We have enough time for me to address something. You are correct that Steve had become aware of the more nefarious aspects of Berkey International upon taking over from his father. And you are also correct that he could not bear it. For this reason, and this reason only, he left Chacala. To return and to make things right. And he did not kill himself."

"I know."

"Good."

"Did Steve have any idea who you are?"

"Do you?"

"I might."

"Doubtful," Vajzh said, turning the mug slowly to examine its opposite side. "But Steve knew enough. And loved me anyway, as you said."

"That's why you came back with him to Atlantis. To help him make it right."

Vajzh sighed and said, "Steve did not wish to involve me. He said he'd make the changes, ensure the Foundation was set for several years, and return to Chacala to be with me for good in a couple of months. He said he would work remotely, if at all, and we could continue as... Well, having some experience in these matters, I suspected he could not extricate himself as planned, so I followed him back. To this place. To—let us say—expedite matters."

"You mean—"

"To speed things along. So that we could return to Chacala. To my restaurant. To our patio overlooking the beach. But Steve did not appreciate the gesture as intended, and he became quite cross with me when I took employment with Ms. Tyson."

"Now I understand the clothes thing," I said, pointing to Vajzh's Hawaiian shirt. "It's a reminder. A tribute to y'all's life together."

Vajzh looked down, confused. "This is what I always wear," he said. "It is festive. And comfortable."

We both looked down at his shirt—a teal background with pineapples turned in different directions and in various sizes. All the pineapples were wearing sunglasses. They looked cool.

"I don't get the Butz angle," I said. "Why'd you let him find out about you and Steve?"

"You are mistaken," Vajzh replied with another smile, less shy this time. "Butz is more than capable at his job. A rarity in this town. In fact, if it were not for Butz and his prowess, I would never have been able to procure the maps you found upstairs."

I made room on my end of the table to unfold them. Despite staring at them for almost an hour before Vajzh showed up, I still couldn't figure much out. "Other than these dots," I pointed, "I'm not sure what they're for. These lines here don't make any sense and these blobs… deposits of some kind? Oil or gas?"

"Both."

"And this nonsense writing… It's not Steve's. Yours?"

"No," he replied. "These marks were made by the agent in question. They are in code."

"What do they say?"

"*Keine Ahnung*," Vajzh shook his head and handed me a stuffed manila folder. "Sadly, I failed cryptography. But the contents of this folder will elucidate matters."

I opened it slowly. It was packed with handwritten notes, more maps, and surveillance photographs of several people, including two I'd spoken with recently. One was Coach.

Vajzh cleared his throat and pointed at another person in some of the photos next to Coach—a younger woman. "You are familiar with this woman," he said. "When was the last time you were in contact with her?"

I looked at the pictures and swallowed hard as the floor dropped out of my stomach. There were multiple versions of the same woman in various photos, taken at different locations in various wigs and types of clothing. Unless someone pointed it out to you, it would be difficult to tell it was the same person. Only in a couple did I recognize her.

BRAVENESS

Coach's foiled backstabbing wasn't hard to see coming. Around the corner from Martin's yesterday, he'd said too much. He knew too much. Like the best jokes, cons are all in the setup, and Coach's details had been too tight, his delivery too convincing and clean. It's one thing to write a hit song; it's another to sing it night in and night out like it's the very first time anyone's heard it.

Coach was right about my phone being bugged. He'd just lied about who'd done it.

I can't say what happened to Coach or Darwin and Derwin after I left them at Nirvana with Vajzh. I only stayed long enough to get convinced that none of them had been involved in killing Steve. It takes surprisingly little work to get the truth out of people when you're good at your job. Vajzh is good at his job.

I drove back to Atlantis alone in Coach's truck with the windows up and ten million dollars in legit cash in the back, security threads and all. I was wearing Coach's whistle. I pulled the Raptor into Steve's driveway, brought the money inside, and dumped it out on top of Steve's enormous table and sat there looking at that ridiculous pile as if it could tell me that what was going to happen next was okay and alright, that everything was going to be alright.

A lot of that cash was already spent. My new arrangement with Vajzh was going to cost me.

I was so exhausted that even my organs were nodding off. I went upstairs to my old room in the attic and fell face down on my bed with my clothes on and fell into a sleep hole so deep it's a wonder I could climb out ten hours later.

I'm downstairs trying to wake up now, loading Steve's French press with the most delicious smelling Italian roast this side of Trieste. I walk into the front room of the house where nobody ever sat and notice that I left the drapes open. The bay window looks out upon the front yard at a scene of a world that makes absolutely zero sense. While I was sleeping, Atlantis was hit with the unthinkable. It snowed.

Snowed is an understatement. For Atlantis, it's an outright blizzard. Not a Minnesota blizzard, mind you, but eight inches of snow and sleet in Caddo County might as well be eight feet. Atlantis is one of those often-mocked places where schools shut down at an eighth of an inch and people hit the streets in panic to stock up on lima beans and fresh water and buckshot at the mere mention of frozen precipitate. What I'm gawking at now is enough to shut down the county for days. Until it melts, the roads will be impassable.

I pull my boots on and step out into the front yard with my coffee and sit down right about where the snow-covered walkway out to Dewey must be. Some giant branches have snapped off the pecans under the weight of the ice and snow, including one the size of a mammoth tusk that's crumpled the hood of Coach's Raptor as if it were made of recycled tin.

For a while, the roads are completely devoid of sound. Then two pre-teens who could be brothers slide down Dewey on their bikes, trying to ski-ride the slope, wiping out every five or six feet, cracking up every time. A couple of cars were left overnight on Falway across the street from the Sheriff's, including my rented Taurus. From here they look like indistinct lumps of animals sleeping beneath their quilts of snow. After the kids and their maniacal laughter fade out down the hill, it returns to a quiet so profound that I can hear the blood moving around in my eyes.

A crow hops down from one of the trees. It starts pecking through the frozen surface of the snow about ten yards away. The crow pops its head up and looks at me for a second before rummaging around again in the snow, poking and rising up repeatedly, burying and lifting, checking me out every time it rises. There's a little pile of snow on its head that sticks there, getting larger with each lift like an expanding white fez.

The last time I remember it snowing more than an inch around here was the day my mother died. I can recall what it looked like outside the trailer that day, but not her face. My mother wasn't anything close to a saint, but she loved me the best she could, and I loved her back the same, as did Steve. He held my mom's hand and read to her while she was dying, which is something I don't know that I could do even now, even after decades of hating myself for not being the one in that chair next to her. I was rarely home in her final days. If I was home, I was in my room, and if I was in my room, I could hear them talking. At some point there was only one of them talking.

By the way he pitched his voice, I'm certain Steve knew I was there, especially when he was reading mom those stories on the last day she was alive. The stories were for me, too. Anyone who's heard Steve's voice—that calm, educated drawl suffused with kindness—will never forget it. I hear it every time one of those stories passes through my mind, as they often do, as this one is doing now:

Snow Bird is a Caddo medicine man who has a son named Braveness. Braveness grows up, meets a mysterious girl in the plains north of the lake, and marries her. She calls herself Buffalo Woman. The new couple lives with Snow Bird and they're happy for a long time, but Buffalo Woman starts to get homesick and wants to visit her people who live on the other side of the hills across the big river. Braveness wants to travel there with her, but Buffalo Woman says he can't—it's forbidden and her people would kill him. But Braveness follows his wife anyway without her knowing it.

Close to the big river is an old pecan tree that Buffalo Woman walks around three times in a circle. She transforms into a buffalo and gallops over to join her people—a herd of hundreds of buffalo roaming the plains on that side of the river. And because buffalo all look pretty much the same to him, Braveness loses sight of her. He just sits there on that hill watching buffalo run around for several days and nights until one morning this lone cow comes back over his way, circles that tree three times again, and turns back into his beautiful wife.

Braveness doesn't let on that he knows. Several moons later, Buffalo Woman gives birth to a son, and Snow Bird names the kid Buffalo Boy. The child grows up big and strong and fierce. Braveness and Snow Bird teach Buffalo Boy the ways of men while he's still young, when most other kids are spending their days running around and helping with the rabbits and acorns and corn. They teach the boy everything they know. He learns quick.

Then, one day when Buffalo Boy is playing with the other kids in the village, one of the other boys chases him around a pecan tree several times as part of some game, and wouldn't you know it but Buffalo Boy transforms into a young buffalo bull right there in front of everybody. The children run away in fear. Buffalo Woman hears their shouts and screams. She sprints over to see this young bull standing there all by himself—quivering, confused, and embarrassed. Right away, she circles that tree three times, turns herself into a buffalo, and she and her son run for the river as fast as they can.

When Braveness comes home from hunting that day, Snow Bird tells him what happened. Braveness is overcome with panic and grief. He heads for the river to look for his wife and son, but all he sees across the water is that same herd of indistinct buffalo. So he waits there for his wife and son to come back. And he waits and waits for moons and moons, just sitting there next to that tree watching the herd and pining for them, hoping one day they'll cross the river and come back. But they never come back.

*

I go inside and shake off the snow. I call Tonkawa Tyson and tell him to bail Red out and then I make more coffee. A half hour later, once I'm warmed up and caffeinated, I ring Sonya on a secure line.

"Howdy, partner. Some weather we're having."

"You're busting Red out," Sonya says flatly.

"Now why would I go and do a thing like that?"

"Exactly."

"He didn't know anything. Red was clueless as the rest of us."

"I wasn't clueless," she replies. "I knew something was off there."

"Well, thanks for warning us."

"I did warn you, just as I warned Steve. Either it was too late by that point or he didn't want to listen. But letting Red out now? Why not leave him in there until we can settle this our way?"

"I'm not sure what *our way* is, Sonya."

"This is one of those *the less you know, the better* things I was telling you about," she explains.

"I'd be better if I knew the whole Mere story."

"Not so sure about that."

"Beginning with her current location."

"You still don't think I'm being straight with you?" she asks. "After all this?"

"I don't know what to think. My head's been fucked eight ways to Sunday, and it's not like it was on straight to begin with. There's not a one of you that's who you're supposed to be."

"Look who's talking," Sonya laughs. "And who am I supposed to be, anyway? Please, educate me..."

"You're not supposed to be somebody who brings in illegals from across the border while Steve's off in Mexico! You're not supposed to be somebody who makes it so Steve has to fly back from his potentially happy life on the beach because he's got to clean up your mess and—"

"I didn't—"

"You're not supposed to be somebody who fails to mention all that before I sign over all those BI shares, Sonya! It doesn't exactly inspire trust. Nor does getting Steve and now me implicated in your sketchy bullshit. So, to answer your question, you're supposed to be somebody who isn't like that."

There's a long pause on Sonya's side of the line. She clears her throat. "Fair enough," she says quietly. "I made some mistakes and I didn't tell you. But you can't blame me for Steve's death. You know that now, right? Besides, we agreed I'd only inform you about major things. Wasn't it you who said you didn't want to know the details? Shit, I wouldn't if I didn't have to."

"Slave labor's a major thing in my book."

"Slave labor? Who the fuck—"

"Threatening Guatemalans with ICE if they didn't stop bitchin? Holding them in shacks behind the BI with terrible conditions, diseased water, and—"

"Stop it," she interrupts. "Just... Who in fuck fed you that bullshit?"

I don't say anything. She already knows.

"That's what I thought," Sonya says. "You're gonna take that deceitful cracker's word over mine? None of that happened."

"None?"

"None," she says. "Do you really want to know more about it?"

"Yeah. I do."

Sonya takes a big breath in and says, "Remember when I said Steve and me didn't end on the best of terms? This is what I was talking about. This and me shutting down Martin's. The truth with the labor I brought across the border was that I owed a couple of favors down south and thought I could run the workers through BI until we found something more permanent for them out west. I didn't see the harm in helping these clients out and turning a profit for BI in the process, you know, win-win for all of us, but it turned out to be too... traceable, I guess you'd say. Especially with the government being what it is these days. And the resultant changes to BI were too quick and drastic. It was a mistake on my part, okay? I got too eager to make a splash. So, yeah, Steve found out, flew back, fired me, and that was that. But we did make a nice chunk of money in the process, and those workers weren't slaves, for fuck's sake. Hell, I put most of them up at the Bestern for close to a month."

"They didn't end up in detention centers when they left here?"

"Some did," she acknowledges. "But only, like, ten of them. And that was only because they split before I found their next stop. And, by the way, Steve made me pay to get them out. Paying off upper-level ICE agents doesn't come cheap."

"Sounds like you made more than enough to pay for it."

"Well, sure..."

"And those profits... they're not what got Steve killed?"

"Their plan was already in motion before that," she replies. "They were playing the long game. They'd never dare come in fast, which is why they took so long with the plant. Speaking of, what's the news on that front?"

"Vajzh is taking care of it."

Sonya goes quiet for a moment. "I sure hate to lose him," she says. "But you'll do good to have him on your side. If I had a couple more like him, I'd be running the whole state in a month's time. But let me give you a bit of unsolicited advice: Make sure you're the one in charge of your tools, Bobby. It doesn't work so well the other way around."

I look outside as the birds and squirrels negotiate the snow for imperceptible goodies below.

"Why'd you shut down Martin's?"

"Fuck, not you, too... Why do you care?"

"Maybe I miss the milkshakes," I say.

"They were tasty. And the burgers and fries and whatever else my mama made back there. You know that building's a fire hazard, right? I don't know what you're planning to do with it, but you better get some good insurance. Anyway, a deal's a deal. It's yours now."

"Martin's was one of the few places that was ever worth a damn around here."

"Maybe so," she says. "But it wasn't your mother who worked for pennies in the back and was fired when you and me were caught making out in the bathroom."

"My mom got fired, too."

"And what did your mom do for work afterwards? What jobs did she have to take as a result of us getting them fired?"

"Okay," I say. "It's not comparable, and I'm sorry it happened. But it wasn't our fault, Sonya, and you shutting down Martin's hasn't exactly ended racism in Atlantis."

"Yeah? And what are you doing about it?"

"I've got some ideas," I say. "Wait and see."

"Thought you were leaving."

"I am, but I'll be around. More than you'd like. And before I take off looking for Mere in all the places she's probably not, how about you stop with the bullshit and tell me what you know."

"You still don't believe me," she says.

"You think I don't know the truth from somebody telling it slant?"

There's a long sigh and another stretched out pause on the line. It sounds like a phone moving from one hand to the other as a door closes in the background.

"Listen," she says. "Do me a favor and say goodbye to Octavia before you split. She might not have let on, but she's one of your biggest fans."

"What's that got to do with the price of biscuits?"

"That's not how you say it."

"Is now."

"How do you think Octavia got that job at the Bestern?" she asks.

"She's got a PBS mind in an MTV world, and she can lie through her teeth like the best of us."

"Partially," Sonya replies, "but she also got that job because she went to school for it, and she went to school for it because I wanted her to come back home and live close by. Her dad never was in the picture, and for years I was... well, driven. Driven, overly ambitious, eyes-on-the-prize... In other words, I wasn't exactly the mother she deserved. There's a lot more to that story. I'm just letting you know that me getting out of a particular line of business and putting all my focus on those long-term plans I mentioned for the BI and the county is a real, honest, sincere fucking thing. Everything I promised Steve I'd do, everything I promised you... believe it, Bobby. And as big picture as all of it sounds, it's always come down to me and Octavia. To our future and what we leave behind for our people. Now that I run the BI, I can finally clean up the mess I've made along the way and maybe fix things with Octavia for real. Hopefully. At some point in life, that's pretty much all that matters—if you've got kids, that is. Hard to understand unless you're a parent yourself. Now you get what I'm saying?"

"Yeah," I say. "I get what you're saying."

THREE THINGS CANNOT LONG BE HIDDEN

By the time she found out what happened to Coach at Nirvana, it was the middle of the following day, which was one snowy, blockaded day too late to escape. She'd always been inclined to chase other scores instead of focusing solely on the task assigned to her, and it had almost got her killed in the past. That's what did it this time.

By early morning, every major road in the county had been shut down. Highway Patrol set up roadblocks up and down 59. The Atlantis airport was an ice-rink. Despite the obstacles, Vajzh tracked her back to the house and set up his perimeter sniper act just as he'd done at Nirvana. She must have known it was coming, but she made a go of getting the rest of her gear and driving out anyway. The Caddy had AWD. If she could just get a trooper one-on-one…

Vajzh watched her through the scope. She tromped out to the XTS, tossed her bag in the trunk, wiped the snow off the windshield, and got inside. Vajzh let her start the engine and warm up the car for a couple of minutes, but when the defroster finally kicked in he fired off two shots that blew out the driver's side tires.

She sat in the Caddy for another minute or two, then stepped out with her hands up. She looked at the useless tires, nodded to Vajzh where he hid in the tree line, and retraced her tiny steps back into Red's house, knowing that Vajzh would allow it. Inside, she dashed off a final text to corporate, burnt the SIM card in the ashtray, and rolled one last cigarette.

Had it been me in her fake-ass moccasins, I would've panicked and ran out the back door, but it wouldn't've mattered. It would've only added frostbite to the inevitable, as she well knew. And had I been in Vajzh's flip-flops after finding out what she'd done to Steve, I would have shot her in the head the second she stepped out of the house, and I would've shot her in the head a couple more times for measure. I also wouldn't be wearing flip-flops in the snow.

Back in Atlantis, Tonk bailed Red out and filled him in, but none of it came as a surprise. Red knew she'd lied about him punching her in the eye and he also knew about the dosing, because the doc had gone over Red's bloodwork with him, shaking his head in disbelief. It was a sedative and anti-psychotic cocktail that would've killed a normal-sized human, and Rain had been upping the dosage steadily over time.

There were other hints: Red's unexpected blackouts, always waking up to find Rain gone; the weekly hair dye job she thought he wouldn't notice; texts in strange code he'd seen on her phone when she forgot to take it out of the room with her; stilted conversations supposedly with her mother; and Rain not wanting Red to ever meet her family, even though she said they lived right across the border in Oklahoma. At the time, none of these things individually meant much to Red, especially considering his drug-addled brain.

Vajzh says that after years in the field you begin to develop a sense of other operatives nearby. Sometimes you can't put a finger on it. It's almost like the absence of a smell that should be there, as if somebody were masking their scent just beyond range of chemoreception, and you catch the vaguest hint that something's missing in the environment. It doesn't usually register until disconnected events begin to link up—unexpected deaths, say, or new players around with detailed backstories. That's when the non-smell gives an agent away.

The file Vajzh compiled on Rain was an inch thick. It included compromised photos of her and Coach at a campground north of town. Her birth name was Christi Tate. She'd grown up in Oklahoma in foster care with absolutely no Caddo ancestry or any other Native blood or ties. By the time she finished high school, she'd lived with 3 families, been in juvie 5 times, spoke 3 languages fluently (and was teaching herself 2 more), and had a confirmed IQ in the low 140s. She was what they call an *exceptional child*, and an exceptionally troubled one, at that. Other than acting and theatre, Christi's interests included running ornate scams on her friends and foster families.

After blowing the roof off her ASVAB test when she was 17, Air Force Intelligence was the first to make contact. Then MIC reached out, then Homeland Security and the DIA, but the Air Force won out by promising a full ride to college with untraceable scholarships, including a bogus entity for kids of Native ancestry, which was perfect for a girl who'd spent her life in Oklahoma in the system. That's where the whole Caddo lie started. It was a backstory she'd build on over the years.

Christi could have gone to school anywhere, but the AF had longterm plans, so they kept her on the DL and sent her to the University of Oklahoma—a mediocre college in the middle of nowhere that wouldn't raise any major flags down the road. But then Christi almost blew it anyway. She graduated with honors in 3 years with a BA in Anthropology and a BFA in Drama, where she stood out at OU's Helmerich School of Drama, starring as Laurey in a touring production of *Oklahoma!* She loved the big stage; she loved attention. She was showing off.

That's when her first handler cut her loose. With the exception of certain semi-retired, beach-wearing outliers, operatives are supposed to go unnoticed. No big stage, no accolades, no front-page pictures. But a different division stepped in and made sure Christi's application for ISR (Intelligence, Surveillance, and Recon) went through, and her new handler steered her to Arabic and Kurdish so they could station her in Iraq. Once there, she excelled. At least for a few months.

It wasn't long until her orphan nature reared its mischievous, attention-seeking, score-hungry head and Christi got caught up with an unsanctioned (and unsuccessful) blackmail scheme concerning Iyad Allawi—the Shia leader who went on to head the Iraqi National Movement. Again, too much lime, too much light. This time, wiser minds prevailed, and Christi was blacklisted. The intelligence community kicked her to the curb.

By then, she'd crossed paths with other nefarious interests in the region. Just as Christi was making inroads with the antiquity-smuggling circuit in Mosul, Halliburton recruited her for Corporate Espionage. They offered five times the pay she'd made at the AF. They wanted her for a project back home.

The oil and gas corps have known about the Northeast Texas deposits for decades, but other than a few dozen derricks on the outskirts of Caddo County, none of them had been able to gain traction where it mattered. Texas landowners had become wise to mineral rights long ago, and dealing with the park system was a bureaucratic nightmare. But with a new administration in place, the race was on, and Halliburton was hell-bent on bending over the major private property owners in the region: Beau Berkey, Steve (after Beau's death), and Red.

Vajzh kept the woman who'd called herself Rain pinned inside the house until Red could get there, which—considering our East Texas version of Snowmageddon—took the better part of the day. Whatever she tried to sell Red once he arrived apparently wasn't vendible.

Red popped out of the house eight minutes later with Christi slung over his shoulder, naked, arms and legs strapped with duct tape. He tossed her in the back of the Bronco and deep-tracked his way through the ice and snow down to the river bottoms. Vajzh followed behind on foot, sticking to the Bronco's meandering tracks and crossing the frozen river in Red's oversized prints like a Christ of the ice floes.

I haven't lost a minute of sleep thinking about it, but that doesn't mean I enjoy thinking about it. Other than running over Chuck in Red's van and then framing Red, Christi did very little herself. That wasn't her style. She'd always found it more interesting to see how much she could get others to do—having Red find her in distress and believing he'd saved her, catching Steve's eye as a member of the Caddo Nation, encouraging his philanthropy, offering to mediate between the Berkey Foundation and her reluctant, secretive people...

It was all going fine until Steve started asking questions—the kind of questions a suspicious person asks who's trying not to reveal how suspicious they are. By then, Christi had made her calculations—about the Foundation post-Steve, about Red and the Padre, about me. I was in the picture long before I even knew there was a frame. When it became clear that Steve was on to her, she had him killed, and it didn't take much to convince Chuck to do it. Putting ideas in Coach's horny old head about the side-scam with me was even easier.

Red toted Christi out to the spot where he first found her—the place she'd faked being lost and so close to dying. He roped her to a tree and waited nearby in the cold without a plan; he just knew it was about to play out and that he'd be going back to the house alone. Christi did her damnedest to stall and keep warm by crying and talking nonstop. She said it was all Coach's idea. She said the CC were the ones who came up with the plan. She said Teisenberg was after her. She said Chuck had raped her, that she was pregnant with his child, that she was pregnant with my child, that she'd been pimped out as a girl by one of her foster moms. She said an Indian had killed her biological father on his farm in Grady County. She said she was being blackmailed by her handler at Halliburton, that she'd been trying to get out of the business for years and they wouldn't let her, that she'd truly fallen for Red, and that she'd done her best to keep him safe and uninvolved in the bigger scheme. She said Red actually had hit her on multiple occasions, that he'd forgotten, that she was terrified of him, that he was under some kind of spell and we had all deceived him into thinking that she was behind everything. And Christi said all sorts of other things a person like Christi will say to manipulate a decent, kind, and forgiving soul, piling up lies and half-truths on top of each other in such baffling fashion that the listener can't tell one side of their brain from the other.

Red didn't buy it, but he also couldn't kill her. So, when Vajzh showed up, Red left her there and went home.

The first thing Vajzh did was build a fire, making sure Christi survived through the night. She drank the water he offered, but she wouldn't eat, and neither would she look at him or say another word. She was all talked out. Plus, she knew the score. Maybe she'd sensed Vajzh as soon as he arrived in town. Maybe she hadn't smelled him, too.

Later the next day, the ice on the river and lake had thawed, and it had warmed up enough for most of the snow to disappear, too. Vajzh waited until dark, bound Christi's mouth with a dishcloth, and zip-tied her into Red's Jon boat. Then he trolled out across the choppy darkness of Lake Atlantis to the spot where that pyramid is said to hide beneath the silted waves. It was the same spot where Chuck was supposed to dump Steve's body on Christi's orders, orders that were technically never fulfilled, because Chuck couldn't do it. During those second thoughts, Chuck saw the pyramid, and as he sat there frightened and amazed, Steve regained consciousness. Realizing where he was and the likely reason for his being there, Steve panicked, upended the boat, and dumped both himself and Chuck over the side. Steve drowned trying to get away.

That's what Chuck would tell us later, anyway. We didn't know any of it until he woke up from his coma. A nurse discovered him crawling around the floor of his hospital room, babbling about his burning hand and looking everywhere for a leg he'd never find.

MAISON DE STÉPHANE

It's a bright day at the end of December—an East Texas encore of warmth that makes Vajzh's former beachwear more sensible. But he doesn't dress like that anymore.

He and I sit on the warped sidewalk across from Martin's as a crew of workers move in and out of the building like a symphony of well-paid ants. I pick grass from a crack in the concrete and listen to the crew speak and whistle and sing in heavily accented Spanish.

"You using Sonya's people?" I ask.

"Hand me a break," he frowns. "These people are specialists, flown in and highly recommended. All legal. No one local could do such a job. Especially on rush."

A woman in her 30s is in charge of the team. She's just inside the new space, pointing at something on the ceiling that's invisible from where we sit. An older man next to her looks up and strokes his salt-and-pepper beard, nodding thoughtfully.

"It's *give* me a break," I say. "*Give*, not *hand*."

"When do you leave?"

"Rude."

"Rude isn't a time."

"Is hassling me part of your new job description?"

"What is this word, *hassling*?"

"Nice try," I say.

"The question is pertinent to our business. Robert departed two days ago and is waiting for you. Still."

"Robert?"

"Butz," Vajzh says. "Former deputy Butz. As soon as your flight details are known, text them to Robert and myself at the number on the back." Vajzh hands me a business card in ornate, French restaurant script: *V. Bavery, Chef Patron, Maison de Stéphane*. There's a hand-written number on the back.

"Maison de Stéphane?"

"Did you expect me to call it *Martin's*?" he asks, eyebrows raised.

Two workers laugh loudly as they unbox an industrial sink in the middle of the street outside the delivery van. Another in a protective yellow suit and hood tosses ratty insulation and water-stained ceiling tiles into the construction dumpster to our left. This block of Stanley Ave has been cordoned off for the entirety of the project, not that the street was in much use before. Vajzh has relocated the front door of his restaurant to the exact spot where Steve's personal booth once was. Just like Martin's, the front of Maison de Stéphane will boast a full glass face that looks out and down upon Stanley Ave like an epicurean pharmacist. A carpenter hammers in trim on the frame.

"Did Steve ever bring you here?" I ask.

"No," Vajzh says quietly. "Ms. Tyson had already condemned the establishment and building—something else enacted in Steve's absence, and to his displeasure. From his reports, I always imagined Martin's to be... rustic."

A worker carries in an armful of antique pendants wrapped in protective plastic. "Burger joint might do better here," I tell him. "You know Atlantis is still Stone Age, right?"

"For now," he nods. "But small-town restoration and destination dining are, as they say, all the rage these days. Besides, we must diverge our activities from the Foundation, yes? Speaking of," he points to the next block down, "I have pondered that old cinema. What would you say to a renovation in the original *Streamline Moderne*? Classic movies only, both European and non?"

"Like a Cinema & Drafthouse thing?"

"What is that?"

"You know, like, watch movies and eat food at the same time? Drink beer, kick back on cozy couches—"

"*C'est barbare*," Vajzh scowls. "Most definitely not. Anyway, returning to the business at hand, it is imperative that you text Robert and myself as soon as you depart. Understood?"

"Why?"

Vajzh stands and dusts off the seat of his gray linen pants. "So that he and the other associate can meet you appropriately upon arrival. And accompany you thereafter."

"I don't need another associate. I don't even need Butz."

"You promised him employment."

"Yeah, but not… Okay, if you want me to have somebody there, I will, but Butz is enough. I don't need two."

"I will not diminish Robert's investigatory prowess, which you will require, but someone else must assume the duties of executive protection."

"What executive?" I ask. "Who protection?"

Vajzh blinks his primordial eyelashes at me and then descends the cracked stairway towards the structure that once held Martin's and whatever memories I've long housed there. He pauses in the middle of Stanley Ave and smells the air again as an animal might—a sophisticated, ninja animal who reportedly makes a mean Tuscan Shrimp. It's only now that I notice his clothes are all black and gray—shoes, pants, belt, guayabera, everything.

"I don't need a bodyguard," I say, following him. "I can handle myself."

"Yes," he replies without turning. "Steve said something similar."

THE ONCE AND FUTURE

I'm two miles out from Red's when I see the smoke. I floor the Taurus over backroad craters and under the blurred cover of loblollies, pines, and myrtles. When I rattle into Red's cul-de-sac, there's a blaze over six feet tall that occludes the front of his Jack-and-the-Beanstalk house, but there's nothing wrong with the house.

The Italian sectional—the one I crashed on after Rain drugged me with the tea—is in the middle of a well-tended fire, the small L portion of the couch sticking out of the flames like the remains of an unfortunate witch. Red steps out of the open door with a cardboard box piled high with bras, panties, and brightly-hued nighties—presumedly Rain's—as well as a freshly shaved head.

"It's you!" he shouts.

"What happened to your hair?"

"Burned it," he says, setting the box down. "Thought you'd be gone by now."

"Without saying goodbye?"

"When did you ever say goodbye?"

"You've got a knobby skull."

Red caresses his scalp with both hands and grins. "Phrenologically speaking, I'm supposed to be criminally inclined. You ever done it? Shaved it all off?"

"Just my face. And one time my balls."

"Feels great," Red coughs and kicks the box of unmentionables into the blaze. There's more of Christi's belongings in the dirt between the front porch and the fire's border, in addition to other objects associated with her touch and purchase: furniture, sheets, towels, toiletries, photographs, etc. All the Native American things, however, are stacked to the left of the front door. Red wads up a crepe-like hippie dress and chunks it into the fire, where it turns into smoke the color and smell of motor oil.

"Truth is, I was hoping you'd stick around," Red says. "For a little bit, anyway."

"Already been here longer than I should've."

"Well," he points down the driveway. "Stay a little bit. Got some folks I want you to meet. Thought you were them when I heard you pull up."

We spend the next half hour turning solid objects into particulated gas. It's more work than you'd think, setting fire to the past.

"Something I want to ask you," I say.

"Answer's no," Red replies, sitting down on the porch and picking his teeth with a twig.

"Here's the thing: I purchased two or three businesses when I was back in Austin and I have, like, zero idea how to run em."

"Sounds like you."

"And I was remembering you had that Toyota dealership in Nashville for a while after you retired."

"Didn't have no dealership," Red spits apathetically at the fire. "Just let em put my name on it. Showed up every now and then for pictures and donuts. You bought a car dealership?"

"Strip club."

"How's that like a car dealership?"

"It's not, I just thought you could help me run it. Either that or my taco joint."

"I do love tacos," he says. "No thanks, though."

"How about with the ladies?"

He shakes his hairless head. "Didn't I hear one of em left you for dead on the strip club floor or something?"

"Sativa."

"That ain't a name."

"Real one's Velvet. Supposed to get married."

"How'd that work out?"

"We're taking some time apart."

"I don't find that type of situation enticing no more," he exhales. "Especially in light of recent events."

"Might change your mind if you met somebody like Sativa."

"Don't want to. Don't want to meet no Sativa, no Indica, no Hybridica, no made-up-named none of em. I'm done with all that. You should be, too. You want my business advice? Sell that titty bar and whatever else you bought down there and donate the proceeds to something worthwhile. Feel good about yourself. Live simple. Settle down or something. Beyond that? I ain't got much to say."

Red goes into the house and comes back a few minutes later with another cardboard box, this one packed with spices, teas, and food from the pantry.

"You should keep that Mac-N-Cheese."

"Keep it yourself," he says. "Keep whatever you want. Is that Coach's whistle you got on?"

I pick out a box of the Mac-N-Cheese. It's the fancy organic kind Meredith likes.

"Y'all retired that old bastard, huh?" he asks.

"Coach retired his own damn self," I say. "You should keep some of this food, Red. Ain't the food's fault that Rain happened to buy it."

"Christi."

"Keep some anyway. How else you gonna get by?"

Red shrugs and hands me a country cool root beer from the bottom of the box. "Same way I used to: catfish, collards, duck, corn, squirrel..."

We drink our lukewarm sodas and listen to the fire talk to itself. Gluten-free smoke fills the air.

"You can't stay here by yourself," I tell him.

"The fuck I can't."

"You need—"

"I don't," Red says, ruffled. "Not yet. I know that CTE is gonna get me one of these days, but I'm way better now I got all that dope she was giving me out of my system. Remember things better. Headaches ain't so bad. Can walk okay..."

"You can't walk worth shit, buddy."

"I walk better than you sing."

"True."

"Tell you what," he burps. "When the day comes I need somebody to wipe my a-hole and spoon me apple sauce, your Louis Armstrong-sounding ass will be the first I call."

I pick up an oddly shaped purple object from the to-be-burned pile. "What's this?"

"Butt plug," he says.

"Why's it shaped like that?"

"To get at your prostate," he hooks his finger to show me. "Want it?"

I toss it into the fire and try not to smell what happens.

"How you know Meredith's in Austin, anyway?" Red asks. "She could be anywhere by now."

"How you know I'm after Mere?"

"The birds talk to me."

"I don't know for sure she's there," I say. "Sonya hinted at it. Makes sense."

"You know Sonya made an offer on my place yesterday?"

"Didn't know you were selling."

"I'm not," Red says. "Not exactly. Marie's still down in Austin, ain't she?"

"Last I heard," I say. "With our daughter."

Red spits out his root beer and I tell him the story. How when I was at Don and Marie's house a handful of details caught my freshly sobered eye: the insanely large pile of Christmas presents, childproof caps on the outlets, the locking front gate, the copy of *Everyone Poops* they forgot to remove from the bookcase where my fireplace used to be...

"Clues all around me the whole time," I say.

"What's that like?"

"Makes a man think maybe he's not as smart as everybody thinks he is."

"Nobody thinks you're smart, pal."

"Red, you giant asshole. Austin would be way more fun if you were down there with me."

"You know not everybody loves Austin like you do, right?"

"I don't even know how to respond to that."

"Look, I appreciate the invitation and all, but..." he looks around at the house and the trees and the yard, "I got stuff to do. You know, while I still can."

"Atlantis doesn't deserve you, brother."

"I ain't talking Atlantis," Red says. "I'm talking this place." He waves his left hand around in a half circle as wide as the fire. "This land. I built a good part of this house. Planted most of the food. Took out the invasives, put natives back in. And I've been getting to know these trees and forest critters for years. I got a life's work of that in front of me, however the fuck long that is. You got any idea how many acres I own? Hell, I ain't even seen it all. It's a big enough chunk for some oil company to come after me with a... whatever she was."

Red pokes one of the burning boxes with a charred stick and the flames rise up to complain, but then they think better of it and fall back down again.

"Remember that village?" he asks. "The one she was supposedly looking for out there? It's real. At least that part ain't something she made up."

"Well, that's what they say, but nobody's ever found it."

"I found it," he smiles sadly. "I just didn't tell her. It was a couple months back. I was saving it for a surprise, for our anniversary or something. But maybe the truth was I was keeping quiet about it because something didn't feel right. I don't know... I wasn't exactly clear-minded when I found it, but I didn't imagine it. It's real. I checked the other day before I called them."

"Called who?"

"It's ironic," he says, glancing down the driveway. "She wasn't but a couple hundred yards from it when I found her. It's just off this side slough, kinda submerged, with these standing rocks on the edge, just like they have on that island near the pyramid, but these are more overgrown and mostly underwater. Hard to tell unless you dive down there. So, in the end, I found something she was never even looking for in the first place, and it was on my property the whole time. My plan was to let her think she found it on her own. I wanted her to be the one, you know? Partially to build her back up, but mostly for her people. The Caddo, I mean."

"She said Steve was gonna give all the BI land back to them," I say. "Is that true?"

"Kinda. Me and him came up with the idea together. Well, she made it seem like it was our idea, I guess. Fine print was funny, though. Wasn't the Caddo Nation, but... I can't remember what the organization said it was, but Steve had it investigated and... Well, it barely had anything to do with real Caddo people. But I made sure this time. This time's legit. This time's gonna stick."

Somewhere nearby in the inviolable forest, a vehicle approaches.

"I wish I would've known about all that before I handed the BI over to Sonya," I say. "Wish I would've known what you were up to. Maybe we could've..."

"Don't much help us now, does it? Anyway, what I'm giving them ain't so bad. It's a start, at least."

It's not one vehicle that pulls up, but two. Crew cab trucks that round into view at the far end of Red's drive—Dodge diesels, white and splotched underneath with mud. Red hands me a kiln-dried pendant on a worn leather cord.

"Here," he says. "Something tells me I shouldn't burn this. You take it. I don't want that shit around here."

The pendant is maybe two inches of polished clay. The figure has two horns and it's hairy all over. There's a crazed look on its face that's furious and frightened and horny at the same time.

"Enkidu," Red says, standing up straighter than I've seen him do in years. "She said it was from Mesopotamia, thousands of years old. Merry Christmas, pal. It's Christmas, right?"

The trucks pull in on the other side of the cul-de-sac slowly and park in a line next to my Taurus. There's a symbol on the passenger side of each vehicle—a bright yellow circle with an outer band of sky blue. In the middle of the emblem, a group of singers in white hats sit around a large drum, mouths open in song. In front, three figures in long dresses and dark braids dance clockwise in a circle—upright, eyes closed.

"Forgot about Christmas," I say, trying to make out the writing on the trucks. "Who's this?"

"New friends," he says, waving as they cut their engines.

I lift the pendant up by the cord and let it turn in the post-solstice light.

"Hey Red," I say. "I think this is supposed to be you."

He snorts and takes another step toward the trucks. He's right—his shuffle isn't nearly as bad as before.

The occupants step out of the trucks slowly—four or five from each. Some wear white hats, just like in the emblem. None look older than thirty. Their faces are unrefined and unusually natural—natural in a way you don't see anymore. There's nothing about them that's out of place, nothing that sticks out of the background.

"That ain't me," Red says, glancing back at the pendant. "That ain't nobody no more. All the wild men are gone."

"Nah," I say. "There's always gonna be wild men. All around the world—Enkidu, Bigfoot, the Green Man... It's all the same story."

Red looks at me as if I just took a dump on his purifying fire. "Who told you that?"

"Told me what?"

"Who told you it's all the same story?"

ACKNOWLEDGMENTS

This novel and those to follow are the result of support, encouragement, and/or invaluable advice from James Michener, Denis Johnson, David Wevill, Pasha Allsup, Eric Gravning, and Colin Whyte.

My high-school friend and fellow offensive lineman, Don Bice, prompted me to resume my devotion to writing and suggested I give fiction a try. So I did. Thanks, Don.

Ain't Never No Snow in Atlantis has gone by several names. All were passed over by dozens of agents and publishers until the manuscript found its forever home with Kallisto Gaia Press, who know what's up. Boundless gratitude to Tony and gang.

I also want to thank my maternal family, especially my grandmother, Velma Burnett, and my great-grandmother, Eula Lee Johnson. Even in death, their love and presence are unwavering.

But mostly I want to thank my beautiful wife, Belinda, for bolstering me in all the ways, and my daughter, Emma-Tara, for simply being herself.

ABOUT THE AUTHOR

Bobby Burnett Lee is a 5th generation Texan who currently lives with his family on an island in the Pacific Northwest where he writes novels, teaches martial arts, and works as a ghostwriter, editor, high school English instructor, and writing coach. He earned his MFA from the University of Texas at Austin as a Michener Fellow and his MDiv from Naropa University as a Lenz Merit Scholar. His poetry and short fiction have appeared in *The Molotov Cocktail, Ponder Review, Black Warrior Review, Field, Florida Review, Iowa Review, New Orleans Review, Quarterly West, Southeast Review,* and other journals, and he is the editor of over thirty non-fiction books, including works by Damien Echols, Apolo Ohno, Paul Conti, and Alan Watts. Find out more at bobbyburnettlee.com.

www.ingramcontent.com/pod-product-compliance
Lightning Source LLC
Chambersburg PA
CBHW030632110125
20180CB00045B/706